Dead Pretty

/ICE

20

DAVID MARK

Dead Pretty

MULHOLLAND
BOOKS
HODDER

First published in Great Britain in 2016 by Mulholland Books
An imprint of Hodder & Stoughton
An Hachette UK company

1

Copyright © David Mark 2016

A CIP catalogue record for this title is available from the British Library

Hardback ISBN 978 1 444 79809 8
Trade Paperback ISBN 978 1 444 79810 4
eBook ISBN 978 1 444 79808 1

Printed and bound by Clays Ltd, St Ives plc

Hodder & Stoughton policy is to use papers that are natural, renewable
and recyclable products and made from wood grown in sustainable forests.
The logging and manufacturing processes are expected to conform to
the environmental regulations of the country of origin.

Hodder & Stoughton Ltd
Carmelite House
50 Victoria Embankment
London EC4Y 0DZ

www.hodder.co.uk

For Xavier – born on the day I wrote 'The End'

'If you are neutral in situations of injustice, you have chosen the side of the oppressor. If an elephant has its foot on the tail of a mouse, and you say that you are neutral, the mouse will not appreciate your neutrality.'

Archbishop Desmond Tutu

'There is no crueller tyranny than that which is perpetuated under the shield of law and in the name of justice.'

Charles de Montesquieu

August bank holiday, last year

She's blonde, near enough. Hair the colour of an old wedding gown. Skin like stripped twigs. Wolfcub eyes behind misted glass.

Flushed pink, she is. Pink and white and pink and white, like a mosaic of seashells. Like a plate of posh biscuits. Like a porcelain doll.

Sticky arms and a sweaty neck, spilling out of a neat white dress: sausagemeat forced through a veil.

Twenty-something. A plump fly in a web of tangled trees and knotted weeds, swinging her legs, toddler-like, over the entrance to a warm, dark hole in the earth.

Leaves in her hair and ladybirds on her skin. Ladybirds everywhere, gobbling up the last of the summer aphids: something from a fairy tale until you look close and see the green slime on their sharp little teeth . . .

Hannah looks at the ladybirds crawling over her knees. She's stopped being amazed by their number. The collective noun for a group of ladybirds is a *loveliness*. That's what he told her and she had been so delighted with it, and with him, that she has not sought confirmation. Everybody else is referring to the colourful creatures as a plague. Hannah cannot imagine being cross about ladybirds. Cannot imagine anything more wonderful. She likes to imagine that they are tiny faeries, flitting and bustling and delighting in the late summer sun.

She shifts her weight on the hard ground. Watches the thick black shadow of the tree bisect her bare thigh, and apologises to

I

the loveliness of ladybirds that takes off, pouting and petulant, as their world goes dark.

He'll be here soon. Here to make it better. To make everything right.

Hannah looks at the sports bag at her feet. Wishes she had made the two-mile walk here in her trainers. She quite likes the new summer dress she bought especially for him and has been surprised at the simple pleasure of walking with her skin touching fresh air. But the new Doc Marten boots have rubbed her ankles raw. She should have worn socks, but he didn't ask for socks. Hadn't ever hinted at a fondness for them. And she wants to please. She wants to please him so badly that she sometimes feels like she is transforming into another person entirely. She has felt desire before, of course. She's a young woman with the same wants and needs as anybody else. But she feels something for him that goes beyond the physical. She wants to be consumed by him. To be enveloped. She wants him to be her chrysalis; to bind and contain her as she disintegrates and reforms. Wants him to be the first thing she sees when she emerges and flaps her beautiful wings . . .

She wishes the ladder weren't here. Wishes, too, that the shadows of the tall trees didn't look so much like prison bars. She wants it to be pretty. To be perfect. Things are going to be better soon. Better for both of them.

The ladybirds land afresh on Hannah's bare skin. She looks up and frowns again at the ladder. Half hidden among the trees, it leads up to a rectangular wooden construction surrounded by chicken wire. He told her it was a 'hide' – a place to conceal oneself to observe the animals. It doesn't look very inviting. To Hannah it looks like the steps to the gallows and she does not want that thought to enter the man's mind when he arrives. She wants him to feel nothing but freedom. To feel relief. And then to kiss her. God, how she wants that. They have talked their way through physical acts but he has never done more than push her hair behind her ear or tuck the label back in her sweatshirt. The time hasn't been right. There have been too many obstacles. He can't give himself to her when he belongs to so many others. She's heard every excuse and wept at each of them, without ever really believing him.

But fate smiles on heroes. The gods intercede on behalf of those with goodness in their heart. That's what she tells herself. It's what he told her too, before she started to piss him off with her texts and letters and her hints and gentle threats. But how else can he see it? This is their chance. The opportunity he needs to get away. And she wants to hold his hand as he runs. She knows he's cross at her. She feels bad about that. Wishes she hadn't had to push quite so hard. But it will be worth it. She knows she can make him happy. Knows how their future will be.

The sound of a car engine from the nearby road causes her to stiffen where she sits. But the driver doesn't even pause. He's not here yet. Might be a little while. She doesn't mind waiting. It's nice here, among the trees. The little church where they first met is almost visible over the brow of the hill. She can hear the trickle of the tiny river. Can hear the birds among the nettles. Fancies she can even hear the badgers snoring in the sett beneath her feet. She likes to think of the animals asleep down there. Can picture them in her mind's eye, snuggled up on crocheted blankets in front of their warm, open fire. Amends the mental picture, in deference to the warmth of the day. Lets out a nervous giggle at the thought of badgers in bikinis, lounging in deckchairs and sipping fancy drinks with long straws . . .

Hannah daydreams for a while. Feels the sweat trickle down the back of her thighs. Crosses and uncrosses her legs. She hopes he appreciates this. She's done it all for him. She's always been such a clean girl. Always brushed her teeth twice a day and showered in the morning. She's shaved her armpits twice a week since adolescence. For him, for them, she has allowed herself to become some kind of cavewoman. She scratches at her armpits. Shudders at the sensation of curly hair. Sniffs her fingers and recoils. Onion skins and unwashed tights. She'd have been bullied for this, at school. Bullied at work, too. And at home. They love her, the bullies. Seem to look at her the way ladybirds look at aphids.

3

She turns her thoughts back to *him*. To what she's done. It's a strange way to win a man. But she would be the first to admit she does not have much experience of the opposite sex. Has had to do her reading.

Give him what he wants. That seems to be the advice on the glossier websites. *Give him what he wants then take it away again.* She hadn't liked that. Wouldn't like it done to her. She'd had to dig further. Had to get down deep into the nature of desire. Of ownership. Has learned some interesting new words.

'We're all Palaeolithic, under a varnish of sophistication. We're cavemen in socks. Take away the iPods and the SodaStreams and we're just cavemen and it's all still about lust and meat, territory and revenge.'

He'd said that to her the very first day. Had blown her mind with new ways of thinking, even if she'd had no idea what a SodaStream was.

Hannah wonders if he will always want it like this or whether some years from now he will have altered his peculiarities sufficiently for her to be allowed to shave, both above and below.

With a start, she realises she has not done as instructed. She reaches into her bag and pulls out her mobile phone. She is under instruction to destroy it: to take out the battery and bury the parts in separate graves. She stuffs her fingernails into the crack at the back of the expensive mobile, and pauses. She needs to see it again. Needs to see what he did for her, what brought them here.

Deftly, naughtily, Hannah finds the video clip. It looks strange, sitting there among the footage of her friend's birthday party and photographs of horses. It doesn't look like it belongs.

She presses play. Watches again with grim satisfaction as the man in the video spits up teeth and begs to be allowed to live. His face is half in shadow and half caked in blood. He's barely human. His cheekbone is sort of caved in and one eye is so puffy that it looks like the cleft in a shapely arse. The thought pleases her. Makes her giggle, as if she has just done something mischievous. The bleeding man's voice is full of snot and tears. It sounds thick and gloopy and puts her in mind of fresh batter mixture being stirred with a wooden spoon. He struggles to get his words out. He looks like he's in more pain than he can endure. It's still not enough for Hannah. But he does get his words out, in the end. It's an apology, of sorts. An acceptance of what he has done and a request for forgiveness. Hannah had given it, but enjoyed making him wait. Had liked knowing she could give the man his life, or signal his death.

Her man had given her that power.

He had taken away her bad dreams. Hannah has never been a brave kind of girl. She's always met friends outside the pub rather than walk in on her own. Would turn to liquid if she found herself on a country footpath and saw a man coming the other way. After *him*, that had gone away. She knew she had a protector. Knows, here and now, that she can kill anybody she likes. All she has to do is make up a story. She won't, of course. She's a good girl. But it's nice to know she *can*.

She could have left things simple, of course. Should have, really – that was the deal. Could have said thank you and moved on. But he had given her a glimpse of something she wanted to possess. And what she wanted, above all things, was *him*.

He was kind in his rejections. Told her about the obstacles in their path and not to think too highly of him. He was no good for her. Too old. Too full of bitterness and anger and a blackness that would only swallow her up if she came too close. He said he had simply done what needed to be done but he could not give himself to her. Would not even try. So she had pushed. Pushed hard.

Hannah pulls her hair back from her face. She wants to tie it up but he has told her he likes it down. She wants to be perfect for him. Wants to be a vision so stunning and sexy that he'll know, on sight, that he has made the right decision. That he doesn't need the others. And then he'll tear at her clothes and bury his face in her scents and she'll spill her blood on the forest floor and he'll move inside her so deeply that it will feel as though they are breathing through the same lungs and pumping blood through the same heart and reaching their climax through one body, here, among the ladybirds and the shadows and the pretty white flowers . . .

The sound of a branch snapping causes Hannah to spin where she sits. The figure is lost in the shade of the tall trees and the glare of the sun as it bleeds through the leaves and the ears of corn that sway in the field beyond the path.

Hannah half stands, wishing she had heard him coming; wishing she'd had the time to compose herself; to lie seductively on the ground and expose the changes she has made to her body just to please him.

She starts to speak. Gives a half-giggle and shakes her head as a ladybird lands upon her lip.

The figure moves forward and Hannah's smile drops from her face like sunlight behind cloud.

'I'm sorry . . . I didn't . . . Where? . . . Look . . .'

And then she sees the knife.

Instinct takes over. Hannah turns to flee. She lunges forward, slipping on her bag, and her dress catches on a gnarled stub of tree root. A long branch whips at her hair and face. Her foot goes into the opening to the badger sett and she feels her ankle twist so violently she half wonders if she has been captured by a snare. It feels for a moment as if she is being pulled into the ground. She cannot find her feet. They slip inside her uncomfortable boots and she feels a toenail tear. She yelps as she tries to stand, and then her face is being pushed into the nettles and the briars, the dead leaves and the earth, and she is shouting for help, for mercy, for forgiveness; one hand suddenly coming free as she twists herself onto her back, revealing the matted hair in the hollow under her arms and the rivulets of sweat that run through the dirt on her skin onto her bra-less chest.

At first she thinks she has been punched. She feels a hard thrust to her bottom rib. She shouts in pain but finds she has no voice. And there is wetness upon her skin. It feels like she has spilled wine on her clothes. She can feel leaves and bracken sticking to her skin. And now there is a weight on her wrists. She is being pinned down, even as the strength pumps out of her onto the

6

forest floor, so that when the sharp, precise pain shoots through her underarms and into her every nerve-ending, she has no way to express it. She just lies on her back, staring through the trees at the distant sun, watching the world fragment into lines and swirls and ladybirds and feeling the figure above her stick a long sharp blade into her guts again, again, again . . .

PART ONE

I

Monday, 2 May, this year

The kiss is sticky. Inelegant. A sensation not unlike biting into a ripe peach.

He feels her hands on his back, her cold fingers applying gentle pressure on each of his vertebrae as if his spine were a clarinet.

Small, neat teeth clamp playfully on his lower lip.

She moves as shadow, insinuating herself into the gap between his broad left arm and the sleeping child he holds so protectively in the crook of his right.

'Let it go, Aector. Just for a moment. Please.'

Detective Sergeant Aector McAvoy pulls his wife close. Feels her settle in his grasp with the same spirit of contentment as the little girl who snoozes against his chest. He strokes the soft skin of her taut, tanned belly and feels her shudder and laugh as he finds her ticklish places.

Her giggling gives their embrace an oddly teenage air; turns this coming together of experienced and familiar mouths into something inarticulate and clumsy. Lips overspill. Take in chin and neck. He feels the blast of air from her nostrils as she exhales, hungrily, into his open face; snorts his breath in a grunt of wanting; tongue like a spoon scraping a yoghurt pot . . . and then she is pulling away, rising like smoke, leaving a fading ghost of scent in the warm air around his flushed cheeks. He breathes deep. Catches the scent of suncream and citrus, of outdoor food and wine. Her skin lotion and cigarettes. He wants her, as he always wants her. Wants to wash himself, lose himself, in her movements, her affection . . .

And then he feels *her*. Hannah. The missing girl. Reaching upwards, through the bones and the splinters and the deep dark earth. Her fingers grabbing at his trouser legs. He feels suddenly cold in his chest and hot in his belly. Makes fists around his wife's hair and ignores her gasp of pain and surprise. Pushes her head back and buries his face in her neck; making a cave for the thudding din of his thoughts.

She's here. Here, beneath your feet. Here, waiting for you . . .

'I'm sorry,' he says, and his refined Scottish accent is dry as ancient bone.

'I like it,' says Roisin, placing a kiss on her daughter's forehead, and then stretching to plant a similar smooch on McAvoy's nose. 'I can handle a bit of the rough stuff. But let her go for a little while, eh, my love? Just try.'

It is bank holiday Monday, just after 4 p.m. A bright spring day. Nap time for Lilah. Above them, the bluest of skies and a round, orange sun. Viewed as a photograph, the image would suggest darting swallows, fat bluebottles. In truth, this valley with its muddy, root-twisted footpath, its gorse bushes and cow parsley, its dandelions and wild garlic, channels a wind that cuts like steel. Even McAvoy, inured to the harshest of elements during a childhood battling hail and snow on his father's Highland croft, suppresses a shiver as the wind tugs at his sweat-dampened fringe. Shivering, they retreat into the shadow of the small, squat church that stands to their rear to find comfort among the headstones and the lichen-covered memorials. Enjoy the distant haze of bluebells, curling around the trunks of adolescent trees like tendrils of cerulean smoke.

The trio hold one another in silence as a chilly gust, unimpeded in its rush from the North Sea, tumbles down the valley. It shakes loose a maelstrom of apple blossom from the overhanging branches. Petals cascade like snow, landing in Roisin's jet-black hair and tickling her skin.

'It's pretty here,' says Roisin. 'I've always thought that if people are going to go missing or get murdered, they should do so in pretty places. It makes it much nicer for me and the bairns.'

'Don't,' says McAvoy, shutting his eyes tight, like a child turning his face away from a spoonful of something unpleasant. 'What if she's here, Roisin? Under our feet, right now. What if we've already stepped on her face?'

Roisin shakes her head and reaches down to pick a daisy. He loves her ability to do something so simple and innocent. Loves that she indulges him his obsession. Has made space in their relationship for the missing girl.

'There are worse places to be left alone,' she says, and starts plucking petals from the flower. 'He loves me, he loves the dead lass, he loves me, he loves the dead lass . . .'

McAvoy isn't sure whether to chide her for insensitivity or kiss her for being so adorable. It is a dilemma he faces most days. Were he not a policeman he doubts he would care much either way. But McAvoy was a policeman in his soul long before he put on the uniform and even today, as acting senior officer on call, he cannot forget that at any moment his phone could ring and inform him of another horrible thing done in the name of passion, revenge or desire. He carries his job with him at all times. Feels the burden within him, and without, like a rucksack full of bricks whose weight only diminishes when he takes his wife and child into his embrace.

Beneath his grey woollen coat, McAvoy has squeezed his considerable bulk into a dark blue suit, complete with yellow shirt and old school tie. His suits are specially made, bought off the internet from a supplier specialising in men of stature. McAvoy has stature to spare. He is a conservative 6 foot 5 inches. He has a rugby-player physique and a handsome, scarred face topped with unruly ginger hair. Grey hairs have begun to speckle his beard and the darkness beneath his eyes betrays the things he has seen. He would look like a nightclub bouncer were it not for the gentleness around his cow-eyes and the freckles that spray across his pink-and-white cheeks.

Roisin, ten years his junior and made all the more elfin by her proximity to her towering husband, wears tight black jeans and a designer sweatshirt beneath the burgundy leather jacket she

13

opened with such excitement on Christmas morning two years ago and has barely taken off since. McAvoy knows that despite the cold, Roisin would be wearing something more revealing were it not for her self-consciousness over the scarring on her legs. She used to love showing off her skin every time the sun pushed its face through the clouds. But an accident two years ago ripped holes in her shins. Left her perfect legs looking like somebody had carved their initials to the bone.

McAvoy looks around him. Marvels at the absence of company. He had not really expected to find an army of Japanese tourists in the grounds of St Ethelburga's church but imagined there would be at least a couple of ramblers and a picnicker or two. Instead, he and his family have Great Givendale to themselves. It has a time-less quality, this place, in this moment. He fancies that he and Roisin could be plucked from their own time, transplanted to a different century and the view would remain unchanged. Reckons they would be unaware they had tumbled through the ages until the locals turned up and started jabbing him with pitchforks and suggesting that both the witch and the giant be burned without delay. In truth, the little church to McAvoy's rear was only built in 1849 and in times gone by, the geese that are busy having a noisy argument down by the tear-shaped pond would be surrounded by onions and sitting in a pot.

'I don't mind,' says Roisin, softly, as she settles back against the wooden bench and nods at his shirt pocket. 'You can tell me again. I won't snore. And if you argue, I'm hitting you.'

McAvoy considers protesting but his left bicep is already sore from the repeated punches she gave him while driving here, and he doesn't think he can take another of her 'love-taps' without making a girlish noise. Roisin does not know her own strength.

McAvoy unfolds the rectangle of paper and waves it at a but-terfly that seems to have taken a liking to Lilah's brightly coloured summer dress. He looks again at the tangle of lines and smudges of forest that make up his satellite map of the area around Pocklington, on the road from Hull to York, where East Yorkshire becomes North Yorkshire and the house prices start to rise.

Lets himself think of her. *Hannah.* The missing girl. The young lassie who was just beginning to live . . .

The Serious and Organised Crime Unit of Humberside Police has been searching for Hannah Kelly since August of last year. Since that time, McAvoy has got to know this rural landscape pretty well. Has snagged his clothes on just about every briar and branch. He knows she's here somewhere. He just doesn't know where to dig. Doesn't know whether it's wrong to bring his family here for picnics. He shivers at the thought that he missed something while lost in a daydream about walking through these woods with his wife and children.

'Make a nest,' says Roisin, nodding at the damp grass.

McAvoy obliges, shrugging off his coat and laying it down. He folds Lilah into its soft, grey arms. He kisses her cheek; his nose touching the tiny plastic device that helps her hear her parents' words and which she has grown adept at blaming for her occasional acts of disobedience.

'Go on,' says Roisin, putting her legs across McAvoy's as he sits down on the bench. 'You'll feel better.'

McAvoy doesn't need his notes. Knows the whole sequence of events off by heart.

'At just after one p.m. on Sunday the twenty-ninth of August, Hannah phoned for a taxi. It picked her up from the back of the Bowman's Tavern in Howden twelve minutes later. Hannah shared a house around three hundred metres away, on Bridgegate, with three friends. She had been invited with them to see a movie at the leisure park at Castleford but had declined, saying she had a migraine. When she ordered the cab, she told the operator she was heading to a village on the road to York but couldn't remember the name. When he picked her up, she said it was Millington.'

'That's the place we had the ice cream, yes?' asks Roisin. 'Pretty little village. Top of the hill?'

McAvoy nods. 'She told him to take her to the Gait Inn. We had a drink and a meal there just before Christmas, remember? Lilah drew on the table with her fork and you called the landlord a fecking eejit?'

Roisin grins at the memory. Encourages him to continue.

'She talked a lot on the journey. Sat in the front and gabbled. Told the driver about her work.'

'What did she do?'

'Press Association in Howden. TV listings for the *Radio Times*. She did two years of an English degree at the University of Hull but didn't finish it and took a job there on a recommendation from a friend. She was pretty good, apparently, though I'm not sure what qualifies as "good". Anyhow, the driver asked her why she was heading out to the middle of nowhere. She said something about meeting an old school friend who was staying at the temple up the road.'

'That's the big place? Looks like Downton Abbey?'

'The Madhyamaka Kadampa Meditation Centre, yes,' says McAvoy, stroking his wife's leg and remembering the gales of laughter that his boss and friend, Trish Pharaoh, had thrown his way when he first read out the name – begging him to repeat it again and again. She makes him do the same with the word 'purple' when she's bored. Apparently the Scots can't say it, though that came as news to him.

'Sounds exotic,' says Roisin. 'A good place to hide who you are.'

McAvoy shakes his head. 'We've checked several times and none of the guests, staff or residents at the temple had any knowledge of her.'

McAvoy tails off. Scans the treeline. Spots his son, still happily beating a sycamore to death with a branch as he fights dragons and defends fair maidens in his mind's eye. He reminds himself to teach the boy the Latin name for the tree when he comes back, sweating and excited and demanding to know where the next sandwich is coming from.

McAvoy looks at his wife, and tries to keep it light as he proceeds.

'So we presume that it was a cover story. The driver said she had a sports bag with her and was wearing jeans, a sweatshirt and trainers. He dropped her at the pub. There were a dozen drinkers outside, enjoying the sunshine and hating the ladybirds.'

'A loveliness of ladybirds,' whispers Roisin to her sleeping child, and looks at her husband proudly. He grins back.

'Aye, the plague of last summer. Couldn't pick up a glass of lemonade without finding a hundred ladybirds using it as a bubble-bath. But the ramblers outside the Gait were willing to put up with it. They saw her get out of the cab and go inside. She gave them this little wave. And not long after she came out again, dressed in a little white tennis dress and Doc Marten boots.'

'Bit of a transformation,' says Roisin, sneering slightly at the very idea of such a combination.

'Not her usual sort of outfit either, according to her friends. Prudish. That was the word they used. Not much skin on show. They couldn't even imagine her wearing something like that.'

'Was her hair up or down?' asks Roisin, chewing on her lip.

McAvoy has to fight the urge to grin. Detective Superintendent Trish Pharaoh had asked the same question.

'Down,' he says. 'The drinkers outside said she looked a million dollars. At first they wouldn't have recognised her as the same girl. Heavy eye make-up too. She gave them a smile. Same little wave. Hoisted her bag. Set off up the road.'

McAvoy turns his head in the direction of the road in question, Grimthorpe Hill. Fastest way from the middle of nowhere to the back of beyond.

'Three different motorists have come forward to say they spotted her walking this way from Millington. The last of them was about a quarter of a mile from here. She was looking at her phone as she walked. Looked a little warm but not unhappy. Certainly not running from anything or anyone.'

'And then?'

McAvoy rubs his face with his large, rough palm. 'Her mobile phone disappeared from the network. There's quite a good service up here, surprisingly. They could pinpoint pretty damn close to where the signal went dead. And that doesn't mean switched off, Roisin. That means somebody taking the battery out. The tech wizards can still pinpoint a dead phone.'

Roisin nods. She knows.

'Her friends didn't report her missing until the next day, and even then it wasn't to the police. She didn't turn up for work and her boss asked one of her housemates where she was. She was as surprised as the boss that Hannah hadn't shown up. Started ringing her and got no response, then realised her bed hadn't been slept in. That night one of them spoke to their parents and they suggested calling the police. So they went to the local station. Got a PC who told them she was a grown woman and probably just with a bloke. It didn't come to CID for four days.'

'What was she like?' asks Roisin, as she nibbles on a piece of hawthorn leaf she picked in the woods and which she said reminded her of being a kid. Why she wants to remember that time is beyond McAvoy, but he doesn't like to make a fuss.

'CID got in to her Facebook account and her emails,' says McAvoy, looking away. 'She had a blog. Nothing much to get excited about for months – it was all favourite films and why she liked cats and whether *Toy Story* was an analogy for life. Just the thoughts of a young girl. She was a romantic. Like a child, really. Used to buy wedding magazines even though she was single. Saw life like a Disney princess.'

McAvoy nods his head in the direction of the cornfield that runs parallel to the woods.

'The screensaver on her computer was a photograph taken in those woods,' he says, looking down at his feet. 'And on her work computer she'd searched Google Maps for the route from Millington to Great Givendale. We haven't found her laptop. She hasn't taken any money from her bank account since she vanished but she made no major withdrawals before her disappearance.'

'Did she have much to withdraw?'

'Not a lot, but a few hundred quid comes in handy when you're planning a new life.'

'And there was no sign of a man?'

McAvoy pushes his hair back from his face. 'Yes and no. She had a boyfriend at university but it wasn't really serious. And the lads she'd been out for drinks with at work were all adamant that she was an innocent.'

'An innocent?' asks Roisin, and enjoys McAvoy's blush.

'She'd still wear white at her wedding, is what I mean,' says McAvoy. 'And not all young men think that's a virtue. I've spoken to a lot of her friends. They were pretty clear that for a long time she was a lot of hassle for not much reward. She was a good girl, Roisin, whatever that might mean. Then things changed.'

'Changed how?'

'I just get the sense that she found somebody. Little things. Her friends said she was acting a different kind of giddy. She was always giggly and happy but she had that little swagger in her step. And the entries on her blog seemed a bit more worldly.'

'You think she lost her virginity,' says Roisin, and this time, she doesn't make fun.

'I think she was preparing to. And she visited peculiar websites on the work computer. Nothing dirty, just interesting essays on different kinds of arousal. And spells, too.'

Roisin gives in to a grin. 'I like this bit. You always go red.'

McAvoy obliges. 'She visited a site about love potions. Ways to get a man to fall in love with you. How to trap them and keep them.'

'Did she never consider good cooking and lots of baby oil?' asks Roisin.

'This was dark stuff. All about scents and using your bodily fluids to create a potion. There was one that talked about getting somebody to drink a coffee laced with your, erm, monthlies . . .'

Roisin pulls a face. 'Not my idea of a Bloody Mary,' she says. 'There are definitely better ways to get a man's attention.'

'She had her eye on somebody. Her phone records don't show much in the way of unusual activity but she did receive a lengthy video message about a month before her disappearance from an unregistered mobile phone. We traced the phone from the distributor. It was sold through a market stall in Goole. The owner kept good records. Remembered the lad who bought it because he was always coming back to complain and whine. He contacted uniform the second the kid came back. It was David Hogg.'

'Who?' asks Roisin.

'The hit and run, a mile down the road from here,' says McAvoy. 'Teenage girl out with her horse on a country lane and a fool in a stolen sports car comes around the corner at ninety mph and takes out horse and rider. Leaves them to die. The girl won't walk again. The horse had to be destroyed at the scene. A nearby farmer heard it screaming. Said the sound will never leave him.'

'Oh yes. Bastard,' says Roisin, remembering the story. McAvoy knows her pity is shared equally between human and horse.

'CID have no doubt the driver was David Hogg. Lives in Market Weighton. His uncle's a hard case and tidied things up. By the time David was arrested the car had been scrapped and there was nothing to link him to the accident. He laughed his way through the interviews. Even answered a few of the questions with neighs and whinnies. Got away with it.'

'And Hannah knew him?'

'We don't know; he wouldn't talk to us. We've found no link between them. Just the video, and we've no way of viewing that. Hogg's phone can't be traced and he mumbles "no comment" no matter how hard you lean on him.'

Roisin smiles, remembering the first time McAvoy told her this story. 'Jaw wired shut?'

'He'll be having his food mashed for years to come. His ankles and wrists were smashed and his face pummelled. Looked like he'd been kicked by a horse, then run over. His uncle had the cheek to demand what we were going to do about it. He put the word around that whoever did it was a dead man. We've had no leads. We've had no indications that the uncle's made any progress either.'

'So what's the connection?' asks Roisin, giving a little yawn.

'I don't know yet. Too many coincidences. Too many unanswered questions. I just can't seem to get past it. I want to hear that she's alive. I don't believe that she is. I can feel her, Roisin. You know I'm not like that. I don't hear voices or believe in clairvoyants. I've never read my horoscope. It's not like that. It's just . . .'

'An obsession?'

He looks at his feet, chastened and ashamed.

Roisin changes her position and snuggles into his chest, poking a finger through the buttons of his shirt to tickle his hair. 'She might be having the time of her life somewhere,' she says. 'You don't have to think the worst.'

He reaches down and kisses the top of her head. Wishes he could convince himself that Hannah is just a missing girl and not a murder victim. It feels like when he was eleven – still trying to persuade himself of the existence of Father Christmas, the Tooth Fairy and God.

They sit in silence for a while, only rousing themselves when Lilah wakes and uses Daddy's leg to right herself and starts bumbling off down the slope to where her brother is running towards them, holding a branch as long as himself. From this distance, he's a kilted Highlander, charging through the heather and the thistles with a claymore in his hand: a miniature of his father.

McAvoy is about to stand up and charge towards the boy, pretending to be an English invader dead set on having his innards sliced open by the noble Scotsman's blade. He knows Fin will like that. Wishes only that the boy wasn't spoiling the overall effect by wearing a Ross County football shirt and a pair of Bermuda shorts.

'Your phone,' says Roisin, nodding at his pocket as she hears it ring. 'The work one.'

He answers with his name, rank and unit, briefly recalling the days when a call from work would set his heart racing with excitement. Here, now, he simply knows that something bad has happened and it is about to interrupt his day.

He nods into the phone. His eyes darken. The colour seems to leach from his skin. He looks up at the sky, at the blue overhead, and the grey to the east.

He takes his keys from his pocket and starts walking up the hill to the car.

Towards Hull.

And an appointment with another dead girl.

2

The two men sit in the front seat of the unremarkable Ford Focus and stare at the convertible parked in the drive at the far end of this quiet, nondescript cul-de-sac on the outskirts of Grimsby.

Inside the sports car, a teenage girl and a curvy middle-aged woman are screaming at one another. The younger one looks like she is ready to do bloody violence. The older one looks tired. Like she's been through a washing machine at too high a temperature. Wrung out, and sad.

Inside the Ford, the two men do not speak. They have exhausted their conversational resources and have learned to feel comfortable in one another's silence. They could be father and son.

The older man smiles as the teenager and the old tart go at it like dogs fighting over a chicken leg. He hopes there will be hair-pulling. Perhaps a top ripped open and an exposed breast. They've had little to entertain them since they pulled up. They listened to the radio for a while but could only get local stations. They don't give a damn about what's happening locally. They're a good way from home. Couldn't care less if the whole east coast fell into the sea.

The teenage girl is getting out of the car now. Her face is flushed and there are tears on her cheeks. She looks like she slept in her clothes and her hair is a mess, but both men have fucked worse. They've fucked younger, too. This one's maybe fifteen. A good deal older than the Eastern European girls that their boss keeps in the back room at his casino and whom they get to enjoy when they are being kept waiting and have read all the magazines in the foyer.

'Nice to see,' says the one called Teddy, as he sips from a bottle of Lucozade. 'You'd have thought a copper's kid would be less highly strung. Gives me hope. No better than the rest of us when you strip it all away.'

He passes the Lucozade across to the man called Foley, who shakes his head without taking his eyes off the scene before him. In his lap sits a wooden figurine. It's carved from cherry wood and exquisitely beautiful. It is no more than the height of a chess piece but breathtaking in its detail. He picks it up and compares it with the older woman from the convertible. The similarity is obvious, though the figurine shows a sultriness that the reality does not currently live up to. The figurine is also unclothed, while the old strumpet in the sports car looks like she got dressed in the dark. Foley holds it up for closer examination and rubs the pendulous breasts. He's pleased he took the box. He hadn't been able to resist. It had been left on the doorstep by a good-looking man with designer stubble and a flat cap. There was no note. No name. Foley had wanted it. Foley had taken it. And now it belongs to Foley.

'Copper kids are probably more fucked up than the rest of us,' he says, moodily. 'Can't be easy, knowing what the people in authority are like when they're at home. Must be terrifying. You grow up watching your mam or your dad fall over putting their socks on or reading a map the wrong way or picking up the ketchup by the top and spilling it all over the floor. You get to see them as a person – y'know, a real, crap specimen, like the rest of us. How are you supposed to believe they turn into a superhero when they leave the house? Must give you a few issues. Must make you almost want to rebel to see how they respond.'

Teddy considers his companion. He's a skinny thing but there are muscles on him like a condom full of billiard balls. He's maybe thirty. Younger than Teddy by a good twenty years but the pair have grown close since they were introduced to one another in the recreation room of Wormwood Scrubs and saw something in each other that they admired. Their relationship was a physical one, on the inside. Pragmatic, if not exactly tender. Since they've been out they have not spoken of what they did for comfort in the confines of the cell they shared. What happens in the Scrubs stays in the

Scrubs. And besides, they have fucked enough girls between them, and together, to know in their hearts they aren't gay.

'You're a philosopher,' says Teddy, warmly. 'Good head on your shoulders, when you're not being a moaning little twat.'

Foley shrugs. He's a moody soul. He muttered and grumbled about the heat in the car all through the drive up from London but has yet to remove his padded coat, hooded jumper or the jeans with elasticated ankles that he has forced into a pair of boots.

Teddy does not dress to impress. He doesn't give a damn about style, or looking like a gangster. In his experience, it's best to blend in. Teddy does this very well. He's a bulky man, but with his receding hairline, double chin and unremarkable clothes, he rarely attracts attention. He's wearing a pale shirt with market jeans and a pair of service-station sunglasses. He urged Foley to do the same, but the younger man had been convinced that the weather up north would be intolerable, and dressed for an Arctic winter.

'Take the picture,' says Foley, as the front door of the house slams and the older one with the dark hair starts punching the steering wheel. 'Let him know we're here.'

'Will do,' says Teddy, and snaps a couple of images with his mobile phone. He checks his messages. 'Nothing new. We're still to hang on until we hear more.'

Foley shakes his head, pissed off and bored. 'Can't we just do it now? We're here. She's just sitting there. And that lass had a decent rack on her. So does the mum. A scare, he said. Why wait?'

Teddy shrugs. He's seen it all before. Has more patience than his young companion. Knows he's on to a good thing. He puts 'debt collector' down on forms when he's forced to explain his occupation. It's a title that covers a multitude of sins.

'He's going to call her himself,' says Teddy. 'Explain things, and then we'll see. She's an important woman. Near enough to being the boss of CID. This has to be done right. Finesse, my young friend – that's what we need here.'

Foley broods. Teddy knows he doesn't like finesse. He likes

24

hitting people over the head with a golf club and stamping on their faces until he can see the pavement through their eye sockets. But he's getting paid well to employ restraint.

Foley lifts the Lucozade and takes a swig. Belches loudly. In response to Teddy's pained look, he opens his window a crack.

'You done a copper before?' Foley asks, staring at a wasp crawling up the windscreen. He leans over and flicks on the wipers, cursing as the wasp flies away before it can be pulped.

'Years ago,' says Teddy, nostalgically. 'Undercover he was. Can't remember which prison it was in. May have been Durham. He was trying to get some pervert to open up to him and tell him where he'd left this kid's body. Me and a lad called Fleetwood didn't know he was a copper. We bunged the guards a fifty to let us have half an hour with one of the nonces. This poor bastard was the one who drew the short straw. He fought like a fucking tiger. Didn't help him though. Not in the end.'

Foley nods appreciatively. Scratches at his groin, then slips his hand inside his jogging pants.

'He get the other nonce to confess?'

'Dunno, son,' says Teddy. 'He never came back from the hospital wing. I think he got a disability pension. Couldn't be a copper after that. Say what you will about coppers, but one thing they all need is teeth.'

Foley considers this. He nods at the woman getting out of the convertible and leers at her ample backside – enjoying the spectacle even more as she seems to change her mind and artfully lowers herself back inside.

'This poor bitch had better start looking for a new career, then.'

Teddy smiles affectionately at his partner. Looks at his phone and lets the anticipation build.

'Oh yes,' he says. 'Oh yes indeed.'

Fat bitch, fat bitch, fat bitch . . .

It had almost been lost, under the slam of the door and the tinny sound of shit music bleeding from her headphones, but there had been no mistaking the mumbled insult as Sophia grabbed her bag (condoms, cigarettes, tampons, a bra and the perfectly sensible knickers she'd been wearing when she left) and stomped towards the front door of the unremarkable semi-detached house on the Scartho estate in Grimsby.

Detective Superintendent Trish Pharaoh sits for a moment in the driver's seat of her sports car. Feels hot tears pricking at her eyes. She can't decide whether she wants to run after her eldest daughter and slap her until she's purple, or go and gorge herself on medicinal red wine and Maltesers.

Pharaoh sniffs. Sucks at her cheeks for a moment. Flips down the rear-view mirror and winces.

Fat bitch, fat bitch, fat bitch . . .

She's forty-six. Dark-haired and curvy. 5 foot 4 inches when she takes her biker boots off. The darkness under her eyes looks like bruising and there is a fine spray of burst capillaries across her cheeks. She's tried to tie her hair back but wispy strands have escaped from the ponytail and are curling up like tiny snakes around a forehead that looks like it has been grooved using a pizza-cutter. There is red in the cracks in her lips. Her eyebrows need plucking. She smells of tobacco and roll-on deodorant, of the clothes she slept in and which she has no intention of taking off today.

Pharaoh hates her reflection so intensely that she's tempted to rip the mirror off and smash it. She resists. Can't afford to have it repaired.

Slowly, she steps out of the vehicle and into the warm spring evening. There's a twinge in the back of her left leg and the base of her spine. She turns to look at the car as she closes the door and sees herself staring back in the darkened glass. Sees the full effect. She wishes she'd put a bra on, that she were wearing something slimming, instead of the jogging pants and man's shirt that she woke up in. Wishes she'd brushed her teeth or eaten a mint before she turned up at the big house near the airport and grabbed her eldest daughter by the hair. Trish could have played the thing a little more deftly. Could have been the cool mum she used to be, giving her little girl a wink as she waited for her to pack her things and disentangle herself from the sleeping bags and beer cans and pizza boxes. Could have told her she'd known all along that she wasn't staying at her friend's house and had in fact gone to a party with older boys. But she didn't. She went in all guns blazing, stinking of last night's booze, demanding to know if any of the slumbering lads had put their hands on her child. She might even have flashed her warrant card. She made damn sure she stepped on the bare thigh of some tattooed halfwit who dared to look up from the floor and tell her to chill. More than anything, she could have waited until she got into the car before screaming at Sophia that she was a dirty little scrubber who was going to be Aids tested as soon as the surgery opened in the morning.

Pharaoh closes her eyes. Shakes her head and wonders just how much her daughter hates her right now. She isn't even cross any more. She did worse when she was young. As she considers this she wonders if, in fact, it is true. Was she a bad girl? She was a big sister herself. Spent her teenage years making packed lunches and cooking teas and walking her younger siblings to and from school. She did her homework, most of the time, and always cleaned up if she threw up in her bedroom. She had been entitled to the odd grope behind the Spar in Mexborough, hadn't she? Did that make her a tart? She didn't think so at the time; isn't sure now. She's been told she dresses like a whore but she's been called most names at one time or another and has never been one to give much of a shit. But Sophia? What the hell is she rebelling against? Is she still a virgin? Oh God, please let her still be a virgin.

Pharaoh remembers her own first time. Andy, he was called. Curly hair and breath that smelled of smoky bacon crisps. He pawed at the fastenings of her bra as if he were wearing oven-gloves. He'd done her from behind in an abandoned council house three streets from the police station where she would one day work. Didn't even take his trainers off. It hadn't lasted long but he'd said she was good at it. Told his friends too, and they told everybody else. She didn't mind too much. It was nice to have a talent, and anybody who used the word 'slag' within earshot quickly discovered that she was even better with her fists than she was at moving her hips. She never gave it away cheaply. Soon learned that having a large chest and pretty eyes and a vaguely exotic look were damn good assets when coupled with a brain as sharp as piano wire. And reputation didn't really matter. She'd never had to lie to her parents because there was nobody to tell her off for the truth. Her mum was too busy trying to keep a roof over their heads. Her granddad seemed to go straight from bright-as-a-button to full-on demented the moment he took early retirement. Life was bloody hard. She'd been bright enough to go to whichever university she chose, but Pharaoh turned down the offers. Hadn't had the money or the inclination. She became a copper, like her granddad, who spent twenty-three years as a community policeman in the days when an ASBO came in the form of a clip around the ear or a good hiding behind the bins. Police Constable Patricia Pharaoh; good in the sack and hard as nails. That seemed enough, once. It hasn't been in a long time.

Pharaoh tries to put a grin on her face. Spots the gap in her smile and feels her stomach heave. Christ, she forgot to put her tooth in. She's been screaming at teenagers with her hair wild and a hole in her smile. Fuck! She left it in the glass of water by her bed. The permanent implant simply won't stay in. She's okay with the falsie but does have a tendency to click it with her tongue when she's thinking. The three younger kids think it's kind of cool. They can tell their friends that their top-cop mum had her tooth knocked out by a gangster in a gunfight at Flamborough Head. They're proud of their mum, even now. They like that their male friends go coy around her and won't trust themselves to wear jog-ging pants if she's wearing a top that offers a view of her cleavage. She needs her girls right now. Needs the people who matter to tell her that she's ace, and pretty, and not the incompetent tart that the newspapers are labelling her as, as they revel in Humberside Police's biggest fuck-up for years.

Not so long ago, Pharaoh was their blue-eyed girl. Her depart-ment's clean-up rate was being lauded at Association of Chief Police Officers get-togethers and the techniques they used to bring down a criminal gang were being exhibited as examples of best practice to other police forces. The *Grimsby Telegraph* even ran a profile on

her and she was approached by a documentary team keen on pro-
filing strong women in male-orientated environments. Pharaoh told
them to piss off. She had no desire to be a poster girl for feminism.
She's never seen herself as that kind of woman, never seen herself
as much more than a copper really. She's experienced misogyny,
but she's never met a sexist bastard who couldn't be made to change
their opinions when you have one hand on their bollocks and the
other around their throat. Pharaoh got where she is by catching
villains. Got her team to respect her by scaring the pants off some
and putting her motherly arms around others. One of the newspapers said that if she were the England football manager, the country
would have a couple more World Cups under its belt and Gazza
would never have turned to drink. She liked that. Didn't agree, but
liked it nevertheless.

Pharaoh flattens her hair down. Tries to act like everything's
okay. It is, really. She still has her job. The shitstorm will blow over
eventually. The Chief Constable is defending her in public, even if
she's in no doubt that he's calling her a silly cow behind her back.
She's still in charge of the Serious and Organised team and has
managed to get rid of the two bad apples who threatened to
scupper the unit before it got off the ground. Shaz Archer is head
of the Drugs Squad now. And Detective Chief Inspector Colin
Ray is probably drinking himself to death under a bridge. It's
months since he last sent Shaz a postcard from his beach house in
Turkey, containing badly spelt instructions that she pass on his
best regards to half a dozen of the good old boys, and to tell
Pharaoh and McAvoy to go fuck themselves. Her unit is doing its
job well. She can't beat organised crime but since the apparent
demise of the Headhunters organisation and its boss, she has at
least managed to contain it. She can't think of the crime outfit
without wrinkling her nose. They were utterly merciless; a group
of professionals who moved in on existing crime families and
demanded payment in exchange for access to their skills. They left
bodies everywhere. Turned her stomach with their creativity. But
Pharaoh and her team brought them down. There have been no
nailgun attacks in nearly two years and the drugs trade seems to

be back in the hands of morons and muscle. Does the Reuben Hollow case matter? Is it worth getting in a state over? She needs to drink less. Smoke less. To start taking care of herself and her girls . . .

There is a shout from inside the house and the thud of a slamming door. Pharaoh realises that Sophia has taken her frustrations out on one of her younger sisters. Olivia, probably. Her youngest is a tenacious little sod who isn't remotely scared of her big sister's hormones and temper tantrums. They spend half their lives pulling one another's hair out while the middle two eat crisps and drink pop and place bets on the outcome. She knows she should go in and break it up. Wonders if the riot squad owe her any favours.

It wasn't always like this. There was a time when she and the four girls lived in a big house on the outskirts of Grimsby. Her husband made good money and he doted on his daughters. He was a charmer. The love of her life. Handy with his fists but a decent dad and damn good at giving her goosepimples whenever he sniffed her neck or slapped her rump as she bent to load the dishwasher. He liked that she was a strong woman, and that she hit him back. He took her to balls and posh restaurants, gallery openings and his private box at the dog track. She didn't know he was financing his business with dodgy loans and that he owed the taxman more money than their house was worth. Didn't find out until he suffered a colossal aneurysm that left him unable to speak or move much below the waist. Trish had got them this place. Trish took care of the court cases and the bankruptcy action and managed to drag herself and the girls through all the unpleasantness without it taking their spirit away. Trish got the garage converted into a bedroom for her husband, where he spends most of his time lying on his crisp sheets, staring at the flickering TV screen and looking like a giant sausage roll. He doesn't even try to speak now. Just turns his head away when the girls come in. Only seems to get excited when his nurse visits. Silly bastard probably still thinks he's a catch, probably has fantasies about them running off together, though his motorised wheelchair only has a top speed of 12 mph and he would need to recharge the batteries before they got anywhere near their love nest.

Pharaoh used to chide herself for thinking harshly of her husband. She knew what he was when she married him and he ran up his debts while trying to give her the life he thought she wanted. It wasn't his fault his brain burst under the pressure. She just wishes the bastard would either get better or die. It's a horrible thought but it's one that she and the girls have almost constantly. She's not a widow. The girls aren't orphans. But she doesn't have a husband and they don't have a father. They have a salami, hooked up to drips and colostomy bags, dribbling into his pyjamas and grunting chat-up lines to the woman who changes the dressings on his bed sores. Each of the epileptic fits that he has suffered since the aneurysm could be his last. But the bastard's hanging on. And he can't do a damn thing to help Trish pay off the one creditor who really isn't troubled by the fact that the courts have written off the family's debts. Her husband borrowed money from somebody who wants it back. The letters have been civil and straightforward, sent to her solicitor from a law firm in London. They speak of a client who loaned her husband a considerable sum some years before. They mention the bankruptcy and the debtor's limited means, and ask that Trish, as his representative, make a sensible offer of restitution. Trish has made an offer but it was not accepted. The creditor was not interested in either a Mars bar or the opportunity to go fuck themselves.

She pushes open the front door and proceeds through to the lounge. It's not a bad house. The walls could do with a lick of paint and there is an assortment of stains on the pink carpet but the furniture came with them from their old house and is worth a damn sight more than Pharaoh put down on the forms when she listed the family's assets. She certainly didn't mention the fact that the painting of the tall man in the bowler hat, which hangs above the fireplace, is an original by the Beverley artist Fred Elwell, and worth more than she earns in a year. The rest of the wall space is taken up with family photos and various certificates of achievement. Olivia's diploma from last summer's drama school almost covers the huge red spray on the wall by the door, wine flung by Pharaoh at her disappearing daughter as the stroppy cow stormed out of the house a few weeks before.

The middle two girls are on the sofa, staring wide-eyed at the laptop, mesmerised by a succession of teenagers falling off trampolines or bouncing over hedges. 'All good?' Pharaoh asks them, warily. 'I'm not going to find any intestines in the bread bin, am I? And please tell me that Olivia isn't trying to make a mace again. I've told you before, a tin of beans in a sock is dangerous. And besides, chopped tomatoes are cheaper.'

Pharaoh gets the grin she hoped for, and a grunt about everything being fine now. Olivia is making herself a drink in the kitchen and there is no sign of Sophia, or blood, so Pharaoh treats herself to a sigh of relief and plonks herself down in the armchair. Picks up the remote control and switches on something mindless.

Oh fuck.

Him.

He's sitting on the comfy chair that the BBC wheels out whenever somebody famous or particularly interesting agrees to appear on *Look North*.

His name is Reuben Hollow, and he's the reason why Trish Pharaoh's life has recently turned to shit.

Pharaoh has to admit he looks good. Prison must agree with him. He was never exactly portly but during his time inside he has slimmed down even further and now he has the sort of cheekbones that most teenage girls would sell their parents for. He's still got the stubble that he kept running his hand through during their interview sessions. Still got the gold earring too, though he's taken off the flat cap that Pharaoh had presumed was stapled to his head. He's wearing a collarless shirt and tweedy waistcoat and there is a pendant of some kind peeking through his dark chest hair. His eyes haven't lost their fire. They're still an almost unnatural blue; glinting like Arctic water as it captures the sun. Christ, he's a handsome bastard, thinks Pharaoh.

And then to herself, *don't you bloody dare*.

The interviewer is doing his best to keep the camera focused on himself but he's fighting a losing battle. Reuben Hollow is more than photogenic. Pharaoh can almost hear the drool oozing from the interviewer's earpiece as the directors order the camera to stay fixed on the man who was freed last Thursday when his murder conviction was quashed by the Court of Appeal.

'You must be feeling very relieved,' says the interviewer, as the camera pans back to let him have his moment. He's a weasel-ly-looking thing. Skinny, with a head too big for his body and hair that looks like it was stuck on at a factory.

Reuben half smiles. Nods. Closes his eyes, as though thinking of the lyrics to a song.

'It's been difficult,' he says softly, in that gentle northern accent that had almost put Pharaoh to sleep in the interview room.

He pauses for breath before continuing his whispered confession.

'I'd never spent more than a night away from my daughter and the next moment I was looking at a whole life in prison. I expected to be punished, but murder was simply the wrong charge. Thankfully, the Court of Appeal has vindicated that. I just want to get back to spending time with my girl and trying to live our lives. We never asked for any of this. I don't like the limelight – I live in the middle of nowhere. I don't like the noise and the chaos of London; even Hull's too loud for me. I like the sound of the birds and my daughter playing her piano. I didn't want to hurt anybody. I just didn't have a choice.'

Pharaoh sucks her teeth and checks her watch. 1.50 p.m. She instinctively reaches for a glass of wine. There isn't one to hand. She clicks her fingers and says 'splashy-splishy' to Samantha, who peels herself off the sofa and pours her mum a large glass of Rioja, which she hands over without a word.

'Why don't you unfasten another button?' Pharaoh mutters at the telly. 'Christ, it's like you're about to burst into song. You're not auditioning, you preening twat.'

On screen, the interviewer is apologising to his guest.

'We're about to show some footage that might be distressing to both the viewers and to yourself but which may illustrate why this has been such a complex case. Now, Mr Hollow, am I correct in thinking that you were sitting outside the Duke of York in Skirlaugh, north east of Hull, when the sequence of events began?'

Hollow nods and looks away, as if it's all too much to take.

'It had been a hot day,' he says, quietly. 'July the twelfth. I'd been working in the sun and felt entitled to a drink. That's one of the pubs I occasionally pop into. It's a family place. My daughter feels safe and the cider's good.'

'And can you tell us, in your own words, what happened?'

'Who else's bloody words would he use!' screams Pharaoh, and her daughters decide to take the laptop through to the kitchen.

'It was probably around seven p.m.,' says Hollow. 'My daughter had been at a friend's in the village. She was going to meet me so we could go home together. I'd had a pint and switched to fizzy water, as my receipts from that night will show. I was talking to a friend at the bar when there was a commotion outside. Then somebody I know from the village put their head around the door and said that Del was in trouble.'

'This is your daughter, Delphine?' asks the interviewer. 'And she was sixteen, yes?'

'She's seventeen now,' says Hollow. 'Had her birthday while I was in prison.'

'And tell us what you saw as you looked outside.'

Hollow licks his lips. A flash of something primal flickers on his face, as though a pike has leapt from a lake to grab a butterfly. He seems to be replaying the moment in his head.

'Del was over the other side of the road,' he says. 'She was crying and her clothes were ripped. She had blood on her lip and running down her leg from a gash on her knee. And three lads were a few feet away, shouting and swearing. One of them was holding half a dozen small stones in his left hand and tossing another one up in his right. I'm not Sherlock Holmes but it was clear they had assaulted Del.'

'And this is in a town you call home, yes? A pleasant community.' The interviewer shakes his head, horrified at the world.

'There's an old boy drinks with me sometimes,' says Reuben, looking up into the camera. 'He was having a cigarette outside. He'd seen what was happening and gone over as soon as Delphine appeared. One of the lads pushed him over. Right there, in the street where he'd lived all his life.'

'And the boys responsible were known to you?'

Reuben laughs a little. 'They were known to everybody. They were a nuisance. I'd stuck up for them a couple of times when people told me what they were like. We've all been young, haven't we? But they were trouble. One older lad and two seventeen-year-olds. Thought they were something special and loved to show off how tough they were. Somebody had obviously told them about Delphine's brother and they thought it was okay to hurt her with that. I don't understand that. Her brother's death affected Delphine and me in a way I can't even explain. They thought it was funny to taunt her over it. And when she did what I'd always taught her to do and stuck up for herself, they attacked her.'

The interviewer nods and the screen fills with grainy CCTV footage, shot from the front of the pub. It shows Reuben Hollow walking calmly to where his daughter is cowering and taking her in his arms. Then the oldest lad throws a stone. It hits Delphine in the small of the back.

And Reuben goes to work.

'Mr Hollow, I am not a parent myself but I can understand the anger that must have gone through you in that moment. That being said, can you condone such violence?'

Hollow has to bite back the laugh that threatens to escape his lips. 'Violence? They attacked my daughter. They mocked the memory of my son. That wasn't violence. That was a little lesson in manners.'

The interviewer's eyes seem to light up. He can see the headline writers having a ball with that one.

'Mr Hollow,' he continues, 'we can clearly see in the video that you struck the eldest man, Barry Mathers, full in the face and then kicked him in the ribs when he was on the ground. You also threw seventeen-year-old Dean Day over a garden wall and hit Stewart O'Neill in the ribs so hard that both his feet left the ground.'

Hollow looks at him, all innocence and charm.

'Yes,' he says. 'I did. And I would do it again, as any parent would. What has happened to us? Seriously? We let these people bully us. Scare us. I taught my children to stick up for themselves. How do we do that? Well most of the time we turn the other cheek and let it slide. But these boys attacked my daughter.'

The interviewer seems pleased. He can clearly see the highlights of this chat playing on the national news.

'Now as far as you were concerned, that was the end of it, yes? You and your daughter went home.'

Hollow nods, and for a moment his blue eyes seem about to fill with tears. Then he regains his composure. Scratches at his stubble.

'I have a gypsy caravan at home,' he says. 'Delphine and I sometimes spend our evenings in there. She reads. I carve. Occasionally we sing songs. It's our little retreat. The first thing we knew about Mathers Senior was when he marched up the steps and tried to take my head off with an axe.'

On the sofa, Pharaoh shakes her head. The bastard sounds so damn plausible.

'This is Wayne Mathers, the father of the man you assaulted in Skirlaugh?'

Hollow nods.

'His son told him I'd attacked him for no reason. He came to sort me out. It was dumb luck that I kicked out and he fell backwards down the steps. I didn't even think he'd hurt himself. He went down with a thud but he got up again. I talked him around and he got in his car and drove off. That was that. It was another fortnight before I was arrested. Another few days until I was charged. My solicitor had no idea that it would be a murder charge. Even then I felt sure a jury would believe me.'

The interviewer takes a breath.

Here it comes, thinks Trish. *Here it bloody comes . . .*

'And it was the statement of Humberside Police Sergeant Alan Cotteril that was the vital evidence during that trial, yes?'

Pharaoh can't take any more. She stamps over and switches the telly off at the wall. She wants to smash the damn thing. She knows the story by heart anyway. Mathers suffered a head injury as he fell down the steps. It caused a haemorrhage that put him in a coma and eventually claimed his life. One way of looking at it was that Reuben Hollow had killed him. Pharaoh considered the evidence far too thin for a realistic chance of a murder conviction. Even Shaz Archer thought the best they could get was manslaughter. Then good old Alan Cotteril came forward with a statement. Reuben Hollow had admitted to him en route to the station for interview that he had given Mathers Senior a good hiding. Had smashed his head off the wheel arch of the caravan and didn't stop until he got an apology. The statement was enough to show intent to kill and the case went forward to the CPS. Hollow was charged with murder. Pharaoh can still remember the look in his eyes. It was hurt and bewilderment and absolute stone-cold despair.

My daughter, he'd said, over and over, as she read the charge. *Who will look after my daughter?*

Despite Cotteril's statement, not all the jury could be convinced that Hollow was guilty. The judge eventually accepted a majority verdict and Hollow was sent down for life. Then the press started to kick up a fuss. Could a man not defend himself in his own home? Could he not stick a punch on the arseholes who had assaulted his daughter? They painted a picture of a humble, handsome man, fighting for the old ways. He was a sculptor. Lived in a cabin in the woods with his prodigiously clever daughter. He was a looker with the eyes of a poet: gold dust for the tabloids. And when Sergeant Alan Cotteril was found dead in his living room having overdosed on whisky and prescription painkillers, Pharaoh's life got worse. Next to his body was an open laptop screen. On it, he had written his deathbed confession. Hollow's confession was pure fiction. Cotteril had made the whole thing up and he knew the truth was all going to come out. Hollow's case was fast-tracked to the Court of Appeal. Then the *Sunday Mirror* splashed with a story it had been working on for weeks. Sergeant

Alan Cotteril was Wayne Mathers' cousin through marriage. The link was the worst-kept secret in Skirlaugh and yet nobody had picked up on it. Least of all Trish. The vultures started to circle and their wings blew up a hurricane of shit, all of it heading for her. How had she missed the link? That was what they all wanted to know. Even McAvoy had allowed one disloyal eyebrow to slide towards the ceiling when the revelations surfaced.

Pharaoh growls at herself as she realises she has allowed her thoughts to turn towards her sergeant. For a while she thought about setting up a money box on the mantelpiece to put a pound into every time she allowed the image of his big stupid freckled face to swim into her mind. Then she realised it would cost her too much. If he'd been on the investigation there was no way the link between Cotteril and Mathers would have gone undiscovered. But he'd been on his bloody holidays, smooching and simpering with that pretty little cow of a wife. Pharaoh chides herself again. *Be nice.* She has nothing against Roisin. Just wishes the bitch was still in protective custody and not around to show up all Pharaoh's faults. Perfect tits, perfect arse, perfect little wife. If she wasn't hard as coffin nails and as fiercely protective of Aector as Pharaoh herself, Trish would probably have nutted her by now.

She drains her red wine and wonders if she should take a shower. Wonders if there are any Easter eggs left in the cupboard. Wonders what she would do if Aector turned up and saw her wearing the shirt that he left here last time he and the family came to stay.

Wonders, for the thousandth time, if she should just tell Aector the truth about the whole damn business. Whether he would understand.

Her mobile phone makes the decision for her.

It's DC Ben Neilsen, calling from Hull's Old Town.

They've got a body, Guv.

Been trying to ring you for ages.

McAvoy said to call you immediately . . .

And this one is *really* fucking sick . . .

3

Millions of pounds in regeneration money has been thrown at this estate but it's still got more anti-social behaviour orders per square mile than anywhere else in the city and a fair number of weddings and christenings are planned around court dates. It's a place where the only way to get rid of unwanted furniture is to put it in the garden with a 'for sale' sign.

Helen Tremberg rubs a hand over her face. She smells talcum powder, antiseptic wipes, egg mayonnaise and bleach. Her olfactory bulb is used to such assaults but today's battering veers close to grievous bodily harm. She shudders. Unearths a packet of extra-strong mints and crunches through two like a horse with a sugar lump, allowing the aroma to fill her head and numb her tongue. She rummages in the pocket of her suit jacket and finds her vanity mirror. Flips it open and gives herself the once-over. Passable. Still not pretty but far from undesirable. Brown bobbed hair, broad shoulders and gentle eyes. Tiny silver studs in her ears. A baggy roll-neck jumper hiding her shape. She's still conscious of the baby-weight. Probably always will be.

Helen is sitting at a round table in the deserted bar. The place shouldn't be open but she spotted the caretaker and persuaded him to let her inside. He'd been happy for the company. Happy to help the police. Happy to tell her that while a lot of people on this estate thought all coppers should be burned alive, he would definitely piss on one if they were on fire.

'I'm sorry about that. It was just, you know . . . not something I ever thought I'd see . . .'

Helen looks up into the pale, pinched face of the young police community support officer. She can't be much more than twenty-five. Frizzy ginger hair, Celtic skin and freckles. Red eyes and nose from the cold and the tears. She's sorted herself out a little in the toilets of this glorified community centre but there is no mistaking the fact that she looks shaky and scared.

'Don't give it a second thought,' says Helen, patting the chair opposite and pushing the packet of mints towards her. 'It would be more worrying if it didn't upset you. Bloody hell, you saw something awful. There's no training can prepare you for that. I just wish I could tell you that you'll never see anything like it again. I'm afraid by the time you retire you'll be able to eat a full fried breakfast from a tray while watching a post mortem.'

The PCSO manages a smile. Her name is Vicki. She wanted to be a social worker when she left university but didn't quite get the grades and couldn't seem to get her foot in the door. Worked in a bar of an evening and an office during the day before her mum showed her an advert in the paper. Reckoned she would make a good PCSO. Reckoned it was perfect for her. It'd allow her to help people and build up her confidence. The advert had been placed to attract people with 'excellent communication skills and experience of dealing with difficult situations'. Vicki wasn't sure she qualified on either front, but telling her mum she was too nervous to apply led to one of those difficult situations, and the experience of it led Vicki to fill in the damn form. She hadn't been entirely sure she even wanted the job when she went for the first of the interviews but has now been in the role for over a year and is enjoying it, truth be told. She likes the uniform and the camaraderie. She's making some headway with the local teens. Some of the mums know her by name. It was the proudest moment of her life when a thirteen-year-old schoolgirl sought her out and asked her advice on what to do about the baby she thought she might be carrying. Vicki didn't know what advice to give, but she knew that by asking, the girl was demonstrating that Vicki was, in some way, a person whose opinion might count. That felt good. She's recently begun to consider applying for the regular police service. She can see herself as a community police officer, can see the attraction of getting villains off the street and helping nice people lead nicer lives.

She was still feeling that way until the early hours of this morning, when she forced the door of the property on Ryehill Grove and found the body of Raymond O'Neill.

'You've done great,' says Helen warmly, using the tone and body language that her former boss Trish Pharaoh seems to manage so effortlessly. Helen feels a bit of a fraud. She's not great at flattery. Gets a bit embarrassed by the whole affair.

'I wasn't sick,' says Vicki, with some pride. 'Well, I was a bit, but not at the scene. There's no contamination, I was careful.'

Helen smiles. Pulls out her notebook. 'You did great,' she says again, and makes a mental note to come up with a better platitude if she is ever called upon to do this again.

'He called me a cunt, once,' says Vicki, looking down at the grey-blue carpet and flicking at something with her clumpy black boot. 'O'Neill, I mean.'

Helen decides not to make a note. She nods. 'From what I've heard, he used that word the way most people use punctuation.'

'He was horrible,' says Vicki. 'I don't mean he was horrible enough to deserve that, but . . .'

'Maybe he was, maybe he wasn't,' says Helen, candidly. 'That's not for us to worry about. Now, I really need a bit of focus from you, okay, Vicki? You've done great. I mean, brilliant. It must have been awful, seeing that. But you'll feel better when you've got your statement down on paper. There's no rush for that. All I need from you is the bare bones, okay? I'm not the expert on this estate. You are. I don't know very much about Raymond O'Neill. You know more than I do. So, fill in the blanks.'

Helen takes another mint from the packet. Gets another whiff of her lunch and her six-month-old baby. She has to fight back the smile that threatens to erupt on her face whenever she thinks of the child. Tells herself not to be soppy when she's supposed to be working. Of course, she isn't actually *supposed* to be working. Not according to the rota. Helen has been back from maternity leave for just under a month and found herself temporarily seconded to the Drugs Squad under the command of the unit's new boss, Shaz Archer. Helen has always detested the snotty cow but is now almost obsessive in her loathing. She hates the fact that Archer is now a DCI. As if she didn't already have everything! Archer should be here now, getting her hands grubby on the Preston Road estate. But Archer has an important polo match today. She's somewhere down in the stockbroker belt, riding her pony and swinging her mallet and drinking Pimm's with blonde, toothy girls and tall men with ancestral quiffs and floppy lips. Helen isn't part of that crowd. Isn't part of any crowd, really. What she is, is a bloody skivvy. She should be watching the Grand Prix with her dad and little Penelope, wrist-deep in a bag of chocolates, wearing jogging pants and slipper-socks and dozing, gently, in a room that smells of gravy. Instead she's here, doing Archer's job, talking about a scumbag whose murder sounds as though it should be celebrated with fireworks and an open-top bus parade.

'Is DCI Archer going to be coming down personally?' asks Vicki, and there is something a little like awe in her voice. Archer is fast becoming a pin-up girl for a certain type of impressionable youngster. She's stunningly good-looking and tough as discount steak, with an arrest record that a lot of coppers would kill for. The *Hull Daily Mail* recently ran a four-page spread on this glamorous face of local policing, painting a picture of a dedicated and determined young woman whose story should be made into a TV crime drama. They made out that she was a feminist's dream and a slap in the face to chauvinists – conveniently forgetting that they wouldn't have bothered giving her any publicity if she hadn't been all fake tits and shiny teeth.

Helen lets her distaste show on her face. 'I think I'll be doing the legwork here,' she says, icily. 'DCI Archer is having a bikini wax in the morning and needs time to emotionally prepare.'

Vicki gives a confused smile. Looks disappointed and trembly-lipped.

Helen has her pen poised over a page full of notes she scribbled on the drive over from North Lincolnshire an hour ago. She found plenty of information online about O'Neill. The local papers were full of him last February and the reports about his trial were a useful précis of his criminal life to date. Helen already feels as though whoever killed him has not robbed the world of one of its great thinkers.

Raymond's extended family was the terror of the Preston Road estate. At his last court hearing, he revealed that he was the father of seventeen children (that he knew about) by eleven different women. The jury heard details of thirty-eight previous convictions, for everything from drunk and disorderly to heroin dealing. At fifty-eight, he had spent a total of fourteen years in various prisons. He had never worked, but somehow managed to own a house, a luxury static caravan and a speedboat. He also had a newborn baby, which was the reason he was spared jail for his latest misdemeanour. He had broken the wrist of a woman who tried to intercede while he was in the process of stamping on his girlfriend's stomach outside a pub on Priory Road. He told the court he was too drunk to remember what had happened but that he had 'probably just lashed out'.

The victim was only twenty-four, a classroom assistant who had just put a deposit on her first home. She was two years older than O'Neill's girlfriend, who refused to give a statement or make a fuss about her own injuries. Such things were par for the course. The judge showed unexpected leniency to O'Neill, who pleaded guilty at the first opportunity and had been expecting a stretch inside. His family erupted with delight when the judge declared he was going to suspend his prison sentence and allow him home to help care for his child. The cries of the victim's family were lost among the roar from the collected O'Neills, and while the local papers went crazy with indignation, the national press treated him like some sort of celebrity. He posed for photographs with as many of his kids as could be gathered together and revelled in his role as a cheeky scoundrel who had beaten the system.

This morning, O'Neill's body was found in a boarded-up house on Ryehill Grove. The door was kicked open by PCSO Vicki Fry.

She found Raymond O'Neill laid out on his belly with so many cracks in the back of his bald head that it looked like crazy paving. The stench climbed down her throat like fingers of fog.

'Why were you there?' asks Helen, and tries to keep her tone inquisitive rather than accusatory. 'He'd never been reported missing.'

Vicki looks down at her feet. A blush creeps out of the collar of her uniform. It reminds Helen of McAvoy. Most things do.

'There was a bit of talk on the estate that he'd done a runner but his family weren't the sort to call the police. But from the state of him he must have been there for weeks. Months, maybe. We certainly hadn't heard from him since the end of February when he got free. What's that – fifteen months? He must have been there the whole time. House hadn't been occupied in a good couple of years.'

Helen stops writing. Indicates she should slow down and start from the beginning.

'I'd worked the night shift,' says Vicki, taking a breath. 'A few of us have volunteered to do some of the less sociable shifts. We go out with the regulars. I finished at eight this morning. Midway through the shift, a patrol car radioed to say there was a drunk lass on Southcoates Lane, puking in the gutter and posing a risk. I was partnered up with a PC and we weren't far away so we went and checked it out. She was off her face but not unpleasant. I got her some water and checked she was okay and she said she had money for a taxi so we called one for her. Waited with her until it came. She sobered up enough to give us her name and address and then she started asking us why we hadn't found O'Neill. Started giving us this stuff about him and his family being the scum of the earth and that the world was better off without him. Then she came out with it. Said that the lad her neighbour buys his weed off had been spreading it about that his body was in a house on Ryehill. He'd been in there, looking for copper. Found a body and recognised him. I asked her why he didn't report it and she just shrugged and said he wanted to keep his head down. Then her taxi turned up.'

44

Helen sits, waiting for more.

'The officer you were with,' she says, carefully. 'He didn't suggest bringing her in for a statement?'

Vicki looks wretched, as though she doesn't want to get anybody into trouble. She pulls a face.

'She was drunk. He said it was just bullshit. Said we had her name and address if we needed it.'

Helen raises her eyebrows. 'You didn't support that view?'

'I thought it was worth investigating,' says Vicki, looking back at the floor. 'So I popped down there after my shift. There are half a dozen empty houses. I didn't think it would take a moment to check it out. So I had a look in the windows. Tried the doors. I opened the letter box at one of them and the smell hit me. Rotting meat and something else. Something like vegetation. Like a fishtank that hasn't been cleaned. There was no mistaking it. I kicked the door in. There he was.'

There is silence in the bar save for the sound of Helen's pen scratching on the page. She deliberately keeps her eyes down in case the young officer is crying again.

'You called it in?' asks Helen. 'Immediately? You weren't concerned about getting into trouble? Not exactly procedure, is it?'

Vicki rubs her thumb against the palm of her hand, as if pushing in a drawing pin. 'I thought that wasn't as important as getting people there. I thought I couldn't get into trouble for doing what I thought was best.'

Helen says nothing. She has found out to her cost just how naïve a perspective Vicki currently enjoys. She is about to press her for more when the phone rings. Her first instinct is to panic that something is wrong with Penelope. Then she realises the ringtone is not the one she has programmed for her father, who is currently babysitting. She answers with her name and rank, hoping that she is about to be told that DCI Archer has fallen from her horse and been fatally brutalised by a stallion. Instead, she hears the voice of Bernard Reardon, the lead science officer at the crime scene on Ryehill Grove. He's a quiet, hardworking and professional man who has never made a pass at Helen or been disciplined for making inappropriate comments. As such, Helen does not expect him to rise much higher in the service.

'DC Tremberg,' he says. 'I'm right in thinking you are looking after things in DCI Archer's absence, yes?'

Helen rolls her eyes and gives a little laugh. 'Your guess is as good as mine,' she says, sighing. 'But yes, I'm down the road at the Freedom Centre, talking to the officer who found the body. You need me to come up?'

'Probably not,' says Reardon. 'Not much to be gained, really. I'll have the photos with you before the end of the day. We're a little strained for resources, what with Professor Jackson-Savannah being otherwise engaged.'

'He's back, is he? Oh goody.'

'Yes and no. He's currently at the beck and call of DSU Pharaoh and her sergeant. I'm pleased we got this one and not the other. Young girl, so I'm told.'

Helen chews on her thumbnail and wonders, for a moment, what kind of case her old unit has landed. She curses Shaz Archer for requesting her transfer to the Drugs Squad, and for a moment, she once again questions the cold bitch's motivations. Shakes away her suspicions.

'Poor cow,' says Helen automatically. 'Is he okay? Actually, sorry, forget that, just tell me your initial thoughts.'

Reardon pauses for a moment, probably about to give his usual warning that nothing he is going to say should be considered fact and that she would be better served waiting for the complete report. Then he gives an audible shrug. He knows there's no way Helen will leave it at that.

'If the body in question is indeed Raymond O'Neill, we can say with certainty that he suffered a great deal before his death. He was tied up, gagged and beaten. It's hard to say at this stage but some degree of care has been taken to preserve the body. We'll have to analyse the organic material but from the lividity it certainly seems he's been there for several months and if that is the case, I'd have expected us to be fighting bluebottles and scooping him up with a spoon. It was professionally done. That's all I can tell you until we get things properly processed. I will email your-self and DCI Archer as soon as I have more, but it may not be till the early hours.'

'I'll probably be awake,' Helen says absently.

'I heard you were now a mum,' says Reardon, emotionlessly. 'Good sleeper? Happy to be back?'

Helen realises the questions are automatic and not really in search of an answer. She makes some vague responses then thanks him for his time, ends the call and turns back to Vicki.

'It was definitely O'Neill, then?' asks Vicki, nodding slightly. 'And he was killed?'

'Seems like it. They hurt him badly.'

Vicki digests this. Looks around, like a schoolgirl about to say a swear word.

'He was a horrible man,' she says, conspiratorially. 'When he was freed after hurting that poor woman, even the real hard cases on the estate thought it was disgusting. He was a proper bastard.'

Helen considers her notes. She fills her mind with a mixture of memories and imaginings. Sees him. McAvoy. His sad eyes and scarred skin; an oak tree whose branches are both shadow and shield. She has a constant desire to impress him. Remembers the feeling that fizzed through her when he brought her flowers and some of his wife's home-made remedies, and first took the baby in his colossal, broken hands.

Beautiful, he had said, and her head had filled with images of Scottish kings and warrior poets and she had felt absurdly pleased that her child measured up.

The memory fragments as her phone beeps and the crime scene photos begin to fill up her inbox. She has to suppress a shudder as she opens the first image. Whoever killed Raymond O'Neill was no amateur. And they had clearly enjoyed their work.

4

The sky is darkening over Hull's Old Town.

Blue lights, fluorescent coats and flickering tape are strobing and spinning at the entrance to Bowlalley Lane. This is the part of Hull that has barely changed in centuries. It's all high buildings, old bricks, and cobbles like freshly baked loaves. A hundred yards away on Whitefriargate, men in blue shirts and girls in short dresses are drinking lager and clinking glasses and trying to pretend that the sunshine is going to come back. Their whispers join the car engines, the breaking bottles, the pleas for spare change, the pigeons rustling in the trees around Trinity Square and the echo of the bells of St Mary's Church. They catch the breeze and rush down this man-made valley, echoing off the boarded-up offices and cut-price studio flats and soaking into the bones and bricks of this battle-scarred city.

The forensics van is parked halfway down, opposite the passageway that leads to the centuries-old drinking den Ye Olde White Harte.

On the other side of the narrow road an archway leads into a courtyard of overflowing dustbins and various kinds of grime. The paving slabs are greasy and the rubbish bags have spilled their contents down the back of the giant bins and into the gutters. Pizza boxes, empty lager cans and the insides of toilet rolls turn to mush beneath the blue-bagged feet of the police officers who mill around awaiting instructions.

The victim's flat is upstairs. It's a one-bedroomed mezzanine affair; the floor carpeted with discarded clothes, unopened letters and plates that look like an artist's palette: blobs of red slowly scabbing over on their cheap white surfaces.

In the bathroom, the tenant stares up, sightlessly. There is vomit in her mouth and on her chin. The curved bruise on her throat reveals the horror of her final moments. She has been strangled between the porcelain rim and the plastic seat of her toilet. Somebody pressed the seat down on the back of her neck and didn't let go until she had choked on her own puke. Then they lifted her arms and scalped her armpits, before emptying a full bottle of bleach onto her corpse.

She was an 'alternative' girl, in life. Tattoos, piercings and thick eye make-up. Petite. Maybe 5 foot, at a push. Her hair is shaved around her studded left ear and long and black everywhere else. She was wearing a little black vest and a pair of purple knickers when she died, showing off elaborate ink around her skinny thighs and sharp shoulder blades, which rise from her pale skin like shark's fins. Her feet are dirty and her toenails need cutting. She has cheap string bracelets around her thin wrists. Her fingernails look expensive; pink and black with tiny diamante sparkles. There are calluses on her fingertips. The ring finger on her right hand is missing, sliced off below the second knuckle. There is a hole in the linoleum floor, among the blood and bleach, that seems to indicate where the digit was severed; a knife going through the skin and gristle and bone with one sharp, practised push.

'Jesus,' says Pharaoh. 'That's bloody horrible.'

She raises a hand to her face and takes a whiff of the blue plastic glove. It stinks like a condom but is a damn sight better than the stench of rotting flesh, blood and chemicals that has been trapped in this poxy little bathroom since a killer closed the door.

She turns back to McAvoy, who is hovering in the doorway and making the place look even smaller than it already is. He's wearing the same white coveralls and blue plastic shoe-bags as everybody else, but somehow his make him look like a statue, while every-body else's make them look like bewildered ghosts.

'Are you coming in here?' she asks, testily.

'Is there room?'

'Would I ask if there bloody wasn't?'

McAvoy sidles back into the bathroom.

'A good few days,' says McAvoy as Pharaoh stands up and turns to face him.

Pharaoh feels like spitting. Her hair is still wet from the shower and her clothes smell of hastily applied perfume and the cigarettes she chain-smoked on the drive over. She's never cried over a corpse before but she spotted a couple of uniforms with red eyes as she pulled up on the cobbles outside and pushed her way under the police tape and past the forensics officers and made her way to the great sad island of composure at the centre of it all; busy directing operations in his low Scottish grumble and apologising every time he stepped on somebody's toes.

'This is her place?' asks Pharaoh. 'We're sure?'

McAvoy nods. 'Ava Delaney. Twenty-one. Lived here five months. No computer or phone that we can find. Neighbour thinks she's got family in Warwickshire but can't be sure. Likes to play her music loud and there's usually a smell of cannabis wafting around the flat entrance.'

Pharaoh looks at the corpse again. 'Pretty one,' she says, pursing her lips. 'Fuck, I need air.'

The pair push back out into the tiny flat and into the corridor. McAvoy follows her down the stairs and out into the little court-yard, where she instantly unzips her coveralls and fishes out one of her black cigarettes.

'Nice day off?' asks Pharaoh, through a cloud of smoke. 'Up until now, I mean? You take Roisin and the kids for a picnic . . . Sandwiches, lemonade, Hannah Kelly's body . . .'

'It's not a day off when you're on call,' he says, bristling slightly. 'And we weren't looking for her body, that would be sick. It's just somewhere nice.'

'Don't correct me,' she says, kicking him on the shin and giving him a smile. 'You've got your obsessions, I've got mine. Is Roisin cursing me?'

'Not your fault,' says McAvoy, looking at the pattern on the brickwork and refusing to meet her eye. 'And it's your day off, if you remember. Have you eaten properly? And have you made that appointment for your back? You can't put it off, you need to take care of yourself.'

Pharaoh holds up a hand. Ash tumbles onto her biker jacket. She wipes it away, as far as the hem of her knee-length black dress.

'Sophia went to a party last night,' she says, with her eyes closed. 'Boys galore. I only found out when I saw her in a picture on Facebook. I shouldn't have been looking. Made a right tit of myself. She's not talking to me.'

McAvoy plays with the zip of his coverall. Tugs at the patch of hair beneath his lower lip. He loves Pharaoh's girls. They each contain something of her spirit. They're strong and feisty, independent and fearless. They love his own children and think Roisin is the coolest grown-up on the planet. Roisin reckons they need a dad, and a good telling-off, but has no intention of volunteering her husband for either job.

'She's a good girl,' he tells her, trying to find something helpful to say. 'It's just a phase. You're a good mum. I can talk to Sophia, though I don't know what good I'd be. Maybe Roisin—'

Pharaoh gives a bark of laughter. 'Yeah, that would do my self-confidence a power of good. Christ, I'm a mess, Aector.'

McAvoy looks at her. He considers telling her she's wrong. He'd love nothing more than to tell her she looks a million dollars and she's everything from his hero to his best friend. He doesn't. Just colours slightly and looks away. He looks at this horrible little courtyard and wonders at the lives of the people who call it home. Wonders if these are palaces and sanctuaries to some, and cells to others. Wonders when people stopped using the words 'slum' and 'hovel' and replaced them with words like 'bijou' and "compact". Wonders if he's being a snob. He never had money when he lived at home on the croft. Had no need for it when his stepdad sent him off to boarding school aged ten. He shared a squalid house in Edinburgh with a couple of fellow psychology students when he was briefly at university, had a room in the house of a copper's widow when he was a young uniformed constable, and only got himself somewhere vaguely presentable when Roisin and Fin entered his life. He spent a whole summer living in a hotel room a couple of years ago, crying himself to sleep. He makes a mental note to keep those memories at the forefront of his thoughts. To remember the pain and isolation of living in a place made smaller by the weight of loneliness and the sense of having somehow failed.

'Tell me about Ava,' says Pharaoh, placing a hand on his arm. 'Boyfriend?'

McAvoy looks at her hand. Stubby nails and a wedding ring. Short, plump fingers and a dozen bangles, disappearing into her jacket. Soft, tanned skin.

'Ben has been chatting to her downstairs neighbour,' he says, rubbing his face so he has an excuse to dislodge her arm. 'Nice girl. Romanian. Antoaneta Osmochescu. Don't ask me to repeat that, please. She speaks wonderful English. Works in a freight office at the docks. She's been for a few coffees with Ava now and again. Apparently Ava wasn't seeing anybody steady but Antoaneta has seen a few people come and go from the flat.'

McAvoy points in the direction of the front door, where a shapeless wraith in a white suit is dusting the grimy wood for prints while two uniformed constables start placing cigarette butts into clear plastic bags, neatly labelling each one and grumbling at the enormity of the task.

'There's no intercom, you see,' he says. 'Can't buzz yourself up. So most people just give out the code to the door and people can let themselves in, if they're expected. A lot of people seem to have had Ava's code.'

Pharaoh makes a clicking noise with her tongue, as if mentally compiling a list of a thousand different things that are wrong with today's world.

'Work?' she asks.

'We found payslips from Rocky's, the clothes shop in Princes' Quay. We've put a call in to their manager but no answer yet. Probably enjoying the bank holiday.'

Pharaoh nods. She turns away, looking at the overflowing bins and the soggy cigarette butts; the damp brick and clogged, loose gutters. She seems about to speak when her phone vibrates. She grumbles a little and looks at the incoming message. Gives a puzzled sort of laugh then puts it away. For a moment, it looks as though a blush is rising in her cheeks, but she manages to suppress it.

'Keyholder?' she asks.

'One of the landlords. She had two. They let the place through an agency. He came to talk to her about overdue rent. Bit of an erratic payer, but he said she was no better or worse than anybody else. He shouldn't really have let himself in but she'd been ignoring his calls and texts for a week. He's got the number of a bloke she gave him when she moved in as sort of a guarantor. He's contacted him a couple of times but got nowhere. Jez Gavan, he's called. Lives up on Ings. Record going back years.'

'Nicely played,' she says, approvingly. 'First stop for you and me, I think. It's also pretty clear she has a phone. What's the wifi hub for this building? Did she have an account?'

'Got a broadband account that comes up as "Avascave" and which is still working, so she must have paid the bills. And according to her landlord she was a formidable texter,' says McAvoy. 'Not backwards in telling people what she thought. He showed me some of her messages explaining that she'd been going through a difficult time and would appreciate his empathy and patience and that she intended to make recompense.'

The two share a look.

'Recompense?'

'That was her word. All correctly spelled. She was a clever girl. Plenty of books in the apartment too. Poetry. Art critiques. A few crime novels.'

Pharaoh nods and waves a hand at the bins. 'We're bagging this up, yes? Every last scrap. If the person who did this is as thick as most murderers he'll have dumped the phone in the first bin he saw.'

McAvoy cocks his head and gives her a look. 'He?'

Pharaoh opens her palms, indicating that it's bloody obvious.

'That's a murder that screams "hate",' she says, gesturing back towards the apartment. 'That much hate comes from love, or at least some obsessive version of it. It's a man.'

'What happened to your rule about foregone conclusions?' asks McAvoy, and is only half keeping it light.

'I'm having one of those days. Maybe it's because I picked my daughter up from a party full of boys,' says Pharaoh, through gritted teeth. 'And every problem in my life seems to have been caused by somebody with a penis.'

McAvoy looks hurt but can find no way of expressing it that would not lead to a blush so intense he could lose his eyebrows.

'But you're probably right,' says Pharaoh, resignedly. 'We rule nothing out. We need to know her. Family. Friends. Need her bloody phone more than anything else. Is Dan pinging it?'

'Getting the paperwork now,' says McAvoy. He has a sudden mental picture of the technical wizard, with his glasses and baseball shoes and his utter, all-consuming lust for Pharaoh. 'I told him it meant a lot to you.'

Pharaoh rolls her eyes but nods in approval. McAvoy has loosened up a lot these past couple of years. There was a time when he would have allowed his request to be processed in the correct and orderly fashion and wait his turn like everybody else. Under Pharaoh's supervision, he has learned to gently push his way to the front of the queue, using charm, persuasion and if necessary by looming over people until they get uncomfortable and will do anything to make him go away. He still fills in the forms in triplicate in case one gets lost, and blushes hugely if reproached, but he is not above using Dan's feelings for Pharaoh to speed things up. Pharaoh reckons he's finally becoming a proper copper, but she knows he has no real idea what that means. He just can't fathom a world in which there could be any excusable delay in hunting down a young girl's killer.

Pharaoh is about to suggest they go and talk to Ava's Romanian neighbour for themselves, when she hears her name. She turns and sees the figure striding towards them and lets out a groan that she makes no attempt to hide.

'Adam,' she says, with a sigh. 'You're back with us?'

Adam Jackson-Savannah is a Home Office pathologist who has just returned from a three-year placement at an American university. Pharaoh can't remember which one but feels sure he'll drop it into conversation within the next ten seconds. He's a tall, white-haired specimen in frameless glasses and a grey suit. His time in the sun has not improved his complexion. He remains deathly pale with a rash of pimples and blotches that runs down one cheek and onto his neck. The story goes that he was licked by a dog once and suffered an allergic reaction that has never cleared up. Add to this his watery eyes and thin, bloodless lips, and Pharaoh has always felt him well suited to the morgue. She would not hold his appearance against him were it not for his absolute incompetence and willingness to turn a blind eye to the occasional acts of corruption and downright evil committed by her predecessor.

'Yale's loss is Humberside's gain,' he says, and his lips form a tight, prissy pout as he speaks.

'Gene not available?' asks Pharaoh, in a voice that suggests she would be happier allowing a toddler with a scalpel to perform the examinations.

'Dr Woodmansey is on holiday,' he says primly, with a little turn of his head that suggests he finds the other man's dereliction of duty unconscionable. 'So you have me. And I have you. A shame for both of us, I'm sure.'

Pharaoh laughs and nods. 'The civil service has a short memory. I don't.'

'I was exonerated,' says Jackson-Savannah, with a sigh. 'A full inquiry concluded that there should be no stain on my record.'

'No, they found the evidence was inconclusive,' says Pharaoh. 'That's not the same thing. You ballsed up on a very important investigation, there's no mistaking that. I just don't know whether you did it because you're crap, or 'cause Doug Roper told you what to put on the report.'

McAvoy stiffens at the mention of the former head of CID. His involvement in the corrupt copper's demise has left him a marked man in some quarters. Roper was popular. His clean-up rate was immaculate and the media loved him. McAvoy tried to expose him, only to be left with scars to his body and career.

'I still receive a birthday card from Doug,' says Jackson-Savannah, like a teenage girl showing off a signed photograph from her favourite boy band. 'He's doing well. Consultancy work, I believe. That's where the money is. Still a young man. Still with very much to offer. A great shame he left without the fanfare he deserved.'

Pharaoh licks her teeth and looks up at McAvoy. 'Do you know Dr Jackson-Savannah?' she asks.

'I've heard of him,' says McAvoy, with the cold glare that Pharaoh has instructed him to practise at home in front of a mirror. 'Interesting CV.'

'I won't hold the past against you,' says Pharaoh, staring at Jackson-Savannah. 'We all make mistakes. You've made yours. But I warn you, it would be a mistake of fucking epic proportions to presume I run my investigations like Doug Roper. I don't want to tell you what to put in your report. I don't want corners cutting. I want a cause of death and a time of death and I want your every finding to be completely bloody bullet-proof.'

Jackson-Savannah pulls a face, growing cross at the very sug-gestion that he might not oblige. He is about to speak when Pharaoh jabs her thumb at the figure to her left, who is standing bolt upright and looking at him with a thoughtful intensity, like a child wondering whether to keep watching the ant squirm under the heat of the magnifying glass, or kill it quickly with a rock.

'The man beside me is Detective Sergeant Aector McAvoy,' she says brightly. 'You've probably heard of him. He doesn't like you. I can see that in his eyes. And McAvoy likes everybody. Thinks the best of them. I've only ever seen him respond this way to people who said mean things about his wife, and Robert Mugabe. So I'd do your best not to upset him. The girl's called Ava. And you're going to be very, very respectful with her body.'

Pharaoh is about to speak again when her phone vibrates. She sighs and takes the call. She looks puzzled for a second then tells the caller she has no idea why they think she would be interested.

Informs them of her rank and advises them to piss off. Then she hangs up. Composes herself. Turns away. Stubs her cigarette out on the brick and deposits the butt in her leather jacket.

From the street comes the sound of more cars arriving. More hails and hellos from officers who know this is going to be a long night. McAvoy hears his own name, and Pharaoh's. Hears grunts and jeers and wonders if they are from his colleagues or the drunks who are gathering at the end of Bowlalley Lane and craning their necks for a glimpse of dead flesh.

Jackson-Savannah looks about to protest but finds McAvoy still staring, hard, at the side of his head. He turns and bustles away towards the front door.

'Wanker,' says Pharaoh, looking up at McAvoy. 'You're getting good at that dead-eyed look, you know. Proper scary, if people don't know you're a pussy cat.'

'Roisin says I'm about as scary as a chinchilla,' says McAvoy, who has never felt comfortable using his size to intimidate. He has the personality of a much smaller man and would probably be working alongside Dan in the tech unit were it not for the fact that test tubes seem to break in his hands and his great big fingers press the wrong keys whenever he tries using one of the fancy tablet computers that Dan seems unable to live without.

Pharaoh considers him. 'Even chinchillas get rabies,' she says. 'And I've seen you foaming at the mouth. It just takes a lot to get you there.'

McAvoy stares upwards through the tunnel of brick into a darkening sky. He sniffs the air. Hull cannot expect to enjoy the good weather in which the rest of country is bathing. A sea fret is set to roll in, thick and grey. There has been a warning to the ships that churn through the waters of the Humber. The fog is going to close over the coast like a corpse's hand. The thought makes him shiver and think of Hannah, and her unknown grave: somewhere among the bluebells and the daffodils in a place that she adored. He feels the weight of it all settle in his gut. Feels the need to bring some kind of balance to things. He hates what people do to one another.

'We're taking this, yes?' asks McAvoy, turning back to his boss. 'With Hannah we haven't got a body. Not yet. But we can link it. A crime against an attractive young woman. We can say that we've got the resources and a potential connection . . .'

Pharaoh smiles tiredly. 'We'll take it,' she says, convinced it won't be difficult to sell the idea to her bosses. She needs to make up for the Reuben Hollow mistakes, to remind everybody how she got where she is. Needs to take her mind off the shit at home and the red letters from the bank. More than anything, she needs to catch whoever just crushed a beautiful girl's windpipe with a toilet seat.

'You got somebody to watch the girls?' asks McAvoy, looking at his watch and seeming suddenly aware that they are unlikely to get much sleep tonight. 'You and your mum talking again?'

Pharaoh shakes her head and looks at the ground. She already knows what he's going to suggest. She nods without looking up. Dies a little inside as McAvoy pulls out his phone and calls Roisin for help.

5

The baby has been sleeping better since she started on solids. She manages a full seven hours some nights. She had clearly just been waiting for a decent meal. If Helen had known that earlier, she'd have stuffed a bacon sandwich in the little bugger's face while the midwife at Hull Royal Infirmary was still waiting for the afterbirth.

Just like her mum.

That's what Helen's dad had said when she phoned him and said that his granddaughter had finally slept through. That all she wanted was something she could get her teeth into.

Detective Constable Helen Tremberg had not planned on having children. When the doctor told her she was three months gone she felt as though she had been whacked across the back of the legs with a hockey stick. It had taken weeks to sink in. Weeks for her to make up her mind. She'd made the appointment for the termination on two separate occasions. Made it to the clinic on one. Even got gowned up and laid down on the bed before the tears spilled out of her. She saw them as vines, climbing from her eyes and wrapping her tight; a chrysalis of pure misery and the promise of endless regret. She had fled the clinic holding her belly. Sobbed all the way home. Ran to the bedroom and lifted her shirt and talked to the creature inside her. Begged her unborn child for forgiveness; heaving and choking on snot and spittle and picturing the tiny sea-horse in her womb as it slumbered and grew and became the very centre of her being.

Helen looks down at baby Penelope. Six months old: too young to be diagnosed as schizophrenic, though Helen still has her suspicions. She's never met any normal person with two such wildly opposing personalities. Awake and fed, she's a bundle of sunshine; all dribbly smiles and sparkly eyes and grabbing hands. Half asleep and hungry, she's a demon. Even though things have recently improved, Penelope is not a good sleeper. Helen has always needed a good eight hours and a fry-up before she can consider starting the day. Penelope needs roughly twenty minutes, followed by an hour of screaming. Mother and child have done well to survive the first few months. Helen came close to utter mental collapse when the child was just a few months old. She found herself in the Co-op in mismatched shoes, leaning on her shopping trolley and staring at the back of a packet of nappies. The letters had stopped making sense. She was past tired. Past hunger. When Penelope knocked a box of cereal off the shelf and it spilled all over the floor, Helen found herself disintegrating. She sort of folded in on herself, like a flower at night-time. The staff found her on the floor, crying softly to herself and saying 'sorry' over and over. The assistant manager had driven her back to her little bungalow and stayed with her for a while and shared so many anecdotes about how she and her friends had been during the first weeks of parent-hood that by the time she left, Helen felt like a model mum. She didn't even cry when asked about the whereabouts of the baby's father. Just smiled, coyly, and said it was complicated. Too right it was complicated. She didn't even know his name. Just remembers a shape in the dark and the smell of Budweiser and Marlboro Golds.

It had happened in her hotel room after a wedding she hadn't even wanted to go to. He'd been from the groom's side of the family. Squat and wide-shouldered but okay to look at. He helped her upstairs to her room when she overdid the vodka. Stroked her hair for a while as she lay in her pretty dress and told him about her two failed relationships and conviction that all men were bas-tards. He'd told her she hadn't met the right guy. Kissed her, even after she'd been sick. He was gone by the morning. She'd woken up in her dress but without her knickers on. Didn't know whether to feel used or triumphant. Had she pulled? Or had she been taken advantage of? She spent the next couple of days feeling dirty and taking more showers than were necessary. Considered making it official and trying to find out who the bloke was. But she knows police stations and a certain type of investigator and that the first impulse among many is to blame the woman. She decided to drink the memory away. She's got good at that. Has pushed down so many terrible recollections that she sometimes sees herself as a taxidermy creation: stuffed too full and fit to burst.

Helen reaches into Penelope's playpen and tickles her cheek. She gets a drowsy, gloopy smile in return. She gets a thousand smiles a day but they have yet to lose their appeal. Helen is so in love with her daughter that she doesn't know how to express it. Sometimes she fears that she will hug her so tight she will hurt her. She's grown used to the knot of terror in her gut; the desperate need to know that her baby is safe and always will be.

Penelope goes back to pressing her face against the mesh of her jolly plastic prison, and fighting a losing battle to keep her eyes open. Helen looks out of the window at the deathly quiet street. She bought this bungalow from her grandparents. It sits on one of the newer estates in the small market town of Caistor, on the road from Grimsby to Lincoln. She has a true affection for the place. Grew up here. Sees it as a perfectly good town in which to raise her child, with its old-fashioned architecture and farming crowd. She likes that people still plan their year around sowing and harvesting crops. Likes that people can go to the fancy wine bar in wellies and drink next to somebody in Manolo Blahniks and not see anything peculiar about it.

She hasn't really done much to funk the place up. The living room is patterned on one wall with a loud, floral paper but is painted white on the others. The curtains are the same as they were when she moved in and she only bought the large paper lantern that cloaks the ceiling light because it cost less than a fiver. Her sofa is a hand-me-down from a neighbour. She can only take a little pride in the artwork. She has a large picture of two salsa dancers on the chimney breast, drawn with a flamboyant hand by somebody who loved black and red. It's a print, but limited edition, and cost her more than she could afford. So too did the reproduction Grand Prix posters which vie for space on the other walls among smaller, haphazard images of her daughter, her mum and dad, and herself in uniform on her first day at work. Pride of place goes to a line drawing, showing the outline of Penelope's hand, inside her own, with her dad's on top. It's only done on A4 and the frame came from Tesco, but it's Helen's favourite.

She turns away from the window. Looks at the clock. It's just after 1 a.m. Penelope should be in her cot, but Helen likes her close. She doesn't want to go to bed. There could be something interesting on the telly. An old crime drama or a repeat of *Top Gear* . . .

The laptop beeps and Helen gives a sigh of relief. Starts absorbing Reardon's report. Admires the man's economy of language and helpful notes, drawing her attention to the bits she needs most urgently. Somebody had sprayed an irritant in O'Neill's eyes. Chilli oil, as far as he could tell. His wrists and ankles had been tied and the shoes that kicked him to death were Adidas Sambas, size nines. He had been in situ for over a year. The fact that nobody had complained about the smell was deemed by Reardon to be 'largely unremarkable'. The house was cold and well ventilated and the body was still a long way from putrefaction. On an estate where people kept their own counsel, the growing stench was still a long way from unbearable when the door had finally been kicked in. Helen breathes out through a shudder and closes her eyes. Wishes there were somebody here she could say 'fucking hell' to.

After a moment, she grabs a few chocolates from the open bag at her side and stuffs them in her mouth as she types up notes for the morning briefing. Reads back the two pages of details she has managed to cobble together. Highlights the line that stood out: *The top palate of his false teeth broke in two from one of the blows to his jaw and the diamond stud in his left ear was found lodged under the skin behind his jawbone . . .*

She corrects her spelling mistakes and emails the lot across to Archer. Copies in Trish Pharaoh too, if only to piss Archer off.

Helen finds herself sneering as she considers her so-called

superior officer. Archer was a surprise appointment. She has replaced a detective superintendent despite only recently rising to the role of DCI. But Deputy Chief Constable Mallett reorganised CID and handed Archer the top job. She'll be a DSU within a year. Helen can't argue with her boss's arrest record or commitment to the job but she still can't find any way to like the stuck-up cow. She reminds her of the worst of the grammar school bitches who used to sneer at her as she made her way to the comprehensive in her trainers and braces. They'd be getting out of Daddy's Range Rover with their flute cases and their designer schoolbags and air-kissing Tabithas and Jemimas. Helen would be passing a packet of crisps between herself and lads called Gary, Nathan and Arran, dragging their Argos schoolbags as if they were made of rocks and slogging up that damn hill to a day of doodling on her maths book and chucking pens at her friends' heads. The grammar school bitches never said a word to her but she always felt pitiful under their gaze. She'd probably named her child Penelope just to spite them, even if Helen's mum had had her heart set on "Brenda".

'Can I use a naughty word please, Penelope?' says Helen softly, to her sleeping child. 'Thank you. Shaz Archer, I fucking hate you.'

Helen grins to herself and shakes her head. She shouldn't let the cow wind her up, not when she's not even here. She just wishes the bitch would disappear, like her old boss Colin. He may have been a feral, physically repulsive sociopath, but he was fanatical about locking up villains. Helen can't believe he would pack it all in. Helen was there that night. She saw the rage in his eyes. He had told Shaz Archer everything they had learned about the Headhunters and she had turned him away. It was a betrayal that undid him. Broke a heart that Helen didn't know he possessed. She tried to console him and received bile and rage for her trouble. He had driven away in search of alcohol. When Helen woke the next morning, the man she and Colin had pegged as the mouthpiece of the Headhunters was dead. Colin had cleaned out his flat and sodded off. Helen had briefly entertained the notion that Colin was responsible but Archer claimed to have checked an alibi. She also spread the word that he wasn't coming back. He'd been in touch and told her he'd had enough. Nobody doubted it – after all, Archer and he were thick as thieves. Only Helen knew she had rejected him and for reasons she has never truly fathomed, she has chosen not to share that information with anybody else. No charges were brought in connection with the gangster's death but it was soon apparent that the Headhunters had decided to leave Hull alone.

In her playpen, Penelope gives a wriggle. Manages to kick one of her toys.

'Goal!' says Helen quietly, as she gets up and crosses back to the child. She wants to pick her up. Wants to wake her up. Can't leave her alone for more than a few moments and finds herself smiling just to look at her. She knows she would be better served keeping her head down, getting on with her work and studying for her sergeant's exams. She can't complain about the way Archer has treated her since she moved over to her unit. Doctor's appointments and sick days are tolerated and Archer hasn't taken issue with the couple of times Helen turned up at crime scenes with baby sick on her lapels and eyes the colour and consistency of blue cheese. After all, Colin Ray used to turn up looking worse.

Helen looks at her watch. It's long past time to take the little one through to bed. Penelope has a cot and her own room but has yet to spend a whole night in it. Helen lets the child sleep with her. She's heard all the advice on the subject she can stomach, every damn cliché. Yes, she knows she's making a rod for her own back, and no, she doesn't care. She likes snuggling up with the little one.

She closes the laptop, finishes her chocolates and flicks the telly on. Turns the sound down low. Decides to leave it another half an hour and then they can both go to bed at the same time. She fiddles with the remote control for a while then puts the news on. A curvy girl with wild hair and freckles is reporting to camera from Hull's Bowlalley Lane. A body has been discovered in an apartment down Courts Lane. Detectives are treating it as suspicious but have not yet formally identified the victim. Neighbours have told reporters that they believe it to be a woman in her early twenties but lead investigator Detective Superintendent Pharaoh declined to comment. Pharaoh was the arresting officer of Reuben Hollow, who was freed last week by the Court of Appeal and spoke to her colleagues about Humberside Police earlier in the day.

The screen fills with the handsome, twinkly-eyed sculptor, with his stubble and his earring and his scruffy kind of cool.

'They have a difficult job to do,' he says, to the earnest interviewer. 'I don't want anybody to think this was some sort of personal vendetta. I've seen the accusations levelled at Detective Superintendent Pharaoh and I know they will have hurt her deeply. She doesn't deserve that. She is an extraordinary, tenacious and compassionate person. It was the Crown Prosecution Service who chose to prosecute and it's they who should be held accountable. DSU Pharaoh is the sort of person I would be proud for my daughter to turn into. And she's a hell of a looker, too.'

In the darkness of her living room, Helen gasps with shock and laughter. Rewinds the TV and plays it again.

Wonders if Pharaoh has seen it yet.

Wonders, too, just how many pieces she is going to break Reuben Hollow into come the morning.

'She seems to have pissed him off good and proper,' says Teddy, looking at his mobile phone. 'I do believe we have to go and do unspeakable things.'

Beside him, Foley stirs. He's been asleep for a good hour, snoring and grinding his teeth with his face against the glass of the Ford Focus, as if staring at Trish Pharaoh's front door with his eyes closed.

'She still in there?' asks Foley, drowsily. 'The pikey-looking one?'

Teddy looks at his young colleague with admiration. Doubts he would be able to go straight from sleep to lustfulness like this. He needs a coffee and a piece of toast before he can even think about anything physical.

'She hasn't come out,' he says. 'Boss says the copper was very rude when he tried to call her just now. He's tried to be nice. She doesn't seem to be listening. She needs to realise this is happening, that the boss doesn't give a shit if she's a copper, a judge or the Queen of fucking England. She owes, and she's paying. Not like him, is it? He seems to be playing roughly. You think he's trying to impress?'

Foley puts his hand down his trousers and gives himself a rub.

'The pikey,' he says, ignoring the question and concerning himself with the pleasant pictures of destruction in his mind. 'She a friend or what, you reckon? Babysitter? She had a couple of kids with her.' He cranes his neck. 'Aye, her car's still there. It's her or the daughter.'

Teddy seems to consider both options. 'There's the fucker himself, in the garage. Been done out as a bedroom for him. Bloody lovely, by all accounts. Must have cost a bit.'

'Money to burn, some people,' says Foley, taking his gun from his jacket pocket and placing it under his seat. He knows himself too well. Knows his tendency to give in to temptation. 'You got the thingy?'

Teddy pats his pocket. Wonders whether the pretty girl with the dark hair will piss herself when the strings of the taser start pumping electricity through her body. Whether a puddle of piss will stop Foley raping her.

'Shall we go say hello?' he asks, conversationally.

6

There are some nice homes on the Ings estate. Nice people, too. It's a down-to-earth kind of place. Most of the cars have tax discs and half the houses have satellite dishes. The kids go to school with their hair brushed and any teenager who kicks their football into a neighbour's garden stands a good chance of getting it back without a kitchen knife through its middle. It has character. A sense of community. Neighbours will plead ignorance if they spot a bailiff asking for directions and adults will apologise if caught swearing in front of somebody else's kids. Luxury items are paid for on credit cards and court fines settled monthly. It sits to the east of the city, a buffer between the problem zones at the far end of Holderness Road and the outer reaches of the Bransholme estate. Keeps the coppers busy with burglaries and arson and the occasional car theft, but it's the kind of place where stolen property can be recovered by going and knocking on a certain door and threatening to do something invasive with a broom handle.

McAvoy and Pharaoh have no prejudices about the people who make their homes here. Would not register a moment's disquiet about leaving their children here overnight. But the properties on Surbiton Close do not represent the wider community. This is a neighbourhood of architectural monstrosities. More than 90 per cent of the homes are boarded up. Most have 'Water Off' signs spray-painted on the walls, though whether this is a useful message from a contractor or an obscure instruction to unwelcome visitors is anybody's guess.

This is a place of weeds and broken glass. Holes have been torn in the steep tile roofs where chancers have punched through in an attempt to steal the copper from the derelict homes. The white-painted wooden porches that were intended to make this development look modern and Scandinavian have rotted in the face of the elements and turned the colour of dead and bloated skin. The windows are shuttered and the pebble-dash is flaking off like burned bark.

There are only a handful of occupied properties and they are squat, cramped affairs. The interlinked terraced homes look as drab as Monopoly houses. Jez Gavan and his partner have burrowed in at number 17 like ticks in a dog's back leg. His home overlooks a car park of pitted tarmac and dead grass. The bulbs in the lampposts have long since been smashed and it takes an effort to find the house. Then it takes a few curse words and an authoritative tone of voice before anybody answers the repeated bangs on the cracked blue paint of the front door. An upper window is thrown open and a woman with a head the size of a normal person's torso bellows something discouraging at them as they stand and wonder whether anybody here would notice the advent of the apocalypse.

Mrs Gavan has no interest in the police or their business. Tells them she's paid as much council tax as she's willing to and has no time for any more of the local authority's bullshit. Doesn't want to hear from no Jehovah's Witnesses either. And if they're here to complain about her daughter Beth, they've come to the wrong house. She's got pregnant by a Kosovan and moved to Dewsbury. McAvoy handles the negotiations. Uses his softest voice and saddest eyes and holds Trish Pharaoh back as she prepares to put her boot to the door. Eventually the woman consents to waddle downstairs and throw open the door. She glowers out from beneath bushy eyebrows and greasy hair and rubs a fat, tattooed hand over her clammy features as she masticates a lump of something neither officer cares to identify. She's wearing a massive T-shirt with a picture of a teddy bear on the front and the message 'hug me' on the back.

'Couldn't get my bloody arms around you,' mutters Pharaoh as the woman stomps off back upstairs to rouse her man, giving them a glimpse of a backside with so many pockmarks Pharaoh wonders aloud whether she's ever been blasted in the buttocks with a shotgun.

For twenty minutes they are left in a cluttered living room with two snarling Dobermans and a toddler who seems to be using his nose as a solution to some impending mucus shortage. His finger is so far inside his nasal cavity he seems to be searching for a shortcut to his brain. The respite at least gives McAvoy a chance to work on his technique for sitting down without actually touching anything. He tries not to judge. His childhood home was tidy and uncluttered because they couldn't afford anything to clutter it with, but at least it was clean. The living room of Jez Gavan's home looks to have been modelled on an overturned wheelie bin. Bottles, takeaway boxes and a mountain of cigarette butts lean against one wall like a ski slope. A light bulb hangs, naked and filthy, from a flex in the centre of the room and illuminates three inflatable armchairs and a coffee table made from Adidas shoe boxes and a sheet of Perspex. A sheet of tinfoil sits next to a bag of tea-lights and a dirty spoon on the makeshift table, alongside a copy of the *Hull Daily Mail* and a half-empty packet of Jammie Dodgers.

'Homely,' said Pharaoh as she entered the small living room, with its stench of stale tobacco, rubbish bags and damp. 'Remind me to Google "Dresden" when we get back.'

For the past twenty minutes they have found themselves becoming slowly hypnotised by the pixelated glare coming off the plasma TV on the far wall. The screen is so large that McAvoy has found himself wondering whether the house was built around it.

The investigation is only a couple of hours old and already he feels the weight of it. To search for justice is to wear damp clothes. He feels the chill of Ava's corpse upon him. Has never shaken off the damp caress of Hannah Kelly. He is a man with two lives. He is able to pursue killers purely because of his wife and children waiting for him. They are his antidote and reason. But the dead slink inside him like shadows. He can feel Ava taking root. Knows that tiny particles of her are lodged within his nostrils, that his shoes carry her dead skin cells. His every breath brings her inside him. He is already building an image of the petite, attractive girl who suffocated on her own puke as somebody pressed a toilet seat across the back of her neck. He can picture her sitting in that tiny flat, stubbing out cigarette after cigarette into a coffee mug overflowing with butts. Can see her playing with her phone and painting her nails and eating chips in bed while watching silly films on the DVD player and supermarket TV that she propped on an overflowing chest of drawers. He has flicked through her music. Felt himself collapse a fraction as he looked at her curling, girlish handwriting and her songs about love, desire and loss. She owned candles and nice wine glasses. Her tea-towel matched her coffee jar. She was somewhere between adult and child; trying to make a home and then letting it tumble into teenage squalor. He pities the forensics officers who must catalogue and test every last fibre of her flat, from the tiny hairs on her razor to the lump of rock on her windowsill.

Pharaoh has been talking. Making comments, under her breath, about the colour of the carpet. Asking whether the yellow stain on the ceiling is from cigarette smoke blown upwards, or piss that has dripped down.

And then Jez Gavan makes his entrance.

House and master suit one another immaculately.

He is dressed in jogging pants and a decade-old Man United shirt stretched so tightly over his gut that McAvoy wonders whether it is painted on. He is every bit as fat as his woman, though where she at least has a face capable of more than one expression, his is so scrunched up and sour McAvoy wants to show him off to Fin and tell him that the old saying is true about what happens when the wind changes. All of his features are gathered together in one little lump in the centre of his bulbous face. It looks like a full English in the centre of a serving platter.

Jez greets them by belching loudly and scratching his short hair so vigorously that it causes a brief halo of dandruff to form around his crown. There is darkness under his eyes and a cigarette paper hanging, unrolled, from his lower lip, like a Post-it note that nobody has taken the time to fill in. He throws himself down on an armchair, sending up a cloud of dust, then sticks both hands down his trousers. He treats both coppers to a smile. Looks appreciatively at Trish Pharaoh's tits. Gives McAvoy the once-over and clearly decides that the big bugger has muscles like an elephant but all the killer instinct of a dishtowel.

'What you bastards want?' he asks, picking up an expensive smartphone from the floor and playing with the buttons. 'Why's it always me, eh? Why can't you find some other poor bastard? How many times do you lot want to fit me up? I ain't done owt. I'm just an easy collar. I told you before, I'm never speaking to coppers again. I was honest with you. Well, not you. But coppers, yeah? I didn't even know what I was doing. I was so pissed I couldn't see. Went in the wrong fucking house, didn't I? Door was bloody open. Fell asleep on the sofa. No harm done. Silly bitch should lock her door, shouldn't she? Shouldn't have come to court. I've got fuck all to say to you.'

Pharaoh is patient with him. Gives him a chance to vent a little spleen. She's never met Gavan before but his record suggests that he knows how this game is played.

'Can I stop you there?' she asks, holding up her hands and standing up. 'You seem to think we're here to cause you grief. The truth is, we're not. We're here because Ava Delaney used to be registered as living at this address. And Ava Delaney is now dead. So stop all this bollocks and start paying us some bloody respect, or you'll be down the cells and bleeding from the nose quicker than you can count to three, which in my estimation is about twenty fucking minutes.'

Jez looks at Pharaoh like a moped driver who has just pulled up at the traffic lights next to three Hell's Angels on Harley-Davidsons. His unhealthy yellow face turns a shade of grey and his tattooed hands turn to fists as he scratches at the arms of his plastic chair. Eventually, he manages to find the enthusiasm for a strange kind of gulped smile, then barks an order at his woman. A moment later, she brings him a battered metal tin. He rolls a cigarette with dirty fingers. It's prison-thin; the habit of a man used to conserving his tobacco. It betrays Gavan's history, his years in a variety of category C prisons and one brief stretch in a category

A. He was the least impressive prisoner at HMP Full Sutton. He was sent down for armed robbery, though the charge sounds more glamorous than it was. The gun with which he held up the post office on Sculcoates Lane was plastic and came free with a magazine for primary-age kids. He ended up in the jail for violent and dangerous prisoners because he defended himself when somebody went for him in HMP Doncaster. Half throttled a prison guard who came to break up the fight. Spent the last four weeks of his sentence among killers and rapists before spilling out on parole at the tail end of last year.

'Ava,' says Gavan, lighting his cigarette and recovering some degree of composure. He looks at the ceiling as if ruminating. 'Not sure that rings a bell. Can you give me a bit more?'

Pharaoh gives a little laugh and turns to Jez's other half. 'Do you want to give his head a bang or should I?'

Something passes between husband and wife. She gives him a look that suggests she will back him whatever he decides but that in her humble opinion, it would be wise to help.

'Dead, yeah?' Gavan asks resignedly. He purses his lips and blows out a cloud of smoke. 'Fuck, that's a shame. Pretty girl.'

Pharaoh turns to McAvoy, who is staring at the small boy in front of the TV with his finger up his nose. He doesn't even appear to have registered the newcomers in his home.

'Shall we send the little lad to bed?' asks McAvoy, softly. 'Not ideal for young ears.'

Mr and Mrs Gavan appear to register the presence of the youngster. 'Bed now, Dylan,' says his mum. 'I'll be up to say goodnight.'

The little boy unpeels himself from the floor. His pyjamas are clean and he has been sitting on a newspaper. He gives both parents a small smile and says, 'Love you,' as he closes the door. McAvoy watches him go.

'So, Ava Delaney,' says Pharaoh brightly. 'And can you roll me a cigarette please? I'm out.'

McAvoy sits quietly on the chair as his boss does what she's good at. She takes a thin cigarette from Gavan's hands as if she is receiving a communion wafer. It's a gesture of appreciation and acceptance. It shows Gavan that she's not so very different from him and that she does not want to cause him any headaches. It also gives him a view down her cleavage, and a couple of other reasons to want to make her happy.

'She really dead?' he asks, lighting her cigarette with a cheap lighter. 'You're a DSU. Can't be a car crash. Can't be overdose. Somebody must have killed her. Fuck, poor cow.'

Pharaoh nods. Picks a piece of tobacco from her lip. Settles back in the plastic chair and makes herself comfortable. Turns to Jez with a smile.

'Ava. How did you know her?'

Jez isn't paying attention. He's looking up again at the stain on the ceiling. Seems to be picturing the small, dark-haired girl. He shakes his head and turns his attention to McAvoy.

'You find out who did it, you rip their fucking head off, yeah? She was a stroppy cow but a nice enough lass. Didn't deserve that.'

'Could you answer my colleague's question, Mr Gavan,' says McAvoy, staring through the short, ratty man's face and focusing on a spot 100 yards behind the back wall.

'Aye, aye,' mutters Gavan, turning back to the warm, open face of Pharaoh. She seems happy enough, smoking her cigarette with her legs crossed and a swoop of dark hair snagged in the hoops of her earrings. Could just as well be reclining in a rocking chair at a big country house after a dinner party.

'I live over the water,' she says. 'Grimsby way. Long way from here. I've got daughters. It's a bit of a trek, to be honest, and it's getting on for ten p.m. already. So, Jez, if you could just give us the basics I can get home and into my pyjamas and try and get a few hours before this all starts getting horribly intense and shitty in the morning. Be a darling and help us out.'

Jez looks between the two officers and seems to decide that he would rather talk to the sexy DSU than the massive, brooding Scotsman with the broken hands.

'I hardly know her,' he says, and his face shows regret. 'Knew her, I mean. I just did the lass a favour.'

73

Pharaoh stays quiet. Lets him fill the silence.

'Look, I got talking to her in the Lambwath. This was months ago. Christmas just gone, that sort of time. You know the Lambwath? Not my normal pub but I was barred from my local so I went to spend my money somewhere else. She was in there with some friends. I don't know what the occasion was. Birthday or leaving do or something. She was dolled up to the nines. They all were. She didn't look like the others. Looked like Morticia Addams with all the black she was wearing and the piercings and the eye make-up. But for all that she was a smiley thing. She asked me for a fag and I said I didn't have any but I'd roll her one. So I did. We had a natter. She told me she was going to have to move away because she couldn't get a flat. Seemed a shame to me.'

Gavan glances at his wife. Her face is stone.

'Look, I haven't always been a good boy,' he says, looking at McAvoy and trying to find an ally. 'I thought she were a pretty thing and I'm a sucker for that. She told me she couldn't get a flat because she had a bad credit history and I said that money talks and if she could put down the first few months' rent then most landlords wouldn't worry too much about the credit checks. I own my own home, see?' He gestures at his living room. 'I doubted I could be a guarantor for the poor cow but I gave her my address and my number and said she could try and use my name on the forms. Could say she lived here, if she liked. I was just being nice.'

Pharaoh raises an eyebrow. Twinkles a little. 'You're a bad puppy,' she says, in a way that makes Gavan seem to grow two or three inches in height.

'I wish I hadn't met the lass, to be honest,' he says. 'Right pain in the arse she became. Called me up a week later and said she'd given my number to her landlord in case there were any problems. Said she'd spent her savings getting stuff for the flat and was stony broke. Wanted to borrow a few quid. I'd just got out of the nick and didn't have enough money for a packet of tobacco. I ignored her. Then she sent a load more, saying she was really in bother and hadn't eaten and that she had to get a train ticket and all the sob stories people use when they're trying to fleece you. I'd have changed my number if so many people didn't have this one. Then her landlord phones me and says she's behind with the rent and that she's given them my name! I was proper fucked off. Wasn't my fucking business, was it? And my wife here puts up with a lot, y'know? I told her about this lass who kept bothering me. She wasn't happy but it was a weight off my mind.'

Pharaoh looks across at the rotund woman. Gives the tiniest of signals for McAvoy to take over.

'Worth their weight in gold, a good wife and mother,' says McAvoy, softly. 'Jez is a lucky man. You must have reminded him of that when he told you.'

Mrs Gavan sucks her cheek, enjoying the attention and the big man's wide, sincere eyes.

'We've been here before,' she says, rolling her eyes and nodding at her errant husband. 'He's a sucker for the pretty faces. Always giving lasses money for a taxi or a few quid to get themselves a pizza on the walk home. Can't help himself, the silly sod. This Ava took the piss. I believed him when he said nothing had happened – especially when I saw her for myself.'

'You actually met?' asks McAvoy, keeping his eyes on hers.

'In town,' she says, chattily. 'Bottom of Whitefriargate. Jez and me were having a drink in the Bonny Boat one Friday night. Don't normally drink around there but he were treating me. I saw him talking to this tiny little thing with half her head shaved and tattoos and piercings every-bloody-where and I thought I should go and save him from himself. Jez were apologising. Saying he had nothing to give her.'

'She wanted money,' cuts in Gavan. 'She wasn't insisting or being a cow or anything. Just really pleading. I said I could spare a few quid but she said she needed a few hundred. Would do any-thing. The missus butted in before I could promise her I'd sell the house and give her the proceeds.'

'I wasn't nasty,' says Mrs Gavan to McAvoy. 'Just told her that she should have a bit more self-respect. Everybody has problems. What does she think we are, a bloody bank? I sent her on her way.

Told Jez to get his number changed and tell her landlord that it was fuck all to do with him.'

McAvoy turns back to Gavan.

'And did you?'

'Didn't change the number but I sent her landlord a text and never heard back,' he says, picking his smartphone from his knee and holding it up like a prop. 'Never heard back. That was that.'

'And when did you last hear from her?' asks Pharaoh.

'Weeks, I reckon,' says Gavan. 'Got a message a couple of days after the missus saw her off, saying she was sorry and wouldn't bother me again. She was just in a state. I wouldn't have wished death on the poor lass.' He chews on his lip. Starts rolling another cigarette. 'What happened? She stabbed?'

'Why do you ask that?' asks Pharaoh.

Gavan shrugs. 'It's what people do, isn't it? Strangling or stabbing. We haven't got guns, have we? It's easy for the Americans. They just pull a trigger.'

Pharaoh keeps her eyes on Gavan's. He looks away first.

'Could you tell us any more about her background? Her friends? Do you have any dates or times or places that may assist us?'

'I might have kept some of her messages,' Gavan tells her. 'I'm not much of a technical bloke. That any good?'

McAvoy pulls himself from the inflatable chair with as much dignity as he can muster. Holds out a hand for the phone. After a moment's hesitation, Gavan deposits it in the large, warm palm. McAvoy's fingers dance across the screen. He turns back to Pharaoh and shakes his head. Gives the phone back to its owner, who shrugs apologetically. 'Not even a contract,' he says, sadly. 'It's a pay-as-you-go.'

On a whim, McAvoy pulls out his wallet. He folds it over so the picture of Roisin and the baby is facing away. Shows the image of Hannah Kelly to Gavan.

'You recognise this girl?'

Gavan looks puzzled but studies the photo. After a moment he shrugs. 'Missing lass from the papers, ain't she? Aye, I recognise her from that. But nowt else. Why? This connected? You not caught anyone for that yet? Poor bitch.'

McAvoy says nothing. Looks at Hannah's face for a moment and then reverently closes his wallet.

Pharaoh taps her fingers on the arm of the chair and reaches out a hand. McAvoy pulls her upright, like she's a granny getting out of a beanbag.

'We'll need a formal statement, Jez,' she says to Gavan, who appears to have discovered some long-dead spirit of chivalry and is standing up to see his guests out. 'And if anything else comes back to you, call me.' She presses a card into his hand. 'She didn't die well. We don't know much about her but unless she's been slicing up babies, she didn't deserve what happened to her. Be the hero, yeah? Help us out.'

Jez nods solemnly and backs up a pace or two as Pharaoh steps out of the front door and back into the glare of the car's head-lights. McAvoy gives Mrs Gavan a smile, then follows Pharaoh across the broken tarmac to the vehicle. He isn't surprised to find it untouched. Reckons that the neighbourhood vandals would rather set fire to themselves than tamper with a vehicle visiting the Gavans.

They stand in the silence for a moment, listening for the shouting to start. When it does, it is a muffled but unmistakably shrill affair. Mrs Gavan is going spare.

'Well?' asks Pharaoh, lighting one of her own cigarettes.

'No doubt about it,' says McAvoy. 'I looked through the wifi networks the phone has stored. Ava's was one of them. It's been in her home.'

Pharaoh rolls her cigarette between her fingers. 'You think he got sick of her demands? Decided to put a stop to them? He can't have shagged her, can he? Turns my stomach.'

'Perhaps he wanted something for his money,' says McAvoy, looking away. 'Killed her to shut her up.'

'Should we nick him?' asks Pharaoh, though the question is directed more at herself than her sergeant.

'We'll have a lot more to bombard him with when we have the

post-mortem completed,' he says. 'He's not scared of a police station or a cell. If he's done it, we want enough to show him how
pointless it is to argue. He's a proper old con and we must have his
DNA in the system so we'll just have to show him we've got the
deck stacked. Make him see the sense in confessing to it. '

'What about her?' asks Pharaoh. 'Miss World in there.'

'Hard to say,' muses McAvoy. 'I can't see her scalping somebody's armpits, though, can you? Seems a bit ritualistic. I doubt
she was as polite to Ava as she claims, but it's hard to see her doing
that.'

'True,' says Pharaoh, and pulls out her car keys. 'Plus, she'd
never manage the stairs.'

The pair climb back inside the car. McAvoy feels a tiredness
settle upon him as he squeezes himself into the passenger seat. A
few hours ago he was sitting on soft grass with his wife and child,
trying to find peace and a place inside him for Hannah Kelly.
Here, now, he wonders if he has the capacity to carry another
pretty girl's ghost. Wants to catch whoever did this, and fast. Wants
to get back to Hannah. He feels as though he has betrayed her by
allowing this new spectre to come between them.

'Back to mine?' asks Pharaoh. 'There's room.'

McAvoy looks at his personal phone and feels a prickle at the
back of his neck, as though cold spiders are dancing on his skin.

Six missed calls and a dozen messages.

He reads the last one. Roisin's words, typed in caps to show
him she means it.

I THINK THERE'S SOMEBODY TRYING TO GET IN.
XXX

7

Bank holiday Monday, 10.17 p.m.

Fog is closing over the east coast like an unwashed lace curtain and drawing a dirty haze across the half-full moon as it shines down on this quiet cul-de-sac. The sound of tipsy conversations bubbles up from back gardens and the air is greasy with the lingering scent of barbecues and mown grass.

A nice place, this. Home to teachers and bank clerks, council workers and bankrupt detective superintendents. A place for dinner parties and jubilee celebrations, where people respect one another's parking spaces but would commit murder if their neighbour planted a leylandii tree without asking first.

Roisin McAvoy: sitting in the darkened kitchen at the rear of the property, holding a meat mallet and jabbing at her mobile phone. There's sweat under her arms and across her forehead but she's not as scared as she should be. She's faced a lot of danger in her life. Fancies her chances whatever the odds. She doesn't like violence but if she encounters those who do, she's willing to kick their heads in.

Sophia opened up to her this evening. Told her about the lads she and her friends had got to know recently. Older boys. One of them has a Peugeot 306, which makes him as moreish as heroin in the eyes of adolescent girls. They like a drink and a smoke and know which quiet lay-bys to park up in when they have female company. One of them got a bit overly friendly with Sophia recently. She told him to back off, in front of his friends. Made him look like a mug, or so he said in the string of vile texts he sent her in the hours afterwards. Worked himself up. Got increasingly descriptive in his threats. Sophia had feared he would turn up at last night's party. She was relieved beyond measure when the person who dragged her from her sleep turned out to be her mum, even if the drama queen had shown her up. Sophia had reacted without thinking. Said some hurtful things. But of course she loved her mum. She just didn't want to get into trouble by telling her about the lad who was threatening her.

Then they heard the noises at the back door.

Now Sophia sits with her arms around her three sisters, quiet as church mice as they huddle on the sofa in the living room and try not to cry. She snuggles in to little Olivia, who's feeling proud because she heard the strange noise coming from the back door.

Upstairs, a red-haired, barrel-chested seven-year-old sits cross-legged on Olivia's bedroom floor. There is an earnestness to his gaze. A sincere devotion to the task he has been given. He has already keyed the number into the cordless phone between his legs. He's just waiting for his mum to give the word and he'll press the green button and demand immediate assistance. His dad is busy, catching killers. Fin is willing to fill the void.

The handle of the kitchen door begins to turn. There is the sound of a thin set of metal rods slipping back into their cases. The careful, practised whisper of a UPVC door easing open.

'You boys lost?' asks Roisin, flicking the light on.

Teddy and Foley look with amused surprise at the young woman who stands in the neat kitchen. She's in her mid-twenties and no more than 5 foot tall. She's model pretty, with dark hair and tanned skin. Neat, bare arms and a six-pack are accentuated by a purple vest. There are tattoos around her belly button and a jewel through the middle. She's wearing leopard-print leggings and the toenails of her bare feet have been painted different colours and adorned with diamanté. She's holding a phone and a meat tenderiser and looks thoroughly unperturbed by their nearness.

'You're a traveller, ain't you, girl?' Foley's voice is pure south London and contains a mocking contempt.

'I'm Roisin,' she says, and the Irish in her accent becomes more

80

pronounced. 'This is a copper's house. My husband's a copper too. We've already called the police. It looks to me like you're most definitely in the wrong place, so if I were you, I'd fuck off while you have the means to do so.'

Foley takes a step forward and Roisin subtly alters her position. She's only got to shout and Fin will call 999. She hopes it won't come to that. Doesn't know whether Pharaoh would want this reported. She knows Sophia doesn't. The poor girl's got herself into a bit of a situation but it's nothing that can't be resolved. These blokes are probably well-meaning and hard-of-thinking uncles or cousins who have had a few cans of lager too many and agreed to help restore the family honour by scaring a teenage girl. Roisin has no time for such things, for these kinds of men. She never had to put up with much in the way of teenage romancing. Travellers don't really date. Many don't get to spend time alone with a boy until marriage is up for discussion. That would have been the plan for her, had she not fallen in love with the big, gentle copper who saved her and showed her how life was meant to feel.

'Got a houseful,' says Foley to himself, rubbing his nose. 'All the girls through there, are they?' He nods at the closed door. 'That one with the long hair looked a peach. Wouldn't mind a play with that, to be honest. Wouldn't mind at all.'

Roisin ignores him. Looks at the older of the two.

'I don't know what you want but you won't find it here,' she says, flatly. 'I reckon you're a couple of blokes who got a bit drunk and took a wrong turn, eh? I reckon you're feeling a bit silly and a bit embarrassed and want to just go and sleep it off. I'm right, eh? What d'you say?'

Teddy keeps looking at her with the same half-smile on his face. He seems to be making up his mind about something important.

'You really married to a copper?' he asks, at length. 'You a stripper, then?'

Roisin consents to laugh. 'I can turn my hand to most things, mister.'

'The bitch still out?' asks Foley, sniffing something unpleasant into his mouth and swallowing it back down.

'Bitch?'

'This bitch,' says Foley, and holds up a tiny wooden figurine. It shows Pharaoh, viewed on her best day. It's a beautiful piece of work, done with a tender, worshipful hand.

'Where did you get that?' asks Roisin, and finds herself hoping that she gets an opportunity to bite the head off the thing before her husband ever gets a chance to see how much unwarranted perkiness the sculptor has added to Pharaoh's bust.

'Lovely thing, isn't it?' says Teddy, before Foley has a chance to answer. 'Flattering depiction but unmistakable. My mate here shouldn't have taken it but he does appreciate the finer things in life. He's not alone in that regard. Take our employer. He loves modern art. I'm not much of a fan myself. Some of the stuff in his office gives me a bloody migraine. But he does like his swirls and his patterns and his big blobs of colour. It's his indulgence. He's indulged a little too much recently. Got himself in a bit of a pickle. So he's asking his old friends to do right by him. Calling in a few old debts, you might say. That's why we're here. Just wanted to see if we could come to some kind of an arrangement.'

Roisin looks from the older man to the younger and back again. She's painfully aware of the children upstairs and in the next room. She will fight to her last breath to protect them but hopes to Christ that McAvoy gets her messages before it comes to that.

'I'm just the babysitter,' she says, with a wink. 'Just me and the kids here. I reckon if it's that important to you then you should go and see her at work. She's a reasonable woman. Probably all a misunderstanding.'

Foley suddenly snaps his head left and points at the door in the far wall.

'That lead through to the garage, does it? He in there? The gimp?'

'Now now, lads, don't be taking the piss,' says Roisin, as if this is all grand craic and can soon be cleared up over a pint of Guinness. 'He's not a well man. We don't go in there. I've only met him a couple of times and he's not one for visitors. Why don't I give Trish a call, eh? See if we can't get this sorted. I'll put the kettle on, shall I? Or would you be wanting a glass of whiskey? I don't know if it's a Bushmills house or a Jameson; or I've no doubt there'll be vodka . . .'

Without a word, Foley crosses the kitchen and turns the handle on the door to the converted garage. Soft blue light spills out, alongside the sound of a cowboy film playing on the flatscreen TV at the end of Anders Wilkie's bed.

Roisin starts forward, shaking her head, bringing up the meat mallet. She'd have no hesitation in bringing it down on the chavvy bastard's arm. Would smash his head open if it comes to it.

'Stand still,' says the older man, and produces a weapon with a yellow barrel and a black handle from behind his back. 'This is a taser, love. Not police issue, mind. Five times as powerful. I shoot you with this and you'll shit your lovely leggings and that means when I take your pants off you're going to be all embarrassed. Stay the fuck where you are. And if you say another word I'll go and use it on the littlest kid I find. That would be yours, I reckon. Saw you turn up with two of them. Ginger one and a black-haired little princess. How do you think she'd cope with fifty thousand volts, eh? I reckon she'd look like she'd been toasted.'

Roisin stands still. Feels a chill creep into her flesh. Tries to send a silent message to the girls in the next room. Begs them with her mind not to come in here, to grab the two upstairs and run for the door.

'Look at the state of this poor bastard,' says Foley, standing in the open doorway. 'This is the bloke, yeah? Fucking pitiful.'

Teddy shows no inclination to go over. He keeps staring at Roisin, like he's considering his options. Like he has the option of doing whatever the fuck he wants.

'A hundred grand,' says Foley, loudly. He's addressing his comments to the gaunt, half-immobile man in the hospital bed, hooked up to fluids and monitors and staring with hollow-eyed boredom at the flatscreen TV above his bed. 'He wants his money, matey. I'd get off your arse and get it, if you can. But I don't reckon you can. So we'll just wait here until your missus comes home and we'll ask her.'

'This is about money?' asks Roisin, quietly. 'They're bankrupt. They used to have a big house. Aector told me. They lost it all. That's her husband's debts, not hers.'

Teddy strokes the taser. Looks longingly at the gap between her vest and her waistband.

'The boss wouldn't normally be fussed about a hundred grand,' he says softly. 'But there have been changes in the way he works. He's got new friends who expect things to be done a certain way. They expect payments to be made regularly. If those payments aren't made, they get upset. Our boss would love to carry on being useful. I'd say it would be fair to assume he's trying to make a point here. You may be a fucking copper, but you still owe what you owe. That seem fair? Oh Foley, you are a bad, bad lad . . .'

In the doorway, Foley is giggling. He's pulled down his jogging pants and is pissing into the bedroom.

'He's not getting up, Teddy. Reckon he's on the level. This bloke was a player once, was he? Christ, how the mighty have fallen.'

Roisin turns away from the sight. She feels temper prickling, though most of it is directed at herself. She'd wanted to show off. Reckoned that the people fumbling with the back door were no worse than a couple of pissed-up teenagers. She'd planned on being the cool grown-up, on delivering a slap or two and sending them on their way. She recognises something in the eyes of Teddy and Foley: the look of men who have hurt her before.

'Shall we give him a zap, Teddy?' asks Foley, tucking himself away. 'It's all brainwaves and shit, isn't it? Might cure him. Or fucking kill him . . .'

Roisin turns as the door from the living room opens. Sophia bursts in, her eyes red and the remote control for the TV in her hands.

Teddy looks at her and begins to laugh. 'What you gonna do with that, you silly cow? Fucking mute me?'

Roisin swings the meat tenderiser like an ape wielding a club. Teddy yanks his arm back before he can fire and with his free hand, delivers a harsh slap to the side of her face. She rocks back and Teddy steps forward, snarling.

Sophia throws herself at him like an angry cat. She claws at his neck and tries to sink her teeth into his cheek. She spits curses in his ear and tries to ram her thumb into his eye socket. Her mother has taught her well.

'Foley!'

The young man grabs Sophia by the hair and drags her off his partner. He hits her twice in the stomach and has to step backwards as she vomits all over the kitchen floor. She drops to one knee, and he goes to kick her in the side of the head . . .

The door to the kitchen opens at the same moment that the lights in the room go out. Teddy turns to the door, yelling, and Roisin staggers back, trying to grab the meat mallet. Something whistles past her. A shape. A scent. All wood shavings and rich tobacco. She hears the sound of flesh on flesh and the sharp, hard crack of bone against something hard. She scrabbles back. Finds the light switch. Bathes them all in harsh yellow illumination.

Teddy is dragging the younger man towards the door. Foley is bleeding from the head and his eyes have rolled back like something from a cartoon.

A thin man in a granddad shirt and soft cords is holding a hand up to his eyes, shielding them from the glare. There's blood on his knuckles. He spots something on the floor and darts forward as Teddy hauls the door open and bundles both himself and Foley into the back garden and the enveloping darkness.

'Mine,' says the man, gathering up the dropped sculpture of Pharaoh. 'Well, your mum's, actually,' he adds softly as he places a hand on Sophia's back and helps her up. 'Give it to her for me.'

Roisin is too stunned to speak. She raises a hand to the hot slap mark on her cheek and then gathers herself. Rushes to Sophia and takes the crying girl in her arms. There's sick in her hair and she seems barely able to walk. The front of her jeans is wet.

'I just wanted to make sure she got it,' says the man.

He looks awkward. Embarrassed. Vulnerable and lost. He also looks like his hand is hurting. One of his knuckles is already starting to swell. Roisin takes his hand and looks at the injury. His hands have been hurt before. His fingers are delicate and olive-hued; their tips hardened but nimble-looking. She looks at him properly for the first time. Recognises him. From the telly. From the papers. From her husband's files.

'You made this?' asks Roisin, taking the tiny figurine from the crying girl. 'It's good. Flattering, but good.'

Reuben Hollow looks at her with eyes so blue that Roisin is put in mind of a Siberian husky. She feels an urge to put a palm on his stubbly face, to smell him, as if they are animals figuring one another out. She lifts his hand and rubs her tiny, warm thumb across the skin, checking for breaks and finding only old injuries. He seems unsure of himself. Looks like he needs a hug more than any man she has ever met.

'Don't tell,' whispers Sophia, holding her fingers to her mouth as if trying to breathe life into a dead mouse. 'Mum, I mean. She'll go mental. She doesn't need it.' She turns to Reuben. 'Please. Don't tell her what happened. This is my fault, I know it.'

Roisin is about to protest but there is a look in Sophia's eyes that she feels unable to argue with. The girl looks as though she has suffered enough. Roisin understands. Knows that the teenager needs to forget what has just happened to her and not spend all night being interrogated. Did the men mention money? Something about Trish and her husband? None of what has happened feels right to Roisin, but she is finding it hard to concentrate. The handsome man is looking at her with an intensity that is making her skin prickle.

'Roisin?'

She turns. McAvoy is standing in the doorway. He looks as though a trapdoor has opened inside his body. As though, within him, columns are tumbling like the ruin of Rome.

Then Pharaoh is pushing past him. Taking it all in. Advancing like a warship and grabbing Sophia to her chest; pushing Reuben Hollow with the flat of her hand and telling him, jaw clenched, to get out of her house.

Roisin comes to her senses the moment McAvoy puts his arm around her and asks if she's okay. Whether the children are okay. Why Hollow was here. What's happened . . .

When she looks up at him, he is staring at his reflection in the darkened glass; almost imperceptibly shaking his head; pitying the hapless fool who didn't hear his wife's plea for help until it was too late.

PART TWO

8

Tuesday morning, 9.06 a.m.

McAvoy stands by an open window on the first floor of Courtland Road police station, an ugly building overlooking the Orchard Park estate; a grey battleship run aground in a hostile harbour. This is a place of empty houses and overgrown fields, roped-off play areas and smashed phone boxes. Soggy stems and dead petals flutter in cellophane coffins on lampposts and buckled barriers. Old twists of police tape garland garden fences. Satellite dishes sprout as fungus on crumbling brick.

He's watching an old lady wrestle with an umbrella. It isn't actually raining but the gathering fog has made the air cold and damp. He watched as she spotted the droplets of water on her glasses. Saw her stop at the roadside to begin the complex process of hauling an umbrella from her bag. She has removed a bag of boiled sweets, a purse, a diary and a hairbrush and does not have enough hands to hold them all while still searching out the errant umbrella. She looks like she's in her seventies but from this distance it's hard to say. McAvoy finds himself inventing a story for her. Decides that she is on her way to the bus stop and is planning a trip into town to buy a card for a poorly friend, or something nice for the grandkids. She's wearing a sensible coat and shoes built for comfort. She's done her hair nicely before leaving the house. Perhaps she has her eye on a man. She never really felt much for the man who knocked her up when she was still a youngster. Fishing stock, probably; one of the families from Hessle Road. He wasn't always nice to her but provided for the kids. Got her a decent enough house but drank it away when the fishing industry died. Moved them to Orchard Park for a fresh start then ran off with some strumpet from the Rampant Horse . . .

McAvoy scowls at himself. Wonders what the hell he is doing? He turns away from the old lady before he has to endure the sight of her dropping her purse and bursting into tears . . .

'Sarge?'

Ben Neilsen has said his name three times already but McAvoy's head was too full of his own thoughts to pay him any heed. Now he spins back towards the assembled officers. Rubs a big hand over his face and manages a smile. Orders his thoughts. Clicks the top of his pen a few times. Looks back at the big whiteboard with its photographs and names, arrows and dates.

The Serious and Organised unit is only half the size it was. For a time, it was made up of more than a hundred police officers and civilian staff and had a brief that covered a multitude of sins. They were the Major Investigation Team – the force's murder squad. Budget constraints have diminished the unit's size and remit but it remains the glittering jewel of Humberside Police. Detectives from across the country want to work for Trish Pharaoh and to be handpicked for her inner circle is to be given the ultimate nod of approval. She has not sought a replacement detective chief inspector since Colin Ray's departure. McAvoy is still a detective sergeant but the team are well aware that in Pharaoh's absence he is the boss. The only person who doubts his ability to do the job is McAvoy himself.

He screws up his eyes and pulls at his collar. Wishes he were lying in his bed in his battered old rugby shirt and boxer shorts. He didn't sleep last night. He and Roisin stayed at Pharaoh's overnight, squeezed together onto a three-seater sofa under a fleecy blanket, Roisin burrowed into him like a kitten. He lay there, cramped and ridiculous; feet hanging over the end and one arm slowly turning grey beneath Roisin's shoulders.

'The link, Sarge?'

Neilsen says it encouragingly, willing his sergeant to do well. He knows how much McAvoy hates this part of the job.

McAvoy follows Neilsen's gaze to the photograph of Hannah Kelly. It's a pretty image. She's smiling, head half turned, as though somebody has cracked a joke as she's leaving the room. She looks sweet. There are no piercings in her ears and she wears only the faintest trace of make-up. She has the kind of English rose quality that the national papers would have gone crazy over if she had turned up dead in the first week of the missing persons inquiry. They've rather lost interest now, though McAvoy senses that is about to change.

'Nothing concrete,' says McAvoy quietly, then repeats it for those at the back. 'This is an investigation into Ava Delaney's murder, have no doubt about that. But Hannah Kelly remains a missing person. She vanished from her home just twenty-six miles from where Ava was killed. They are of a similar age. Statistically, serial violent crimes against women occur with several months' hiatus. I don't want you to make any assumptions about this case but I do want every possibility to be in your thoughts.'

Neilsen nods. Gives him a smile. McAvoy smiles back and immediately feels a fool. He feels ill. He couldn't face the McDonald's breakfast that Roisin and the kids wolfed down on the drive back over the bridge this morning. Had hushed Roisin's questions with soft little smiles. *Just tired,* he said. *Overloaded.* His brain feels like a saturated sponge. But he knows that in the coming days he will need to absorb more and more. He wishes he could compartmentalise, that he had the capacity to vent and offload. He sickens himself today. His every thought should be stuffed full of Ava Delaney, but his mind keeps handing him an image he never wants to see again. For all the horror of what was done to Ava's corpse, it is the sight of Roisin holding Reuben Hollow's hand that most turns his stomach. She looked at the man the way she looks at McAvoy. He had helped her. *Saved* her! McAvoy should be grateful. Should be shaking Hollow's hand and buying him drinks. Acting like a normal man about the whole bloody thing. Or he should have hit him in the face so hard that he flew out of his shoes. Either option would have been better than the one McAvoy chose. He just stood there like a great bloody idiot, staring at himself in the darkened glass, steadying himself on the back of a chair, as Roisin explained what had happened.

A couple of teenagers, Roisin had said. Just boisterous lads. This nice man had heard a commotion and come to see if they were okay. Sophia had been feeling a little rough and thrown up with all the drama. No problems. All fine now. Sorry for worrying you . . .

McAvoy knows Roisin loves him. Knows she will always be loyal. But he has never believed he deserves her, or that she is with him for any other reason than a sense of gratitude for saving her so many years ago. She wasn't even a teenager when they first met. She was a feisty, free-spirited traveller girl, temporarily camped up on a farmer's land near Brampton in Cumbria. Some bad men had taken her, and young Police Constable Aector McAvoy had taken her back. Years later they fell in love. His life before her seems like it belongs to somebody else. She holds his whole heart. Owns his conscience and soul. He is not angry at her for looking at Hollow with simpering eyes, just quietly broken-hearted.

'Medical records are through,' says DC Sophie Kirkland, spinning back from her computer screen. 'Give me a tick . . .'

While he waits, McAvoy looks back at the board. They won't know much about where to start until the post-mortem exam is carried out. Ava will be on the table right now, scrubbed and sliced: a Y-shaped incision from sternum to pubis and her flesh peeled back like the flaps of a tent. The top of her head will have been opened with a circular saw and her organs removed and weighed. The dirt beneath her fingernails and toenails will have been removed for analysis. Her vagina and anus will have been probed and swabbed for DNA. McAvoy has witnessed such indignities before.

'Busy girl,' says Sophie, with a note of disapproval in her voice, as she scans the report and gives the other officers the highlights. 'History of self-harm. Suspected overdose last June. Admitted to Hull Royal Infirmary and had her stomach pumped . . . was referred for psychological evaluation. Prescribed anti-depressants . . . referred to a counsellor but the referral wasn't followed up. She last saw her GP two months ago for something to help her sleep. Said she hadn't self-harmed for a long time.' Sophie looks up from her screen. 'I'll go back to when she was in nappies. Shout up if I find anything.'

McAvoy nods. Taps his pen on his lips and turns to DC Andy Daniells, who has been waiting his turn to speak like a six-year-old who knows the answer to a teacher's question. He's a young, round-faced Welshman with a comfortable gut and a pleasant, chatty personality. He's a good listener and works like a dog. Most importantly, he has a habit of bringing a picnic hamper full of luxuries on surveillance jobs and is more than happy to share. His dad runs a fancy delicatessen in Cardiff and sends his son all manner of indulgences. It's made him popular. He recently entered into a civil partnership with his long-term partner, a painter and decorator called Dean, and even the most hard-bitten homophobes in the department chucked a couple of quid into the collection for a present.

'Andy?'

'Been Facebooking since about half four,' says Daniells, eagerly. 'I know that isn't a verb, Sarge, before you start. We haven't got her password yet but should be in soon enough. Her profile settings aren't particularly private so we've been able to get a good idea of what she's into.'

McAvoy nods encouragingly. A Facebook photo of Ava has already been printed out and stuck to the board. It shows a funky, sexy little rock chick in a black halter-neck top with piercings, tattoos and a pleasing naughtiness in her eyes.

'Last used her account on Monday evening,' continues Daniells. 'Commented on a picture of a baby elephant. Said, "Aww – so cute." Prior to that, a bit of banter with a friend down south. Arguing over who's the better guitar player. All friendly, but we've sent a local uniform to talk to him. She was a regular Facebook user, that's clear. Took a lot of selfies. Posted lots of pictures she liked. Sunsets and treehouses, aurora borealis and stuff like that. Took the piss quite a lot. One thousand, three hundred and twelve friends. Interested in films, music, poetry, travel. Used to be in a band called Donkey but I don't think they troubled *Top of the Pops*. Posted a lot of motivational messages about tattooing. On January twenty-first she had an argument with some girl from Coventry who said she was an ugly bitch with tiny tits. Ava's reply was very reasonable, though she did sign off by calling her a cunt. Eight messages in all. Ava's were the better spelled. No threats to kill but a lot of people "liked" Ava's response.'

McAvoy nods, as his brain swallows it all down. 'Usual stuff, then, yes?'

Daniells gives a vigorous nod of the head. 'She took a brilliant selfie where she'd wrapped her head in Sellotape, but I think she was just bored. Got a lot of "LOL" responses. People have a lot of free time, don't they? I'm going through each friend in turn and cross-referencing them with HOLMES and doing a swift Google search. I've roped in a couple of support staff for help, if that's okay. Let me know if you need them back . . .'

McAvoy waves a hand, admiring the young constable's tenacity. 'Anything so far?'

'One of her friends from Coventry – that's where she's from, originally, if any of you were wondering – has a record for possession with intent to supply, and some bloke she talks to about music was done for wounding a couple of years ago. And she's commented on a memorial page to a lad called David Belcher. Something about everything happening for a reason, which struck me as a bit ambiguous. I'm looking deeper, don't fret. He died in June last year. Knocked down and killed walking home out near Wawne. His profile has been "memorialised", which means the page stays active but sensitive information is removed. We've been able to get on there.' Daniells pulls out a folder from under his seat and flourishes a colour printout. 'If that's not her then I've got a thirty-inch waist.'

McAvoy takes the proffered picture. It shows a thin-faced, unscrubbed lad of around twenty, gurning for the camera while a smiling Ava Delaney plants a kiss on his cheek.

'Relationship?' asks McAvoy.

'That picture was taken last May. Nearly a year ago. I'm thinking that perhaps we should go and see the lad's family, maybe ask a couple of uniforms to swing by . . .'

McAvoy looks back out of the window. The old lady has gone. A tree beside the chain-link fence is showing the first signs of blossom. The petals show as a fuzzy swirl of pink between the earthy tones of the damp branches and the gathering grey of the sky. The blossom is late this year; the result of a winter that bit to the bone.

Neilsen refreshes his computer screen. Pushes in before Daniells can speak again.

'There are two entrances to the courtyard and both are covered by CCTV. That's the good news. Bad news is that almost everybody who knows Hull's Old Town knows that you can use it as a cut-through from Bowlalley Lane to Alfred Gelder Street, so there are maybe twenty people every fifteen minutes going in or coming out. We've got all the recordings going back a fortnight. Once we get a vague time of death it will narrow things down a little.'

McAvoy rubs a hand through his hair. Looks past Ben at the score of men and women, notebooks in hand, ties unfastened, lines in their foreheads and weary resignation in their eyes. They expect to catch whoever did this. Expect to find an angry boyfriend behind it. They've heard what he did to her and hope the same gets done to him once he's in the cells.

Another day at the office.

Another dead girl.

'Family?' says McAvoy. 'Friends?'

Ben hits some buttons on the keyboard. The printer at the far end of the room whirs into life.

'A précis of what we've got will be in your hands in a moment,' says Ben, to the team behind him. 'For those of you who struggle to focus on big words this early in the day, here are the highlights. Ava was twenty. Born and raised in Coventry. Lived with mum and stepdad until she was eleven when they split up and Mum moved to Germany to be with a squaddie. Ava went too. Went to a squaddie school in a place called Paderborn. We've requested her records. At sixteen she moved back to live with her gran in

97

Coventry. Bit wild, but nothing that should have you losing any sympathy for her. Got into music. Goth stuff. Indie. She started at a local college but dropped out. Did some work in call centres and clothes shops. Arrested during a drugs raid on a house in Wood End but released without charge. Started a couple of apprenticeships. Beauty. Hairdressing. Didn't finish either. Had a couple of boyfriends but according to what her mum told me through the tears when I spoke to her in the early hours, nothing serious. She was a bit lost – that's what her mum said. Had a big brain but didn't seem to be able to stick at anything.'

'Who broke the news to mum?'

'Military police,' says Ben promptly. 'She'll be looked after. She did say she thought Ava was getting things together. New job. Seemed a bit more content. Played a song down the phone to her a few days ago and it was less dark than the stuff she used to write when she was cutting herself.'

'The suicide attempt? The financial problems?'

Neilsen nods, consulting his notes again. 'Mum had helped her out. Stepdad too. But if they transferred her five hundred quid she'd go and get a tattoo or buy six pairs of shoes. Her mum thought the suicide attempt was a cry for help, but she was adamant that help was always forthcoming.'

'When did she last see her?'

'Christmas,' Neilsen replies. 'They came to London for a few days and she went to see them there. Had a nice dinner. Nice day, so it seems. Nothing to worry her mum, anyway.'

'Stepdad?'

'Engineer. Glowing record. Seemed to think of her the way a stepdad should. Did his duty.'

McAvoy purses his lips. He feels a pressure in his chest. Wonders if he should force himself to eat. Whether he should call Roisin. Text Pharaoh. Drive out to Reuben Hollow's place and shake his hand. Finds himself scowling, and wonders what the team make of it. He starts to turn red and snaps his head in the direction of a young civilian officer when she opens a can of pop that has been shaken in her handbag. Sighs above the curses and the hiss of spilled cola as it soaks into the dirty grey carpet among a million other stains . . .

'We'll regroup at two p.m.,' says McAvoy. 'PME will be in by then. We'll know a damn sight more than we do now, which, let's face it, won't be difficult. The boss will be back too, so let's give her something to smile about, eh? And if anybody forgets to ask any witnesses about Hannah Kelly, I will give their name to the boss, whose mood today should not need explaining.'

There are glances and mutterings among the assembled officers. There is no secret about Pharaoh's current whereabouts. Most of them will have watched Reuben Hollow's appearance on *Look North* last night. All will have read the newspaper articles tearing her apart for incompetence. They know that, even now, she's sitting in the Chief Constable's office with representatives of the CPS and Police Federation, looking over their options if Hollow decides to take legal action against the force. Pharaoh doesn't want to be there. She looked as if she was going to drive straight off the Humber Bridge when the call came through this morning, demanding her presence at HQ. She wants to be here, looking for Ava's killer. And McAvoy knows that they have a better chance of catching the murderer with Pharaoh in charge than with him.

McAvoy turns away as the hubbub returns to the room. The team spin back to their desks. Bottles of Lucozade hiss open. There is the rattle of fingers on keyboards and the rustle of fists being stuffed into crisp packets. He crosses back to the window. Tries to find pleasure in the pink among the grey, but feels as though something is squeezing his lungs. When he looks at the blossom he sees only the certainty of death. Knows that within days, the petals will be mulched beneath feet and tyres, rotting in pitiful little drifts at the side of the road.

Angry at himself, he turns back into the room.

Locks eyes with Ava Delaney.

With Hannah Kelly.

Makes another promise to the dead.

9

Trish Pharaoh looks at the palm of her left hand. Peers, intently, at the grooves and lines. Tries to make out a shape. The curve of a neck, perhaps. The angle of a jawbone. The hard, firm bullet of a nipple.

She looks again at the wooden sculpture she holds between the finger and thumb of her right hand. Wonders if she really looks like that. Hopes to God she does.

She takes a deep, angry drag on her black cigarette. She has smoked it down to the filter and uses the last burning ember to light another before inhaling so deeply that stars appear and explode before her eyes. It improves the view a little. She's leaning against the dirty glass of the smoking shelter at the rear of the Police HQ on Clough Road. The building is a thoroughly modern construction, painted in bright colours and designed to look like a cross between a community centre and an office for a funky marketing company. It hasn't got much character. Pharaoh likes old police stations, buildings that smell of the role they were built for. She likes a police station to carry with it the tang of tears and disinfectant, spilled whisky and a billion cigarettes. It's a comforting smell. She wouldn't wear it as a perfume but it has always made her feel at home. Here, in this palace of pastels, lumbar-support swivel chairs and ergonomic desk placement, she feels like a tramp in the lobby of a posh hotel. This is just about the only place she can stomach. A glorified bus shelter in a car park full of Audis and Land Rovers; the vehicles of the senior officers and the shiny, well-groomed people who hold their coat-tails.

She looks at the tip of the cigarette. Wonders if she should grind it out on the little wooden figurine. Knows, immediately, that she will not. She already owes it a favour or two. It kept her quiet in the meeting. Gave her something to focus on as the menfolk spouted shit and the cold stones in her chest turned white-hot with temper. She squeezed her wooden likeness until it almost burst the skin. Focused all her energy on crushing herself. It was a strange, voodoo-like experience, but it helped. She will come through this storm as she has come through others. For now, she has to just take whatever is thrown her way. She's a career officer. She's made it higher in her profession than any other woman in the history of Humberside Police. Might be Head of CID before the end of the year. Could be Assistant Chief Constable by fifty, though she doesn't like the idea of wearing uniform again. Or she could retire on a half-decent pension and spend her time being a mum. The idea seems appealing, sometimes. But she's fought too hard and too long for what she's got. She likes catching criminals. Doesn't trust anybody else to do it properly. She judges herself by how many murderers she has put away and she's pretty proud of her ratio. Besides, she doesn't want to give the top brass a sacrificial lamb to slaughter. Let one of them take the heat for a change. Let the CPS admit that they were the ones pushing for the prosecution. Let ACC Mallett admit that he knew about the link between the victim and the sergeant who nicked Reuben Hollow. Pharaoh had only come to the case at the last. Why the hell wasn't Shaz Archer at the meeting? And it wasn't even as if Hollow was threatening legal action against the police. He had every right to feel aggrieved. Had every right to show the world what a good man would do to protect the people he loves.

Pharaoh lets her thoughts turn to the man of the hour. Bites her lower lip and grinds out her cigarette. Catches sight of a nice-looking Volvo and wishes she'd ground it out on the bonnet instead.

Reuben bloody Hollow.

Pharaoh looks again at the figure he carved for her. They have been arriving for the past six months. He's got good at recreating her. He didn't have particularly good tools or wood to work with when he was inside but he still managed to craft something beautiful out of a nub of chair leg. It had arrived at work, delivered by a big, embarrassed-looking drug-dealer who had been released from Full Sutton the day before. He dropped it off at reception and muttered something about it being from a friend. Pharaoh had opened it in secret. Hadn't known whether to be flattered or furious. Chose to ignore it. They kept coming. Half a dozen figurines, one every few weeks. They started out in the outfit she had worn during her interviews with Hollow. By the last one, she was fully naked. Hollow had let his imagination run away with him but she would be lying if she said she didn't look forward to seeing his creations. It felt like a very slow seduction; her disrobing done a piece at a time and each step immortalised. His hands had caressed that wood. He had freed her. Found her likeness within the grain and moulded her into something enduring and beautiful. He had found a way to communicate with her that required no words. And he had slipped into her thoughts like blood beneath a door.

What the hell had he been thinking? He had talked about her on TV. Complimented her. And he had come to her house! He'd given a naked sculpture to her daughter. Sophia even had the good grace to blush when she explained what had happened the night before. He'd seen off a couple of tearaways. However he'd imagined the evening working out, it hadn't gone according to plan. She'd barked at him as if he were a vagrant who had wandered into her kitchen and started making a sandwich. She'd tried to focus on tidying up Sophia but her daughter would only allow Roisin to come near her. McAvoy had stood there like a great bloody lemon, no doubt dying a little on the inside because his perfect little wife had gone all doe-eyed at the sight of Reuben's cheekbones. She'd all but kicked Hollow out. Told him that he was trespassing and that it was a criminal offence. She appreciated his help but didn't need it, or want it. Told him he was a fool for coming here. What if there had been photographers? What was he thinking!

Pharaoh tuts at herself and makes a mental apology to the McAvoys. Roisin was a diamond last night. Cleaned up. Gave hugs where they were needed. Made everybody a drink and a bite to eat. She could tell she'd upset Hector but he was doing his best to hide it. He looked even more cow-eyed than usual. Pharaoh hadn't known whether to hit him or give him a cuddle. She settled on neither. Went to bed with a bottle of Zinfandel and dreamed about Jez Gavan and his fat wife. The latest figurine was on her pillow when she woke. There was a cup of strong black coffee on the bedside table. Sophia's apology, she hoped.

Pharaoh knows she has to go back in. Has to sit there while they push around shit like so many scarab beetles in uniform. She's not even dressed for the occasion. Had thrown on a black dress from the laundry hamper as she came down the stairs at 6 a.m. Was pulling on her biker boots when she realised Aector was still in her home. Briefly thought about pretending she had forgotten, and walking in on him while wearing just bra and tights. What was happening to her? She felt like she was losing control of some vital piece of herself

Pharaoh looks around her and feels the fog drawing in. It would be nice to just let it take her. Would be nice to turn away from the station and disappear into the curtains of damp air. Already some of the vehicles on Clough Road are switching their headlights to full beam. The cloud has stooped to take Hull in its embrace. She can barely see the brightly coloured gym that stands next to the police station, or the discount furniture store across the road.

She squints.

Sees *him*.

Reuben Hollow is leaning against the wall at the back of the police station, across the car park from where Pharaoh stands and smokes and snarls at herself.

He's been here a while. Saw her emerge from the building and stamp between the cars to the dirty glass and metal construction where the smokers have been exiled to.

He watched her fumble with her lighter, suck smoke into her lungs and breathe out a cloud of black and grey. It coiled around her. Touched her hair and skin. Drifted away, to mingle with the fog and the cold damp air.

He cannot see what she is looking at so intently but hopes it is the sculpture he made for her. He hopes she isn't offended by the creations he has diverted himself with. She has been on his mind ever since she first came to his house and consented to drink his home-made sloe whisky. She smoked the cigarettes he rolled for her. They talked about children. About loss and duty. He thought he had made a friend, and then she arrested him for murder.

He bears her no ill will. He has never wanted to hurt her. He wants to protect her, from that which is within her and also without. He likes to take women under his wing. Likes to be there when they need him, like last night. He doesn't know who the men were but it was right to hurt them. He's sure she'll tell him everything, soon enough. They'll become confidants. Friends, even. He sees something in her that he wants.

She's crossing towards him now; angry, surprised.

'What the hell are you doing, Hollow? You can't be here. This is stalking.'

He raises his hands placatingly. He's dressed the way he likes, in old jeans and a collarless shirt, leather jacket and flat cap. He's holding a copy of the *Hull Daily Mail*.

'Ava,' he says, pointing to the front page. 'I might be able to help. My daughter . . .'

Pharaoh stops. Scowls. Pats her pockets for her cigarettes then reaches up and takes the hand-rolled one from between Hollow's lips.

She looks at him with eyes that are almost as blue as his. Almost as tired, too.

'You have information pertinent to the case?'

He shrugs. 'It may be nothing. But I thought if we could talk . . .'

Pharaoh looks at the object clutched in her palm. Her lips become a thin line but there is no disguising the smile she is trying not to give in to.

'Why don't you come back to mine? We can talk. We have so much to talk about, Trish.'

Pharaoh says nothing. She looks, for a moment, as though she is about to fob him off. To tell him she can't just leave work in the middle of the day and that she doesn't have the time. She seems to catch herself before she can do so. Seems to make a decision that here, now, she doesn't give a fuck.

And then she follows him through the fog to his car. Climbs inside the battered old Jeep, and lets him drive her away.

10

10.16 a.m.

The police station on Grimsby's Victoria Street. A long, two-storey building in three different shades of brown, bordered by the magistrates' court on one side and a supermarket on the other. It's a busy road, and all the buildings around here are occupied.. There's a little retail park, down towards the old docks. An all-you-can-eat Chinese buffet. An electrical retailer and a tile warehouse. A furniture shop for people who don't buy their sofas on credit and don't baulk at paying £500 for a coffee table. A Kwik Fit and a JobCentre are neighbours to the snooker club and the car wash. A couple of solicitors have offices in the older buildings at the top of the street, just before the crossroads that lead on into Grimsby's town centre and its chain pubs and sandwich shops. If there were room for a brothel and a place to buy fried chicken, it would be a masterclass in urban planning.

In a drab office painted the colour of sour milk, Helen Tremberg sits at her desk and holds the telephone so tightly that there is a danger of leaving grip marks in the plastic.

'So what was the actual point, then?' she asks, through gritted teeth. 'I should have been in on it! I'm not made of glass. Am I part of this or not? No . . . look . . . of course I appreciate that . . . of course . . . Yes, I'm grateful . . . it does make things easier, yes, and . . . no, no, that's not what I'm saying. Look, I'm sorry I snapped. Yes, yes I'll let you know. Thanks. Thanks. Bye.'

She bangs the phone down hard in the cradle. Does it twice more for effect. The two civilian officers with whom she is currently sharing an office have popped out for a cigarette so there is nobody to see the tear of frustration that betrays her and spills from her tired eyes. She sniffs. Rips open a bag of Cadbury's Buttons and stuffs a handful in her mouth. She swallows without tasting. Imagines, for a moment, what it would feel like to sit on Shaz Archer's chest and hit her repeatedly in the face. Knows, without question, it would be bloody lovely.

Finally, she takes a deep breath. Closes her eyes. Lets them flutter back open, like butterflies coming back to life. Stares out of the window . . .

As part of her return from maternity leave, Helen is allowed to work the majority of her shifts from Grimsby HQ, rather than over the water in Hull with the rest of the Drugs Squad. It makes life easier in terms of childcare and travel-to-work time, and keeps her out of Shaz Archer's way. Normally, that means her working day is relatively peaceful and she can at least get away at a sensible hour. She'd also fooled herself into believing that she was making a valuable contribution to the team.

This morning's edition of the *Hull Daily Mail* has made a mockery of that.

Last night, DCI Sharon Archer led a series of raids on three properties on the Preston Road estate. She and her team confiscated cocaine, heroin, cannabis and cash. They arrested six people. It was described in the press as a 'crisp, clean and efficient' operation. The pictures showed a short, tubby man with bad skin and short hair being led away in handcuffs and aiming a boot in the direction of the camera.

The reporter had clearly enjoyed being invited along for the ride.

Helen was not extended the same invitation.

She had managed to read to the fourth paragraph of the article before her temper bubbled over. The death of Raymond O'Neill had been the lead item on page five.

It took an hour of increasingly insistent demands before Archer returned her phone call.

All happened last minute, she said.

No time to contact you.

We needed you dealing with the O'Neill case.

It wasn't lying. I don't lie . . .

Helen rubs her hands through her hair. She should have been on the damn raid. Should at least have known about it. Christ, Archer must have been laughing her perfect bloody tits off. That was why the cow hadn't come to the O'Neill murder. That was why it had landed with Helen. Archer had been too busy planning her latest media masterclass. She had told Helen she had a polo match. A bloody polo match! And all she'd had to say in response to Helen's work on the murder was that it didn't sound like one for her team and should probably be bounced over to Pharaoh. Helen had wanted to pull Archer through the phone by her hair extensions and beat her unconscious with her expensive shoes.

She takes another breath. Looks at the photo of Penelope on her desk. It's a sweet picture. Penelope with a headband pulled down over her eyes so it looks as if she has been blindfolded, gummily grinning at the unexpected darkness. She's wearing a *Top Gear* T-shirt declaring 'I Am The Stig'.

Right, bloody calm down.

Helen gathers her thoughts. She has to work out how to proceed. Played right, this could work out okay. If the O'Neill murder is going to Serious and Organised, she could, perhaps, go with it. Catching whoever killed O'Neill is going to take a lot of legwork. It's the kind of case that will only be solved by good fortune and knocking on doors, and she has no desire to start walking around Preston Road with a picture of the deceased, asking people if they know who smashed a bastard's skull to pieces. She needs resources. Needs Pharaoh and McAvoy. Needs to get away from Archer before she lets her mouth run away with her.

Breathe, Helen. Calm down.

Taking another handful of chocolate buttons, Helen fiddles with her computer. Finds herself on the gossip section of the *Daily Mail* website. Discovers that an actress she has never heard of is struggling with cellulite and that a footballer's girlfriend has started bleaching her anus. Helen wonders why these pieces of information are so much easier to remember than passwords and PIN codes. She works her way back to the *Hull Daily Mail*. Curses Archer and stuffs another chocolate in her mouth. She clicks on the other stories on the news site's homepage. Reads a little about the death of Ava Delaney. Poor lass. Sounds as though a boyfriend did it. Shouldn't be that hard to catch. A nice collar. A chance to do something useful. Pharaoh will probably kick him in the bollocks by accident before she cuffs him.

She clicks on another link. A feature on the growing list of unsolved crimes in the Humberside Police area. One of the losing candidates in the police commissioner election is having a pop about the police not being able to get to the bottom of half a dozen violent incidents over the past year. He mentions Raymond O'Neill and wonders why it took so long for the body to be discovered. Why had nobody been looking for him? How could a body lie undiscovered for so long? Mentions the shoot-out up at Flamborough Head a couple of years back. Bodies have yet to be recovered and the situation adequately explained. And what about the hit and run at Wawne? The debacle over Reuben Hollow. It's a scathing piece and one that will have the top brass squirming. Helen can't find many factual inaccuracies in it, though she does feel like mentioning that Pharaoh was doing a bloody good job catching villains until her resources were slashed in two.

Helen finishes the chocolate. Scowls again. Wonders if she should just bugger off home. Her dad's looking after Penelope again. Taking her around Tropical World at Cleethorpes. Helen would rather be there. He took Helen there when she was little too. They could take a ride on the little steam train. Maybe eat some fried chicken and go to the soft-play area near the cinema.

An email alert drags her out of her reverie. She's set up a filter on her system so that key contacts are automatically flagged as 'urgent'. This one is top of her list.

For the next hour, Helen does not take her eyes off the computer screen. Her notes would be illegible to anybody but her, written without looking away from the passages of text that scroll before her eyes; a Spirograph of blue ink on lined paper. Her civilian colleagues return and ask her if she would like something to eat or drink and she waves them away with a dismissive flap of her left hand. They leave her in peace. They like Helen. Everybody likes Helen. She's tall and strong and funny and committed and she sometimes brings her baby in for them to coo over. Used to be a big-hitter, apparently. Saved the life of a copper's wife a couple of years ago. Got more scars than a blind carpenter's thumb, if you believe the rumours . . .

At around noon, Helen pushes herself back from the computer. She breathes into her hand for a while, her finger hooked over her nose; elbow on the desk, knees touching the underside, biting her lip.

Helen had almost forgotten that she had requested the information. She phoned it across yesterday afternoon, driving back over to Caistor with the smell of antiseptic and sandwiches on her skin. She asked one of the civilian officers to make a formal request to every force in the country, asking for information on all cases that carried any of the same signatures as O'Neill's murder. Under Pharaoh, such requests were standard procedure. They had made a similar request of Interpol. She wanted data on violent incidents occurring within a month of the victim being freed from jail or walking out of court without a custodial sentence. She wanted information on any cases where the victim had previous convictions for violent crimes. She wanted information on any cases where the victim was bound and beaten. Any cases where the victim had irritants in their eyes.

One of the civilian officers put in some hard yards to get the information back to her. Had spent the morning sifting, scrutinising and putting it into something cohesive and understandable. They had done a brilliant job. Helen would offer them a chocolate, were there any left.

Helen feels her pulse racing. She should take this to Archer. Should throw it in the bitch's face and tell her that she has missed a golden opportunity to cherry-pick something career-defining. It's nothing to do with drugs and everything to do with vengeance.

O'Neill's killer has done this before.

Done it well, and often.

She picks up her phone again and chews on her lip as she wonders whom to call.

Replaces the receiver and gets her bag.

She has to be certain. She only has circumstantial evidence and a hunch.

But she's pretty sure she's just identified a serial killer.

11

'You're looming a bit, Sarge.'

'Sorry. Should I sit?'

'If you like. You'll still be taller than me though.'

McAvoy pulls up a swivel chair and eases himself down onto it. Andy Daniells is right. Even seated, he casts a shadow over the constable's desk.

'This feels a bit like driving in front of your dad,' says Daniells, as he flicks swiftly and expertly through the swirls of text and colour on the screen. 'Y'know, where you make sure you check the mirrors properly and don't run any amber lights.'

McAvoy smiles a little. He quite likes the thought of Daniells wanting to impress him.

'I'm not sure I've ever driven my dad anywhere,' muses McAvoy. 'Up the wall, perhaps.'

'Was that a joke, Sarge?'

'Sort of.'

'It was okay. Not terrible. You should make more of them.'

McAvoy studies the cuffs of his shirt. Roisin and Pharaoh tell him the same thing. Tell him that he can be funny, when he tries. That he should try a little banter with the lads, now and again. It might help. Might make people a bit less wary of him, make him seem less like an old warrior king and more like a functioning human being with a wife and kids and a house by the river. He keeps meaning to try it. Just can't seem to find the nerve. He feels like a politician who has been instructed by his public relations team to smile more during interviews and who ends up grinning like a Halloween lantern and being ripped to bits on satirical panel shows. Best just keep quiet, he thinks. Don't take the risk.

'Here we are,' says Andy. 'This is where Ava's boyfriend, David Belcher, died.'

The screen fills with an image of a stretch of country road. A wall of trees on one side, barbed wire fence and open green fields on the other. Metal railings up ahead, sticking out of a low brick wall. Pylons in the distance. Sky like dirty glass. Orange cones and police tape visible in the corner of the shot. A marker and identification number propped on the tarmac, marking the spot where Belcher's body went over the wall, through the trees and into the brown water of the slow-moving drainage stream below.

'Mum thinks he was taking a walk to clear his head,' says Daniells. 'Mates say he was going to visit a lass. Either way, he left the Waggoners pub in Wawne at a little after ten p.m. He'd gone there with two friends.'

'How? Where did he live?'

'He was living with one of them at a house in Wawne. Do you know Wawne? Tiny place. First village you see if you come out of the Bransholme estate on the back road? Used to be a monastery there, I think. Or an abbey. Actually, why am I telling you? You told me! Ha!'

McAvoy gestures for Andy to carry on.

'He'd had four pints of Stella and two vodka and Red Bulls by the time he left but it seems he had been drinking at home for most of the day before that. He was pretty far gone. He was in an okay mood. They'd split up, you see.'

'Andy, try and keep this in some sort of order,' says McAvoy, grimacing. 'He and Ava were an item, yes?'

Andy pulls a face, chastened. 'They started seeing each other last spring. Met in Spiders. Alternative club. All ripped black tights and eyeliner.'

'I know Spiders,' says McAvoy tiredly. He was called there plenty of times while still in uniform. Saw teenagers dressed as vampires and enough black make-up to stage a minstrels show.

'What did he do for a living?'

'Apprentice joiner. Cottingham firm.'

'Serious relationship?'

'He fell for her hard, according to mates and mum. He'd had a couple of girlfriends before but he was besotted with Ava.'

'Happy relationship?' asks McAvoy, though he knows, even as he says it, that such a thing is impossible to quantify.

'Seemed so. They were looking at getting a place together. They spent a lot of nights staying over with his mates who had this place in Wawne. Anyway, it didn't work out.'

'Details, Andy . . .'

'He was a jealous sort. Got his temper up after a few drinks, and anybody who drinks Stella has temper to spare. She was hard work, according to his mates. Used to go into these moods, and they knew she had a history of cutting herself. They weren't really suited. His mum met Ava once and thought they weren't right for each other. She said he was a simple lad, but she didn't mean it nastily. I got what she meant. He wanted a house and a job and Sky TV and a wife and kids. Maybe a fortnight in Majorca once a year. Wanted to drink lager and play football. Ava seems to have wanted more than that. She liked poetry and music and she analysed the world. His mum said she was a moody cow. She messed with his mind a little. Ended it and broke his heart.'

'And when was this?'

'It ended last June. They hadn't been together very long. He didn't take it well. Really didn't know if he loved her or hated her. You know how they get.'

McAvoy almost pushes Andy for more information on what he means by 'they' but he feels he already knows. 'They' are the men who lose their temper and attack their partners. 'They' are the people who take up most of a police officer's working day. *They* are the fucking bastards.

'The night he died,' says McAvoy, staring again at the image on the computer screen, taken by accident investigators last summer. 'He'd left the pub, worse for drink . . .'

'He had an ex-girlfriend lived in Bransholme. It's a couple of miles on foot. He'd had a skinful, wanted a shag. Sorry, boss, but that's what his mates said.'

McAvoy nods. He's holding a can of fizzy orange in his hand and realises it's getting warm. Takes a swig. Licks the stickiness from his lips. Presses the can to his forehead and is half surprised not to hear a sizzle.

'Looks like the vehicle came around this bend,' says Andy, pointing at the screen, 'and hit him hard enough to send him over the wall. He was in the water three days before anybody found him. Bloody horrible conditions and even in that space of time he was bloated as hell by the time the forensics boys got their hands on him. The car hit him from behind. No way of knowing what vehicle – there are no paint traces. He hit the wall on his way over. Smashed his kneecap and tibia. Two ribs.'

'Cause of death?'

'Multiple injuries. There was water in his lungs.'

'He was still alive when he went into the water?'

'Very briefly.'

McAvoy nods. 'Any sign it was deliberate?'

Andy gives an unsatisfactory shrug. 'No witnesses. Nobody's come forward. No enemies to speak of.'

'Record?'

Andy flicks through his notes. 'Police were called twice to a previous girlfriend's home. Her mother called us in.'

McAvoy waits. He feels a headache nagging at his temples, a stiffness in his jaw.

'He was violent?' asks McAvoy.

'Domineering, you could say. But yeah, he was a bully. He'd grab her wrist and yank her about. Shake her. No punches or slaps but just enough intimidation to show he was in charge.'

McAvoy looks at the image of Ava on the whiteboard. Recalls the details of her hospitalisation.

'Do we think he bullied Ava?'

'It would explain why she ended the relationship. She doesn't seem like she'd take that for long. Could explain why she approached Jez Gavan for money. She'd rather be poor than bullied.'

'Was she interviewed after his death?'

Andy looks sheepish, even though he had nothing to do with the investigation.

'His mum told investigators he had recently ended a relationship but she had no address for Ava, or a surname. There were some attempts to track her down but for whatever reason, they came to nothing.'

McAvoy tries not to let his disapproval show. Investigations are complex affairs. Information gets lost. Leads are not properly followed up. People go on holiday and forget to finish all the jobs on their to-do list. McAvoy has been on cases so shoddily handled that it seemed they would only make an arrest if somebody walked into the police station with 'I did it' written on their hat. Even then, there would be a good chance somebody in the evidence store would lose the hat.

He looks at Hannah Kelly, glued to the edge of the board like an afterthought.

'Hannah,' he says, quietly. 'You said you had something.'

Andy grins and takes the empty can from his sergeant. Drops it in the full wastepaper basket and makes no move to pick it up when it hits the stack of takeaway boxes and old papers and bounces onto the floor.

'What day did Hannah disappear?' asks Andy, even though he knows the answer. He wants McAvoy to act as his prompt as he divulges what he has learned.

'August bank holiday.'

'Look at this,' says Andy, and brings up Hannah's Facebook profile. It shows a 'friend' request, sent on 6 September, from the account of Ava Delaney.

McAvoy takes a deep breath. Holds himself steady. He's about to speak when he feels a presence behind him. Hears a familiar voice say a few hellos. He turns and sees Helen Tremberg. She looks agitated. She's smiling, but it's her serious smile. He wants to ask her what's wrong but he feels as though he is moving closer to something. He holds up his hand to ask her for five minutes. She mouths the word 'canteen' and heads back the way she has come, a large sweat patch blotting the back of her pale blue blouse. He screws up his eyes. Forces himself to concentrate.

'A week after she vanished,' he says, turning his attention back to the screen. 'It was in the papers on the Friday before. How many other friend requests has she received since she vanished?'

'A dozen,' says Andy. 'People do that, though. They read about a missing person or a dead person and they try and find them on Facebook. I don't know why.'

'Any indication Ava had done that before?'

'Once,' says Andy, with a grin. His fingers move over the keyboard and a memorial page opens up. McAvoy recognises the girl at once.

'The girl David Hogg ran over. Near Great Givendale. The girl on the horse.'

Andy nods. 'Smashed into her when she was out on a hack. Horse was called Alfie. Horse dead, girl never going to walk again and has so many head injuries she doesn't remember her own name, let alone anybody else's. Hogg's uncle crushed the car so we couldn't get him for it. And Hogg got his head kicked in by some third party, if you remember that particularly joyous day.'

'The message that was sent to her phone,' says McAvoy, impatiently. He knows all this. Knows that a video message was sent to Hannah's phone from a number registered to David Hogg. Hogg has refused to explain it. McAvoy has screwed himself into the ground trying to get answers from Hogg and his uncle about their connection to Hannah, but without success.

McAvoy chews on his lip.

'The rider.' He can't recall her name so reads it off the screen. 'Alice Winter. We spoke to her family when Hannah went missing. The proximity between the last place Hannah was seen and the scene of the crash made it seem worth checking out. We know a video was sent to Hannah from Hogg's phone, but we couldn't establish any kind of connection. This is like knitting with water. Where are the statements?'

Andy rummages in the sheaf of printouts by his desk and finds a two-page witness statement in which the distraught mother of Alice Winter explains she has never heard of Hannah Kelly, but wishes them every luck in finding her. It was of no importance, at the time. May still not be.

McAvoy stares at the printed page, and then at the screen. Alice's Facebook page is full of horses, just like Hannah's. It's sweet and pretty and heart-breaking.

'What are you thinking?'

McAvoy isn't listening. He's looking into the eyes of a brown-haired girl in full equestrian show-jumping gear, nuzzling her face into the neck of a handsome brown horse. He looks back at the picture of Hannah on the board.

'Sarge?'

McAvoy has never taken drugs. Has always been terrified to try. But he suddenly feels an endorphin rush and a bolt of energy as his mind opens like a flower. He takes the case files from Andy's desk and starts leafing through. Turns back to Ava.

Three girls. One injured in a random horse-riding accident. One missing. One dead. Two pretty, well-adjusted girls and one a little wilder. Nothing to link all three. Hannah walked into the woods of Great Givendale and disappeared. Ava was killed in the bathroom of her squalid flat by somebody sick enough to scalp her bloody armpit . . .

He fumbles through the notes. Finds a witness statement, given to a police constable a week after Hannah was last seen, by one of the drinkers outside the Gait. Hannah had waved as she emerged onto the main street, lovely in her tennis dress and Doc Martens. He'd thought she was maybe a foreigner.

McAvoy finds the line that has been nagging at him, glimpsed months before and stored alongside so much else.

He thought she was a foreigner because she hadn't shaved her armpits.

McAvoy feels the ground lurch. Feels sick.

He imagines a killer, bent over the pretty girl who has haunted his days and nights. His imagination fills with mixed horrors and memories as Hannah blends with Ava in his mind. He sees her killer taking a blade to her as she screams and squirms. Sees dirty fingers at her throat and her innocent brown eyes popping and exploding as he throttles her and her blood pours over her white dress and into the dirt and leaves of the forest floor . . .

McAvoy stands a little too quickly. Takes a step back. Doesn't know what he has found but knows it matters. Looks back at the screen in a bid to fill himself with anything other than the images that are tumbling, over and over, in the eye of his imagination.

Looks at the horse and remembers the faintest whiff of something he was told, years ago.

He shushes Andy and starts dropping witness statements on the floor. Finds the number again.

McAvoy uses his softest, most compassionate voice as he introduces himself. He does not do it for effect. He can only imagine what Mrs Winter is going through, the sadness and terrible rage that must fill her every time she looks at her daughter. McAvoy asks his questions quickly. Apologises if it sounds strange. Apologises for asking her the same questions she answered once before. He stands, silently for a moment, as Mrs Winter goes away to check out his request. A moment later she is back. His face changes as he tells her not to apologise. Not to blame herself. She was under too much pressure at the time to be able to recall a stranger's name on a random document.

He hangs up and turns to Andy.

'The horse,' he says, under his breath. 'Hannah didn't know the rider. She didn't know Alice Winter. She used to own Alfie. It says in the equine passport.'

'The what, Sarge?'

'She wouldn't . . .' he says, half to himself. 'She might want him hurt but she wouldn't know how to make it happen. She's not like that.' Frantic, erratic, McAvoy pushes his damp fringe out of his eyes and moves the keyboard to his side of the desk. He feels a vague sense of disappointment and has to fight with himself to feel something else. He's found a link but he wishes to God he'd found something else.

He pulls up the crime scene photos from the hit and run that killed the horse. Grimaces. Logs in to the *Hull Daily Mail* site and navigates his way through the photo archive.

White and pink carnations, left among the wildflowers and the bigger bouquets. A scribble in a looping, girlish hand he knows like his own. Three kisses and a love-heart. He'd been too damn overwhelmed to think of this before. Too full of tears and loss and grief for a girl he never met.

I never forgot you. You'll always be in my heart.

'That was what first brought her out there,' says McAvoy, bright-eyed, red-faced. He turns and looks at the silly, sweet girl on the whiteboard. 'She'd gone to say goodbye to her old pony.'

12

'Looks like a volcano has erupted,' says Hollow, looking in the rear-view mirror.

Hull is behind them. They're heading up the coast, through fields of lurid yellow rapeseed and damp green grass.

Pharaoh turns in the passenger seat and looks out of the back window. The sky above the city is an avalanche of dirty grey. She understands his meaning. It does look as though something has erupted. She half expects to see ash falling like snow.

'First time I came to Hull it had seven different skies,' he says, in response to her silence. 'Every direction I looked there was another season. Stand on the Humber Bridge some time and look around you. It's breathtaking. You need a glove on one hand and suncream on the other.'

'That explains the bloke in the flip-flop and the snow-shoe,' says Pharaoh, turning back to the road.

Hollow glances over at her and smiles, then turns his attention back to the road.

Pharaoh feels a strange blurry emptiness inside her. She doesn't know what she's doing, and she *always* knows. She wonders if she's sickening for something. She's uncomfortably warm. Can feel sweat beading on her forehead and in the small of her back. Her feet feel slippy inside her boots and her hair is starting to go curly. She wishes he would put some music on. She can hear her own breathing, even over the hum of the tyres on the quiet road.

'You ever come out this way before?' asks Hollow. He gives a self-deprecating smile. 'Before me, I mean.'

Pharaoh shakes her head. 'I've passed through, on the way up to Bridlington. Went to Hornsea a couple of years back to see a suspect. Real big fat bastard. Looked like he'd been carved out of discount ham.'

Hollow laughs. It's a warm, guileless sound.

'You should be on the stage,' he says.

'As what? Freak show performer?'

'You're funny, I mean.'

'Funny looking.'

'Funny in loads of ways. And yeah, a bit funny peculiar.'

'What does that mean?'

'You're not like other people. It's a good thing. I tell my daughter the importance of individuality. You're a hell of an individual, Trish.'

'Did I tell you that you could call me Trish?'

'No.'

'Well, you can. But just not, y'know, in front of anyone.'

'I think I may have called you Trish in one of our interviews.'

'You actually called me "Princess" at one point. That went round the station like a stomach virus, I can tell you.'

'Sorry. I'm sure I meant it affectionately.'

'People don't tend to be very affectionate when they're being interviewed in connection with a man's death.'

'I had nothing to fear. I knew I hadn't done anything.'

'Yes, you had. You kicked him and he banged his head and he died.'

'I kicked him because he came for me.'

'Because you beat up his son.'

'Because his son attacked my daughter.'

'And your daughter didn't provoke them? Angel, is she?'

'She's the whole world. She's everything I'm not. She's wonderful. Better than all of us. Don't you feel that way about your children?'

'What are you saying? That I don't love my kids?'

'No. I can see you love your kids. I can see you love your job.'

'You're a fucking clairvoyant, aren't you? What else can you see about me?'

'That you're lonely. That you get scared sometimes. Scared that if you let go a little, the world will collapse.'

'You don't know a damn thing about me.'

'I thought about you a lot. Every day in prison. Every night. Did you like what I made for you?'

'You shouldn't have done that. Were you taking the piss out of me?'

'No. It helped me feel closer to you.'

'Why did you want to feel close to me? I put you in prison.'

'You didn't want to. In a different place, a different time, we could have been friends.'

'Do you know how much trouble I'm in because of you? You came to my house! You're sending me sculptures of me with my clothes off! You're talking about me on the news. I'm a serious career officer. I'm not a simpering little girl. What am I doing here?'

'You need to get away. To get to know me a little more. To know I shouldn't be in prison. It might make it feel a bit better when you're getting shouted at.'

'People don't shout at me. I do the shouting. They cower and wait for me to stop.'

'I know. I've seen you in action. It's beautiful.'

'Don't start . . .'

'I've never seen such passion in a person. You're like the sky over Hull; a hundred different kinds of powerful and sublime.'

'You talk so much shit. Do you know how many women came forward to give statements about your character when we arrested you? Bloody dozens. I've met your sort before. You're a charmer, I can see that. But don't think I'm going to fall for you. I'm here to investigate a murder.'

'Remembered that, have you?'

'Don't smile at me like that.'

'You're smiling too.'

'I'm not. That's a wince. That's . . .'

'I like you smiling at me.'

'Tell me about Hannah. I mean Ava. Ava Delaney.'

'Who's Hannah?'

'Somebody else. A missing girl. Vanished last year. My sergeant thinks she's dead.'

'Is she?'

'Looks like it. Sad case. We may never know what happened to her. I can take that. He can't. Everything hurts him. He carries it all.'

'Sounds a good man.'

'Yeah, he's a fucking saint. Tell me about Ava.'

'That's the girl from the papers, yes?'

'You know it is.'

Hollow closes one eye, as if thinking. A solitary bird sings a repetitive, two-note refrain that sounds pleasant for about ten seconds, and then becomes as annoying as a ticking clock.

'I want to be honest with you, Trish,' says Hollow, looking at her in a way she is not used to. 'If I tell you something that I should probably keep to myself, will it help you trust me? That's what I want most. I want you to trust me.'

Pharaoh is suddenly grateful for the bird in the trees. It allows her to look past him and say something that will lighten the mood.

'I would love it if people told the truth,' she says. 'And shot that fucking bird.'

'I saw her at Hull Royal last year,' says Hollow, looking directly into her eyes. 'I probably shouldn't mention it, given all the bother I've been through, but if it helps you I'll tell you. She was in there with some lad. Delphine had a horrible migraine and I was panicking that it was something more sinister and took her to get checked out. That girl was on a trolley in the corridor, curled up like a puppy. She looked tiny. A lad was with her. Young. Short hair. Bit dirty-looking. He might have been her boyfriend.'

Pharaoh rubs her hands together. Her palms are clammy.

'You spoke to her?'

'She was asleep. I just glimpsed her.'

'And yet you remembered her face.'

'I know faces. I'm a sculptor, remember.'

'Part-time, the way we heard it,' says Pharaoh, with a little nastiness. 'More of a carpenter and handyman, according to some.'

'People say horrid things. If they said something like that to my daughter I'd tell her to blame jealousy. Never listen to bullies.'

'Do you remember the date you took her to the hospital?'

'I can find it. I'll check. Last summer, before you turned my life to crap. Oh, here we are.'

Hollow turns the car onto a muddy, uneven driveway. Tall, silver-green trees form a triumphal archway. Light gutters in the space between the leaves and the tangled branches. Patterns dance on Pharaoh's face and clothes and skin.

A hundred yards from the main road, the woods thin out. The car emerges in a clearing, where Hollow's house sits like something from a nursery rhyme. It's an old-fashioned, tumbledown affair with exposed brickwork and old timbers. A paradise, of sorts. Rusty trampoline and home-made swing in the front garden. Wildflowers scattered in the tall grass, thrown like handfuls of paint. Disordered headstones, mossed over and illegible, half sunk beneath nettles and cow parsley, flaxweed and bluebells. Beehives, long since abandoned, their wood a shade of green that makes Pharaoh think of corruption and decay. She listens and hears the chirrup of starlings and the tic-tic-tic of the cooling car.

Pharaoh summons up what she can remember about the place. It used to be a chapel. Belonged to a landowner who used it as a place of private reflection. His reflection failed to pay off his gambling debts and the chapel was sold along with the rest of his estate 160 years ago. It's passed through many hands since then. Spent years abandoned and derelict. It was bought by a charity in the 1970s. The architect meant something to them, though the name meant nothing to Pharaoh. They tried to restore it but ran out of money. Sold it to one of their members, who started repairs then got sick and had to sell. It ended up in the hands of a family named Fox. Terry Fox was a writer, of sorts. A former Oxbridge professor, he had family money and was happy to spend his share of it on turning the run-down old building into somewhere he could drink wine, grow vegetables and put his feet up. He converted it into a home, though it was never a particularly comfortable place for his family to live. He retained the narrow windows and stone floors. Kept the centuries-old font as a feature in the guest bedroom. Installed a heating system that worked for roughly three days every winter. Kept the graveyard, too. His kids grew up playing football and picnicking among the headstones. Their father found it rather quaint. Mum was too mashed on home-made wine and cannabis to give much of a damn either way.

Pharaoh looks around her as she climbs from the vehicle. The breeze is cool and the sweat on her skin turns instantly chill. She shivers, but hides it. Concentrates on recalling the details of the complex family tree. Professor Fox's daughter, Marissa, was living here when she met Reuben Hollow. She was thirty-five. Bohemian. Had travelled the world and not learned very much about it. She made a living selling home-made jams and flavoured oils, though in truth, it was the last of Daddy's money that paid the bills. She had two children. Delphine was just two when the twenty-two-year-old Reuben entered her life. Aramis was a year younger. Pharaoh pictures a feral little thing in biodegradable nappies and hand-knitted romper suits that made his skin itch. Reuben had just left art college. He'd got a decent enough degree. Didn't know what he was going to do with it. Agreed to spend a summer working for the family of a friend from university. Bumped into Marissa in a pub in Old Ellerby and found her captivating. Wooed her. Wed her. Nursed her when she got ill. Raised her children. Took what work he could and put his own stamp on the house. Marissa died of cirrhosis of the liver when Delphine was eleven. Reuben was both mum and dad from then on.

'This way,' says Reuben, sticking his hands in his pockets. A hand-rolled cigarette is smouldering between his lips.

Pharaoh lights one of her own black cigarettes. Looks around her again and wonders how she would have felt growing up here. It's not quite sinister but it does have a timeless, otherworldly quality. The world could end and the residents of this ramshackle house would likely experience no interruption to their lives. It's completely sheltered from the road. A thousand trees stand sentinel between its residents and the nearest neighbours. It's a cool, quiet, secluded place. A person could either find peace here, or lose their fucking mind.

The gypsy caravan is a red-painted, bow-topped affair. It looks like something from a painting. The shafts for the horse are a gaudy yellow and the net curtains across the leaded windows are brilliant white.

Pharaoh has seen all this before. Hollow walked her around the crime scene months ago. Showed where he was when Wayne Mathers attacked him. Showed where he fell. He'd expected it all to go away soon after. Had never thought he would go to prison.

'We're not going in the house?' asks Pharaoh, as Hollow opens the doors at the rear of the caravan and starts filling the old tin kettle from the tap that sticks out of the leaf-covered ground.

A tip of logs and twigs is already made up at the centre of a circle of blackened stones.

'Delphine will be doing homework,' says Hollow, as he strikes a blade against a piece of flint and lights a piece of bog cotton that he has taken from his pocket. It smoulders in his hand. He places it at the base of the twigs and blows on it gently. The fire comes to life.

'She's an angel,' says Pharaoh, unsure whether to sit, stand or walk home.

'Can I get you tea? There's loads of old wine from Marissa's dad's time. Or I have lager, if that's your thing.'

'Tea will be fine. No, fuck it. Lager, please.'

Hollow reaches into the wagon and grabs a small bottle of lager from the tub of cold water beneath one of the sofa beds. He rubs the moisture off the side onto his shirt. Chucks it to Pharaoh. She catches it and opens it in a frothy spray. Takes a deep swallow. Looks at him, sitting there on the steps of the caravan with a fag between his lips and an earring in his ear and that bloody twinkle in his eyes. She wonders if she's being charmed. Hates that she might be.

'What am I doing here, Mr Hollow?' she asks. 'Really.'

He looks at her for a long moment. Stares into her so intensely that she wonders if he is viewing her thoughts like a show-reel. She burns under his gaze. Feels like she is trying to out-stare the sun.

'I've wanted to talk to you properly since we met,' he says, taking a long pole from the rusted wheel of the gypsy wagon and poking at the fire. 'Come and sit down. You're safe. I promise.'

'I know I'm safe. Do I strike you as a scared person?'

'Honestly?'

'Yeah, just for the laugh.'

'Not scared, no. Sad, maybe. Overwhelmed, perhaps. How's your daughter?'

'Sophia? Fine. Shaken up. I should say thanks.'

'I didn't do anything.'

'Fuck off. I saw blood on your hand. You hit one of them, didn't you?'

'I wouldn't be able to say.'

'Well, thanks. But please, don't come to the house. My husband . . .'

'Yeah, you keep him quiet.'

'I didn't have any reason to tell you about him.'

'What's wrong with him?'

'He had an aneurysm. Pressure of work. Pressure of a lot of things. I don't like talking about it.'

'He's a lucky man, to have you care for him.'

'I don't care for him.'

'He lives with you.'

'He lives in the garage. He doesn't even try to get better. He's not my husband.'

'You used to love him.'

'Love's a funny thing. It's just a word, isn't it? I've locked up a lot of people who've killed for love.'

'Why don't you boot him out, then?'

'He's the girls' father. But it's more than that. Duty, maybe. He gave us a good life, once.'

'He was kind?'

'Generous, maybe. Not kind, no.'

'Tender?'

'Exciting.'

'Loving?'

'What is this?'

'Did he ever hurt you?'

'Fuck off, Hollow.'

'There are tears in your eyes.'

'It's the smoke from the fire. I'm not a scared person, whatever you think. I can give as good as I get.'

'Nobody should have to suffer from bullies. Least of all people that matter.'

'Everybody matters.'

'You don't believe that. Nobody believes that.'

'He'll never be an old man. This isn't forever.'

'How often do you check on him in the hope he's stopped breathing? How often do you pray for him to just switch off?'

Pharaoh feels something buzzing around her head. Feels like she is being attacked by bluebottles and ladybirds. Feels herself swaying slightly. It's all too green, out here. Too natural. Too organic. She feels like if she lay down she would be eaten by the earth.

'You're a cruel fuck,' she says breathlessly. 'Take me back to the station.'

'You've just got here. We're just talking. I want you to meet Delphine. I'll show you where I work. I've been making something . . .'

Pharaoh finds herself desperate for a drink. Imagines pressing a cold can to her forehead, chest and neck. For all that she wants him to stop digging into her mind, she does not yet want to leave. This place seems timeless, somehow. Feels hot and lethargic and far removed from all the shit of the everyday. She hasn't yet got what she came for, and is not even sure she knows what that is.

'Give me another lager then.'

'You haven't finished that one.'

'I'm planning ahead.'

'Tell me everything. You know me and I know so little about you. All I see is a beautiful, intelligent, passionate woman who's held her burdens alone for so long. That big guy with the red hair and the muscles. He's your friend?'

'He is.'

'He has feelings for you.'

'You don't stop, do you?'

'And that was his wife? The little one? Who wants to be you?'

'Wants to be me?'

'You can see it. She envies you – your looks, your success. You should be flattered. But she should stop now. She'll never be you. There's only one you.'

'Does this work on your pathetic women, does it? I've read the statements. You're a charmer. You've got women across the parish all wet for you. I'm not one of them.'

'I don't want that from you. I just want to get to know you. Here. This is pear brandy. Take it slow, it's potent . . .'

'The sculptures. How do you know how I look naked?'

'I imagined it. I have a good imagination.'

'What do you want from me?'

'Whatever you're willing to give.'

A curtain twitches at an upstairs window. Delphine Hollow watches through the stained glass as the curvy, dark-haired woman drinks brandy from the bottle. She's the copper. The one he likes. The one who arrested him and took him away.

Delphine watches her father reach down and take the copper's hand.

He pulls her up onto the step of the gypsy wagon.

After a time, the copper leans her head upon his shoulder. They smoke and drink and watch the fire. He looks happy. She looks unsure. Flushed. She seems to have lost a piece of herself some-where on the drive.

Delphine is seventeen. She's tall, with red hair and freckles. She's wearing a towel and a pair of flip-flops and the heat of the shower has raised red patches on her pale skin.

She picks up a pot of moisturiser from the bedroom dresser and begins to rub it into her skin.

She's smiling as she watches the lady try and kiss her father. He's so *good* at this . . .

Delphine realises she is being rude. Turns away from the

window. She knows what's about to happen and it would be unfair on both of them to have a witness.

She walks, damply, to the big double bed. Lies down and stares up at the familiar pattern on the ceiling.

Puts her hands over her ears as the shouting starts and a solitary bird rises up from the swaying, silent trees.

13

Helen can see her own face reflected back in the screen of the laptop. Can see herself swimming on top of the crime scene photos, her hands with their long, chubby fingers, coated with salt from the packet of crisps, hovering over the keys like the legs of some great hairless spider. She can see the mirror image of the sickly green paint and big windows behind her. Sees the gathering fog: an unwashed lace curtain bunched in rumpled and unruly folds.

She scowls at herself and feels the beginnings of a cold; a pressure across her sinuses and behind her eyes.

She looks up as McAvoy enters the canteen. He pulls at the door for a moment. Remembers he's meant to push. Pushes too hard. Stumbles into the wide, nearly empty, brightly lit room. He's red-faced. His ginger hair is dark with sweat at the temples. He's still buttoned up to the throat; old school tie knotted in a perfect double-Windsor. Grey waistcoat and trousers. Crisp white shirt. He's not wearing his suit jacket but Tremberg knows that he will not have removed it until somebody told him he was allowed.

'Helen,' he says, making his way over to the table. He looks for a moment as if he is about to offer a handshake. The notion of a hug and a kiss seem to flicker over his big, broad face. Eventually he manages a smile and stands there, looking uncomfortable.

'Sarge,' says Helen. She realises he's waiting for permission to sit. He would never dream of doing so without being invited. He will stand up again when she rises. He'd still be pulling her seat out for her had Pharaoh not told him to stop a couple of years ago. 'Sit down, please.'

'You're looking well,' he says, lowering himself into the seat opposite. 'Motherhood agrees with you.'

Helen releases a grin. It comes out with a little snort of laughter.

'She's sleeping through at last. Got a good appetite. Like me.'

McAvoy nods. 'She must miss you during the day.'

Helen feels a flash of annoyance. She is sensitive to any suggestion that she is failing in her duties as a mother by going back to work. One of the desk sergeants at Scunthorpe told her he thought it was a disgrace that she had returned to her career. She was a mother now. Should act like one.

'Fin and Lilah must miss you too,' says Helen flatly.

McAvoy nods, not spotting the challenge. 'They do,' he says, sadly. 'Not as much as I miss them.'

Helen looks into his deep brown eyes and reprimands herself for doubting him. He would never criticise her for returning to work. He's helped her do so. He's been there whenever she has needed him and not even asked her who the father is. He respects her decisions. His own wife may not have a career but he would support her if she chose to. He's proud that she's a mum. If she suddenly decided to become a table dancer, McAvoy would carve grips in her stiletto heels so she wouldn't slip.

'You're working on the Old Town murder?' asks Helen, in a rush. 'I only know what I heard on the news. Twenty, was she? Poor thing.'

'We'll get somebody for it,' says McAvoy, with certainty. 'There's a peculiarity. Possibly a signature.'

Helen studies her sergeant. He looks tired. There are flecks of grey in his beard. Tiny red lightning flashes in his eyes.

'Go on,' says Helen, curious.

'The armpits have been removed,' says McAvoy, quietly, looking at his cuffs. 'Cut off.'

Helen pulls a face. 'Sick bastard.'

'We're waiting for the post-mortem. A lot of material to be gone through. She must have let him in. He seems to have choked her with the toilet seat. Crushed her windpipe.'

'Fucking hell,' says Helen, then registers his distaste. 'Sorry, Sarge.'

She chews on her lip. Screws up her eyes. Goes through all the little rituals of thinking.

'Hannah Kelly?'

McAvoy nods. 'There may be a connection, of sorts. I don't know. It's just a whisper in my head at the moment. Some similarity.' He considers her quizzically. 'Can I ask you something?'

Helen nods, pleased to be of use.

'If you were meeting somebody for a romantic assignation, would you shave under your arms?'

Helen laughs before she can stop herself. Sees the colour bloom in McAvoy's cheeks. She knows how difficult such a question must have been for him.

'Sometimes ladies don't have a shave before they meet somebody so they won't be tempted to jump into bed with them,' says Helen, pushing the laptop away so she can't see her reflection as she says it. 'It's a way of controlling yourself. If you don't want to spoil things by having sex straight away, then you give yourself a reason not to be seen in the nude.'

McAvoy nods thoughtfully, as if the same thought had occurred to him.

'Hannah had hairy armpits, according to one witness,' he says quietly. 'Ava's were chopped off. Is that a connection, or am I just swatting at nothing?'

'I don't know much about the case,' says Helen. 'Was it a political thing? Was she a feminist? Some people don't shave as a statement. Some people just don't bother because they can't see the point. Not everybody hates it. Very popular in the Mediterranean, I'm told. I knew a bloke once who actually preferred it when I didn't shave . . .'

McAvoy coughs and puts his arms down on the table a little too heavily, causing a teaspoon to rattle in the saucer of Helen's cold cup of tea. She pulls a face at him.

'You did ask.'

McAvoy manages a smile in return. 'It's a hard question to

bring up in interviews,' he says, holding her gaze. 'I'll have to ask her friends about it again. Her parents. You'll be able to toast muffins on my face by the time I'm through.'

'Can somebody else not ask?'

'Hannah's my responsibility,' says McAvoy, and saying it out loud seems to add a weight to his shoulders. He sags a little. 'You should be in Grimsby, shouldn't you? Is this just a social call or was there something you wanted me for? Roisin would love to babysit if you need her to.'

Helen shakes her head. Pulls the laptop back towards herself.

'I wanted your opinion,' she says, as matter-of-factly as she can. 'The boss's too. Is she around? I figured not. Getting a bollocking at Clough Road, is she?'

McAvoy nods; his face flooding with disappointment and outrage on behalf of Trish Pharaoh. 'More dramas over Reuben Hollow,' he says, and it seems to pain him to say the name.

'I saw him on TV,' says Helen cautiously. 'He even said she did her job properly and shouldn't be blamed. That's like a football manager getting a vote of confidence from the chairman – you know they'll be for the chop within a week.'

'He's a saint,' says McAvoy, with a flicker of something that Helen has not seen before. 'What was it you wanted my opinion on?'

Helen takes a breath. Checks the clock and decides that she should do this quickly, efficiently and without embellishment. Hopes that McAvoy trusts her enough to let her finish.

'Raymond O'Neill,' she says, typing quickly. 'Found in a former stash house with tied wrists, an irritant in his eyes and injuries to his skull consistent with having his head beaten off the floor. He was every type of bastard. Got away virtually untouched after a violent assault. Was laughing at us, at the system. He was hurt professionally.'

McAvoy nods, waiting for more.

'This is a crime scene from Ipswich,' says Helen, spinning the screen to show her sergeant. 'Dennis Ball. Body found in an industrial skip behind an electrical store. Bruising to the throat and a smashed kneecap but again with an irritant to the eyes. And here.' She pulls up another image on the screen. 'Bruce Corden. Found dead in south London in November the year before last. It looked like he'd slipped on ice coming down the steps outside his house. Huge amount of damage to the base of the skull. But the post-mortem found a patch of hair missing from the front of his scalp that suggested he may have had his head smashed against the stone steps. Coroner recorded an open verdict.'

'Irritant in the eyes?'

'No, but it did match the other criteria.'

'What other criteria?'

'He had recently been given what many considered a rather lenient sentence for drink driving. Knocked a local woman off her bike while three times over the limit. Drove off and left her dead in the road. Spent some time on remand so when it got to court, he was sentenced to time already served and allowed to walk free. The victim's family gave an interview to the local paper talking about justice and how they had been robbed. He didn't even show any remorse, they reckoned. Stood in the dock smug as you like. Grinned at them when the judge said he could go.'

'The other case. Dennis Ball. He'd been inside?'

'Nothing recent,' says Helen, grimacing. 'No actual court case. But his son was up for arson and witness intimidation about a month before Ball was found dead. Ball had a record long as your arm and it seems his son was a chip off the old bollock. The judge even said so when Ball Junior got sent down. I've spoken to the investigating officer and he reckons it was an open secret that everything Ball Junior did, he did on his dad's orders. They just couldn't find anybody willing to say so in court. They had forensics on the boy, so they charged him. His dad still put the word out that if he went down, half the estate he ran was going to go up in smoke. Real nasty piece of work. Was done for rape when he was seventeen and doesn't seem to have changed his attitude to women much since then. The DCI I spoke to said that Ball sexually assaulted one of his officers when she tried to arrest him over some stolen goods he had in his house. Ended up being his word against hers because her partner didn't actually see the assault. You'd think he'd have backed her up, eh?'

McAvoy says nothing. Helen takes a deep breath and pushes on.

'This from the Turkish police,' she says. 'Paul Dean. Forty-six. Found dead at the bottom of his empty swimming pool two summers ago. He's a Brit. Ran a restaurant in Sheffield; owned a holiday house in a place called Kalkan. No record and no negative press. But he was found with irritants in his eyes. The Turkish authorities filed it as an accident – reckoned he'd got something in them and drunkenly fallen into the pool.'

'And why do we doubt that?'

'Because of this,' says Helen, and presses play on the video clip on her screen. It shows a short, snappily dressed man with a shaved head and pointed features. He's in his mid-forties. He's sitting at the end of a long bar in a quiet, modern pub. There are several empty glasses in front of him. The image is black and white and there is no sound but McAvoy watches, his chest beginning to constrict, as the man starts dropping his empty glasses onto the floor. A barmaid, dressed in black, appears and begins waving her hands. The man lunges forward and grabs her. Smashes her face onto the bar. Glasses break and fall. He pushes her away. Her hands fly to her face and come away bloody. A second figure appears and drags the first man away. A bar stool topples. The video cuts to black.

'Paul Dean,' says Helen. 'The victim was an eighteen-year-old. Jessica Heaney. That was in a bar in County Wicklow, Ireland. He'd been drinking all day. She refused to serve him and he went batshit. She needed microsurgery for the cuts to her face. Will have scars for the rest of her life.'

'He was arrested?'

'Went to his holiday home with his boyfriend. It took the Garda weeks to identify him from the footage. He'd been over to Ireland on a golfing holiday. By the time they got a name, he'd had his accident in the pool. The footage of his attack on the barmaid was posted onto his Facebook page. They didn't want anybody grieving for him.'

'Who posted it?'

'Victim's sister. She lives over here. Goes to the University of Hull, the Scarborough campus.'

'You've spoken to her?'

'I thought I'd see what you thought before going any further.'

McAvoy plays the video again. His nose wrinkles as he watches the violence.

'Has DCI Archer been made aware of this?' he asks cautiously.

'She's got O'Neill's death down as drugs related and nothing's going to change that.'

'You believe somebody is targeting bullies,' says McAvoy, thinking aloud. 'Are we talking a vigilante?'

Helen shrugs, not certain. 'I know it's thin. I know I may have found connections because I was looking for them and saw what I wanted to. There's a good enough reason to kill anybody, you know that.'

McAvoy rubs at his forehead. Breathes hard through his mouth.

'There was a hit and run at Wawne,' says McAvoy. 'He was a bully too. And he was the boyfriend of our murder victim from the Old Town.'

Helen raises her eyes, unsure if the connection is relevant, or merely interesting.

'It wouldn't do any harm to talk to some of the victims' families,' muses McAvoy. 'The families of the people who were hurt, I mean. Not everybody is able to leave it to the courts. People have their own ideas of justice. Hogg hurt something that mattered to Hannah but I don't know who she would ask to beat him half to death in revenge. I don't think that kind of viciousness is in her.'

'It's in everybody, Sarge.'

'I don't believe that.'

Helen sighs, exasperated with him. She casts around for the right words to describe the victims of a killer who may not exist. 'These men all seem like they deserved pain,' she says. 'If anybody deserves pain, it's men like this.'

McAvoy looks at her. 'We don't think that way. We can't. Everybody does things wrong. We can't deserve death as a consequence.'

Helen finishes her crisps and considers her companion. He has seen people die. Has found bodies and saved lives. He carries guilt and self-doubt as constant companions. He lives to try and make the world a little nicer for the people he loves. She wants to be like him but knows the price he pays for holding his emotions so close. She has never seen him let go. Not even when she was in the hospital, having saved the life of his wife and child. Even then, his tears were held inside. She fears he will break one day and wonders what he will become when the tears flood out. She wishes he were able to free himself of the barbed wire of conscience that he has wrapped in and around himself. Helen has suffered at the hands of bad men, and she feels no remorse for being glad that somebody is serving up a different kind of sentence. She will still try and catch whoever is doing it, but she will not grieve for those they have killed.

'Look for connections,' says McAvoy. 'Do it quietly. Don't boot down any doors. I'll clear it with the boss when she's back. Call me at home tonight and let me know what you've found. If there's enough to take things forward, the boss will bring it under the unit's purview. The Wawne link will be enough to sell it to the brass.'

Helen looks doubtful. 'You think she'll come through this unscathed?'

McAvoy looks momentarily displeased, like a schoolteacher who has seen a favourite pupil put an apostrophe in the wrong place.

'She's the boss,' he says. 'She's done nothing wrong. We won't catch anybody without her.'

Helen looks at him again. Sees in him a desperate desire to do good and a terrible fear of getting things wrong. He needs Pharaoh to remain an unsullied icon, somebody to look up to and impress. He needs Roisin to be his symbol for goodness and wonder, and his boss to be an example of how to behave. McAvoy is not an overly religious man, but Helen suddenly feels that he thinks of the two women in his life the way Christians think about favoured saints. They are his channel to something greater.

'I'll take the blame if there's any comeback,' says McAvoy, standing. 'Say I told you to do it and you were powerless to resist.'

Helen grins and feels an urge to punch him on the arm.

'That wouldn't actually be a lie,' she says, packing her things.

McAvoy looks at her, all sad eyes and tired smile.

'I'm not irresistible,' he says, confused.

Helen turns away, shaking her head.

You've no idea.

14

Teddy has never drunk in a place like this before. Never sunk pints in a boozer where the toilets have ultraviolet lights so that heroin users can't find their veins, or drunk whisky from a bottle that simply has the word 'whisky' written on the label in marker pen. It's not that he is particularly sophisticated. It's just that pubs with slices of bread and dripping on the bar seem to come from a different time and place. Teddy has just discovered that the time is now, and the place is Grimsby town centre.

He carries the drinks back to the table. Two pints of lager and two chasers. He didn't specify which lager. The lass behind the bar didn't ask. He was busy chuckling at the menu, wondering how an all-day breakfast could only be served between the hours of nine and three.

'Get that down you,' he says to Foley. 'Chaser first – put the cart before the horse.'

'Cheers,' Foley grunts, and downs the whisky. He grimaces. 'Tastes like raw potatoes.' He is brooding. Pulling on his electric cigarette. Teddy considers him. The younger man has a nasty purple bruise from the hinge of his jaw down to the little dimple in his chin. It's obviously fist shaped. Anybody looking can tell that he's been thumped. Foley seems to be feeling a little precious. He's used to being glimpsed with bruised knuckles and blood-stained shoes. To be seen as such an obvious victim is upsetting him. He's been difficult company all day.

'Good seats,' says Teddy, trying to cheer his companion. He rubs the old, stained mahogany of the curve-backed and rickety chairs. From here they can see out through the big glass double windows. Can see the dark grey mass of Grimsby Minster and the semicircle of teenagers who sit on the grass with their backpacks and their outlandish hair and who read their schoolbooks in the warm spring air.

Foley just sucks at his cheeks and scowls. He's wearing a tracksuit top and jeans, white trainers and a baseball cap, and two sovereign rings and a chain thick enough for a mountain bike. He smells of expensive aftershave and cigarettes and the sausage roll he ate for lunch. And also, ever so faintly, of the tea-tree stick he uses on his spots which Teddy does not admit to knowing about.

'Might be a good place to watch the boxing,' muses Teddy, looking around and up at the huge, pull-down screen. He feels quite at home here. It's a place for serious drinkers, a place to drink in ones and twos. An old boy with hair like dirty meringue is seated at the table to his left. The bottom of his pint glass is the same thickness as his spectacles and every time he raises it to his lips he looks like he has three eyes. His suit is the colour that black goes when it has been boil washed too many times. He hasn't spoken since he walked in. Just sits, and drinks, and reads the classified pages of the *Grimsby Telegraph*. Circles the dead that he once knew.

'She's had enough bloody hugs,' snorts Foley, staring intently at the crowd of teenagers. His eyes are fixed on Sophia Pharaoh-Wilkie. She looks striking in her school blazer, grey skirt and white knee-socks. She back-combs her hair for school and wears just enough make-up not to be told off. She's sitting with the older kids. Lads from Grimsby College. She's reclining against a tall, androgynous-looking specimen who keeps flicking his hair out of his eyes and occasionally tickling Sophia's ribs. Lots of the girls have given her cuddles over the past hour. She's been telling them some sob story about the nasty men who came and hurt her last night. Has probably updated her Facebook status and taken a selfie looking violated. Foley wants to smash her face in.

'Chill your boots, son,' says Teddy, placatingly. 'The boss is thinking things over. He's a man of patience. He says the word, we can enjoy ourselves. He says no, we sit and drink in this lovely place. Life's a peach. We're on expenses. Don't get so upset. He hit you in the dark, mate. You'd have fucking broken his spine if you'd seen him coming.'

Foley seems briefly mollified by his companion's words. Were they still inside, Teddy would give his cheek a stroke. He'd hold his face in his hands and stare into his eyes and tell him he's the man. Not to get upset. Then he'd lead him to their bunk beds and spoon him for an hour. Maybe slide a hand inside his jeans. Make him feel better. Here, now, he can only try and make the grumpy sod laugh.

'The boss is fucking losing it,' says Foley, slumping lower in his seat and rolling a mouthful of phlegm with his tongue. 'We should have gone back there last night. Burned the fuckers to the ground . . .'

Teddy sighs. He has worked for many men over the years and is quietly fond of his current employer. For the past six years he's been a fairly decent boss. He runs the Krakatoa Casino in Blackwell and a private members' club in Mayfair. Lends money at an interest rate that puts most credit cards to shame. Offers security services and occasionally gets his hands on shipments of cheap booze and cigarettes. He helps people reach the UK. Helps employers find cheap labour. He's an agreeable enough man in his late fifties and he earned his stripes when the serious gangsters still ran London. He doesn't like to hurt people. Teddy has only had to open one throat since he began working for him. He's cut the fingers off a couple of late payers and sliced a whore from her eye socket to her chin, but he took only minimal pleasure from it, and his boss none at all. The whore hadn't even been a looker to start with.

'Why are we here, Teddy?'

Teddy turns to his companion and gives him a warm, indulgent smile. 'Getting philosophical again, my friend?'

'Fuck off – you know what I mean. This isn't worth it. She's a copper. It's not that much bloody money. Barely worth paying us to come all this fucking way.'

Teddy shrugs. Finishes his pint. He's been around long enough to know that times change. Sometimes, your boss on a Monday is in the ground come Tuesday. By Wednesday, you're working for somebody else and refusing to look back.

'You've heard the same stories I have,' he says flatly. 'The boss has bowed the knee.'

'Them?' asks Foley, cautiously.

Teddy shrugs. They have both heard the rumours. For the past two or three years, an organisation of ruthlessly efficient mercenaries has been taking over territory from established criminal outfits. Those that have refused to join them are dead or in prison. Nobody knows where they came from or how much influence they intend to assert but those who have crossed them have been hurt beyond enduring.

'They did it to Carruthers,' says Foley quietly. 'His dad runs Blackpool. He was doing a spell in Lincoln. When the screws found him they'd nailed his hands to his knees and blowtorched his fucking chest . . .'

Teddy says nothing. He's heard the stories. Knows what he will say if they approach him and ask him to join up. He'd shoot his mother in the face before he'd submit to such tortures.

'You think they've asked to see the boss's books?' asks Foley. They've never let themselves talk about this. They're feeling one another out like chess masters.

Teddy shrugs. The thought has occurred to him. If the boss has lost territory to a new outfit, perhaps the new chief is demanding more than he can realistically expect. The boss has been lending money to lost causes for years. Nine times out of ten, they pay up or sign over something useful. In the case of Anders Wilkie, the boss never expected to see it again. The debtor was a cripple. He had nothing to offer. His missus was a copper. The boss gave it up as a learning experience. This past month, the boss hasn't been himself. He's been drinking more. Losing his temper. Demanding swifter and heftier payments from his underlings. When he despatched Teddy and Foley to Grimsby he couldn't meet their eyes.

'Maybe whoever the boss is paying has it in for coppers,' says Foley.

Teddy's smile breaks the ice. Foley relaxes a little. They both seem to be on the same page. They both harbour the same doubts. Their boss is on borrowed time. Whoever is making demands of him has ordered that Pharaoh be hounded. And that suits them fine.

'Speak of the devil,' says Teddy, and answers his phone.

The man at the other end of the line is their boss, Dieter Helfrich. He grew up in East Berlin, under the boot of the Communists. Played the black market as a teen. Hurt people where he had to. Sold vaguely useful secrets to the West until his life became difficult and then enjoyed the hospitality of his British paymasters when they helped him defect in 1986. He sold guns to gangsters in east London. Channelled money into clubs and security. Played the game. Brought over a couple of old pals after the fall of the Berlin Wall and became a player in south London. He's pushing sixty now and looks like a geography teacher. He's short, with unkempt grey hair and big, square glasses. He tried smaller, frameless spectacles but they made him look too much like a German caricature. He used to spend his spare time at his riverboat home by the Thames, but then the Headhunters entered his life, hurt his businesses, and told him he now worked for them. His Ukrainian mistress disappeared. They demanded a set sum each month. They looked through his books and recognised a name. And then a voice in his ear told him to go and make Trish Pharaoh's family pay.

'You're looking at her?' asks Helfrich. 'The girl?'

'I can see her now,' says Teddy quietly. 'My friend here is feeling a little put upon. He's just itching to take out his frustrations.'

'Tell him to rein in his impulses. This isn't about anything more than money. You played it wrong. Pharaoh should have been on the phone begging to be allowed to pay back what her husband owes. You've missed your chance. Don't go for the daughter first. Find somebody else in her life and squeeze.'

Teddy sucks his teeth. 'A friend?' he asks.

'Do what you do best. But the money is the key, Teddy. I have commitments. This is important.'

Teddy looks at the phone quizzically as his employer hangs up.

He wonders how he will break the news to Foley. The lad has been so looking forward to making the copper's daughter beg. He feels bad that his young friend will be disappointed. He pulls a face as he works out a compromise, then his face splits into a big grin as he remembers the pikey. She ticks all the boxes. She'll be perfect, in fact. Pikeys don't tell the police. They don't matter, truth be told. She said her husband was a copper but that was obviously bollocks. And by Christ she had some spirit. Shouldn't be hard to find, neither. He turns to his friend and puts a hand on his shoulder. Looks across the blackheads and bruising around his nose.

Grins as he speaks.

'Foley, my lad, there's good news and bad news . . .'

In the back room of his casino, Dieter Helfrich dabs at his forehead with a silk handkerchief. The fourteen-year-old Ukrainian girl remains spread-eagled on his desk, reading a magazine. He pats her backside, absent-mindedly, as he mulls things over.

He's growing poor under the Headhunters but if he can prove his worth he'll survive and flourish. They'll make him rich. He'll be able to retire years ahead of schedule, pockets bulging with a payday that they promise will be like no other.

He pulls the thong from the perfect white buttocks of the girl. She mumbles a word of thanks in her native tongue then apologises for not using English.

He's grateful to the Headhunters. They have sent him girls worth far more than the dead-eyed addicts who proved good enough for his customers for years. But, like all their gifts, the girls have come at a price.

Look after him.

That had been their instruction. He'd done as he'd been told. Found a room in one of the houses he owns and deposited the yellow-toothed, sallow-skinned zombie on a stinking mattress under the eyes of two East European guards. He was barely human. Long teeth, dirty nails and greenish skin. Must be pushing sixty. Slack jaw and features like a dead rat.

He'd barely been able to say his name when pressed by Dieter's men.

Fuck you, he'd managed, then coughed on bile.

His captors had made a mess of him. Shot him full of a chemical mix that turned his skin into a patchwork of sores and his mind to a sack of screaming snakes.

I'm a policeman . . .

15

'I'm sorry.'

'If you say that again I'm going to elbow you in the throat.'

'Really. That wasn't what I brought you here for. I'm sorry if you misunderstood . . .'

'Stop talking. Save your life.'

On the steps of the caravan, Reuben Hollow hangs his head. He's been rolling and unrolling a cigarette for the past five minutes. It's starting to annoy Pharaoh and she's annoyed enough already. Annoyed and hot and embarrassed. Burning with shame.

'Do you want me to roll that?' she asks, through gritted teeth.

Hollow notices the cigarette, seals it shut with the tip of his tongue and lights it with his black Ronson lighter. It's a classic, expensive-looking object. He plays with it nervously. Raises his head and stares at Pharaoh. She's standing by the fire, chain-smoking. Her hair is stuck to the sweat on her head and neck. The right leg of her tights is laddered and there is dirt on the back of her black dress.

'If you tell anybody . . .' says Pharaoh, her teeth clamped around the filter. She softens her face a little, then hardens it as tears prick at her eyes. 'Why did you carve those figures? What did you expect me to think?'

Hollow scratches at his stubble. He'd only let her kiss him for a moment. She came at him hungrily. Her mouth was hot and wet and tasted like his own. Her body felt warm and her breasts had squashed against him as she pulled his mouth onto hers and grabbed a fistful of his shirt.

It was when her tongue slithered against the roof of his mouth that he reacted. Pushed her away as if she were a vile thing. Pushed her too hard. She had fallen backwards. Snagged her tights and landed on the ground among the dead leaves and the scuttling, crawling things. She had looked up through a veil of hair and her face had contained more hurt than he had ever seen.

He had rejected her. Led her on just so he could say no. Had played with her like she was a schoolgirl. She hadn't even known she was falling for him. Had surprised herself as much as him when she clamped her mouth onto his. It has been so long. So long since somebody has touched her. So long since she felt beautiful.

Here, now, she repels herself. She has never felt so unclean.

'I thought you might like something to drink.'

She turns, wiping her eyes and trying to hide her laddered leg behind the good one. A girl is walking towards them through the grass, holding a thick green bottle and two glasses. She's good-looking. Red hair and freckles. She's wearing a man's jumper and a pair of denim shorts, her hair tied back with a scarf that puts Pharaoh in mind of munitions factories and overalls. She's wearing glasses with a chunky frame and her features are pleasingly mischievous. Delphine.

'That's so thoughtful,' says Hollow. He comes down the caravan steps and greets his daughter with a kiss on the forehead. He lingers there, sniffing her hair. Gives her a squeeze. 'This is Delphine. You've met before, yes?'

Pharaoh's throat feels dry. She raises her cigarette to her lips and realises it has burned down to nothing. She and Delphine have never spoken but she saw her every day during the trial. She sat in the public gallery with a quiet dignity and took notes. Every night she took two buses home. Walked the last mile to this lonely place, with its headstones and ghosts. Didn't cry when he was sentenced. Only let her tears go when he was released. Then she held him on the steps of the Court of Appeal and sobbed into his chest as he held her and the scrum of photographers snapped their pleasure and pain from every angle.

'I'm going soon,' says Pharaoh, in as kindly a voice as she can manage. 'If you could call me a taxi, please.'

149

Hollow stands with his arm around his daughter. 'I'll drive you,' he says. 'Here, have a drink.'

Pharaoh feels so out of place she's tempted to simply run off through the woods. It's all suddenly too much: the buzzing of the flies and the rustling of the trees and the chirruping of the songbirds on the headstones and high branches; the shadows of the leaves moving over her face; the emptiness in her gut and the hot, angry sense of having let herself down . . .

'Are you okay? You look like you're sweating. Drink this.'

Pharaoh feels unsteady on her feet. She takes the proffered glass. Smells Delphine as she puts her arms around her and steers her to the steps of the caravan. She smells like a teenager, of sweat and mown grass. Cheap shampoo and junk food.

'Daddy, help me get her sat down. Is she okay? I heard shouting . . .'

'Don't worry, darling, she's just overworked. Needs a rest. Here, Trish, drink some more. I'll take you back soon, I promise.'

Pharaoh can smell something else. It's an oppressive, thrusting scent and spears into her mouth and nose like the fingers of a grasping hand. She can smell corruption. Can smell the earth, the leaves turning to mulch beneath her feet. She's suddenly overcome by thoughts that are alien to her. Is consumed by the knowledge that all things end. Feels tiny. Feels for a moment her place in the order of things and realises that if she catches a thousand murderers she will still have failed to matter.

This place, she thinks. *Here, among the dead. It's a window into something that we should not see.* She imagines growing up here. Watching as chicks hatch and fledge and fly away. Finding their pathetic bodies among the snapdragons and bluebells. Seeing them feast on wriggling things; gulping down spiders and moths, squawking and fighting, begging for life . . . Pharaoh cannot stand it. She would grow mad here inside a week under the weight of seeing nature as it truly is.

'I'm okay,' she says, and tries to mean it. 'I'm sorry. I'm just tired. Too many late nights.'

'I'll get the car,' says Hollow. He seems pleased to have

something to do, a little lost in the face of Pharaoh's embarrassment and sickness.

'Don't worry,' says Delphine, sitting next to her. 'I can make you something. Have you eaten? Did Daddy take you for something? There are some nice pubs. We could go.'

'I'm fine. I just need to get back to work.'

'Will you come again? Daddy likes you.'

Pharaoh turns away. Doesn't like the word 'daddy'. Doesn't want to be seen. .

'I came here to talk to him about a murder inquiry.'

'I thought that was all over.'

'Not that. That's done. He told me he'd taken you to hospital and you saw a girl. Ava Delaney. She was found murdered last night.'

'That's horrible. How?'

'I can't tell you that. But do you remember anything about her?'

'I had a migraine that night. I don't remember very much. That's so sad. How old was she?'

'Do you know the name Hannah Kelly?'

'I don't think so. No, no, I do. Is she the one who's missing? Why? Did Daddy say we'd met her too?'

'No, we're just asking everybody. I'm sorry to trouble you.'

'I don't blame you, y'know. You were just doing your job. But those lads did attack me for no reason and Daddy just did what everybody should do.'

Pharaoh looks into the eyes of the pretty, earnest girl and sees a love for her father that she has never seen in any eyes other than Fin McAvoy's.

'It must get lonely out here,' says Pharaoh, gesturing around her. 'Just you and your dad.'

'It wasn't always just us. My brother died – you know that, don't you? Killed himself. And Mum drank herself to death.'

'I'm sorry. About both of them.'

'Aramis used to get sad all the time. He drank polish. Poison. It was a horrid way to die. Nearly broke Daddy's heart.'

'And yours, I expect.'

'Of course. I talk to him a lot. It's nice to have him close by. It only got lonely when Daddy was gone. But he's back now.'

Pharaoh closes her eyes for a long time. When she opens them again, Reuben Hollow is standing in front of her holding out his hand.

'I carved the figures because you're beautiful,' says Hollow softly, as he helps her down the steps towards the car. His hands are warm and his breath upon her neck threatens to take the strength from her legs. 'Too beautiful to be sullied by me.'

Pharaoh allows herself to be steered into the passenger seat. Closes her eyes as the shadows dance upon her and the warm leather seats burn her skin.

'Come again,' says Delphine, as the car jerks away over the uneven grass. 'Please.'

Pharaoh catches something in the voice. A plea. A hint of something she cannot place.

She looks across at Hollow. Handsome and charming, with his blue eyes and gentle hands. Reuben Hollow, who refuses to touch her because she's too damn beautiful. Reuben Hollow, with his arm around his daughter's shoulders and a kiss that lingered a second too long upon her head.

She closes her eyes and hopes sleep will take her.

Hopes that when she wakes it will be into a world where her thoughts do not make her feel so sick.

16

Tuesday evening, 9.18 p.m.

A row of terraced cottages, white-painted and timeless; little front yards and potted plants blooming in window boxes. Overhead, the mass of the Humber Bridge; so many tonnes of concrete and steel, rising out of the fog and the coffee-coloured waters of the estuary.

Aector McAvoy, sitting on the stretch of grass opposite his home, phone under his chin and notebook on his lap, watching through the darkness and the clouds as his children throw stones in the water and his wife plucks daisies with her dainty toes to drop them in his lap one at a time.

'No earlier than Sunday,' he says, consulting his notes. 'No later than Tuesday. He'd say later rather than sooner, if you pushed him.'

At the other end of the phone, Pharaoh snorts. 'If I pushed him he wouldn't get up for a month. Carry on.'

'Cause of death was asphyxiation. Low levels of oxygen in the blood, high levels of carbon dioxide. Evidence of significant cyanosis. That's the purplish colouring.'

'I know what it is.'

'Crushed hyoid bone. Do you know—'

'Yes.'

'Vomit in the mouth and throat. Not much stomach content left but she had been drinking red wine shortly before her death. A spirit too, though he's struggling to identify it. She had eaten from a bag of toffee popcorn and had a microwave moussaka for her lunch. We found the packaging in the carrier bag she was using as a bin.'

'The scalping,' says Pharaoh, sighing. 'Get to the scalping.'

'A sharp blade. Well maintained. Polished with a normal household chamois. Equally sharp on both sides of the blade. Perhaps six inches long. Not like anything found at the flat. This was an impressive weapon.'

'Was it after death, Hector?' asks Pharaoh. Her voice suggests this is the thing that matters most.

'Yes, thankfully,' he says, closing his eyes for a moment. 'He held the hair in his fist and sliced through the axilla. That's the technical name for an armpit . . .'

'I know.'

'. . . left a tiny patch under the left arm. Enough to suggest at least a month's growth. Possibly more.'

'The bleach,' says Pharaoh.

'Used as a crude way of destroying anything of forensic value. Caused severe burns to the skin and meant we couldn't get a print off any part of her. It was done by somebody with some understanding of forensics but no real expertise. Basically, nothing you wouldn't know by reading a lot of crime books.'

McAvoy hears the neck of a wine bottle hit a glass. Hears Pharaoh swallow and then a deep breath as she takes a drag on her cigarette. He has so much to ask her. He expected her to walk into the incident room all day. Had expected at least a phone call. But he has been left to run a murder inquiry without her guiding hand. Jackson-Savannah delivered his findings mid-afternoon and McAvoy held off briefing the team until he was damn sure Pharaoh wasn't going to show. He has been calling her all evening. Was about to give up when she finally called back, just as McAvoy and Roisin were telling the kids it was time to cross the road and go back home for a bath and bed. They were delighted when McAvoy took the call and signalled they could have another few minutes on the little patch of rocks and mud that they insist upon calling 'the beach'. It is where they spend most of their evenings. The house is already too small for them. They only moved in a couple of years ago and it has spent much of the time since under tarpaulin and scaffolding, being renovated and largely rebuilt. It is a newish property, built to look old. It shouldn't have ghosts yet. But it has witnessed death and destruction. People died in the living room during an investigation that almost cost the McAvoys everything. They would have moved out were it not for the view. McAvoy adores it here. Loves the water. Finds the drone of tyres on tarmac comforting as it drifts down from the colossal bridge. Likes the chatter of the drinkers who make their way to and from the Country Park Inn; the sound of the ice-cream vans and the squeal of children playing football on the grass. Likes to hear the splash of the lifeboat as it hits the motionless water. There's a park nearby. A large, decorated farm cart, filled with flowers that spell out the words 'City of Culture' in a riot of reds, yellows, blues and greens, poems by Philip Larkin etched into the spokes of the great wheels. It soothes him. Helps him to breathe.

Roisin holds a buttercup under his chin, clutched between her toes. She grins at him. She looks spectacular: leggings and a leopard-print vest, hoop earrings and a riot of gold and garnet at her throat. She's been more affectionate than ever tonight. Still feels bad about upsetting him. Has told him half a dozen times how good he looks today. Made him a lemon meringue pie this afternoon. She hasn't needed to do any of it but the fact that she has makes McAvoy feel a little more whole. She is his antidote. He fills himself with her so he can face the horrors of his days.

'How did it go?' he asks Pharaoh, when the silence stretches out. 'Today?'

'Peachy. I buggered off at lunchtime. Had a lead worth following.'

McAvoy waits, curious. This is not how she normally operates. 'Anything?'

'Nah. Well, maybe. I'll tell you when I see you. My head's a shed right now. You can email me Ava's medical records if you like but I doubt I'll get to it before morning. I have a report to write for the brass. Complete breakdown of the investigation into Hollow. Why I did what I did. Who said what. What I knew. They're covering their arses but they're still onside. We just have to weather it.'

McAvoy turns to his wife. Puts his hand on her bare ankle.

Admires the delicate ink that winds up to the scarring around her calf.

'Jackson-Savannah found something else,' he says, stroking Roisin's instep with his rough thumb. 'He found traces of an organic material in her stomach. Something he wouldn't expect.'

'Yes?'

McAvoy looks again at Roisin. She told him about the properties of the substance, what it could be used for.

'Houseleek. Sempervivum. Do you know what that is?'

McAvoy can hear the scowl in Pharaoh's silence. 'Go on,' she says.

'It's the British aloe vera. Can be used to treat burns and skin complaints. Increases your blood pressure and is good for earache, the heart and digestive system and has been known to have a positive effect on shingles and haemorrhoids.'

There is silence. Pharaoh takes a glug of wine. 'You're telling me this because . . . ?'

'A trace of it was found in Ava's stomach. Recently ingested. It may have lots of good properties but you do not want to swallow this stuff. It causes serious stomach problems. Vomiting. People used to take it as an emetic to make themselves throw up. Can be used with large amounts of parsley to bring on a miscarriage.'

'Parsley? You use that in fishcakes, Hector.'

'Yes, but it's all about the dosage and the part of the plant you use. If you have skills with herbs you can knock up a tincture that tastes of nothing which will make you throw your guts up in next to no time.'

Pharaoh breathes out her cigarette smoke. 'Roisin told you all this, I presume.'

McAvoy looks at his wife, blithely polishing her fingernails on her Lycra-covered chest and beaming with affected pride.

'If somebody went to the trouble of concocting this stuff then we aren't looking for somebody who lost their temper and killed Ava in a fit of rage. They got her to ingest it. Followed her to the bathroom. Suffocated her with the toilet seat then cut her and took their trophy.'

156

Pharaoh stays silent for a moment. 'Do I remember something in the Hannah Kelly disappearance about her waving to a group of ramblers and them thinking she was Mediterranean?'

McAvoy takes a breath. Wonders how the hell she stores it all in a mind so full of politics and children, wine and medication.

'There's a witness statement to that effect. It didn't seem to make much difference at the time but if somebody has a fetish . . .'

'Quite,' says Pharaoh. 'Ava's body – was the rest of her unshaved?'

McAvoy doesn't need his notes. 'No. Shaved legs. Waxed bikini line. Forensics found some of the used strips in the bathroom pedal bin. She waxed herself only a day or two before she died.'

'And Hannah?'

'We obviously don't know for certain but she had a used razor in her shower bag and one of her housemates remembered seeing her with smooth legs not long before she disappeared.'

McAvoy finds himself rolling up the ankle of Roisin's leggings. Strokes her smooth skin.

'You're not a secret expert on fetishism, are you?' asks Pharaoh. 'You couldn't tell me off the top of your head what sort of man likes a woman to be smooth everywhere but under the arms?'

'I think it may have something to do with scent,' says McAvoy, and turns away from Roisin's quizzical expression. 'There are some websites. I've requested a call from one of the registered clinical psychologists first thing. They may be able to shed some light.'

'Does Jez Gavan strike you as the sort of person who would be able to set anything like this up?'

McAvoy considers the scabby little dealer. He doubts it.

'This is somebody with a cool head. They either knew her or charmed their way in. Slipped something in her drink. I've requested that any drinking vessels or empty bottles be tested first by the lab team. They have so much to go through. The flat was a rubbish tip. Do you want to see the instructions I sent regarding how to prioritise?'

'I'm sure it's fine,' says Pharaoh dismissively. She seems tired. Her voice is a little slurred.

'Are you okay?' he asks her again. 'Helen Tremberg came to see me today. Has an idea she wants to run past you. I thought we could maybe bring it under our umbrella . . .'

'Whatever you think,' says Pharaoh with a yawn. 'Fuck, I'm no use to you tonight. I feel rotten, to be honest. Can you run all this past me again first thing? I need to sleep. You need to read about armpit fetishes.'

McAvoy smiles. 'Is Sophia okay?'

'It's all peachy, Hector. Sleep tight.'

She hangs up and McAvoy is left staring at his phone.

'She out of sorts?' asks Roisin, standing up and brushing herself down. She peers through the fog and calls her children. They emerge like soldiers, bursting out of the mist. Lilah bumbles along beside her brother, who is holding her hand and pulling her a little too fast. Both are giggling.

'Just office politics,' says McAvoy, hauling himself upright. 'She plays the game well but this thing with Hollow . . .'

Roisin drops her eyes. Puts her hand in the small of his back and moves closer to him.

'I don't know how he charmed her, if that's what he did,' says Roisin. 'He's nothing special to look at. Not when you're in the room.'

She stiffens for a moment, as if she is preparing to say something else. He knows her noises and movements. Knows them like his own.

'You know the other night?' she asks, quietly. 'That business at Pharaoh's? I've been thinking about it. Maybe there was more to it. Maybe I should have said something. But I thought it was just some bother with Sophia. She's been in a state recently and I said she could talk to me. Look, I promised her I wouldn't say anything and I know how you feel about promises, but I have to tell you this or I won't sleep. It was nasty, Aector. They were men, not boys. And they wanted Trish. They weren't just local thugs, babe, they were the real thing. I'm sorry, I should have said, but Sophia begged me not to. Those two need to talk.'

Aector sucks his cheek. Wonders if she is over-reacting. But he has never had any reason to doubt her.

'A promise is a promise,' he says, at last. 'I understand why you played it down. But nobody would be daft enough to go after Trish. I'm sure it's just a mix-up. You've told me now. Leave it to me.'

Roisin seems relieved. Reaches up and strokes his beard.

McAvoy wants to push her for more details but fears spoiling the moment. He wants to sit on the toilet seat reading a story to Lilah as Roisin baths her. Wants to drink hot chocolate and finish the lemon meringue pie, to catch Fin reading under the covers with a torch, going over the letters that his granddad has been sending him almost daily since they returned from the family croft last summer after a holiday that mended a lot of the broken bridges of McAvoy's past. He wants to make love to his wife as the breeze plays with the curtains of the tiny bedroom. Wants her to muffle her shouts against his neck. Wants her to fall asleep covered in sweat so that when she wakes she will be scented the way he likes. He half smiles to himself. He could have told Pharaoh that yes, he does know a little about what some men want. He likes for Roisin to sometimes smell a little less of perfume and more of flesh.

'This way, Fin,' shouts Roisin.

The boy has run off towards the park. He stops and looks back, impish, as he tries to persuade his parents to let him have five minutes on the giant spider-web of ropes that he can scale in moments. Roisin points at her watch. Shakes her head. McAvoy walks towards his son, Lilah still in his arms.

He gets a whiff of it. That sweet, cloying odour of decay. Of rotted meat. Turned earth. It comes to him through the fog; a faint whisper of something putrid, hanging in the mist.

'Fin. Fin, come back.'

The boy thinks it's a game. Runs into the mist. It closes around him. He becomes a charcoal blur, covered over with pencil shading.

McAvoy sniffs. Takes a deeper breath. It's unmistakable. He's smelled death too many times not to be able to recognise it. Knows how the corruption of skin and tissue climbs into the mouth and throat like frost on a bitter morning. He sends Lilah trotting back to Roisin.

'Fin!'

The boy stops short as his father raises his voice. McAvoy runs into the mist and almost collides with his son. He takes him by the arms and pain crosses Fin's face.

'Go to your mother,' says McAvoy, insistent. 'Now!'

McAvoy turns from his boy and pushes on into the fog. Feels the stench permeate deeper inside him.

He hears Roisin shouting but it is all just static. His blood rushes in his ears. The stench in his nostrils is sliding greasy fingers up and down his thorax.

McAvoy sees the shape of the farm cart. The smell may as well be painted on the grey air.

He steps forward and looks down into the cart.

Her features have sunk down. Her eyes are closed but they have dropped down into the canyons in her skull. Her cheeks cling to her jawbone. There is skin missing on her shoulders and knees. Tendons show through the putrid meat of her bare feet.

Hannah Kelly.

Hands touching at her waist, laid out on a bed of flowers, wrapped in a plain white sheet.

Hannah Kelly.

Skin like rancid ham. Dirt on her skin and worms slithering in her hair.

Hannah Kelly.

She's been dead for months. Dead and buried.

Now exhumed, and laid out like a fairy-tale princess.

Before he turns away, McAvoy notices the staining between her arm and torso. Sees where the blood has pooled, after her killer lifted her arms and sliced off her skin.

PART THREE

17

Yvonne Turpin has the devil horns of a red-wine drinker emerging from her pale lips. She's dressed for comfort in a cheap polo neck and jogging pants. Wears no rings and has bitten her nails so close that her fingers look like pink and painful tentacles.

On the threshold of the flat above the bookies on Nottingham's West Bridgford estate, Helen Tremberg has to stop herself from glancing at her notes to make sure she has the right woman. The lady before her bears little similarity to the straight-backed, dark-haired woman who stood on the court steps and railed against the injustice of releasing the man who had killed her sister.

'Sorry about the mess,' she says, as she leads Helen into a living room that she seems to have stopped redecorating halfway through. Some of the loud wallpaper has been painted over in cream and a large chunk of the dirty, paint-spattered wooden floor has been sanded clean. She seems to have simply given up on the project, content to live in a room that carries her own stamp as well as that of its previous owner.

'Tea?' she asks, sitting down on a chintz sofa and picking up a magazine and wine glass from the cluttered coffee table. 'Or wine? You might have to drink the white stuff. It may be a bit vinegary but it's okay.'

Helen considers the frail, mousy woman before her. She has rarely seen somebody in such desperate need of a good hug. She puts Helen in mind of a beaten dog, shaking and flinching at every loud noise and looking out at the world with eyes that have seen too much sorrow.

'Difficult journey?' asks Yvonne.

Helen puffs out a fed-up breath. 'Fine until I got into the city. Then it was just bedlam.'

'I don't go into the city centre much,' says Yvonne, drawing a circle on her knee with her finger and then repeating the gesture in the opposite direction. 'Shops around here are enough.'

'You're a driver?'

'I can but I haven't got a car. Taxis are too expensive. The bus is okay if you don't get the nutters.'

'I can't stand the bus. There are always people coughing on you.'

'I've noticed that. I don't like to wear a coat with a hood in case people are putting their dirty tissues in it behind me.'

They stop. Look at each other. Helen spots the vinegary white wine and a clean-ish glass by the coffee table and pours herself a little measure.

'I'm sorry to trouble you,' says Helen, as she sips the wine and tries not to demonstrate that this particular Sauvignon Blanc is now only suitable for stripping the paint from armoured cars. 'As I said on the phone, it's really good of you to talk to me. Your sister's death must have been horrendous and the sentence her killer got is a joke. Feel free to shout and scream and bellow and I'll listen to all of it.'

'I don't really understand what it is you're after,' says Yvonne, then looks down at her belly, as if appalled by her own rudeness. 'And my screaming's all been done.'

'Look, I can't say too much. But there are certain cases that have one or two similarities and we're trying to pick our way through some of the murky bits,' says Helen, keeping it vague. She can't give much more in the way of specifics because she isn't sure of them herself.

'And Toni's death is one of them? But we know who was responsible for that, even if you wouldn't know it from the sentence he got. And they can't exactly dig him up and try him again, can they?'

Helen raises her hands a fraction, urging Yvonne to slow down and let her speak. She takes a breath. Settles herself.

'Tell me about Bruce Corden, please, Yvonne. Tell me from the start.'

Yvonne seems to be swilling spit around her mouth. Her eyes darken and her nostrils flare for a moment. She shakes her head, ever so slightly. Rubs at her lower lip with the index finger of her right hand. She looks like she wants to dissolve.

'He killed her,' says Yvonne. 'My Toni. My little sister. Sweet as a chocolate button, that's what Dad always called her. She was, too. Pretty as a Christmas card. Better looking than me.'

Helen wonders if she should butt in or let Yvonne talk. Decides to simply smile.

'We lived miles away from each other most of our adult lives but we were still close. She was always sending me pictures she'd found online. Funny stuff. Pugs in Sherlock Holmes hats. Kids falling off trampolines. She was a bit of a scamp. Loved giggling. Knew how to make me laugh. I was godmother to her daughter, you know that? I mean, I was always going to be in the kid's life but she still went to the trouble of asking me to be godmother because she thought it was important. It meant a lot to me. She was such a good person. If she'd died for something that mattered I could deal with it, or at least find some comfort. But she just died. Died horribly, because she got in somebody's way.'

Helen flicks a glance at her notes. Checks there are no crime scene photos spilling out of her file. Fears that Yvonne would fall apart if confronted with such an image.

'She had a flat in a place called Catford. Do you know it? South London gets a horrible time of it on the TV but it always seemed nice to me whenever I went to stay, and I went to stay a lot. I'd go down every couple of months. Help her with Stephanie. That's her daughter. She's six now. Living with her dad. I don't see much of her.'

Yvonne chews on her lip. Scratches her bare foot against the cheap cord carpet.

'The bicycle was a Christmas present from me,' says Yvonne, into her chest. The words drip with guilt and remorse; they are greasy with regret.

'You couldn't have known,' says Helen, aware that the words are not enough.

Yvonne manages a weak smile, as if she has heard such asinine nonsense a thousand times before. She ignores Helen's comment.

'She was spending so much on bus fares and she kept saying that she was feeling a bit fat and flabby and needed some exercise. I got her the bike. Ordered it off the internet and had it delivered with a big bow. She was squealing when she rang me. Couldn't believe it. She was like a kid with a shiny tricycle. I made her promise to wear a helmet. She was thirty-three and I was making her promise me! But she did and she stayed true to her word. She loved that bike. Always wore a helmet. Not that it did her any good.'

It will be three years in May since Bruce Corden's Ford Transit van ploughed into Antonia Turpin as she cycled home from work on Shooters Hill Road. Corden was three times over the drink-driving limit. He made his living as a removals man, though rumour had it that not all of his clients were aware he planned to remove their possessions. He was a bloated, flaky-skinned abomi-nation of a man; a walrus in knock-off jeans and a hooded top. He'd spent the day sitting at home with a crate of beer and a carton of imported cigarettes, watching a DVD box-set with his hand in his trousers. Decided he needed a little more booze. Set off for the off-licence. Didn't hear Antonia Turpin's shriek as he ploughed into her. Didn't register her presence beneath the wheels for another half a mile and even then, figured it was probably just a refuse sack. He put his foot down. Cleared the blockage. Went to the off-licence and got himself a bottle of cheap bourbon. Drove home past the growing crowd of onlookers who were standing around the mangled remains of a once bright, bubbly mum.

'I didn't really understand it when the call came through,' says Yvonne, quietly. 'I hadn't heard from Antonia's boyfriend in a couple of years. They'd split up, you see, though they were still on good terms. He was down as her next of kin. The police contacted him and he had to phone around. There weren't many people to call. Mum and Dad both died ten years ago. They went within six months of each other. Maybe that's why Toni and me were so close. Anyway, he told me what happened. Said she was dead. I don't know what happened after that. I think I went blank. It was like somebody had flicked a switch and everything was suddenly dark and silent. I sleepwalked through it all. They were good to me at work but they couldn't let me stay off forever. I was working at the university, did you know that? Quite a good job in admin. They had to let me go, of course. I wasn't turning up and when I was there I was like a lunatic, staring out of the window or crying.'

Helen nods, closing her eyes. 'You did her proud when it came to court,' she says encouragingly.

Yvonne takes a moment's comfort. Smiles her thanks. 'I put what energy I had into representing her well at the trial. The police didn't really communicate with me about where they were at with the investigation but they told me when they charged Corden. They expected him to plead guilty.'

As Yvonne speaks, Helen glances down at her notes, stitched together from a dozen different news websites. Toni's killer didn't plead guilty. Claimed that the accident was the fault of the cyclist. She had ridden into him, he said. Maybe it was a suicide attempt. No, he hadn't been drinking before the accident but he had opened his drinks as soon as he got home and that was the reason for the positive breath test. The Crown Prosecution Service felt the case slipping away from them and offered him the chance to plead guilty to a lesser charge of causing death by dangerous driving. He agreed and was sentenced to two years in prison. He had already been on remand for eleven months and it was not considered in anybody's best interests from him to return to prison, only to be released a couple of weeks later when he had served half of his sentence. So Corden was unshackled and allowed to walk from the dock. He blew a kiss at the Turpin family as he did so. Celebrated on the court steps with a six-pack of lager that his mates had brought. Walked off to the pub and drank himself insensible. Told every reporter who questioned him that he had been set up. Said she should have been wearing high-visibility clothing. Said he wasn't as drunk as they made out and it was probably prescription medication that had thrown the breathalyser off . . .

'I've never felt as empty,' says Yvonne, draining her wine and casting around for the bottle. 'It was like a trapdoor had opened in me and everything I thought and believed about the world just fell through it. He had killed my sister and he was out on the streets. I'm not a violent person, I promise you I'm not, but I swear to you, if I'd known who to ask I'd have paid somebody to drive over his head.'

Yvonne shivers. Pulls her knees up close. Wraps her arms around herself and whispers, 'Bastard.'

'I'm so sorry,' says Helen, and wonders how many times in her career she will have to say that. 'I can't make any excuses for what occurred. Sometimes the system fails.'

Yvonne raises her head and there is a spark of challenge and defiance in her wet irises.

'There are different kinds of justice. That's what he said. That's what he got.'

Helen pauses a moment. Runs the sentence back.

'That's what Corden said?'

Yvonne shakes her head, agitated. 'No. The punter. The bloke.'

Helen sits in the absolute silence of the living room for a moment. Orders her thoughts. Stays quiet in the hope Yvonne will keep on talking.

'I'd lost my job, like I said,' Yvonne continues, into her knees. 'I needed work. Managed to get some bar work. The Blue Bell. Nice old pub in the city centre. It was good for me, I think. When you work in a bar and hear people's problems you realise that you're not the only one in pain. They knew, you see? The regulars. I'd given an interview to one of the national papers, and the local paper here and in south London both did pieces on it too. I thought it might change something. It didn't. The job helped, though. People talk to a barmaid, don't they? And it was nice to have so many people telling me I was doing good and that I shouldn't reproach myself for grieving. But it was all the same stuff, you know what I mean? The same phrases. They meant well but while it might have put a little smile on my face, it didn't change what was on the inside. He saw that. Really helped put me back together.'

Helen wonders where this will lead. Wonders if she already has enough to start making her excuses or if there is something more to be learned by letting Yvonne carry on with her recollections of the man who helped her feel better.

'This is your boyfriend we're talking about, yes?'

Yvonne gives her a sharp, angry look. 'I haven't got a boyfriend. I haven't for years.'

Helen lets her confusion show on her face. 'I'm sorry, I don't understand.'

'Nobody did,' says Yvonne, and she is talking to herself more than Helen now. 'He was just a punter. Pint of ale and a scampi and chips. No peas. Two rounds of bread and butter, and extra lemon. He told me to get myself a drink with the change. He was nice. Watched me while I worked, but not in a creepy way. Finished his lunch. As I was getting the plates he asked me where my sadness came from. Just like that. Came out and asked. You don't often get people asking questions like that so I tried to make light of it. Then he turned his head and looked right into me and I swear, it felt like a ghost was passing through me. Next thing I was dizzy and sick and all the grief I'd held back was bubbling up and there I was, snuffling against his chest and sobbing in his arms like a crazy person. There are a couple of booths in the Blue Bell and he took me into one of them. Sat next to me, holding my hand. Told me to talk, to share it. So I did. Told him all about Toni and Corden and how my life was just this constant battle to stay a step ahead of all the black thoughts that were pulling me in. I told him the truth. I couldn't get Corden out of my mind. All I could see was his face; that smile as he walked out of court. I wanted to hurt him so badly I could taste it. He listened to me. I'd swear he was a bloody guardian angel if I hadn't stopped believing in those things. But he told me it would all be okay.'

Helen does not know what to say. Says nothing. Waits for more.

'It worked out okay,' says Yvonne, brightly. 'He was right, though he won't have known it. I don't even know why I'm mentioning it; I just feel it's important that a stranger helped me. He made me feel better. And then karma slapped Corden in the mouth. He fell down some steps near his house. Cracked his head like a boiled egg. I got a call from the police who investigated Toni's death. It was just a courtesy really. They said it was an accident – just like what happened to Toni. Just one of those things. It felt bloody glorious.'

Helen lifts her notepad. Doodles some concentric circles as she lets the possibilities swirl.

'Who was the man?' she asks, keeping her tone light.

Yvonne gives a tiny shrug. 'He was just there that one time. Talked to me. Made me feel better.'

'You didn't think he might have done something to Corden?' asks Helen, as gently as she can.

Yvonne shakes her head. Makes a face. 'That's typical, isn't it? A nice man does a nice thing and the next thing he's the bad guy. I wish I hadn't told you now.'

Helen changes her expression. Tries to win her back round.

'I didn't mean that. I'm sorry. You're right, sometimes people come along and they just make things better. I didn't suggest anything else. Just for argument's sake, though, do you think you would know him again? For our records . . .'

Yvonne looks at the wine bottle. Seems to shrink a little when she realises it is empty.

'I hope I was helpful,' says Yvonne. 'Two accidents, that's all. Toni died and the man who killed her ended up with his brains all over the ground. Maybe there is a different kind of justice than the one you get in courts, but I tell you what, if there is, I hope you don't do a damn thing to stop it.'

Helen cannot find it in her heart to disagree.

18

Assistant Chief Constable Bruce Mallett pulls aside the curtains. Sees his own head staring back at him. Stares through himself into a bleak sea of swirls and spits, blurs and nothingness. Hates Hull to his bones.

The fog is so thick that it seems as though a steam train has chugged past the window, belching swirls of grey-black cloud. Mallett can barely see the blue lights. Can only just make out the outline of the white tent that the science officers have erected around the floral cart where Hannah Kelly lies, dumped atop the peonies, petunias and gerberas like compost.

'We're quite sure?'

'It's her, sir.'

'There's no room for doubt?'

'It's her. I know her face as well as I know my children's. I stare into her eyes every time I close my own. It's her, sir.'

He turns back into the little living room. McAvoy is standing to attention, his face the colour of fog. His wife is sitting on the arm of the sofa, lips pressed together into a bloodless line. She hasn't looked at him since he arrived. Doesn't seem to like coppers. He'd been at a function at Beverley Polo Club when the call came in. Had been enjoying champagne and vol-au-vents; the plunging necklines and sparkly dresses. Had been enjoying the smell of Shaz Archer and the absence of his wife. He's still wearing his dinner suit. He unfastened his bow-tie on the drive over, chewing on extra-strong mints and barking angry orders into his mobile phone.

'Sit down, for God's sake, McAvoy.'

'I'm fine, sir.'

'Christ.'

Mallett plonks himself down on the sofa. Roisin immediately stands. She crosses to her husband. Takes his hand. McAvoy begins to colour.

'It's appreciated, love,' says Mallett. 'Can't see a bloody thing out there. Should be a uniform here soon with some proper clothes for me and then I'll be out of your hair. Another cup of coffee would be a treat.'

Roisin's smile falls well short of her eyes. She is doing her duty. Playing the good hostess. Speaking when spoken to. She doesn't like this man. He's big and loud and rude and can't keep his eyes off her chest. He makes her husband feel uncomfortable and is stopping them from doing what they want to do, which is cuddle up and have a good cry.

'There's lemon meringue pie, if you're hungry,' she says, taking his cup.

Mallett's eyes dart down her top. He gives her a big smile, all capped teeth and pastry crumbs. 'Best not, love. Watching my figure.'

Roisin gives a courteous smile. Heads to the kitchen. Wonders if she should pretend they have a proper coffee machine. It would give her a cover story if overheard hawking up spit.

'Great one you've got there,' says Mallett as Roisin departs. 'Worth their weight in gold, a good wife. That's what I'm told, anyway. I don't think there's enough gold in the world to equate to my wife but that's because she's a fat bitch.'

McAvoy doesn't smile. Can't. If he parts his lips he fears he'll be sick. His mind is full of her. Full of Hannah, gift-wrapped and laid out for him just a few feet from his home. He can still smell her. Knows his children can too. He's lit candles in their bedroom and sung them a lullaby; told them that sometimes bad people do bad things but that they are safe and should not be afraid. They believed him. He wishes he had their conviction. He doesn't know how anybody can believe themselves safe. Doesn't know why they accepted his kisses as he tucked them in. They should be turning away from him, disgusted that their big, strong, policeman daddy could do nothing to stop a beautiful, innocent young woman being butchered. He hopes they're asleep dreaming of better places and happier times. Knows they won't be. They'll be sitting at their bedroom windows, watching the swarm of men and women in luminous coats and white overalls cordoning off the area from their row of houses down to the waterfront.

'Second wife, actually,' says Mallett, trying to make conversation. 'First one was nice enough. I was the problem, I think. Couldn't get used to just one woman, that was the trouble. Maybe we married too young. I don't know. Cow took the kids with her when she left. I don't see much of them. Youngest's a wild one. Seventeen now. Where does the time go, eh?'

McAvoy nods. Tries to look at his watch but realises he can't do it without it seeming obvious. He looks to the door, wishing himself selfish enough to have allowed Pharaoh to drive over here when it was clear she was in no fit state. He hates being around anybody from the upper strata of the force. Mallett may have a reputation as a decent, old-school copper but McAvoy knows that if he had to, he'd throw any one of his officers to the wolves. He knows from personal experience that promises count for nothing in the glare of the media spotlight. Men like Mallett made McAvoy a pariah. They safeguarded a corrupt officer's pension and legacy and let him swan off without a stain on his permanent record, while McAvoy was labelled a grass and encouraged to quit. Pharaoh had saved him. Believed in him. Convinced him he was a good copper and a better man. He'd almost started to believe it himself.

'You think it's coincidence?' asks Mallett, hopefully. 'The killer may not have known you lived here.'

McAvoy shakes his head. 'She was left for me to find,' he says, teeth still clamped together. 'Me and my children. Somebody who knows that I'm investigating her disappearance.'

'So you must have interviewed her killer,' says Mallett, crossing his arms over his fat belly.

'Perhaps.'

'That won't look good,' says Mallett thoughtfully. 'Has anybody followed you? Have you given anybody your home phone number? Are you listed in the phone book?'

'We're not listed. A few people have my home phone number. I haven't noticed anybody following me.'

'Could you relax a little, McAvoy?' asks Mallett, exasperated. 'You look like the central pole in a circus tent.'

McAvoy relents. He slumps down in the armchair where Fin usually sits to pretend he is a king. He feels a vibration in his pocket and pulls out his phone. Another message from Pharaoh. Another query about his wellbeing. She would be here had McAvoy not insisted she stay home. He does not need Mallett to see her in the state he knows she will be in by this time of night. He needs to safeguard her reputation, even if he leaves himself rudderless without her.

'The business with the girl in the Old Town,' says Mallett, thoughtfully. 'You think it's linked?'

McAvoy stares at the picture above the fireplace. Loses himself in woods and sunsets for a moment. Balls his fists as he speaks.

'There are two ways of looking at it,' he says, in little more than a whisper. 'Either it's the same killer, and he got tired of waiting for us to find Hannah's body so made it easier by dumping her outside my house. Or we have two killers. Hannah's murderer displayed her as a rebuttal to the Ava Delaney killing. Showed whoever it is they're trying to impress that he's the real sick bastard and the murder in the Old Town is the work of some amateur.'

'Or it could be coincidence,' says Mallett.

'It could be.'

'But you don't think so.'

'No.'

Mallett is about to speak when Roisin returns. She hands him a coffee and a smile.

'Cappuccino? Lovely.' Mallett takes a large swallow and then sighs. 'Where are you at with Delaney?' he asks. 'The Press Office will be here in a bit and they'll need something useful. Can you help with the statement?'

'Of course, sir. We do have a suspect. Jez Gavan. Dealer. Bit of a villain.'

'An arrest would be a help. Bit of good news to wrap around the bad, eh?'

'Detective Superintendent Pharaoh has a good relationship with him,' says McAvoy, improvising. 'We can bring him in first thing. Press him. But I would urge caution on suggesting we've got our man. I don't think Gavan did it.'

Mallett pulls a face. 'That's not for you to decide. We build a case and see what happens.'

McAvoy can't help himself. Lets his irritation show.

'DSU Pharaoh did that, sir. She built a case against Reuben Hollow. The CPS decided to prosecute. And now she's having her name blackened all over the news.'

Mallett looks briefly affronted. Then he regains his composure. 'Pharaoh's a big girl in a senior role, Sergeant McAvoy. It comes with the territory. If you want promotion you'll learn to take a few lumps for the team.'

A hiss emerges from behind Roisin's locked teeth. 'A few lumps? Have you seen what he looks like when he takes his shirt off? He's got more scars than a fecking lion-tamer! And he's not the only one. Do you know what his being a copper has cost us? Do you? You sit in our house and drink our coffee and talk about taking your lumps? What was the last lump you took?'

McAvoy begins to put a restraining hand on Roisin's arm but pulls himself back. He's horrified to hear her saying these things to his boss but can't bring himself to make her stop.

'Mrs McAvoy, don't think we're not grateful for the contribution your husband has made in one or two investigations . . .'

'One or two investigations? Get your fat arse out of my house while you have the fecking legs to carry you! When I come back I want you gone. I'm going to check on my kids. You want another coffee you can wear it.'

She turns her back and storms from the room, slamming the door behind her. Mallett and McAvoy sit in silence. McAvoy's face is stone, though there is the faintest smile at the corner of his mouth. He has kept Roisin away from his fellow officers. He feared their prejudices and remarks. It never occurred to him that it was his bosses who should be scared.

'She's under a lot of pressure,' says Mallett to himself. He sits back on the sofa and adjusts the front of his shirt. He looks embarrassed. Scolded.

'It wasn't very nice for any of us,' says McAvoy. 'She knows how much it mattered to me to find Hannah alive. She knows what it means that the body was left here. It means there's a personal element to this, and we've been through things like that before. It's hard. Hard for us as a family.'

'No apology necessary,' says Mallett. He checks his watch. 'Where's that bloody uniform, eh?'

They sit in silence, listening to the muffled voices of the officers on the path beyond the front door. There is no laughter. Just workmanlike conversation and the occasional shout when one of the local journalists tries to breach the cordon.

The door opens and Savannah-Jackson enters the living room. He is still clad in his white suit and his face-mask has been pushed up onto the top of his head. He looks red and tired. He nods at Mallett but addresses himself to McAvoy, who pulls himself out of the chair.

'Nice place,' he says, looking around the small room and giving a nod of appreciation at the tasteful pictures and spotless skirting boards. His eyes linger on the collection of horse brasses on the mantelpiece and the sculpture of a horse's head on the marble fireplace. 'Exceptional craftsmanship,' he says, indicating the horse. 'Are you an equestrian family?'

McAvoy is thrown by the sudden enquiry. He shakes his head. 'My wife used to ride. The brasses are hers. My father sculpted the horse.'

Jackson-Savannah purses his lips as though looking at a Caravaggio in a gallery. 'A gifted man. Is he an artist?'

'He runs a croft and works as a caretaker in the village hall,' says McAvoy. 'He just has a knack for this kind of thing.'

'People would pay good money for pieces like that.'

'Not where he lives they wouldn't.'

'Do you sculpt?'

McAvoy lets his confusion show on his face. 'Not really. A bit. When I was younger.'

Jackson-Savannah purses his lips. Claps his hands, as if returning to business. 'Dead for over six months,' he says dispassionately. 'Multiple stab wounds to the face and torso. We'll be able to count them when we get her washed. She's been buried for months too. We're taking soil samples.'

'The armpits,' says McAvoy, dry-mouthed. 'Were they . . . ?'

'Scalped,' says Jackson-Savannah. 'Same as the other girl.'

'Christ,' says Mallett, standing up. 'So it's one killer?'

'That's not for me to say.'

'Who's co-ordinating?' asks Mallett. 'McAvoy here's raring to go. Is the house-to-house under way?'

Jackson-Savannah gives the Assistant Chief Constable a haughty glare. 'I am a Home Office pathologist, not a police officer. But if you expect me to answer your every query I will be glad to do so. The duty CID inspector is bumbling his way around. Tim Graves. He was making noises about DSU Pharaoh's unit no doubt cherry-picking this one as well. Shall I inform him he is to be vindicated in his suspicions?'

Mallett smiles at the pathologist's pomposity. He turns to McAvoy. 'Your team is already on the Delaney case. This is coming under that banner. It will take some careful management of the press but I'm sure you can handle that. And when your boss has the grace to show up you can tell her I want a full précis of where we're at. Get this Gavan chap arrested. I'm going to go and find out where my bloody uniform is.'

He nods at the pathologist and winks at McAvoy. Opens the door and lets in the cold and the fog.

'The sculpture,' says Jackson-Savannah, nodding again at the creation on the fireplace. 'Gift, was it?'

'We stayed with him last summer,' says McAvoy, distracted. 'He gave it to us as we were leaving.'

'Was it a whittling knife he used?'

'Just a regular knife,' says McAvoy, frowning. 'He's had it years. You're not properly dressed up there unless you've got a pocket knife. Why?'

'I need a comparison for the weapon,' he says, matter-of-factly. 'It's hard to see but I'd suggest the wounds on Hannah's body were made with a small blade. A knife sharp on both sides, with a hilt. Perhaps four inches long. It's hard to tell but one particular wound is almost textbook. I think the weapon could be missing a portion of its tip. Not a rare weapon, by any means. The sort of thing one uses for whittling.'

McAvoy stares at the sculpture. Wonders just how many other things he cares about will be tainted with the blood of others before his work is done.

'It should set the cat among the pigeons, that's for certain,' says Jackson-Savannah, chattily. 'A political nightmare, I imagine, and not one that will look good for your DSU Pharaoh. She should be careful whom she insults. She won't have many friends when the news gets out.'

McAvoy nods, then realises he has only been half listening. He turns angry eyes on the pathologist.

'What news? What are you talking about?'

'The report should be in your inbox, Detective Sergeant. I am not your secretary.'

'What report, Doctor?'

Jackson-Savannah gives a last glance at the sculpture and then turns and walks out of the room. McAvoy stands alone, eyes closed, wondering what the hell to do next.

Slowly, as if diffusing a bomb, he looks at his phone. Finds the report sent from Dan in the lab.

Skin cells and trace DNA have been discovered on a handkerchief stuffed in the pocket of Ava Delaney's little black leather jacket.

The knife used to scalp her armpits was perhaps four inches

long with a double-sided, hilted blade, commonly used in wood carving.

McAvoy feels his heart fold in on itself as he reads the name at the bottom of the report.

Reuben Hollow.

19

'*About 6 foot tall, medium build. Good-looking, yeah. Blue eyes, nice smile, smelled like, I don't know, like my granddad's garden shed used to, if that makes any sense . . .*'

Helen is just past Lincoln, on the windy road that will have her home in around forty minutes. If not for Penelope she would have stayed overnight in the pretty town where she spent the evening. Stamford, in south Lincolnshire, is the sort of place Helen would like to retire to. It's all manor houses, mullioned windows, ancient stone bridges and quaint little shops. She spent a weekend here a few years ago, testing the limits of the four-poster bed in some boutique hotel with a married man who made her feel desirable and exciting for about five hours, and then ashamed of herself for the next two days. She'd like to come here with Penelope when she's a little older. Would like to sit down for a five-course dinner somewhere posh, to make her daughter giggle by calling the waiter 'my good man'. She imagines Penelope, swilling Tango around her mouth and testing its piquancy as she imitates a connoisseur.

Helen grins in the darkness. Turns on her fog lights as the first whispers of cloud stream past the windscreen. Turns her thoughts away from her daughter and towards the purpose of her lengthy round trip.

She had left Yvonne to her tears and her wine. Managed to inveigle the most half-hearted of physical descriptions out of her before she did so. She acted like it really wasn't important. But her mind was sizzling with possibilities by the time she got back to her car and followed the spark of an idea through to its conclusion. She called the other names on her list as she drove.

Spoke to the sister of the barmaid attacked by the thug who wound up dead in his swimming pool in Turkey. The sister was a chatty, bubbly Irish girl who was thrilled to be talking to a police officer, even if it was about such a horrible thing. Yes, she'd been delighted to hear about the death of her sister's attacker. No, she didn't recognise the physical description. But her mother might. Helen had called the number she gave her. Spoke to a tired-sounding and wheezy woman in her fifties, asked her the same questions and got the same replies. She'd been about to hang up when the woman had said something that she should have bitten down on. Was he in trouble? Would he be okay? Helen had hung up. Made a note to contact the Garda and get somebody to take a more formal statement first thing in the morning. Then she'd driven to Stamford to speak to the ex-copper who arrested Dennis Ball for menacing the closest thing the pretty little town had to a rough estate. Ball had grabbed her. Pinned her down and forced her mouth open with his dirty hands before spitting down her throat and grabbing great fistfuls of her thighs, buttocks and chest. He'd looked into her eyes and grinned. Licked her face and pulled out a lump of her hair. He was only prevented from raping her when the other officer from her patrol car caught them. They were behind a skip outside an electrical store. Nine months later, Ball's body was found in the same spot; his skull smashed to pieces. The officer had quit the force by then and was trying to make a new start. She'd told a lot of people what had happened. Maybe the guy that Helen described was among them but she didn't know or care. And if he'd been involved in hurting Dennis Ball, he should get a bunch of flowers and a trophy.

Here, now, Helen feels a pulse of exhilaration beating inside her. She imagines telling McAvoy what she has found. Imagines telling Pharaoh. She needs to digest it all. Needs to make sense of it, to figure out how a charming, softly spoken vigilante has been killing people with impunity for God knows how long.

Helen picks up her phone and checks her messages. Calls Vicki back and pulls over at once.

'Vicki? Hi, this is Helen. Yeah.'

The PCSO sounds as though she has been running. She's breathless. Her voice sounds small.

'Helen, hi. How's things?'

'Not bad,' says Helen, hoping that the other officer has rung for more than a chat. 'Did something occur to you about O'Neill?'

Vicki's pause lasts almost ten seconds. And then she starts blurting it all out.

'Honest, I swear if I'd remembered this the other day I'd have told you, but, look, I was watching a bit of telly tonight. Mum had taped a programme and I was having some food and fast-forwarding and there was a bit of the local news at the start of the programme. And look, I don't normally watch the news. But this guy was on. And I remember speaking to him. He'd done a bit of work at the Freedom Centre, fixing some of the flooring in the function room.'

'Go on,' prompts Helen, with a finger in her ear.

'Raymond O'Neill was drinking in the bar area with one of his lads and a couple of mates,' says Vicki, still talking too fast. 'They were celebrating.'

'Celebrating?'

'Him getting released.'

'So this was last February?'

'Must have been. Anyway, there was a bit of a to-do. Nothing major, a bit of bother.'

'Vicki, you can tell me.'

The PCSO sighs. 'You know I told you he called me a c-word? This was the day. There was a nice family drinking in the bar and Raymond and his mate were being really loud and swearing and it caused a bit of an argument. We were in the neighbourhood. We came in and tried to calm things down. Ray was really in my face but that was just Ray. The man who was on the news tonight – he was watching it all. I spoke to him when it all calmed down. He said Ray was an animal. I told him he didn't know the half of it. Told him about Ray getting released from prison. I swear, I never thought of it again until tonight. Remember, we didn't know Ray was missing so at the time it didn't seem relevant. But when I saw him interviewed and realised who he was . . .'

Helen manages to convince Vicki she has done a great job. Calms her with kind words that seem to flow naturally from her tongue. Her heart is racing as she hangs up. Her knuckles are white around the steering wheel; the words scored into her open notebook have penetrated a dozen pages. She doesn't know what she thinks or what she should hope for. Can't remember if she came out with any decent platitudes before she hung up.

She opens a text from Ben Neilsen.

Hannah Kelly's body has been found outside McAvoy's house.

Helen's hands go to her face. She can picture the devastation in his eyes. Can imagine the fire and ice in his gut.

She starts to call him. Stops herself. Starts again.

He's quiet when he answers. Quieter than usual. Manages his name and a breath.

'Sarge, I heard . . .'

'Thanks for ringing,' he says, and sounds grateful. 'Not very nice here at the moment.'

'No. Shit, Sarge, I'm so sorry.'

The phone rustles by her ear. She can hear McAvoy readjusting his own phone, brushing it against the grey and ginger bristles on his cheeks. She wonders if they are damp. Whether he has cried or is holding it all in to fuel the promises she knows he makes to the dead and those left behind.

'How did you get on?' he asks. 'Are you okay? You're not still on the road, are you? What about Penelope?'

Helen keeps her eyes on the road. Realises that despite herself, she is smiling.

'There's so much to tell you. We're on to something, I swear.'

McAvoy grunts his interest and approval and seems to be making up his mind about something. Finally, he comes out with it.

'There's been a development with the Ava Delaney case. We've found DNA at the scene. It belongs to Reuben Hollow.'

Helen turns to look at the road signs as he says it. Sees her eyes widen in the darkened glass of the driver's window.

'Hollow? Christ, wait until you hear what I just found out . . .'

McAvoy makes a noise as she recounts the contents of her conversation with Vicki Fry. Helen wishes she were better at reading his sounds.

'Can you make yourself available first thing tomorrow? I know it's a lot to ask. But I could use a steady pair of hands. And I want to hear how your interviews went.'

Helen gives a proper smile then bites it back.

'What are you thinking? Hollow was still inside when the girl died, wasn't he? And what about Hannah? Were there any similarities? I mean, psychologically. Sorry for asking, it's just . . .'

She hears McAvoy sigh. It's not a dismissive or disappointed sound. He's just too full of questions and sadness to contain it.

'I'll leave you to it,' says Helen, trying to cover up and cursing herself for rambling on.

'Thanks again, Helen. Kiss Penelope goodnight for me.'

He ends the call. She can almost feel the soft, powerful pressure of his thumb upon the button of his phone.

She turns off her music and drives home in silence. Makes a promise to herself that tonight, she will hold Penelope extra tight.

Knows, to her very bones, that for every knight in shining armour, there are a million dragons to slay.

20

Wednesday morning, 7.14 a.m.

Pharaoh didn't sleep much last night. Got a couple of hours of absolute blackness before waking in a tangle of twisted sheets and sprawled-out children. It took her a few moments to realise which bedroom she was in. The middle two children had pushed their beds together and made a nest of eiderdowns and pillows. They'd told her they'd made her a soft cocoon where she could do something about the bags under her eyes. She'd hugged them both and taken up the offer. Hadn't even felt them climbing in beside her when they tiptoed up the stairs. When she woke, her mouth had tasted of wine and garlic, cigarettes and lip-gloss. The room was spinning from the drink and her tiredness. She could have just slumped back on the pillows. Could have fought her way back to sleep. But she chose to check her messages. Chose to read what McAvoy had sent her. Chose to let him enter her thoughts.

Pharaoh knows that she's doing something silly.

Here, now, pushing her sports car too fast through the fog on the grey road that winds through green and yellow fields towards the coast.

Here, on the road to Reuben Hollow's home.

She feels light-headed. Muzzy around the edges. Her thoughts feel somehow slurred. She has never been an enthusiastic user of recreational drugs but does remember the feeling of smoking sticky black resin behind the Spar with a couple of older lads when she was a teen. Wonders if she has somehow ingested something. Could Sophia have slipped something into her morning coffee?

Pharaoh grimaces at herself for even thinking it. Hates being a copper sometimes. Hates what it makes her imagine.

Rubbing her eyes, she plays with the blowers on the dashboard. Tries to remove some of the mist from the windscreen. It makes no difference. The condensation is outside the car, thick and grey as old mashed potato. She keeps seeing shapes emerging from the gloom. Half expects a flock of bats to encircle the car. She feels twitchy. On the verge of something. She feels as though there are angry birds inside her skull, pecking their way out as if through a pie crust in a nursery rhyme.

Pharaoh eases her foot off the accelerator. The fog still hasn't lifted, though it is thinning out as she leaves Hull behind her. She has the radio on low but is barely listening to the breakfast show. She heard the news at 7 a.m. as she drove through the quiet, mist-wreathed streets, heading east through the city centre. A young woman's body found at Hessle Foreshore. Speculation that it might be missing Howden resident Hannah Kelly. Police refusing to rule out a link between her death and the discovery of a body in Hull's Old Town. Some soundbites from a defeated candidate for the role of police commissioner, smugly spreading fear over the rise in violent crime.

Pharaoh wants to close her eyes, to pull over and go to sleep in a lay-by. She wouldn't give a damn if a lorry flattened her car with her in it. She feels like a stranger to herself. Knows that she has been unravelling for months now. She's always liked a drink but for the past year or two she's needed one to soften her world. Has felt as if she is staring into bright sunshine whenever the pleasant shade of red wine and vodka have left her system. She knows when it began. She made a deal that cost her far more than she gained. Compromised what she believed in and made a pact with a very bad man. Her oldest friend is still walking with two sticks because of it. People are dead. She was not to blame, and she tidied it all up better than anybody else could have, but Pharaoh feels as though she let the devil inside her and has been drinking as if trying to drown him.

She hears her phone vibrate inside her handbag. Knows

instinctively that it will be McAvoy again. He needs to talk to her. Needs advice. There have been significant forensic discoveries. Helen Tremberg has unearthed some connections that need a senior detective's input. But more than anything, is she okay? That was what he'd asked, over and over, in the messages she scrolled through with mounting panic in her chest. She wonders what he is demanding of her now. Has she eaten? Does she need a uniform to come and drive her into work?

Pharaoh chews on her cheek. Checks the rear-view mirror and looks away quickly when she catches her own eyes. She looks wrecked. She's still wearing the same things as yesterday. Hasn't washed her hair. Didn't even remember to splash her perfume on when she left the house. She smells of stale cigarettes and sweat-dampened clothes.

Something brown and sleek bounds across the road and Pharaoh has to swerve to avoid it. She gets a glimpse of spindly back legs and a flash of white tail. Takes a breath as adrenaline floods her and feels beads of perspiration prickle on her forehead and chest. She slows down. Turns right and goes through the village, past the pub where Hollow interrupted a pleasant day's drinking by beating the crap out of three little bastards.

She turns the car onto the bumpy track through the trees. She can't make up her mind whether she likes the feeling of being enveloped in nature. It could be a peaceful place, this. Could be secluded and private. A fairy-tale cottage of flowers and trees, birds and wild herbs. But she cannot get past the feeling of being swallowed. Of being somehow folded within something. Sees the forest as a single living organism, closing around her as if she had alighted on the leaves of a Venus fly-trap.

She winds the window down. Breathes in the smell of damp grass and sawn timber, bluebells and dew. Breathes in and shivers as the cool air chills the sweat that clings to her skin.

'What are you doing, Trish? What are you bloody doing?'

Her voice cracks as she speaks. She wishes she had something to drink.

She slows down as she nears the cottage. Spots the gravestones to her left. The flowers have yet to wake under the caress of the sun. Their petals are folded inwards like the wings of birds. A plume of smoke drifts upwards from the chimney that juts from the red tiles. The downstairs curtains are open but the ones in the upper floor are closed. She stares up at them for a time. Imagines him, sleeping beneath white sheets. Wants to press her face into the pillows and breathe in his scent. Wants him to push her face down into sheets that stink of them both.

Pharaoh grimaces again. Rubs her forehead. Drops her chin to the steering wheel and closes her eyes. She has always known what to do, always been on top of things. Right now she feels so lost that she fears she will never find herself again.

Should she call McAvoy? She knows that he will give her some small comfort. His voice will soothe her. He'll tell her what she wants to hear. She's a good copper who did her job. Mistakes were made but none malicious. She just needs to hold it together a little while longer and things will work themselves out. He'll help her. She's done it for him often enough.

'Detective Superintendent?'

Pharaoh jumps as she hears her name. Looks up to see Delphine Hollow walking towards her through the long grass. She's wearing a man's dressing gown and green wellington boots. Her hair is ruffled at the back and she is looking at Pharaoh with a half-smile on her face. Pharaoh pushes her hair back and takes off her seat belt, opens the door. Puts her right boot down on a clump of pretty flowers. Disentangles herself from the car and stands up straight.

'Were you looking for Dad? He's out the back, sawing wood. He'll have his earphones in so there's no point ringing him. He shouldn't be long. We have felling rights to a small portion of the woods, you see. Dad hates chopping them down but there's no point being a sculptor if you haven't got anything to sculpt with. He'll come in looking like he's been bereaved, you see if he doesn't.'

Pharaoh spots the mug of tea in the girl's hand. Delphine sees her looking.

'Shall I make you a cup? You must be exhausted. Have you been down at Hessle? I heard it on the news. Awful, isn't it?'

188

Pharaoh walks around from the far side of the car and stands in front of the girl. She's good-looking, in a rumpled sort of way. Has a tomboyish quality that suggests mucky knees and dirty fingernails. She smells of the outdoors. With her naughty eyes and freckles she looks the way a cartoonist would draw an independent spirit.

'Coffee would be lovely,' says Pharaoh, and is surprised at how soft her voice sounds. She's not a quiet person. Isn't used to having her words drowned out by song thrushes and bees.

'We were both sorry you couldn't stay for dinner last night,' says Delphine, beckoning her towards the house. 'Dad's a great cook.'

'Is there anything he can't do?' asks Pharaoh, distractedly, as she picks her way around the headstones. 'You sound like his publicist.'

Delphine turns and throws Pharaoh a big broad smile. 'He's not much good at maths. And if he puts a shelf up I guarantee it will fall down.'

'Really?' Pharaoh feels oddly pleased by this. She's good at putting up shelves.

'Yeah, he can carve you some stunning shelves but ask him to drill a hole and put up a bracket and he'll go white as a sheet. He can't do his tax returns either. Starts fretting about them around six months before they're due. Mum used to do that for him, apparently.'

Delphine leads them into a low-roofed kitchen. The ceiling is striped with chunky old timbers and painted a cheerful shade of yellow. There are jam jars of herbs and flowers on the windowsill and dirty plates in the deep sink. A long wooden table stands in the centre of the room, set for two. The room is rich with a pungent aroma, medicinal and earthy, sharp and aniseed.

Pharaoh looks down for something to wipe her feet on. Stops short as she reads the names on the gravestones beneath her feet.

'Don't let them put you off,' says Delphine cheerfully as she fills the kettle and puts it on the old-fashioned stove. She takes a box of matches from her dressing-gown pocket and lights the burner.

The smell of smoke briefly eclipses the combined scents of the herbs.

'Unusual,' says Pharaoh, stepping lightly across the headstones and leaning against the table.

'It's a better way to recycle than washing out Marmite jars,' says Delphine, scooping coffee into a striped mug. 'They'd all fallen down and we needed a new floor. Dad and me did it together. Aramis was very good at offering words of encouragement.'

Pharaoh hears the note of sadness in the girl's voice. Were she feeling more like herself she would already be giving her a hug. She's a tactile person, able to motivate her officers with nothing more than a squeeze on the arm or a pat on the arm. Right now, she feels as though she would turn to stone if she touched anybody.

'You must miss him,' says Pharaoh. 'I'm sorry; that sounds silly. I just mean I'm sorry you had to go through that.'

Delphine gives a nod of thanks. Scoops sugar into Pharaoh's mug without asking.

'I miss him, of course I do. I miss Mum too. I've still got Dad though and it pays to be grateful, don't you think?'

'He's got you too,' says Pharaoh. 'Seems like you're a good team.'

Delphine beams, delighted at the compliment. 'It was horrible when I was here all by myself.'

Pharaoh looks away. Reads the inscription on the flags beneath her feet. Alice Mainprize. Died in 1873, aged just twenty-six.

'I wasn't having a go,' says Delphine, suddenly realising how her words could have been construed. She pulls a face of self-reproach. 'He's back now, isn't he? You had to investigate. People can't just drop down dead without some kind of authority getting involved. That's the way of the world.'

'You've got a good head on your shoulders for somebody so young,' says Pharaoh, taking the coffee from her outstretched hand. 'I guess you had to grow up quickly.'

'I don't feel like a grown-up,' Delphine tells her, leaning back against the work surface. Her dressing gown falls open, revealing pale, freckled skin.

'You're planning on going to university, aren't you?'

'Dad's planning on me going. I'm not so sure I want to.'

'No? You're clever enough. He told me about your grades when we chatted the first time. He's very proud of you.'

'I don't think I'd like being around all those people. I didn't like school much. I always just wanted to get back home. I like the woods. I like helping Dad. I don't know why I have to go to university when I could just read the textbooks at home.'

Pharaoh breathes in the scent of the coffee.

'You sound like you've had this argument before.'

'We don't argue. We just have different opinions.'

'And he thinks you should go to university.'

'He wants what's best for me. We just disagree on what that is.'

'You don't want to stay here forever, though, do you? What if you meet a boy? You're pretty and clever and good company. You'd do brilliantly at university.'

Delphine looks bashful. She jumps up onto the work surface and bumps the heels of her welly boots together, face in her hands, elbows on her knees.

'What is it you're after Dad for?' she asks. 'I mean, with these murders, I'd have thought you'd be here, there and everywhere. There's no problem, is there? With Dad, I mean?'

Pharaoh chews her lip. Tries to find the right words and fails.

'There are still some loose ends,' she says at last. 'You probably know how seriously Humberside Police is taking what happened. There are people who think he's going to sue us. I couldn't blame him if he did, though for his sake I hope he doesn't. It would be best if it all blew over. The papers are going to make him some sort of superhero otherwise, and then when they get bored of that they'll turn on him.'

Delphine's smile fades a little. She wrinkles her nose. 'Is this you warning him to keep his mouth shut? Because that wouldn't go down well with his solicitor.'

Pharaoh can't help but give a little laugh. She likes this girl. Admires her devotion and loyalty. Wonders, briefly, how her own girls feel about her. Knows already how they feel about their dad.

'I wouldn't dream of threatening you or your father,' she says, finishing the coffee. 'I've explained it to him and I'll say the same to you – the prosecution could have gone either way. There was no malice. He was found guilty, and freed on appeal. We didn't know about the conflict of interest. Under different circumstances, it could have all come to nothing. Under others, he could still be inside. We just have to deal with the political fall-out from it all.'

'I don't know how much he's enjoying the attention,' muses Delphine, mollified. 'The phone doesn't stop ringing. He's got another two chat shows booked in for Sunday morning. He can't say no, that's his trouble. Can't say no to women, anyway.'

Pharaoh's expression flickers for a moment.

'He told me in interview that he was raised to admire women. His mother died when he was a teenager, yes?'

'Younger than I am now.'

'Does he have brothers or sisters? I can't recall.'

'No, he was an only child. Just him and his dad, and he's dead now too. A lot of people around him have passed away over the years. He doesn't let it get to him too badly. We help each other.'

'He grew up in a place like this, didn't he?'

'In the countryside, you mean? Yes, sort of. It was a modern house but in an old-fashioned town, surrounded by mountains. It was lovely. He took me and Aramis there once. I don't know why. Just wanted to share it with us, I think.'

'It can't have been easy for your mum – his inability to say no to the ladies.'

Delphine shakes her head, a swift, angry gesture. 'I didn't mean it like that. He makes women feel good and likes them liking him but he's never had a girlfriend since Mum. I don't think he wants one.'

Pharaoh says nothing. Feels the colour rising in her cheeks. She swallows down the burning sensation in her chest as she remembers the way Reuben turned his mouth from hers as she tried to kiss him.

'It must be nice, knowing that there's somebody there to swoop in and save the day when you're in trouble. I suppose I've got a friend like that. He'd hold a building up with his bare hands if he thought I was trapped underneath.'

'Sounds a good person to know. Is he a policeman too?'

'Yes. A good one, though he doesn't realise it. We've kind of swapped jobs since we became friends. He used to be the sparrow with a broken wing. Now he's a great bloody eagle and I feel like the vulnerable little chick waiting for him. It's pitiful. Don't get old, Delphine. Trust me.'

Delphine smiles. 'You're not old. You look great. Dad thinks so, anyway. And yeah, you're right – it is nice knowing he'll be there. I've always known that.'

'I've seen the video footage of that day,' says Pharaoh gently. 'I saw how scared and upset you were. I've read your statement. That must have been horrible.'

Delphine taps her welly boots together again. Fiddles with the bracelets on her wrist.

'They used to be horrible to Aramis, too. They're village kids. Inbred morons, Dad calls them. We're the weird family that lives in the woods. They were one of the reasons Aramis did what he did.'

'One of the boys said that on the day in question, you were the aggressor.'

Delphine barks a laugh. 'Me? Oh yeah, I'm forever picking fights with three big lads. Honest, I was just walking back from a friend's and they started having a go. Started talking about my brother. Then they got really nasty. Talking about Mum. Dad. Me. Saying stuff about us. Sick stuff. I told them to shut up and they started throwing stones. The next thing I was on the ground and bleeding and getting kicked in the stomach. My top got ripped. I didn't know what to do.'

'But you made it back to your dad.'

'He saw me. Saw what had happened. He did what everybody would want their dad to do.'

Pharaoh nods. Absorbs it all. Wonders, for a moment, what McAvoy would have done. He has probably asked himself that same question more than once.

'If it were me, I'd have killed the lot of them,' says Pharaoh. 'He did the right thing by his family and by his conscience, even if the courts would disagree.'

'He did the same thing later when that bastard turned up and tried to go for him. I swear to God, Dad just pushed him and he fell and hit his head. It was nothing. He shouldn't have gone to prison for that, and you know it, no matter what you have to say to the papers.'

Pharaoh realises she has been feeling a little better. Her head has cleared. She's thinking in straight lines. Might be ready to face Hollow. Might be ready to go to work and pick up the reins of the murder inquiry. Might be able to look at McAvoy without seeing her own shame reflected in his big brown eyes.

She takes her phone from her top. Wipes the moisture off the screen. The signal is terrible here but she can see she has had several missed calls. The last, from Helen Tremberg, was just moments ago.

'I may have to catch up with your father another time,' says Pharaoh, sighing. She rolls her eyes. Enjoys the little smile she gets from Delphine in return. She wonders for a moment whether she and Sophia would be friends. Whether Delphine is the sort to go to a party at a big house and not tell her mum there would be boys there. Wonders what Hollow would do to anybody who put their hands on her.

There is a sudden knock at the door that makes them both jump. Delphine pulls her robe around herself. Crosses over the headstones, skipping over memorials and dates, prayers and psalms, long since chiselled from smooth, unfeeling rock.

She pulls open the wooden door and begins to ask her father if he forgot his key.

Then she opens the door wider and Pharaoh looks past her at the two familiar figures in the doorway; their tired faces.

McAvoy and Tremberg: two giant paper cut-outs, blocking the light.

21

A small, heart-shaped clearing amid a blanket of trees.

Three figures, half lost in fog, standing in a loose triangle among the graves and the wildflowers in the shadow of a small, red-roofed cottage; light flickering across their faces as a watery sun plays with the shadows of the looming evergreens.

'We tried to ring. We've been trying all night and all morning. We didn't know what to do when we saw your car.'

Helen stops talking as Pharaoh turns cold eyes upon her.

'Boss, we couldn't wait any longer. I didn't know what else to do. Sophia said you left early and I literally had no clue where to find you.'

Pharaoh looks into McAvoy's earnest face. She can see him fighting with his emotions. He wants to ask her what she's doing here. Wants to know where the hell she's been. The last time they spoke he was telling her not to come to the murder scene for fear of her bumping into Mallett. Why hasn't she replied to his messages?

'I do seem to recall that I'm the senior officer,' snaps Pharaoh. 'I can follow up lines of inquiry without checking with my sergeant or somebody else's detective constable, can't I?'

McAvoy looks down at the grass. Runs his tongue around the inside of his mouth.

'There have been developments,' he says finally. 'There's lots to tell, Guv.'

Pharaoh scowls at him. Sucks half an inch off her cigarette. He holds her gaze. There's temper in his eyes. She rather likes it.

'Maybe we should go somewhere else and talk,' says Helen, flicking her gaze between the two. She has never seen them argue. It's like watching her parents fight.

'No, no, if it was important enough to track me down for then there's no time to waste,' says Pharaoh, pushing her hair behind her ear. McAvoy looks away and she enjoys a moment of victory. Then, just as quickly, she feels remorse. Feels as though she has just given a rabbit a Chinese burn. 'Are you okay, anyway?' she asks, softening her tone a fraction. 'Hannah. It must have been horrible.'

McAvoy stares into the trees. Focuses his attention on the back wheel of the gypsy wagon, peeking out from between the trees.

'Is Roisin okay? What did the kids actually see, Hector? You know I would have been there. It was you that bloody insisted . . .'

McAvoy manages a little smile.

'It was hard,' he says. 'That was supposed to be our home forever. It's already experienced too much bloodshed. All I want is for the kids to have nice memories.' He waves a hand, indicating that there is too much to say. 'I just wish she wasn't dead. I knew she was but I wish there was still hope.'

'Somebody knows how personally you took her disappearance,' says Pharaoh. 'They left her there for you.'

'ACC Mallett asked me for a list of enemies. Where do I start?'

Pharaoh gives a dutiful laugh. Some of the tension leaves her shoulders. She looks as though she'd like to reach out and give him a squeeze on his forearm.

'I bet he and Roisin got on like a house on fire,' says Pharaoh, winking. 'Uncomfortable?'

McAvoy blinks, long and slow.. 'She told him a few things he won't forget.'

Pharaoh pulls a face. 'Bet he loved that. I hope to Christ you didn't apologise for her.'

'I wouldn't dare.'

'Did you manage any sleep?'

'I'm fine, Guv. What about you? You must have been up and out early.'

Pharaoh kicks distractedly at a dandelion clock, her boots sending tiny ghosts spinning into the grey air. 'I got a couple of hours. The girls made me a nest.'

'And Sophia? Any better?'

Pharaoh shrugs. 'We'll talk. Somehow, we'll talk.'

Helen stands between them, turning her head from side to side like a tennis umpire. She wishes they'd either hug or have a fist fight.

'Have you read your emails yet, boss?' she asks diplomatically. 'There's a lot to take in.'

'Crap signal here. Are you going to tell me what's so important that you had to turn bloodhound?'

'We came to talk to Mr Hollow,' McAvoy says. 'I should have said. My head's a muddle, sorry. We didn't know you'd be here.'

'Reuben?' The word comes out sharp and shrill and she curses herself for using his first name. 'Hollow, I mean. Why? You're not running errands for ACC Mallett, are you? Are you doing some goodwill shit, mending bridges and making Hollow feel less inclined to sue? Because if you're doing that during a murder investigation I'm going to poke your eyes out with your own thumbs.'

McAvoy shakes his head. His lips become a thin line.

'Hollow's DNA has been found on one of Ava Delaney's possessions. More than that, Helen has established a connection between a possible vigilante and several suspicious deaths. And that vigilante is starting to sound more and more like your friend.'

Pharaoh stares at her sergeant. She looks more like a wife being told her husband is being arrested than a senior police officer following up a lead. She gives a shake of the head. Tries to become herself again. There is a redness to her cheeks; a flame in her eyes.

'He met Ava Delaney at Hull Royal Infirmary. I'm aware of that.'

McAvoy looks confused. 'That information hasn't been distributed . . .'

'I'm a fucking superintendent, Hector. Me knowing something is often enough.'

McAvoy looks up, past the trees. Snaps his head to the left as a bird begins its two-note call.

Pharaoh forces herself to hold his gaze when he finally turns to look at her.

'Well I don't know how well he got to know her at Hull Royal but we found traces of his saliva on a handkerchief in her pocket.'

Helen looks away as Pharaoh starts forward. For a moment, she seems about to slap him.

'What?' asks Pharaoh, so softly that it comes out as little more than a growl.

'A handkerchief,' he repeats. 'Trace DNA evidence.'

'He probably wiped her eyes! That's the sort of bloke he is. And this is from Jackson-Savannah, yes? Probably bullshit. What else is there in her house? What connection have you found between them?'

'Between Hollow and Ava Delaney? Nothing. But Helen has been investigating several suspicious deaths. Men who appeared in the newspapers having got away with something. Whenever there's a vulnerable woman seeking justice he seems to swan in like a superhero and the next moment somebody is dead. We've got a growing number of cases in which men who have escaped justice have been killed not long after, and always when there's a vulnerable woman to impress along the way. Ava's boyfriend was a bully. He ended up dead in a ditch. Hannah Kelly received a video message from David Hogg's mobile not long after he killed a horse she used to own and love. Yvonne Turpin's sister, Toni, was killed in a hit and run and he all but got away scot-free. Next thing he's dead too. And the whiff of Reuben Hollow is all over at least one of the cases. Raymond O'Neill had a connection to him. And Ben is pulling Jez Gavan's prison records right now and I already have a pretty damn good idea what he'll find . . .'

Pharaoh rubs a hand across her nose. Makes fists. She shakes her head. Fumbles in her bag for her cigarettes and tries to light another. She can't turn the wheel on the lighter. She curses, shaking like a drunk going through withdrawal. McAvoy takes the lighter from her and lights the cigarette. She gives a small nod of thanks and breathes deep. Regains some composure as she smokes.

'Whatever you think you've got, you don't have enough to talk to him,' she says, in a voice more like her own. 'Not now. He's right in the eye of the storm, Hector. Humberside Police is being called every name under the sun and I'm having my name dragged through the mud because he got sent down for a murder when the press think he's a hero. Now is not the time to start questioning him over the murder of a young girl or a bunch of random bastards from all over the place. Trust me.'

McAvoy opens his mouth to speak but clams up when Pharaoh shakes her head.

'People know how loyal you are,' she says, some warmth creeping into her voice. 'If word gets around that you've come and hauled Hollow off for questioning on some other charge it will seem like a vendetta. Like we're closing ranks. You know I trust you and your judgement but have you considered the fact that maybe you're looking for stuff against Hollow because you don't like him?'

'I don't know him!' splutters McAvoy, reddening. 'I just know what's he costing you.'

'I'm a big girl,' says Pharaoh, smiling. 'Maybe, just maybe, there's more going on than you know. I'm not saying we won't ask him some questions. I'm just suggesting that softly-softly might be better. Mallett would go spare if he knew you were here.'

'And what about you being here?' asks McAvoy, his nostrils flaring. 'Where is he, anyway? Off carving you a bunch of white roses in his fucking caravan?'

Pharaoh's face tightens. Helen gives a little hiss of surprise. Neither woman has heard him speak this way before. Neither has ever seen him look so much like he wants to hurt somebody.

Pharaoh grinds out her cigarette. Straightens her back and looks at the side of McAvoy's face until he looks at her.

'Tell me about Hannah, Detective Sergeant. The injuries.'

'It's the post-mortem this morning,' says Helen, when McAvoy does not reply. 'But her armpits were scalped.'

199

Pharaoh does not turn her head. 'You can't scalp an armpit. Scalping involves the removal of the scalp.'

'Okay then, the armpit was removed with a knife.'

'A sculptor's knife,' says McAvoy, under his breath.

Pharaoh gives a laugh that contains no mirth.

'I'm going to go and get in my car and have a little think,' she says, after a moment's silence. 'Then I'm going to go and do my job. I suggest you two follow up some of these leads and concentrate on finding a link between Hannah Kelly and Ava Delaney. I suggest you do your jobs like professionals. I will have my phone with me for the rest of the day and I will be putting out some fires at HQ. If you need me, ring me, but make damn sure that it's worth my time. And Hector, if you knock on Hollow's door when I'm gone, I will suspend you. Are we clear?'

McAvoy breathes deeply. His face has gone white.

'Where was he last night?' he asks quietly. 'Seriously, Guv. Where?'

Pharaoh gives a shake of her head. 'We'll talk later. I know what you went through last night. I know you're hurting. Don't let your emotions get on top of you.'

McAvoy watches as she turns away, her shoulders a little stooped and dandelion spinners in her hair.

'Jesus, Sarge,' says Tremberg, under her breath. 'I thought she was going to hit you.'

McAvoy turns and looks at the red-roofed cottage. Takes in the ivy and the wildflowers, the gravestones and buckled railings. Imagines, for a moment, how it would feel to wake in this place. How it would feel to see Roisin sitting on the steps of the old bow-top gypsy wagon, hoops in her ears and dirt on the soles of her dainty feet. Wonders how Pharaoh looked, last night, moving on top of Hollow as McAvoy and his family coughed on the stench of Hannah Kelly's body outside their home.

'You don't think there's anything going on between them, do you?' asks Helen, pulling a face. 'I mean, she wouldn't. She's Pharaoh.'

McAvoy shakes his head. Remembers all the nights he has held her hair back while she has thrown up red wine and vodka. Remembers the slurred conversations at 2 a.m. and the miles he has put in to ensure she never drives the children to school when she's too drunk to see.

'No, she's not,' he says, shaking his head. 'Not any more.'

22

Roisin doesn't understand the motivation of the teenagers who lounge on the damp grass outside Grimsby Minster. It's a ghastly day. Although the fog has not taken this part of the east coast in its fist, the sky is an endless smear of grey and the air is speckled with a misty rain, a billion tiny raindrops hovering like flies.

'This is Webbo,' says Sophia, indicating a tall, jointy specimen in a black hooded top, heavy white foundation and eyeliner. 'He's studying drama at Franklin.'

Roisin gives Webbo a parental once-over. Underneath the Goth make-up he seems to be quite freckly and she spots red roots peeking out through the black hair around his temples. He flicks his hair out of his eyes and nods a hello. Roisin smiles politely.

'Nice to meet you, Webbo. Eyeliner, eh? What's the word for that look? Emu, isn't it?'

Webbo sneers, flaring his nostrils contemptuously. 'I don't do labels,' he says. 'I'm just me, man. I'm no emo.'

'Emo, that's it,' says Roisin conversationally. 'I heard you're into slicing your arms with paper clips and razor blades and stuff. What's that all about, then?'

Webbo looks to Sophia for support. Turns back to Roisin.

'When the blood flows, your pain leaves with it, yeah? When I'm in pain inside, I just take a razor to my arm and let it out.'

Roisin considers this, nodding and sucking her cheek.

'It's not for me,' she says at last. 'If I'm feeling sad I have a good cry or cuddle somebody I love or have a bit of a shout and a bar of chocolate. But if you like slicing yourself to bits, that's up to you.' She turns to Sophia and gives her a hard look. 'You're not into that shit, are you? Because if you're cutting yourself, I swear, I'll save you the bother. You won't need to self-harm – you'll be in enough pain from the slapping I'll give you.'

Sophia shakes her head, colour rising in her cheeks. Webbo looks between the two women and makes a poor decision.

'It's her body,' he says, indicating Sophia. 'She's her own person. She wants to deal with her pain, that's up to her, nobody else.'

Roisin ignores him for a moment, continuing to stare at Sophia. Slowly, she bends down and attends to Lilah in her pushchair. Her voice takes on a sing-song quality as she addresses her child.

'This is Webbo, Lilah. He's an emo. Can you say, "Emo"? He dyes his hair and puts on make-up and likes to cut his arms. What a silly man. Is he a big silly? Yes, he is. Do you know what would happen to Webbo if you brought him home to our house and said he was your boyfriend, Lilah? You do, don't you. Your mammy would cut his legs off and bury him in the back garden, that's what she'd do. And Daddy would probably be cross and give Mammy a bit of a telling-off, but deep down, he'd know that it was for the best, because Webbo is a total knob and should probably feck off while I'm distracted. Do you want to sing "Old Macdonald Had a Farm"? You do? Good girl!'

Sophia finds herself torn between a desire to turn crimson, and to throw back her head and laugh. She likes hanging out with the older lads but thinks of Roisin as the coolest adult she has ever met. Loyalty to Roisin wins out, and she turns her back on Webbo. She crouches down next to Roisin and together they sing a verse or two of Lilah's favourite nursery rhyme. The child grins, gummy and delightful, and by the time Roisin and Sophia stand up again, Webbo has slouched off to join the throng of black-clad, disaffected teens.

'Is he the one from the party?' asks Roisin.

'He's okay,' says Sophia. 'He's a friend. Sort of.'

'Have you done it with him?' Roisin asks her.

Sophia shakes her head. 'I told you, I'm not ready for that. The lad who wanted to at the party isn't even from around here. It all got blown out of proportion anyway. And I shouldn't have led him on.'

Roisin looks at her teenage friend. She feels like lighting a cigarette but is making an effort not to smoke around the children. Instead she reaches into the pocket of her leather jacket for her lip-gloss. Applies a liberal coat and smacks her lips together. She's fond of Sophia but doesn't really know how far her duties and responsibilities should go. Although she wishes that Trish Pharaoh spent less time with Aector, she respects her. She doesn't want to piss her off and make things awkward for Aector by overstepping the mark with her eldest daughter. But she has been stewing these past couple of days. She should have told Trish what happened, about the two men who turned up at her house with a taser and threatened bloody violence. Sophia had been so insistent. *Please don't tell.* And in the moments after it happened, Roisin reacted instinctively. She may be married to a copper but she was brought up thinking of the police as a threat. She was brought up to handle things herself and never to tell anything to people in uniform. Instinctively, she had downplayed the incident and her part in it, and Sophia followed her lead.

In the days since, she has grown increasingly worried that she has put Trish and her children in danger. The two men didn't seem like local thugs. They had a look in their eyes that she has witnessed too many times before. The horrors of last night have shaken Roisin. The body of Aector's missing girl was left virtually on her own front lawn. Danger is encroaching on the safe little island of happiness where she and Aector and the children try to live. Aector's work has cost them dear in the past. They both bear the scars of his need to secure justice for both the living and the dead. She accepts this. She would never ask him to be anything but the man she fell in love with. But she fears what could happen to those close by. Her friend, Mel, lost her life a couple of years ago because of her relationship with Roisin. Pharaoh's old boss, Tom Spink, has to walk with two sticks after being caught up in an investigation. Now it is Sophia whom Roisin fears for. She has come here to check that she is okay, and to warn her that they must now tell the truth. She has come to tell her that the other night, they got it wrong.

'Did you say you think you led him on?' asks Roisin, fixing Sophia with a hard glare. 'Christ, girl, don't you ever bloody think like that. You can be naked and underneath a fella and still say no. Don't you understand that? Your body's your own. Not everybody gets the chance to choose who they share it with, but you're a strong, intelligent girl from a good family. You don't have to give yourself away and you don't have to feel bad if you decide not to sleep with a bloke just because he's got himself worked up. What was it he called you on Facebook?'

Sophia looks at the floor. 'A prick-tease,' she mumbles.

'A prick-tease? Christ. Sounds like he teases his prick all day and all night. Don't you realise, that's not an insult. You're a pretty girl. You're sweet and charming and likeable. He wanted to do it with you and you said no. That's all there is to it. He can go on Facebook and say shit about you if he wants – you're still the winner here. You stood your ground. Now, tell me once more, just so I'm doubly sure, he did accept it, didn't he? There's nothing else you need to tell me? Because there are ways and means of making sure he never does it again.'

Sophia shakes her head and Roisin looks her full in the face. Sees the truth in her eyes. Nods, satisfied.

'Right, so, that's one problem solved. Now, about those dickheads who came to the house the other night. What have you told your mammy?'

Sophia seems relieved to change the subject. She gives a half-smile and starts digging at a piece of stuck-down chewing gum on the pavement outside the church.

'I haven't seen much of her,' says Sophia. 'But when she asked, I said the same as you did. Couple of idiots who wandered into the wrong house. That man told them to get out. That was the end of it.'

Roisin starts wheeling the pushchair away from the church, past the Fishermen's Memorial with its polythene-wrapped tributes placed reverentially on the black steel. Roisin looks at the face

205

of the bearded trawlerman as she passes. It is hard and weather-beaten, his expression one of grim determination. Fleetingly, she wonders if the figure ever truly lived; whether he was sculpted from life or from photographs, or is just a work of the sculptor's imagination. She wonders if other people ask such things. Knows one who certainly would.

'You know those men were more than local idiots,' says Roisin, as they pass the window of the run-down boozer beneath St James' Hotel and into the main square. A tramp is asleep on one of the stone benches, steadfastly refusing to open his eyes despite the attentions of two police community support officers, several pigeons and a seagull. An old woman shelters in the doorway of the hardware shop, smoking a cigarette and eating a sausage roll. Food containers and betting slips chase each other on the breeze, tangling around the legs of the half-dozen office workers and listless shoppers who cross the drab grey forecourt.

'Why do you say that?' asks Sophia, cautiously. 'I've been telling myself it was my fault. What do you think?'

'It's just the things they said. The way they were. I don't want to know about your money worries or your mam's past or anything like that but they seemed like they wanted more than a bit of trouble. I was wrong to try and keep it from your mam. We need to tell her. I've told Aector. We don't have secrets.'

Sophia says nothing, just trudges alongside as they leave the square and start to pass the nicer shops. There's a sale on in House of Fraser. A two-for-one offer in Specsavers. Five sausage rolls for a pound in Greggs.

'Tell her, Sophia,' says Roisin. 'I'd just mention it, in passing, like. Say I've been thinking about it and that maybe there was more to it. I won't say anything about them roughing you up or what they threatened to do. But she's a good copper and a good mammy and she's better placed to sort it out than me. Is that okay?'

Sophia stares at the ground as they mooch down a side street, past a charity shop where a woman in her eighties is standing in the window trying to put a leather jacket on a mannequin. The windows are steamy with condensation and through the smeary, damp glass, it looks to Sophia as if two corpses are preparing one another for a night out.

'It could have been nothing,' says Sophia in a low voice. 'We don't know.'

'No, we don't,' says Roisin. 'But if anything happened to you I'd fill a bucket with tears.'

Sophia gives a genuine smile. Walks a little closer to Roisin. Considers her for a moment. She's extraordinarily attractive; her eyes the blue of the water in a well-kept tropical fish tank. There are holes for several earrings in her dainty ears and a tangle of inked stars and flowers disappears down the tanned skin of her neck and shoulders beneath the collar of her leather jacket. She exudes something – a strength and confidence; a self-belief. Sophia has so many questions for her. Wants to sit her down and demand to know what it feels like to be her.

'She'll kill me for not saying anything,' says Sophia flatly. 'It will be my fault. You should have heard what she said to me after the party. She hates me sometimes.'

'Not true,' replies Roisin lightly. 'She worries. She's bound to worry. She had good reason to worry.'

'I called her a fat bitch,' says Sophia, and there is guilt in her voice.

Roisin pulls a face. 'If I said that to my mam I'd have been in hospital for a month, and I'd have deserved it, too. Don't say that to her again.'

'She makes me so bloody angry,' says Sophia.

'She's your mammy. She's meant to. Here, do you want a lift back to school or are you done for the day?'

They have reached the ugly grey car park on the outskirts of the town centre. It's a four-storey construction and looks as if it was built purely to get rid of a job lot of leftover breeze blocks. Few people park here. Roisin parked her vehicle on the top floor because she wanted to hear the end of the song that was playing on the radio and it made Lilah giggle to hear the wheels squeal as

Mammy wound the car around the tight turns, up through the darkness and into the grey light of the open top floor.

Sophia checks her watch. Roisin thinks school must have started by now, but the girl seems in no hurry to head to class.

Together they manoeuvre the pushchair up the stairs to the top floor. They swing open the yellow doors and are halfway across the grey tarmac towards Roisin's car when they hear the voice, cheerful and playful, like a game show host welcoming viewers to another fabulous edition.

'Well, hello there, ladies. Mighty fine day for it, eh – whatever "it" might be. You've no idea how pleased we are to see you. We were despairing.'

Roisin and Sophia turn back towards the doors. Teddy and Foley are standing there like sentries. Teddy is panting a little, having taken the stairs two at a time. Foley is grinning, his gold necklace pulled up and wedged in his smile, carving shiny jewels into his cheeks.

'That's what I love about small towns,' says Foley, pushing the chain out of his mouth with his tongue. 'Everybody knows everybody. People bump into each other. Not like this where we're from. You can go your whole life and never so much as run into your next-door neighbour in the local shop. But the north? I think there's only a dozen people live here. I'm getting an authentic experience, that's for sure. I've only been an adopted northerner for a few days and already I'm running into a couple of old friends.'

Without thinking about it, Roisin stands in front of Lilah's pushchair. She puts one hand across Sophia and gently moves her backwards.

'We were just talking about you,' says Roisin conversationally. 'Honestly, right at this second. Funny old world.'

'I bet you were,' says Foley, moving forward. 'I fucking bet you were talking about me. I bet you've been dreaming about me, you pikey bitch.'

Roisin gives Foley a withering look and then turns to Sophia. 'People always go for the low-blow, don't you find? It's just rude. I mean, there are all sorts of things he could call me but he has to

208

go straight in there with the "traveller" thing. As if I think it's an insult! I mean, if I was going to insult him, I'd mention the spots and the piggy eyes and the appalling clothes but I'd never have a pop at his heritage. That's just uncalled for.'

Teddy takes a deep breath. Reaches out and puts a hand on the younger man's shoulder. Whispers something in his ear and then steps forward, taking the lead.

'We got off on the wrong foot the other day,' says Teddy, addressing his words to Sophia. 'We were rude. Truth be told, we came up here to do a job. That job involves recovering a debt of your poor crippled father's. A very important man wants that debt paying and given that your father's too busy shitting in a bag and withering away to dust, it means your mum's liable. Now, we understand she's a copper but that isn't a get-out-of-jail-free card, if you'll pardon the pun. So she needs to pay up. And I can't think of a better way of getting her attention than letting my friend here bend one of you over the bonnet of that car. Can you?'

Sophia turns teary eyes on Roisin, who is fiddling with her tobacco tin and making a roll-up on the handle of Lilah's push-chair. She takes her time. Fixes her eyes on Teddy's as she licks the cigarette paper closed. Picks a piece of tobacco from the shiny gloss on her lips and lights her fag with a cheap lighter. She blows out a cloud of smoke and appears to be thinking.

'A lot of money, is it?' she asks Teddy, at length.

'Not an unmanageable sum,' he says, still looking at Sophia. 'Not for somebody with a good job and a sports car. She doesn't have to write us a cheque straight away. We'd just like a gesture.'

Roisin considers this, then gives a rueful smile.

'You had the money in your hands, lads. You don't even know what you let go.'

Teddy drags his gaze away from Sophia. Considers Roisin. She's a tiny little thing but nothing about her suggests she is afraid. He's dealt with pikeys before. Wonders whether she's connected to anybody important. Whether there would be hell to pay if he threw her off the roof.

'In our hands?' asks Foley. 'What d'you mean?'

'Her fella,' says Roisin, taking another drag. 'Bloke who saw you off the other night.'

Foley scrunches his face, as if struggling with algebra.

'Her fella? Her fella's the cripple.'

'Don't ask me to explain the politics of it all,' says Roisin, waving a hand. 'She's more of a carer for her husband. She leads her own life. She's been seeing Reuben for as long as I've known her. He's an okay bloke. You wouldn't know it to look at him but he's worth a bloody fortune. He's an artist. Made the statue in the square that you passed. I think Victoria Beckham owns one of his pieces. He could pay any debt with the fluff from his bloody pockets and you let him slip through your fingers. If I was your boss and I heard that, I'd be bloody livid.'

Foley and Teddy exchange a glance. Slowly, Teddy whispers in the ear of the younger man, who flashes a look of defiance.

'You know him well, do you?' asks Teddy, slyly.

Roisin shrugs. 'Well enough. Like I say, he's okay. My husband knows him better than me. I'm not sure you saw my husband, did you? He's a detective sergeant, though that's not really the point. He's what you might call *massive*. Pussycat to me and the kids, of course. Loveliest man you could wish to meet. But very protective. Fierce, you might say.'

'Am I supposed to be scared?' asks Foley, taking a step forward.

'No, you're supposed to be sensible. Reuben Hollow. That's the name. Lives east of Hull. Little place in the middle of nowhere.'

Teddy has his phone out, swiping his fingers over the surface.

'Hollow,' he says, half to himself. His lips move as he reads. 'Says here he's been inside. Just got out. Manslaughter. Says your mam's the one who put him away.'

Roisin gives an indulgent smile. 'I'd have thought a clever man like you could read between the lines. How do you think they met? How do you think he got out? Do the sums, mate. How much money do you think he got for being falsely imprisoned? He got a settlement from Humberside Police that would make your eyes water.'

Foley flicks a glance at his colleague. They are both thinking the same thing. Thinking about how much traction a decent score would buy them with their potential new employers. They could make some serious waves. They could catch the eye. hey could be Headhunted by morning.

'We've found you once, we could find you again,' says Foley, spitting on the ground in front of Roisin. 'You say a word and I'll cut that baby's fucking throat.'

For the first time, Roisin's façade falters. Her lower lip trembles and she has to make fists to stop her hands from shaking. With an effort she forces a smile.

'You want money, I want an easy life. Seems simple to me. If I were you I'd have fucked off already.'

Teddy has the good grace to smile. Foley blows her a kiss. A moment later, the double doors are banging and the two men have disappeared down the stairs.

For a full minute, Roisin stares at the doors. Then she turns away and crouches down in front of Lilah, stroking her soft, pink face. When she stands up, there is a tiny tear running down the side of her nose and onto her lip. She pays it no heed. Just looks up at Sophia and stares, hard, into her eyes.

'I'll tell your mum,' says Roisin. 'She can tell Hollow. This is what she does. It will be okay.'

'You were making it all up as you went along,' says Sophia, her voice cracking. 'I thought they were going to . . .'

'I was thinking on my feet,' says Roisin, and is surprised to hear her own voice so steady. 'Look, I'll take you home. Phone in sick this afternoon, yeah? I'll call your mum now.'

Sophia says nothing as she lets herself be put in the passenger seat of the little car. She's white-faced. Paler than an emo, drained of blood.

Outside the vehicle, Roisin talks quietly into her phone. Trish isn't picking up. Neither is Aector. She tries them both again and again. Eventually, she decides to leave the briefest of messages. Leaves Pharaoh a voicemail, asking her to call her; telling her it's important. Some bad men threatened her and Sophia. She might have let them think Reuben Hollow had money. She might have put him in a spot of bother.

Roisin ends the call. Starts to count to ten but is calm before three. She climbs into the driver's seat and places her phone on the dashboard, hoping it will ring. Hoping that she can unburden herself. Hoping that she has not just placed a man she barely knows directly in the firing line.

As she drives out of the car park, the phone seems to mock her.

Dark.

Black.

Silent.

23

It's quiet in the main reception of Hull Royal Infirmary. The fog is keeping visitors away. The handful of people who do linger in the Chez HEY café are staff and patients. McAvoy sits at a round table, sipping hot chocolate from a cardboard cup. Two porters in blue T-shirts are waiting in line for bacon sandwiches, chatting with the short, wire-haired woman who operates the till, and who gave McAvoy his drink at staff discount prices because she liked the look of him. An old woman in a floral dressing gown is reading a novel at another table, pulling faces when she gets to the juicy parts. She has a healthy colour in her cheeks and seems sprightly enough. McAvoy wonders what's wrong with her. Can't help wondering if she's faked some mystery illness so she can have a few days looking at a different set of walls to the ones she's grown tired of at home.

McAvoy wipes the chocolate from his moustache. Has to make an effort of will not to recoil at the chemical smell on his hands. His mind becomes a mouth, biting down hard on the memory that floods his vision. He checks his phone. Stares at the picture of Roisin, Fin and Lilah, smiling at him from behind the date, time and the jolly little icons that tell him just how many messages are awaiting his attention. He opens the file of pictures. Scrolls through until he finds Hannah Kelly. Stares into her eyes and smile and tries to use it to wipe out the scene playing in his imagination. Fails, utterly.

McAvoy managed to stay for the first ten minutes of the autopsy. Remained quiet, clad in his white coveralls, plastic shoe-covers and face-mask. Kept his own counsel as Dr Jackson-Savannah combed the dirt from Hannah's hair onto a long sheet of white paper. Kept his lips locked as the mortuary assistants took sample after sample and washed her down. Endured the sight of Jackson-Savannah massaging her joints so he could move her into a position that would allow him to begin cutting her up. He stood, back to the wall, the smell of meat and dirt and chemicals in his nostrils, telling himself that he could do this – that it was his duty. He left the moment that Jackson-Savannah took the circular saw to her head and began cutting the top off her skull. It had felt like watching the dismantling of one of his own children. The sight had grabbed his heart and lungs and squeezed something from him that he would never get back.

He takes another sip of his hot chocolate. Looks up at a commotion by the double doors. A family, rushing in. Trainers squeaking on linoleum. Hurrying to the front desk and relaying what little they know. A name. Vague details of a collapse. They'd been told to come. Feared they would crash in the fog. What's happening? Please, what's happening . . . ?

McAvoy isn't sure he can stand it. Doesn't know how the blonde, friendly lady on reception manages to spend her days shepherding people to the floors and wards where their loved ones wait, wrapped in green sheets and hooked up to drips and machines; clinging to life or preparing for death.

His phone beeps. A message from Roisin. He gives a tiny smile as he reads it. She loves him. Can't wait for him to come home. She has stuff to tell him when he has a moment. Would love to spend some time with him if he can slip away . . .

She's spelled penguins with a "w". Has put an entire screenful of kisses on the end.

The words give him a little strength. Galvanise him. Help him do what he must.

McAvoy reads his emails. Nods as he processes the information and rings a number he knows by heart.

'Sarge? You still at the mortuary? Don't know how you stand it.' Ben Neilsen's voice is reverential, as if he's talking in church.

'I didn't stay for all of it,' says McAvoy, using the voice of the confessional booth and barely moving his lips. 'I couldn't.'

'Who could?' asks Neilsen. 'Is it over, then? What have we got?'

'Professor Jackson-Savannah has sent a brief note of his findings. There will be a fuller one across in due course.'

'And?'

McAvoy takes a breath. Closes his eyes.

'Seventeen separate stab wounds,' he says, cupping his hand over the phone to cover his mouth. 'Mostly to the face and chest. The tip of the knife broke off in the bone beneath her left eye.'

'Jesus,' breathes Neilsen.

'Patches of skin removed from beneath both arms,' continues McAvoy, swallowing. He can't stop now. Needs to share some of this before the weight of it overwhelms him.

'She's been buried in manure. Horse dung. Has been for months.'

'Fucking hell.'

'Been dead as long as she's been missing. We were never going to find her.'

'Sexual assault?'

McAvoy drops his head to his hands. 'She was a virgin,' he says.

Neilsen says nothing for a while. Finally, he asks his boss if he's all right.

'He can't say whether she was still alive when the skin was removed,' says McAvoy, ignoring the enquiry. 'She may have still been breathing but would have been largely unaware. There are scratches on her back and legs consistent with a struggle taking place in woodland. The samples have been sent off for analysis, as has the tip of the blade.' He stops, composing himself before passing on the last line of the professor's brief email. 'There was a ladybird found in her throat.'

Neilsen pauses before speaking. 'He doesn't mean it was put there on purpose, does he?'

'No,' says McAvoy, his throat closing up. 'It probably crawled in as she lay on her back.'

There is silence on the line for a spell. Eventually Neilsen clears his throat.

'We're in to Ava Delaney's email account,' he says, when it

seems enough time has elapsed to move on to the next dead girl. 'Financial records, too.'

'Yes?'

'Messages to friends. Occasional line or two to family. Going back, she forwarded quite a few sexy pictures to her ex, David Belcher, when they were still starting out. She also sent a couple of messages to an Outlook email account. Deadpretty@outlook. com. I've Googled it. Got nothing. We requested the user details from the provider but it's all fake. Registered in the name of Brian Jacks. I've Googled that, too. He was a judo champion. Hero in the eighties, apparently – I've never heard of him. It's a fake address, anyway.'

McAvoy screws up his face. 'What do the messages say?'

'They're asking for money. I'll read you one. Hang on. "*I'm so grateful for all you've done for me but I can't have a happy ever after with nothing to my name. I would never threaten the person who has done so much for me but if you could consider the financial implications of being young and alone, you would see why I have no option but to request a little monetary assistance. I appreciate the difficulty, but a person of your abilities should be able to resolve such an issue without too much delay.*" She'd swallowed a dictionary, by the sound of things. That was the first one she sent. February of this year. Sent two more a week later, a little nastier. I've cross-referenced the dates with her bank records. Nine hundred and ninety pounds was deposited at the Whitefriargate branch of HSBC the day after the third message. Two ten p.m. I reckon she got a grand in cash, and kept a tenner for her tea.'

'Any more?' asks McAvoy.

'Last Monday. Same again. "*I'm thrilled things seem to be working out so well for you. I would hate for anything to spoil what must be a great time for you. Sadly, my own wellbeing remains stymied by financial troubles. I am behind on my rent and have several debts mounting up. If you could see your way to assisting, you would find me extraordinarily grateful and willing to show my appreciation however you so desired.*" Like I say, Sarge, she was wordy. Anyway, this email contained an attachment. Taken with her mobile in the bathroom of the flat. One hand behind her head. She's topless but her breasts aren't in shot. One armpit is, though, and she's not shaved for the photo shoot, I can tell you that.'

McAvoy controls his breathing. Wonders at the arrogance of youth.

'Whoever did this, they did it because she was a pain in their arse, Sarge,' says Neilsen, as tactfully as he can. 'And before you ask, I've rechecked all of Hannah's emails. She's got no connection to that email address, though the computer geeks are trying to find the ghosts of any she may have deleted. We'll do the same with Ava's.'

McAvoy looks around him. The old lady in the dressing gown has gone. The cashier is cleaning the complicated metal tubes of the coffee machine. The porters are sitting at a table, reading matching copies of the *Sun* as they finish their breakfasts.

'Sophie has spoken to Sabine Keane,' says Neilsen. 'She's the psychologist.'

McAvoy screws up his eyes. Has a memory of his mandated sessions with the unkempt, straggly therapist who tried to take him apart and put him back together a couple of years ago. Remembers how their sessions ended. He doesn't doubt her competence, though her integrity came with some grey areas.

'Some interesting insights,' says Neilsen. 'Like we thought, this could be about one-upmanship. Hannah's killer may have laid her out to get our attention in the wake of Ava's murder. And the way she was laid out suggests reverence. Tenderness. But the manner of her death and the taking of the armpits would seem to be a crime of anger. And if you're saying she was buried in horse shit for months, then he can't have been thinking about her particularly reverently. Dr Keane was interested in the flowers. Said it could be a symbolic act.' Neilsen lets a little eagerness bleed into his voice. 'Horse shit is used for roses, isn't it? You think there's something in that? He planted her. Was trying to see what grew?'

McAvoy shakes his head. Gives a small growl of dissent. 'What about Ava? There was no tenderness there.'

'That's what Sabine said. Have you heard from the boss? She's had no end of phone calls. A few from the National Crime Agency, though those buggers can keep on waiting, if you ask me. They're not taking this one off us, are they? A lot of people have invested a lot of themselves . . .'

McAvoy manages a smile. Reassures his constable. Ends the call without a goodbye.

The world seems a little unsteady. McAvoy cannot work out what he actually thinks. The team remain unaware of the cases that Helen has been digging into, unaware that on top of everything else, they may be hunting a vigilante. He kept the information from them at the briefing this morning. Knew what Pharaoh would say if he opened his mouth about his suspicions. He has never questioned Pharaoh's abilities before but cannot bring himself to let go of his concerns about her judgement. She seems to have a blind spot. Her head is full of Reuben Hollow. He knows the man is attractive and charming but Pharaoh has never allowed anybody to get the better of her. And yet she's behaving as if she's smitten. Won't listen to reason. Hollow's DNA was found at the Ava Delaney crime scene. That alone should be reason enough to bring him in.

McAvoy plays with his empty cup. Tries to order his thoughts about Hollow. The DNA is compelling but proof of nothing. Hollow had already told Pharaoh about his brief connection with Ava Delaney, so it would not be difficult for him to say that his DNA got onto her handkerchief at that brief meeting. If the investigation were being conducted without any media glare it would be enough to haul him in and ask him some searching questions. But Hollow has Humberside Police in the palm of his hand. McAvoy forces himself to think calmly. Does he truly believe Hollow capable of killing a string of bullies and bastards, and then killing two innocent young women as well? McAvoy studied some psychology at university before switching to computer sciences and eventually dropping out. He cannot imagine one person capable of such disparate crimes. He can just about believe Hollow capable of killing men who have abused women, but a whole different set of motivations would be involved for whoever killed Ava

Delaney and Hannah Kelly. Despite the brutality of its execution, Ava's killing was a crime of expedience. She was becoming a nuisance; asking for money. And Hollow was still in prison when she died, on the verge of his triumphant release at the Court of Appeal. Could he have received email messages inside? It's possible. It's not hard to get hold of a mobile phone if you know the right people. Could he have sent somebody to do his dirty work for him?

He tries to clear his head. Starts at the beginning again. Hannah Kelly used to own the horse that was killed in a road traffic accident. She visited the site where it died. Laid some flowers at the scene. She received a video message from the phone of David Hogg. Hogg was almost certainly driving the car that hit the horse. He was attacked shortly afterwards. Brutally beaten . . .

McAvoy runs his hand through his hair. It comes away damp.

He is staring at the plastic tabletop when he feels a presence looming over him. Looks up into a face he halfway knows. He's early sixties but looks older. Big. Scruffy polo shirt, jogging trousers and shoes. Old-fashioned glasses and iodine tattoos on bare arms. Thick white hair, formed into wedges at front and back, as though made of bubble-bath. His face is the colour of old paper and there is a tiny groove in his lower lip where his teeth have bitten down hard. He is extending his large right hand.

'Sergeant McAvoy,' he says.

'Mr Kelly,' McAvoy replies, looking into the face of Hannah's dad. ',

McAvoy begins to stand as he takes the older man's hand. Les waves him back down. Stays still for a moment, then sits down on the plastic chair to McAvoy's right. He pulls a leather pouch from the pocket of his trousers. Says nothing. Stares at it for a moment and then begins rolling a cigarette. Licks it shut and places it on the table. Starts making another.

'I feel like lighting this,' says Les, nodding at the roll-up. 'Feel like causing a scene. You think the security guards would come and throw me out? I'd love that. I'd love to smash my fist into somebody's head.'

McAvoy considers the man. He can see that he is holding himself in check. There is a strangulated quality to his voice, as though something is constricting his throat. It is grief and pain and suffering, and it will be there until the day he dies.

'I won't say that lashing out wouldn't help,' says McAvoy gently. 'It might, for a moment. But getting arrested would just cause more problems and pain. So resist, if you can.'

Les looks up from the task at hand. Everything about him screams grief. There is a stillness to him, an economy of movement, that suggests he is calcifying before McAvoy's eyes.

'She's here, then?' asks Les, looking at McAvoy with eyes the same colour as his daughter's. 'Have they cut her up yet?'

McAvoy doesn't know how to respond. He feels like shuddering at the stark language but can't help but admire Les's unwillingness to find sweeter words for what is being done to his child. McAvoy knows himself guilty of trying to sweeten brutal news with euphemistic descriptions. He has heard himself say 'lost the fight' and 'slipped away' to desperate people, when what he meant was 'died'.

'Dr Jackson-Savannah has concluded his examination,' says McAvoy, forcing himself to look directly at Les as he says it. 'We'll have his findings soon.'

'Knife, was it?' asks Les, and his face quivers slightly as his mind hands him a show-reel of horrors. He bites on his lip again. 'Or were she strangled? Those seem to be the ways to kill young lasses. I read the papers. That's how young girls die in this country. Stabbed or strangled.'

Once again, McAvoy doesn't know what to say. The rules and regulations insist he cannot share details of the investigation. In the eyes of the law, Les Kelly is still a suspect. In time, members of McAvoy's team will need a breakdown of his movements around the time of Hannah's disappearance. But here, now, he looks like a sculpture of dust and tears.

'I know you can't say,' mutters Les, saving McAvoy from needing to speak. 'I probably shouldn't be here anyways. Just felt the urge to be near her. Silly, isn't it? You'd have thought I'd be used to the absence, but something made me come here. It was good of you to tell me personally she'd been found. Hard, like. Hard to hear. And I could tell it were hard to say.'

McAvoy plays with his empty cup. He didn't tell Les where Hannah had been found. Just that a body matching her description had been located. Les won't be allowed to see what's left of her unless he truly begs and pleads, and McAvoy doubts he is that kind of man. Hannah was a late arrival for him and his wife. He was often mistaken for her grandfather when he picked her up from school. He spent his younger years in the Merchant Navy before getting a job as a boilerman at a tyre factory near Stoke, where Hannah grew up. Good, solid family. Semi-detached house and two cats. Hannah's room still looks just as she left it when she went off to university.

'Your wife?' asks McAvoy, tactfully. 'Has she come up with you? Did you request the family liaison officer I recommended?'

Les shakes his head. 'She's home. A friend of ours is with her. She's already shed most of her tears, like. We always knew she weren't coming back. When you called last night . . . I don't know . . . it was almost like relief. But it weren't relief.' Les grimaces, angry at himself for not being able to articulate it properly. 'She were such a bloody sweetheart,' he says, and his face tightens, as though bracing himself for a punch. His eyes dampen for a moment but by effort of will, tears do not fall. 'She were never any bother to us. Such a good girl. I think I told her off no more than half a dozen times in her life and even then it weren't for owt bad.' He smiles at a sudden memory. 'When she were seven they had one of those assemblies at school about feeding the starving in Africa. It really hit home with our Hannah. They had to bring in shoeboxes of stuff that could be sent over to these poor villagers who didn't have much to their name. Do you know what Hannah sent them? My wife's jewellery! She reckoned they could sell it and buy food. I only found out when the school phoned me and said they wanted to double-check that we had said it was okay. I went bloody spare at her but she was just upset that she wasn't going to be allowed to help. How do you get cross at somebody like that? Honestly, she were pure gold.'

McAvoy enjoys the smile on Les's face as he loses himself in the memory. He wants to put an arm on the older man's shoulder but fears that any physical contact would shatter him.

'You look like you sound,' says Les, out of nowhere.

'Yes?'

'The wife said you had a voice for poetry, whatever that means. I thought you sounded like a football manager. Whatever. We're grateful for you keeping us informed. All the calls. I've spoken to a few coppers in my time and they don't all cover themselves in glory when they deal with people. It were good of you. You didn't have to. So thanks.'

McAvoy wonders if he should say something. Decides not to. Watches as Les picks up the half-dozen hand-rolled cigarettes and tucks them into the leather wallet. He puts the pouch back in his trousers.

'I'll light up outside,' he says, as if his earlier threat may have been playing on McAvoy's mind. 'I'm sure you're doing something important, anyway. Thinking, or something. I just wanted to shake your hand. Don't really know what to do now. You think that will change?'

McAvoy looks into Les's eyes and sees Hannah. Sees the same blue irises he has stared into a thousand times. Wonders how it would look if he, the policeman, were the first to break down and sob.

'There's no advice I can offer you,' he says, wishing there were. 'Some people take comfort in justice. I can promise you, I will do everything in my power to make sure you get that.'

Les considers him. Nods. 'I know you will, son. I could tell that from the first time I spoke to you. I can see it in your eyes now. I'm not angry yet. Is that strange? I did my anger when she vanished. Tied meself up in knots imagining what might have happened. It were hard when you told us she'd got herself all dolled up for some bloke. That were never her style. But they get older, don't they? And she were such a romantic. Whoever took her, they picked a girl from the pages of a fairy tale. I can't let myself imagine what she felt in those last moments. I can't. What if she were looking for me, eh? Looking for her dad to come and save her?'

Les sniffs. Locks his jaw and grimaces, as if trying to suck the disloyal tears back into his eyes. 'You think they'll let me see her?' he asks, wiping his nose with his hand.

McAvoy softens his face. Shakes his head. 'You don't want to remember her that way.' Something passes between them. Les reads McAvoy's meaning. Nods as he bites his lip.

McAvoy considers him for almost a full minute before speaking again. He has to know.

'Did Hannah ever mention a man named Reuben Hollow?' he asks.

Les appears to think about it. 'Bloke on the telly? Just got released? No. Not that I can think of.' His gaze hardens. 'Why? He involved?'

McAvoy pushes on. 'Her horse. Alfie. We think that's what led her to the Great Givendale area the first time.'

Les nods. 'She loved that bloody nag. Cost a fortune to stable but we'd never have sold him. It were her suggestion when she went off to university. Said he needed full-time love. She sold him to some lady she found on the internet. It broke her heart when she heard he'd died.'

McAvoy tries not to let his body language change. 'You knew about Alfie's death?'

'Oh, aye. She rang the wife in tears. She were sick to her stomach. Course, she never said where it happened or anything. All we could do was comfort her and say the usual stuff about him being in a better place. Some bloke joy-riding, wasn't it? Aye, well, the wife suggested she lay some flowers or something and Hannah liked that . . .'

He stops. Seems to recall something.

'She met a bloke,' he says quietly. 'Rang the wife in a fit of giggles. Said she'd talked it through with some nice man. Sat in the church grounds and had a natter. It made her feel better.'

McAvoy makes a conscious effort not to look agitated. 'You never mentioned that before,' he says, trying not to make it sound like a reprimand. 'We asked about significant men in her life.'

'That weren't significant,' says Les, a flash of annoyance in his voice. 'How do we know what significant means? She phoned every day and there was always something to report. She just said she'd met a nice man who made her feel a bit better. The wife teased her a bit, but all in fun.' He screws up his face as if trying to drag forth a memory. 'The wife asked her if he was husband material. You know, was he a doctor or a lawyer or something? She laughed it off.'

McAvoy waits for more. Watches Les fight through imaginings and recollections.

'Did she say what he did?' asks McAvoy, trying damned hard not to put the word into Les's head.

'Sculptor,' says Les, nodding. 'Something that didn't pay much. Said he were a nice man and he was a sculptor and he was proper upset to hear about that prick who got away with killing her horse.'

McAvoy closes his eyes. Reaches out and claps Les's hand.

'He put her in a cart of flowers outside my house,' says McAvoy softly. 'Laid her out like a princess. If you have to think of her dead, think of her like that. But please, Les, try and think of her alive. Alive and pretty and full of smiles.'

He pushes his chair back from the table and turns to nod his thanks to the cashier. Notices the price list stuck to the wall. Does some mental arithmetic and works out that she undercharged him. He puts a pound coin on the cash register and gives a weak smile in the face of her protests. Walks from the hospital with his shoulders stooped and an ache in his gut.

Outside, into the silence of a city shrouded in grey.

24

'You're sure you won't get in trouble, darling?'

McAvoy would like to turn his head so he can answer Roisin properly but the country road to Market Weighton is too windy for him to take his eyes off it. He just gives a tight-lipped smile. Keeps his eyes on the strip of blurred grey that cuts through the damp green fields and the hazy air. Tries to order his thoughts over the sound of tyres on tarmac, and his daughter's pleasant babbling from the back seat.

'I don't really mind,' he says. 'Not this time.'

'You're turning into a maverick,' teases Roisin, reaching across to stroke his face with the back of her soft, tanned hands.

'Me? Yeah, I'm a regular rebel.'

'I like it when you're a bit of a baddy.'

'Aye. I know.'

It's mid-afternoon. The fog is less thick here. It seems to be reserving its intensity for Hull. Here, 15 miles north of the city boundary line, it manifests itself as a misty rain; the droplets too fine to fall as raindrops should. McAvoy doesn't know whether to turn on the windscreen wipers or whether that will just make things worse. He tries anyway. Watches the blades smear dirt and flies and moisture across the glass of the sensible Volvo that he bought for its safety features, and has yet to persuade himself to like. He should be alone on this drive. Alone, or with another copper. Shouldn't have brought his wife and child. He knows already what a defence barrister would make of his actions. But McAvoy's thoughts are a tangle of guilt and rage. He suddenly finds his devotion to duty laughable. Finds his conscience a risible indulgence. He can barely bring himself to speak in case he finds himself shouting, can hardly hear what Roisin is saying above the sound of rubber on tarmac and the dull hum of Radio Humberside dribbling from the radio and bringing the local house prices down with each fresh bulletin.

'I'll be quiet,' says Roisin with a sigh. She pouts, petulantly. Leans her head against the window. Stares out at the trees. 'Dead rabbit,' she says, pointing.

'It was just sleeping,' says McAvoy, driving around the sad little grey carcass and trying to be himself.

'In the middle of the road? Dangerous.'

'He's a dangerous rabbit. Proper hard. Kicked the shit out of a badger in his younger days.'

Roisin giggles. Puts her hand on her husband's as it vibrates on the gear stick. 'Do I have to stay in the car? I could help. You can be good cop and I can be fecking horrible cop.'

McAvoy strokes her fingers with his thumb. Looks down at the mobile phone in his lap. The sat-nav function says he's nearly there.

'You can't get out of the car, Roisin. It wouldn't look right. You just keep your head down.'

Roisin pouts again. 'You're no fun.'

She had called him as he was leaving the hospital. Told him he sounded too sad to be on his own. Told him she couldn't stand looking out of the window at the coppers and reporters, gawpers and wankers who have taken up residence on the grass outside their home. She met him by the ice-cream van at Hessle Foreshore, dressed in a red leather jacket and painted-on jeans; holding Lilah's hand and looking forward to a drive in the country with Daddy.

McAvoy looks at the phone again. Still nothing from Tremberg. Nothing from Pharaoh, either. His head hurts from everything he's trying to keep inside it. He had needed Roisin as if she were medicine. Picked her up from home and decided that he would be a better policeman if she were by his side. She'd held him close when she got in the car. Told him that she'd had a tricky morning but she'd left Trish a message and that everything would be fine now she had got things off her chest. He hadn't pushed too hard, though he had felt jittery at the thought of Roisin and Pharaoh having conversations he was not there to referee. Besides, his head had been too full of Pharaoh and the way she spoke to him to focus on his wife's peculiar behaviour. His cheeks burn at the injustice of it. He knows Pharaoh's been concealing something from him. He would not object to secrecy from any other senior officer but he thought he had proven himself to her. Thought they were more than boss and minion. He will never be less than grateful for all she has done for him but cannot help but feel betrayed. Somehow, Hollow has got a hold on her. She is not behaving like she should. He knows that the drink is starting to take its toll but thought the woman he knew was still in control. He cannot help but wonder whether Hollow has seduced her. He hates the thought. Gags on it. Shakes his brain as it offers up a more distressing question: why hasn't he told her about Hollow's connection to Hannah? Why does he feel so compelled to prove his theory to himself before proving it to her?

'There might be more to it than you know,' says Roisin, tactfully. She would love to criticise Pharaoh just for the sheer fun of getting one over on her, but in truth, she knows her to be a good copper and an even better person. 'She's a superintendent, Aector. She had a good career even before you came along. She wouldn't have got there by allowing herself to be fooled by every charmer.'

McAvoy shakes his head. 'We had good evidence. She blocked us. Made it clear he was off limits.'

'He's been in all the papers,' says Roisin. 'He's made her life difficult. She knows about this stuff. Maybe she's right when she says you have to play it carefully.'

McAvoy snaps his head to the left. Temper flickers in his eyes. 'What is it about him? He's got you all under his spell.'

Roisin looks hurt and McAvoy immediately regrets his words. He tries to say sorry but the word turns to ash upon his tongue.

'I'm not under his spell,' says Roisin quietly. 'I didn't even like him. He had something missing in his eyes.'

'I don't even know why he was there,' says McAvoy, slowing down as the sat-nav tells him his destination is on the right. 'He shouldn't even know where she lives, but that's today's world for you – two clicks on a mouse and you know everything about everybody.'

Roisin seems about to speak. Seems about to confess something she has withheld. But McAvoy is turning the car into a gap in the line of trees, pulling into a large parking area where three cars are parked in a loose fan-tail. The doors are open and music is pumping out of the central vehicle, a souped-up Subaru with an exhaust pipe the width of a fire hydrant. The other two vehicles are sporty hatchbacks. This seems to be a place where the Volvo will not blend in.

'Which one is he?' asks Roisin, nodding at the youths who are lounging, languidly, on the bonnets of the vehicles.

'Curly hair. Afro-style, but mucky blond. Probably wearing a tracksuit.' McAvoy is reading from his notes. For all of his personal involvement in the hunt for Hannah Kelly, he has not yet had the pleasure of meeting David Hogg. He phoned the local police sergeant before setting off. Found out where Hogg was likely to be at this time of day. The sergeant had been a solid, dependable character who had been absolutely honest with McAvoy. 'Little shit,' he'd said. 'Better off in the ground. If you get the chance, run over his fucking head.'

McAvoy parks the Volvo. Turns to shush Lilah, who has started whimpering at the sound of house music.

'Wankers,' says Roisin, shaking her head. 'It's such a lovely place. Make them turn it down.'

McAvoy looks around him, peering through the car windows. Green hills roll gently upwards both before him and behind. Behind the grey, a cold blue light strives to be seen. An unfinished triangle of geese arrows artfully across the distant cloud.

He looks at the youths that loiter around the vehicles. Can see four lads and a couple of young girls.

Drops his eyes.

Car tyres have pulped leaves and blossom into the gravel.

'You will stay put, yes? It won't take long. I just need to try.'

Roisin grins. 'Leave me your phone. I'll play Angry Birds.'

McAvoy climbs from the car. He makes sure to walk with a straight back. Makes sure they can see just how damn big he is. Covers the distance in half a dozen strides. Gives a jerk of his head; a northerner's hello.

'Could you turn that down, please?' he asks, polite but firm. A fat, round-faced lad of around twenty years is sitting in the driving seat of the central Subaru. He gives a snort of derision at the request. Turns to his companion and says something he thinks is clever.

McAvoy looks at the semicircle of youngsters who are lounging on the car bonnets. They are looking at him with interest, eager to see what will happen next. He senses that their days play out to a pattern and that today, he is the note of variety.

'I'm Detective Sergeant McAvoy,' he says, raising his voice. 'I'm looking for David Hogg.'

Instinctively, several pairs of eyes flick in the direction of the passenger seat of the Subaru. McAvoy peers in. Spots the lad who crashed his car into horse and rider on a country road and then left them both for dead. He still looks battered, and the way he moves his jaw suggests there is still wire holding it together. He has fleshy lips and a constellation of spots and blackheads across his nose. His hair is a tangled mop, sprouting from a thin head. He may be wearing designer labels but he looks as though he has stolen the garments. Nice things do not sit well upon him. He has not replaced the earring that was torn from his ear during the attack that left him in hospital with bones pulped and jaw smashed. His earlobe still sports a scar.

'You would be Mr Hogg,' says McAvoy, leaning past the driver and fixing his gaze upon the unsmiling lad. 'Could I have a word?'

Hogg mockingly raises a hand to his ear, miming an inability to hear. Then he looks through the glass to his friends for confirmation of his brilliance.

McAvoy sighs. Takes the keys from the ignition and enjoys the shouts that follow the sudden silence. Pockets the keys.

'You can't do that, that's fucking theft!'

'Give them back!'

'You're fucking dead!'

McAvoy turns to the group of youngsters who are glaring at him but making no attempt to move forward. The oldest looks around nineteen. The two girls look like they should still be in school. He wonders what their parents think they're up to. Wonders what he would do if he learned Lilah was out with a group like this, spending her free time drinking cans of Red Bull in the back of a hatchback with the kind of lads who walk down the street with their hands inside their jogging pants.

'Mr Hogg,' he says, turning back to the car. 'It really would be easier if you gave me a moment of your time.'

Hogg looks like he wants to spit. Locks eyes with McAvoy for a long moment. Finally, he hisses a curse and gets out of the vehicle. McAvoy walks around to the far side and holds the door open for him. Rather enjoys watching him struggle to manoeuvre a right leg that still seems to pain him.

'This is harassment,' he says, once he has extricated himself from the vehicle. He says it loud enough for his friends to hear.

'Why is it that everybody the police want to question thinks they're being harassed?' muses McAvoy aloud. 'I'm not harassing you. I'm going to ask you some questions and you can answer them if you want, or be awkward about the whole affair and cause both of us to have a tedious day.'

'You a Jock?' asks Hogg, making the word sound like a sneer. 'My mam used to shag a Jock. He was a fucking prick as well.'

McAvoy closes his eyes. Lets his weariness show in his posture and face. Looks at the audience that Hogg has decided to play to. It's clear Hogg is the alpha male among his cronies. He's the nephew of a big deal. He's got a bit of money. Got a reputation. Seems intent on playing up to it.

McAvoy moves closer to Hogg. Gives him a pleasant smile.

'Did you hear we found her?' he asks. 'Hannah.'

'Hannah who?' says Hogg, as his face falls into its default setting of confused and hostile.

230

'Hannah Kelly,' says McAvoy. 'You were questioned about her death. I'd have thought you'd remember.'

Hogg gives a laugh. Turns to his friends. 'That was fucking months ago. And I told her what I'm telling you. Leave it.'

McAvoy keeps his eyes on Hogg's. Breathes out through his mouth. Clicks his tongue against his palette. Nods.

'Come with me,' he says, and grabs hold of the young man by his stripy blue T-shirt. In the face of Hogg's protests, McAvoy drags him a dozen feet away from the cars. Pulls him forward and presses his lips against his ear.

'I don't do this, Mr Hogg. This is not how I like to conduct my investigations. I believe that people are fundamentally okay but that sometimes they do wrong. When they do, it's up to society to make sure that balance is restored. Somebody did something very bad to Hannah Kelly. I don't think it was you. Nobody ever thought it was you. You were in hospital. That's a pretty damn good alibi. But I know for a fact you ran your car into the back of a horse she used to own and I know for a fact that somebody used your phone to call her not long before she disappeared. All I want to know is the details of that call. And I can't think of any other way to demonstrate my strength of feeling than this.'

McAvoy releases the smaller man, who makes a great show of smoothing down his shirt and glances back at his friends. Then Hogg looks over at the blue Volvo, where a pretty young woman with dark hair and incredible assets is leaning against the bonnet smoking a hand-rolled cigarette.

'Who's that?' asks Hogg.

'Doesn't matter. Not to you.'

'You're not a fucking copper, are you?' says Hogg, suspiciously.

'I told you I was.'

'No, no, I mean, I don't reckon you are. Who are you? Do you work for him?'

McAvoy pauses, thinking fast. 'Him?'

'Him, yeah.'

McAvoy isn't sure whether to let Hogg continue to believe he is somebody other than who he claims to be.

'If I was, I wouldn't say, would I?'

Hogg grows a little pale. Shakes his head and his breathing becomes ragged.

'I never told. Tell him. Please. I swear to God.'

McAvoy stares into the young man's eyes. Wonders, for the merest fraction of a second, whether it would turn Roisin on to watch him punch the little shit in the chest.

'Tell me about the call,' he says in a low voice. 'It will be better for you.'

Hogg seems unsure, torn between calling his mates over and trying his luck against the big guy, or spilling everything he knows. After a moment, his shoulders seem to sag.

'He made his point the first time,' says Hogg. 'Fuck, I was in hospital long enough. I did what he said.'

'And what was that?' asks McAvoy, trying to maintain his composure.

'I apologised!' spits Hogg. 'He owes me for that. Owes me the video.'

McAvoy's mind races ahead; hands him a picture, fully formed. He glares at Hogg. Lets some gravel creep into his voice.

'He made you apologise, yes? To Hannah.'

Hogg looks down at his dirty white trainers. Nods. 'I was pissed when he grabbed me,' he says, as if defending his lapse in dominance. 'I'd smoked a fucking orchard of weed. I was walking home. Still didn't have a car . . .'

'Because your uncle had the last one you stole crushed,' says McAvoy.

Hogg shrugs. 'Whatever.'

'And?'

'He sprayed me with something. A little water bottle, straight in my eyes. Stung like fuck. I couldn't see. Next thing I'm on the floor somewhere. A garage, I reckon, but I couldn't say. I'm bleeding from my mouth and I can barely see. He's got my phone . . .'

'You saw his face?'

'Are you listening? I couldn't see a thing.'

'He hurt you?'

Hogg swills spit around his mouth. Sucks it through his teeth.

'He described what he was doing as he did it. Didn't seem excited. Just calm, like he'd done it before. Said he had a horse-shoe in a sock. Said he thought it was symbolic after what I did. And then he hit me with it. Whipped me around the ribs. The face. I've never felt pain like it.'

McAvoy cannot disguise the sound of his breathing or pretend to be anything other than energised by this sudden misguided admission.

'He filmed you,' says McAvoy.

Hogg nods. 'Used my own fucking phone. I was lying there, bleeding and hardly able to move, and he videoed me. Told me to apologise. Told me to say I was sorry. To beg for my life.'

McAvoy looks away. Turns back to where Roisin is picking loose tobacco off her tongue and smiling at him.

'He sent the video to Hannah,' says McAvoy.

Hogg shrugs again. 'I didn't know her. Didn't know why it was happening. But she saved my life. Phoned him back. I heard him whispering. Whatever she said, he left me alone after that. Came back and gave me one last smack. Took my jaw off the fucking hinge. Told me that if I spoke about what had happened he'd send somebody after me. Told me to be nice to the princesses, whatever that might fucking mean.'

McAvoy sucks his cheek and looks up, past the trees, to where a sudden strip of sunlight has managed to permeate the gloom.

'Your phone,' he says. 'He took it?'

'I was unconscious,' says Hogg. 'My uncle found me. Told me to keep my mouth shut, like I had any choice. They had to wire it shut until it healed. Broke all of my ribs. I can't even drive again yet.'

McAvoy lets his irritation show as Hogg stands and feels sorry for himself.

'You were interviewed by the police,' says McAvoy. He decides

233

to get into character. Snarls a little, like his old boxing coach had shown him years before. 'He knows you told.'

'I never!' protests Hogg. He glances back over his shoulder. Seems unsure whether to start kicking out or to burst into tears.

McAvoy takes out his phone and finds the picture. Shows it to Hogg, keeping his eyes fixed on his. 'You know him?'

Hogg concentrates. 'If I did, I wouldn't say. Tell him that. Tell him I never told her. I didn't recognise him then and I don't now. Only from what she showed me.'

McAvoy feels his world grow still. Feels everything slow down. Imagines, for a moment, he can hear the beating of every wing as the pheasant takes off from the trees. Imagines he can hear the ladybirds, scuttling over damp leaves.

'She?'

'The copper. Superintendent something. Cleopatra, or whatever. She showed me. I told her to leave it alone.'

McAvoy continues staring. Burns a hole through the centre of Hogg's head.

'She showed you his picture?'

'When I was in hospital. Months ago. But I never told her owt.'

'And who has spoken to you since?'

'Coppers? None.'

McAvoy's heart is banging against his chest. He can feel sweat in the small of his back and at his hairline. Wonders whether there is a breathing technique that would help him right now. Wonders whether it would be best to pull out his warrant card, arrest Hogg and make this all official. He shakes his head, as if making up his mind.

'Did she mention his name?' he asks softly.

'Never said. But I saw him somewhere. Telly, it was. Got locked up for something and they let him out on appeal. Saw her, too. Told my uncle and he didn't even believe me . . .'

McAvoy cannot help himself. He pushes forward and looms over Hogg like an oak.

'You're lying,' he says. 'You never met her.'

Hogg scrambles back, fumbling in the pocket of his jogging

pants. Pulls out an object and swings it wildly at McAvoy's face. It connects with a noise like a hammer hitting a wall and McAvoy staggers back; spots of light fill his vision and warm blood runs into his left eye.

'Fuck you!' screams Hogg, swinging the object again and connecting with McAvoy's left forearm. 'Tell him he's not getting me again. I haven't got a horse-shoe in a sock but I can sure as shit put a couple of snooker balls in one. You like that? You like that, you big Jock fuck?'

McAvoy wipes his hand across his face and opens his eyes just in time to see the object arcing up again. He throws his head back. Flings out his right hand. Opens his fist at the last moment and catches Hogg with a slap that will leave the younger man's ears ringing. Hogg shouts and stumbles and McAvoy starts to reach into his pocket for his warrant card. Before he can, a weight lands on his back. McAvoy realises the other lads have joined the fight. Somebody is pulling his hair. He can feel inexpert, ineffectual punches scudding into his ribs. He fights like an elephant being attacked by tigers. Throws one figure at another. Tries to warn them off but finds his mouth full of somebody's sleeve. He wants to fight back properly. Wants to swing the kind of punch that can snap a neck. But he forces himself to remain a policeman. Fights like a grown-up being set upon by youngsters on a bouncy castle. Hooks legs and pushes chests. Refuses to do damage until he has no choice . . .

Tyres screech across gravel. In the gap between two arms, McAvoy sees a flash of blue. Then there is a crunch of metal upon metal. He reacts first. Spins inside the grasp of the teenager behind him and pushes him away with both hands. Sees a space between the fallen figures and darts for it.

'Come on,' shouts Roisin, her eyes wide with exhilaration.

McAvoy throws himself into the passenger seat. Hears roars of anger as Roisin flings the Volvo into reverse and crunches back from the smashed bumper and boot of the expensive Subaru.

'We'll fucking kill you!' comes the scream, but it is lost almost at once in the sound of rubber hitting tarmac, and in an instant, the Volvo is picking up speed and flying around the bends in the road.

'You okay?' asks Roisin, reaching across from the driver's seat and pressing her hand to the wound above McAvoy's eyebrow. 'Fuck, that's deep. Sorry, Lilah – Mammy didn't mean to swear.'

There is a ringing in McAvoy's ears. His head is throbbing. There is blood on his face and on his shirt. None of it matters. The only thing he cares about is the lies that Pharaoh has told him. The only thing that matters is the sure and certain knowledge that Reuben Hollow killed Hannah, and that Pharaoh has always known.

25

Foley is listening to the song he always fills himself up with before he hurts somebody. It's a simple little melody, played entirely on the black keys. It's from a zombie film, apparently, and it's certainly sinister. It builds to a crescendo that always sets Teddy's teeth on edge. It's right for the conditions. In this fog he can half imagine an army of the undead staggering towards their vehicle. Wonders what he would do in such a set of circumstances, though really he knows, without a shadow of a doubt. He'd shoot Foley in the kneecaps and leave him to be eaten. Not now, though. There's no need. It's going to be a blast watching Foley get his revenge. Teddy suspects he'll only break a sweat when he has to help his young companion lift the body into the boot.

'I'm sticking it on again,' says Foley, sitting in the passenger seat, and he skips back to the beginning of the track. Settles moodily in his seat. Fills himself up with the mournful tune and thinks of murder.

'You'll give yourself an ulcer,' says Teddy. 'I can hear you grinding your teeth. You haven't done that since prison.'

Foley says nothing. There are a lot of things he hasn't done since prison. A lot he won't ever be doing again.

'Save your petrol,' says Teddy. 'You're going to burn your engine dry.'

'The fucking engine's off.'

'No, in you, I mean. We only get so much fuel. You'll be knackered by the time you get to him. He's no slouch, we know that. Chill a little. You want a sweet?'

Foley turns furious eyes on the older man. He looks for a moment like he wants to raise the gun and put a hole in the face of his old cellmate, like he wants to stick a knife in the world and watch it bleed to death.

'Easy, son,' says Teddy. 'I give you a long rope. I'm fond of you, but don't look at me like that. You're hurting. You've no need. Chill.'

Foley looks for a moment like he is going to argue. Then he unwinds. Sniffs up something vile and solid; swallows it down. They located Reuben Hollow within moments of leaving the pikey and the teenager. Their boss has a tame copper on his payroll and with only two phone calls he had accessed the national number-plate recognition software. Reuben Hollow's vehicle had just passed through the town of Beverley, heading inland. It had taken Teddy and Foley an hour to reach the location and another hour to pick up his tail. Foley hadn't really expected to find him so easily but fortune had been kind. Despite the thick mist that has pulled a cloak over East Yorkshire, they'd stumbled on his battered old car in this pretty little hamlet that looks to Foley like an exhibit at a history museum. Teddy fancies that if he pushed his arm into the cloud, his hand would come out in another place and time. The air smells of the sea; of dog food and cold. He misses London. Misses people knowing that he is a man to respect and avoid. They're all fucking backwards up here. Northerners throw punches without giving a shit whom the recipient is connected to. In the Grimsby pub that he and Foley warmed to, a bloke in his seventies threatened to smash his face in just for looking at his pint with disrespectful eyes. Teddy had actually found himself apologising. He hasn't said sorry to anybody in years.

'We should take him now,' says Foley, moodily. He's nodding along to the music. Picking at a spot on his neck.

'In a church, lad? C'mon, the boss takes that shit seriously.'

'He wouldn't know.'

'That's not the point.'

They are parked beside a field, opposite the low boundary wall of St Mary's Church in South Dalton. The fog has obscured the ornate spire but the low gravestones are given the power to unnerve by the grey mist that swirls around their ancient inscriptions.

'No signal,' says Teddy, looking at his phone screen.

'How do people live in places like this?' asks Foley. 'What do they do for a laugh?'

'There's a good restaurant,' says Teddy, hoping they will start talking a little more companionably. 'Michelin star, according to the website.'

'Here?' Foley waves a hand at the landscape of nothingness. 'For who?'

Teddy shrugs. Lights himself a cigarette. 'Must be money here somewhere. You know how country folk are. Won't redecorate for fifty years but then they go and buy a Range Rover with the change they found down the back of the sofa. Country folk with country ways.'

'Cuntish folk,' broods Foley.

'Touché, my friend.'

Foley presses play again. Lets the music fill him. Reuben Hollow's Jeep is parked a few feet away. The small cottages which overlook this quiet road are lost to fog. There's little risk of any-body seeing what they have planned for the man who humiliated them when they were getting ready to enjoy themselves with Sophia. Even if the boss hadn't given the go-ahead they'd have been tempted to come back for him. They can dress it up any way they want; he got the better of them.

'How was he?' asks Foley, opening the window.

'The boss? Harassed.'

Foley sniffs. Seems about to say something, then decides against it.

'He says he's got something else for us as soon as we get back,' says Teddy, half interested. 'Babysitting job. Somebody the boss is looking after for his new friends.'

'Friends?' Foley manages to make the word sound like an insult. 'They're riding him like a bitch.'

Teddy raises his eyebrows. 'Easy, lad. He's your meal ticket.'

'He's finished.'

'Yeah? Why we doing his bidding, then?'

'How do you know we are? This new outfit could have his balls in a vice for all we know.'

'I've known him a while. He doesn't scare.'

'Who's this prick we're supposed to babysit?'

Teddy shrugs. 'They've been moving him house to house. Christ knows how long they want him for but I don't reckon he's enjoying himself. Some Russian connection, that's all I could get out of him. We can hurt him but not kill him. And he needs his medicine three times a day.'

Foley picks his nose. Inspects the back of his finger and rubs it on his trousers. 'I'm not touching that horrible shit. Rots you from the inside out.'

They sit in silence. They don't know how long Hollow will be. He'd been climbing out of his vehicle when they pulled up. Had taken a bag of tools and a camera bag with him into the church. Had a key to let himself in. Pushed open the great double doors and walked inside its cool stone embrace. Even took his cap off as he did so. It seemed to Teddy and Foley as if he gave a shit about such things. They have already speculated whether or not he will call for God when they get him back to the isolated farm building they pinpointed early on in their trip north. It's a quiet, out-of-the-way sort of place, where human screams will be lost amid the screeching of the nearby pigs.

'And the boss was happy, yeah? This bloke's been in the papers a lot. On the telly. If he's been screwing a copper and ends up dead there'll be a hell of a racket.'

'The money's what matters. If we do it right, everybody's happy. Well, maybe not Hollow, but the people that matter. We take enough to clear the debt and a little more besides, and we show the new outfit that we can move with the times. The boss understands. He's the one who mentioned the nailgun.'

'It's not his style, though. You're sure he wants it done like that?'

'That's what he said. We nail his hands to his knees then have a party with the blowtorch. Dump him where we like but it has to be in plain sight.'

Foley pulls a face. 'I'd rather just kick him to death.'

Teddy shrugs. 'I'm sure we can put the odd boot in, my friend.'

'Were they serious, you reckon?' asks Foley. 'I mean, that's horrible shit.'

'Boss said if we didn't do it there would be another team up here before the day was out. Said they might not be as squeamish.'

'Squeamish? Fuck that.'

'You'll show them, lad. You're staunch, I know that.'

Foley seems mollified. Stares through the fog at the row of Tudor almshouses that serve as the first and last properties in this one-road town on the way to nowhere. They haven't seen another person since parking up. They're getting uncomfortable and cold in the nondescript car.

Ten minutes later, the two men hear the sound of footsteps on stone. The hinge of the wrought-iron gate creaks and through the fog, the figure of Reuben Hollow emerges. He's a slight man. Unremarkable, from this distance. Doesn't seem like the answer to so many riddles.

'Quietly,' says Teddy, as he eases open his door. 'Show him the gun and get him in the car.'

Foley looks like he is about to protest but eventually gives a little nod. He tucks his chain inside his black jumper, pulls his cap down low, springs from the vehicle and walks forward with the gun held out straight in front of him.

'Stand the fuck still,' hisses Foley, when he is half a dozen steps from his target. Hollow freezes. There is silence, save the sound of Teddy moving quickly behind his prey. He doesn't have a gun, content with the length of pipe he holds in his right hand. He isn't worrying. Has done this more times than he can count.

'Thought you'd fucking put me down, did you?' spits Foley.

'Fuck you, pretty-boy. It was dark. Do your fucking worst.'

Hollow's face is half in shadow. The peak of his cap obscures his blue eyes, though the hand-rolled cigarette wedged in his mouth glows bright red as he sucks on its filter.

'It's light now,' he says, quietly. 'You won't have any excuses. Give me a whirl.'

Behind him, Teddy moves into position. Sticks his fingers into the small of Hollow's back. 'Don't be trying that shit. Get your hands behind your back.'

Hollow keeps his eyes locked on Foley's. The cigarette points upwards as Hollow gives a tiny smile.

'This your dad?' he asks, nodding over his shoulder at Teddy. He slowly begins to raise his hands, still holding the toolbag. 'He keeping you safe? Poor lamb.'

Hollow winces as Teddy hits him sharply on the back of the head. 'None of that. Give me your wrist. You're not getting out of this shit.'

Foley is looking at his target down the barrel of the handgun. His eyes almost glow with venom. He flicks his glance towards Teddy, pleading, and receives an imperceptible shake of the head in return.

'C'mon, Teddy, let me fight him, he's a fucking pansy. We can do the blowtorch shit later.'

Teddy throws a glare at his partner. Loosens his grip on Hollow's wrist for a fraction of a second. It's long enough. Hollow spins, bringing up the toolbag. The leather sack full of hammers, chisels and a score of blades slams into the side of Teddy's head and sends him flying backwards, clattering down hard against the stone. Foley gasps a curse and brings the gun up but Hollow has ducked back and the fog has closed around him like water. Foley starts forward. Slips on something. Looks down and finds the strap of the camera bag under his trainer. Raises his head and realises he has fucked up. Hollow is somewhere nearby. Teddy isn't saying a damn word. Inside him, fear and rage slosh against one another like two tides. He moves to his right and sees the church looming through the grey. Shivers as the gravestones come into focus. Turns back in the direction of the car, deciding that enough is fucking enough.

He screams as the water splashes his face. In an instant his eyes feel like they are ablaze. He raises his hands to his face and suddenly his ears are ringing and the world is a place of dizzying echoes. He realises he has discharged the gun right next to his head. Something warm trickles down his jawline as he tries to cover both eyes and one ear with two hands.

Foley does not have the problem for long. A moment later, he is on his back and Reuben Hollow is sitting on his chest, knee upon his throat and a fist holding a handful of his short hair.

Hollow still has his hand-rolled cigarette. He doesn't look like his heart rate has increased by more than a beat or two.

'Well,' says Hollow, smiling down at the squirming, half-blind figure beneath him. 'You sure fucking showed me.'

'I'm okay at this, for a beginner,' he continues, bringing the back of Foley's head down on the road with a sickening crack. 'You think maybe I've done it before?'

'Fuck you,' hisses Foley, feeling the blood begin to run behind his collar.

'No, thank you,' says Hollow, lightly. 'That would be wrong. It would be an aggressive, bullying act, and I hate bullies. Hate them like most people hate cancer and fruit flies. You don't get to behave like this. You're the one who tried your hand with Trish's daughter, aren't you? Thought so. She wouldn't have liked that. I have my rules and I do tend to wait to be asked, but I don't reckon there would be much opposition to me spreading your head all over the ground. You'll thank me for it. You're blind now. That's chilli oil in your eyes, if you were wondering. Stings, eh? I've never seen anybody look as if they're enjoying it. I don't use it as some kind of torture, you understand. It's just really helpful for quietening people down when their blood's up . . .'

Hollow looks up suddenly at the sound of running footsteps. Sees the metal pipe only a second before it crashes down on his skull.

He falls upon Foley to form the shape of a perfect cross; face upon the wet road and gravel sticking to his skin.

Teddy looks down at his partner. Wonders if there is anything to be done to save him. Locks eyes with the dying man and regrets all the things unsaid, and some of those that were.

He opens the car doors and begins to drag Hollow towards the vehicle, enjoying the soft shush of flesh being pulled over concrete.

It is more than twenty minutes before the first patrol car turns up. It contrives to run over Foley's legs as it comes to a halt outside the church in this quiet hamlet where nothing ever happens.

Foley doesn't say a word. The neural receptors that identify pain are usually found at the base of the skull. Foley's aren't. They're all over the road.

26

Jez Gavan is shouting. He's been shouting for the past twenty minutes. His hollow face has gone a kind of rust colour and there are two blobs of greenish spittle at the corners of his mouth. He is still more attractive than his living room.

'Do you think I'm further away than I actually am?' asks Pharaoh, quietly. 'I can hear you. Dial it down. Your eyes are going to explode.'

Gavan turns to spit on the floor then seems to realise he's in his own house. Swallows down whatever he's just hawked up. Swills it down with the last of his lager and then crushes the can with fingers like tattooed spider's legs.

'It's harassment,' he says, a little softer. 'Fucking harassment.'

'Yes, Jeremy. You said.'

Gavan throws himself down on an armchair and glares at Pharaoh. She's sitting opposite him, smiling sweetly. She's smoking a black cigarette and she has the arm of her sunglasses down her cleavage. She's applied make-up. Brushed her hair. Smeared the hem of her skirt across her teeth and put perfume on. Gavan can't help but leer. She's a good-looking lass. Maybe a little mumsy, but sexy with it. Confident, too. They're alone in the house and he's a known criminal who likes his women plump. He doesn't think she should be feeling so bloody cocksure. She should be feeling nervous. Shouldn't be looking at him like she could smash his face in any time she so chose.

'Don't call me Jeremy,' he says, opening another can of lager. He looks at her and raises an eyebrow. 'You want one?'

Pharaoh seems momentarily conflicted. Seems about to nod. Pulls a face and shakes her head. Gavan makes a mental note: the bitch likes a drink.

'You don't always have to be so aggressive,' says Pharaoh, sighing. 'I know you feel that conversations are for the weak, but if you'd just tell me the truth in an indoor voice, I could be on my merry way.'

'I've told you the truth!' shouts Gavan. Then he drops the volume to a more cordial growl. 'I met Ava in the Lambwath. Helped her out. She wanted more than I could give her and eventually I told her to fuck off. That's that. I'm sorry the poor cow's dead but I don't know any more than that.'

Pharaoh grinds out her cigarette. Shakes her head.

'You've been in her flat.'

Gavan shakes his head, eyebrows bunching together.

'Your phone has her wifi network stored as one of its recognised connections.'

Gavan pulls a face. Blusters a little. 'She lived down the Old Town. I have a drink in a couple of pubs down there. My phone will just have picked it up. I've no bloody clue about technology.'

'And what about your prints? We've found all sorts of things in her flat, Jez.'

'Bollocks,' blusters Gavan. 'You're fishing.'

'You've done time. You can handle prison. But do you want to handle it for the next twenty years? Longer, maybe? You think your lovely wife will wait that long?'

'She'd wait forever,' hisses Gavan, spit landing on his chin. 'But she won't have to. I'm not going back inside. I haven't done owt.'

Pharaoh stares at him, tongue wedged in her cheek. She's considering him the way a scientist would look at a new species of toad.

'Jez, I'm going to talk for a couple of minutes and I want you to listen. I mean, really listen. Okay? Look, I'm tired. I've had a shitty few days. There's stuff swirling around in my head that would make most people fall over and start blubbering. Now, I'm just a normal lass from Mexborough. I've got four kids. My husband's mentally handicapped after having a fucking massive stroke. He lives in a room in the garage that we had converted for him. I have to put ointment on his bed sores sometimes, and once in a while I try and do what the doctors advise me to do, which is to go in there and talk to him. But I don't like doing it, you see. He was a bit of a shit to me and the girls. He was a real flash sod and I used to love him, but you can only get punched in the belly so many times before you start to go off a person. And if he hadn't had the stroke, I'd have probably divorced him. I'd maybe be married to somebody else by now. Or not. I don't really know.'

Gavan looks confused. He keeps jerking his head upwards as though invisible hands are yanking his hair. 'Why are you telling me this?'

'I'm being honest with you, Jez,' says Pharaoh with a sigh. 'I'm treating you with common courtesy. I'm sharing because I want you to understand the person you're dealing with. I'm not a brilliant person, or a terrible one. I'm a normal person. But I'm a normal person who will stop at absolutely nothing to find out who killed Ava Delaney, and maybe Hannah Kelly too.'

'Hannah Kelly?' barks Gavan, spilling his lager. 'The lass from the paper?'

'We mentioned her last time, remember? Her body was found outside my sergeant's home last night. You remember my sergeant. Big man. Ginger hair. Muscles on him like a pop-sock full of melons. He's a sensitive soul. He's taken Hannah's disappearance very seriously. He's understandably pissed off that his kids had to smell her. Now, you might not realise it, but McAvoy's probably the scariest bastard I've ever met. Don't let the sad eyes fool you.'

Gavan takes a gulp of lager. Tries to act the hard man.

'You trying to threaten me?'

'No, Jeremy, I'm trying to protect you. You see, if you don't become a little more helpful, I'm going to call for backup. Three or four patrol cars will turn up. When they get here, I'll be looking like somebody who is trying their very best not to cry. And the hairy-arsed coppers who come barging through that door will know in a flash that you've been trying it on. And they're going to let their emotions get the better of them. Eventually, you'll be handcuffed and taken to the station. You might dislocate your shoulder a couple of times on the way. A long while later, we'll have our first interview. You'll tell us your version of events. Then you'll go back to your cell. The second interview will be a little more intense, where you tell us your story again. And then the third interview will be where we start picking holes in your story and laying on the pressure. None of this sounds much fun to me. But the thing you have to worry about most is the fact that McAvoy will be present for all of it. And he'll be looking at the side of your face for the entire time. He'll be looking through your skin and your muscle and your bone and into the very centre of your brain and if he doesn't like what he sees in there, he's going to express himself. I'm probably not exaggerating when I say that there aren't enough coppers in the station to hold him back when his temper's up. They call him "Psycho" at his old precinct, though not loud enough for him to hear.'

Gavan starts rolling himself a cigarette. Manages to light it. Makes a noise like a child who can't think of a reply to an insult.

'You're a fucking bitch,' he says at last.

'And you're a ratty little fucker. But you're not a murderer.'

Gavan brightens. 'So you know it wasn't me? What about the fingerprints?'

'I never said we found your fingerprints. I said we found all sorts of stuff. Don't leap to conclusions.'

'You're a bitch,' Gavan says again, but it sounds as though he means it as a compliment.

Pharaoh looks him up and down. 'If you shagged her, Jez, I won't judge you. I'll probably be quite impressed.'

He shakes his head, dragging deep on his cigarette and scratching at his spotty, shapeless arms. 'She were a kid. I don't fancy them that young. Or that Goth-looking.'

'So why did you go to her flat?'

Gavan sighs. Looks up to the ceiling.

'I've had my team speak to the bar staff at the Lambwath,' says Pharaoh. 'Gone right through the CCTV. You never got talking to a girl matching that description.'

'I did!' says Gavan, though he is looking at the backs of his hands as he says it.

Pharaoh raises a hand. Presses a knuckle to her nose. Breathes in perfume and the light scent of wildflowers and woodsmoke. Scratches her head. Clicks her false tooth distractedly, as if making a decision. With a sigh, she reaches down into her handbag and pulls out the previous day's copy of the *Hull Daily Mail*. She tosses it across to Gavan, who drops his cigarette as he catches it.

'Page seven,' she says.

Gavan opens the paper and finds the page.

'The man,' she says. 'Handsome devil.'

Gavan shrugs. Closes the paper.

'You were in Full Sutton towards the end of your last stretch,' says Pharaoh. 'Did your paths cross?'

Gavan retrieves his cigarette. Lights the tiny roll of paper and tobacco and recoils as the loose end of the roll-up catches fire.

'It's a blur,' says Gavan.

'Let me help your memory. You know he was there because I've got witness statements from the guards who said you two were inseparable. He helped you out, so I'm told. Funny, that – you being the experienced con and him being the one who kept you safe.'

'Bollocks,' says Gavan, weakly.

'And when you got out in November, you did him a favour or two. You paid off a lass who was making life difficult. But the thing I can't work out is whether you actually killed her. I can imagine you losing your temper and strangling her but not cutting her armpits off. That's not your sort of thing at all.'

Gavan has gone completely still. The colour is leeching from his face, sliding down his body like a lengthening shadow.

'I never killed her,' he says, quietly. 'I swear I never.'

'The money you gave her. Did you give her all that he gave you?'

'What?'

'We both know what Hollow is capable of. If he finds out you stole from him . . .'

Gavan makes a fist. His mouth seems to shake. 'You were the copper he wouldn't stop talking about!' he says, as if he has just worked out the answer to a difficult quiz question. 'He made little statues of you out of soap. Used the edge of his phone card. Kept saying you were beautiful. That meeting you was worth getting arrested for. But he says you stitched him up. You used your looks to get him to talk and then you fucking charged him with murder.'

Pharaoh's smile remains in place though her eyes lose their lustre.

'You know what he did with the statues? He washed himself with them. Rubbed this little replica of you in every nook and cranny.'

'Did you kill Ava?' asks Pharaoh again.

'I gave her every last penny he gave me.'

'You went to her home?'

'Yes.'

'Was she grateful?'

'She said thank you. Counted it out in front of me. Pretty thing but not my type.'

'Did she say anything else?'

'Just the usual shit. Meant a lot to her. Felt awful having to ask. Tell him I'm sorry . . .'

'And when was this?'

'Weeks back. Christmas time. She were a nice lass. I wasn't lying about trying to help her.' He stops, collecting his thoughts, and when he speaks again it sounds as though he is reading a script. 'I gave her my number and said she could use me as a guarantor if her landlord kept giving her problems. It were stupid – I was just trying to do the right thing.'

'Where did you get the money?'

'Picked it up from behind the bar in Bonny Boat in the Old Town. Gift-wrapped, it was, a box tied with a bow.'

'Who left it there?'

'I don't know. Just said what I'd been told to say. That I was picking up a parcel. Landlord thought it was a birthday gift.'

'What else was in the box? You said she counted the money out in front of you.'

'Just a rock! Don't fucking ask me what that was all about.'

'And then?'

'And then I left. That was that.'

'And the story about meeting her in the Lambwath, giving your name to her landlord – was that Hollow's idea?'

'I didn't want to get my name involved but he said it would be fine. That it was just a cover. I told the missus the story about the Lambwath when the landlord kept phoning me about the rent.'

'You couldn't just tell her the truth? Or me?'

'I didn't want to be involved in any of it,' says Gavan, looking smaller somehow. 'I saw what he could do. And I owed him . . .'

Pharaoh sits back in her chair. Stretches and gives a contented sigh, as if she has just taken off her shoes and tights on a hot day.

'How come he's out?' asks Gavan quietly, suddenly looking more afraid. 'He killed that bloke. The one who attacked his daughter.'

'The evidence went away,' says Pharaoh, holding his gaze.

'I've met a lot of bad people,' says Gavan. 'I don't know what to make of Hollow. I never heard him raise his voice. Never saw him get angry. But when I was in Full Sutton and that big black fucker went for me, Hollow took him down like he was nothing. Hit him again and again and again and I don't think he broke a sweat. He's dangerous.'

'You think he hired somebody to kill Ava?'

Gavan shrugs. Looks at her with hooded eyes.

'I don't know why he would. I don't know what she had on him. Anyway, he's obsessed with you. I saw the carvings he did in the woodshop. Saw the way he looked at the little soap figurines. I wouldn't want him on the streets if I were you.'

Pharaoh leans forward. Pulls her sunglasses from her blouse and puts them on.

'He's not dangerous,' says Pharaoh. 'He's something else. He's handsome and charming and clever, and he's very, very arrogant. He's not as clever as he thinks he is but he's a lot cleverer than you. Don't be frightened of him, Jez. You're not his type.'

'His type?'

Pharaoh stands and crosses to the sofa. Takes the can of lager from Gavan's hand and takes a long swig.

She is about to say something else reassuring to Gavan when her phone bleeps and she gives a beery sigh as she answers. She says little but her face turns pale. She looks like a poker player who has laid down a triumphant hand, only to be presented with the barrel of a gun.

Pharaoh leaves without saying another word. Her mind is racing. She fumbles with her phone and feels like swearing as her head fills with Roisin's soft, lilting voice. Something about men at her home, and letting people think the wrong thing about herself and Hollow. Her brain is too frazzled to process it. She has a pain between her breasts. Can feel her heart. She starts ringing Hollow's phone, only for it to go to voicemail. She can see herself reflected in the windows of the car. Doesn't see a strong, confident woman in sunglasses and biker boots. Sees mutton, dressed as sham.

It takes her only a moment to decide.

He answers on the second ring.

'I'm sorry,' she says, by way of greeting. 'I need to see you. Hollow's been taken. I need to tell you everything.'

27

Pharaoh leans her face against the cool metal of the van door. Starts to count to ten. Makes it to three before running a hand through her hair, scoring grooves in her scalp with her fingernails with the sound of somebody ripping cotton.

It's just after 7 p.m. She's leaning against the side of an unmarked white van, parked outside a Gothic church in the tiny village of South Dalton. Blue lights are flashing through the damp muslin of fog. Uniformed officers are fastening police tape to fence posts and dry-stone walls. A man in a tweed cap is arguing with a sergeant in a high-visibility jacket, demanding to know why he can't go into the church grounds and visit the grave of an ancestor he has driven from Norfolk to see. Science officers in white suits are taking pictures of a body with a crushed head, an abandoned black gun, and Reuben Hollow's Jeep.

She looks around her. It's a gorgeous place, despite the gathering darkness and the weather. It's as English as she can imagine; all red-brick and bunting, parish council meetings and hump-backed bridges. She remembers coming here a few years ago. Anders was celebrating a new deal and wanted to splash some cash on his wife and daughters. It had been a fun night. They'd hired a private room and giggled their way through five courses and wine. It had only soured on the drive home. Anders hadn't liked how she'd looked at the waiter. Had drunk too many shots of brandy after the coffees and had lost the ability to control his insecurities. Simmered all the way home. Woke her an hour after she'd dozed off, pulling her out of bed by the hair and kicking her in the ribs with his bare feet. Sophia had stopped him. Took a smack to the mouth for her troubles.

McAvoy is still sitting in his car, looking like a kicked puppy, trying to work up the courage to come and tell her he's sorry, or that he's not, or that he hasn't got a bloody clue who he is or what he wants and needs her to make it all better.

Pharaoh turns too quickly and feels dizzy. She's weary to the bone. Can smell her own exhaustion. Can taste nothing but cigarettes. She's ignoring her bleeping phone.

Pharaoh hasn't had a drink since last night but she feels half drunk, ephemeral and half formed. She hasn't eaten all day, save the three ibuprofen she necked with a cup of machine coffee at HQ. Her fingers feel trembly. She fancies that if she were asked to type up a report, the page would fill with duplicated letters.

She needs him.

Through the darkened glass she catches his eye. Gives the tiniest jerk of her head. Tells him to get his arse inside the fluttering police tape.

In the blue darkness he is just an outline; a big, lumbering thing made of rocks. As he gets close, she sees how tired he looks. Sees the darkness beneath his eyes and the alabaster pallor of his cheeks.

She holds his stare. Manages something like a smile.

'I'm sorry for questioning you,' he says, and she can see how much he wants to turn his head away as he says it. Instead, he focuses too hard; stares, intensely, into her eyes. His damp fringe flutters in the breeze and he seems to be suppressing a shiver. Pharaoh wants to put a palm on his cheek, though whether tenderly or violently, she is not completely sure.

Pharaoh waits a moment. Closes her eyes and sorts herself out. Jerks her head and they begin walking, slowly, up through the village towards the church.

'He was working on a pew, we think,' says Pharaoh. 'He's a specialist when it comes to church work. Lecterns and lintels and all sorts of words I had to look up on Wikipedia. That's when they came for him. He went down fighting. Knows how to fight, does our boy.'

Beside her, McAvoy says nothing. He feels lost. Doesn't know how he feels about anything right now.

Pharaoh kicks at a pebble as they approach the church. Breathes out.

'You know what the Americans say about things being above people's pay grade?'

'Yes.'

'I hate all that shit,' she says, and pauses to light a cigarette. She sucks on it as if it contains answers she can absorb. Inhales it like a prayer.

McAvoy wishes he could think of something to say. He knows she is about to tell him something. Knows that if he keeps his mouth shut, he can't mess it up.

'Privilege of rank,' says McAvoy.

'Burden of it,' says Pharaoh, wryly. She shakes her head. Looks up at the church. Decides she can't bring herself to go in. Leans against the wall and looks up at her sergeant. At her friend.

'I pushed to be allowed to tell you,' she says, through a veil of smoke. 'I wanted you on the team. Turned out I was lucky to be on it myself, if lucky is even the right word. I stumbled into something. They saw a chance to draw him out. They played mind games with a psychopath and they lost.'

McAvoy waits for more. He has to stop himself from reaching out and taking the cigarette from between her lips. Has to stop himself stroking her hair and telling her it will all be okay. She doesn't even smell like Pharaoh any more. She's supposed to smell of Issey Miyake, little black cigarettes and bacon sandwiches. Here, now, she smells of lager, cheap fags and unwashed sheets.

'They think he's killed half a dozen people,' says Pharaoh, looking down. 'More. I've been building a case. He would never have fallen for an undercover operation and the only copper who tried it ended up half dead. So they picked me. Hid me in plain sight. Vulnerable. Needy. Alone. They set me up to look like a Big Mac to a starving man, and Christ, he took the bait. I had no choice. I've had nobody to talk to, Hector. Christ, I've wanted to talk.'

McAvoy stares into her eyes. Fears, for a terrible second, that she is going to let the tears overflow. Gives a tiny smile of relief when she gets control of herself, even as a hundred questions flood his brain.

'I don't even know if I believe it,' she says, grinding out her cigarette on the wall of the church and wrapping the butt in tissue. 'It's all been guesswork and supposition. This case is a career-maker, that's the trouble. They weren't content to let him go down for manslaughter. The bloke who went for him? The bloke Hollow knocked lumps out of? That wasn't an eye-catcher, not for these buggers. They wanted a headline-making case. "Britain's FBI Catch Serial Killer." You know the bollocks.'

McAvoy nods. He is beginning to understand. Knows how the National Crime Agency operates and how its worth is judged.

'The lead detective's name is Aberlour,' says Pharaoh, with a faint snarl. 'Political animal. Utter twat. Acted like I should be grateful for an opportunity to work with the elite. That was his phrase. Elite! They came to me after Shaz Archer arrested Reuben. And my life turned to shit.'

McAvoy waits for more. Holds his hands in fists as Pharaoh plays with her phone and finds the document that Aberlour sent her when she started asking the right questions of the wrong people. It was culled from psychological reports, probation papers, court hearings and intelligence work. She hands the phone to McAvoy with a small nod of warning. Lights another cigarette and watches him read.

Reuben Hollow was not so named until he was twenty-two years old. Prior to that he had been Oliver Millichamp, born in 1974. He grew up in a pleasant, rural environment and was known as a cheerful and attentive student at the village school where he was an above-average student. At eleven, he passed the exams required to allow him to attend a decent school in central York. He excelled. Displayed extraordinary abilities in the arts and English. In 1986 he was involved in an altercation in his village. He was attacked by a group of local, older teens. Oliver grabbed a paintbrush and stuck it in the neck of one of his attackers.

Though the attacker survived, Oliver was tried for unlawful wounding. Went to a juvenile detention centre for the next two years. At seventeen, he brutally beat a man he thought was harassing an elderly woman in his local Co-op. He was sent back to prison. Finished his sentence in adult jail.

Pharaoh loses patience. Can't stand to watch McAvoy read. She snatches the phone and begins spitting information at him without even looking at the text.

'Oliver Millichamp began calling himself Reuben Hollow when he got out,' she says. 'Changed his name by deed poll and disappeared from the system. It was years before he resurfaced. A Nigerian people-trafficker was found with the back of his head smashed in and pepper spray in his eyes. The victim was known to the National Crime Agency. His name was Adejola Bankole, though women called him "the devil". He was involved with an organised crime gang that brought young women over from remote parts of Africa and forced them into prostitution. A month before his death, Bankole met a young Nigerian girl off a plane at Gatwick Airport. She might have come to Britain expecting work as a cleaner or a maid but Bankole was nothing more than a pimp. He was a fucking slaver. He told her that if she didn't do as he said, her family back home would be raped and burned. She never even got out of Gatwick. He'd already sold her to some contacts in Rome. Sold her like she was meat. He gave her a new passport. Fake. Put her back on a plane – this time to Italy. They wouldn't let her in. Sent her back to her point of origin, which was Gatwick, in their eyes. She didn't know what the fuck to do. Just sat in the bar at the airport and cried into a glass of alcohol that she had no intention of drinking. And then she met a stranger. Told him, despite herself, about the devil who would do terrible things to her when he learned she had not made it to Italy. He listened. Told her not to worry. Within the week, the young woman had handed herself in to the authorities and was co-operating with the NCA in cracking the network. And Bankole was dead. The NCA used all of its toys. Facial recognition software was used on CCTV footage taken in the bar. It came up with a possible match: Oliver

Millichamp. The NCA thought they had found a major player in the organised crime world. Presumed they had identified an assassin. They tracked Millichamp to his new life as a woodcarver and caring stepfather, living in the wilds of East Yorkshire. None of what they saw added up.'

Pharaoh takes a breath. Scratches at her forehead and leaves vertical lines. 'The NCA green-lit an investigation,' she says, and the memory seems to pain her. 'Profilers were used. Cameras and recording equipment were placed in his home in the hope that Millichamp or Hollow or whatever the fuck you wanted to call him was going to start naming his gangland employers. The results were unexpected. Hollow was nobody's hired muscle. He killed when he felt it was warranted. Killed only those who deserved to die. And that's when it all got really interesting. Detective Chief Superintendent Aberlour reckoned he had identified a pattern. And that meant he had carte blanche to do what he wanted. Serial killers are recession-proof.'

McAvoy looks at Pharaoh, who is grinding out her second cigarette.

'Helen has unearthed the same thing,' he says. 'There's definitely enough to build a case.'

Pharaoh examines him. Looks upon him like a dog-lover who has just seen a Yorkshire Terrier perform an impromptu back-flip.

'They *were* building the case,' says Pharaoh, looking away. 'Aberlour's lot were getting ready to move on him when Mathers died. Archer arrested him. She didn't expect the case to get anywhere. He'd been defending himself and his victim had fallen. It was always going to be a hard one to prove. Archer lost interest so they brought me in to advise. I looked into his past. Found gaps in his back-story. Found the legal documents that Aberlour had been so excited about. Then Aberlour himself and his pet poodle, DCI Dawn Leather, got in touch with me. They were so cloak-and-dagger it was almost funny. But as soon as they got my assurances that the conversation would go no further, they played me a recording of Mathers' death. They'd bugged

258

Hollow's place, you see. Had the lot. And it was clear Hollow was telling the truth. It had just been an accident. They had struggled, and his attacker had hit his head. Aberlour had audio footage of Hollow telling the man to calm down and apologising for attacking his son.'

Pharaoh pauses. Considers another cigarette and decides against it.

'That's when they started filling me in on his past,' she says. 'They were damn sure Hollow had killed. There was circumstantial evidence by the bucket-load but they were scared. They had to remove any chance he'd wriggle free and embarrass them. They needed something concrete to pin him to one of the unsolved cases that various police forces across the UK had on their books. They told me that they were going to put an informant in his cell with him and get him to open up. But to do that, they needed to make sure he was in prison to begin with. It was up to me to make the case for Mathers' death stick. You can imagine my response.'

McAvoy gives a small snort of laughter. He can see it perfectly. Can see his mentor and idol telling them where to shove such an idea.

'I told them to get fucked,' she says, waving a hand as if this piece of information should be obvious. 'I couldn't put an innocent man away. They laughed at that. Laughed at the idea he was innocent. And then they showed me the photos of his alleged victims. I saw the damage he had done.'

'He only hurt bad people,' says McAvoy, half to himself. 'You were torn.'

'It wasn't that I agreed with Hollow,' says Pharaoh forcefully. 'I didn't think he was some sort of hero and that the streets were a safer place with him free. I just wasn't sure I believed the evidence against him, and it seemed as though Aberlour was only interested in the positive headlines it would bring his team. I honestly didn't know which way to turn, and you weren't around.'

Pharaoh shakes her head as McAvoy begins to protest.

'It wasn't your fault, Hector. You were away, building bridges with your dad. And like I say, they wouldn't have let me talk to you about it anyway. In the end I decided that the only way to know for sure would be to allow the operation. He had to go to prison so they could get answers. I had to build a case that would see him remanded into custody awaiting trial. I never expected him to be convicted. Cotteril's statement was only ever meant to be the icing on the cake. When he was found guilty, Aberlour was pretty much doing cartwheels. He hadn't been able to get his man anywhere near Hollow while he was on remand. They had him in a category C prison where the governor wouldn't play ball. But when he was convicted they sent him to a category A, and his new cellmate just happened to be a detective sergeant from Aberlour's team. The sergeant had been briefed by profilers. Had been told to make himself seem like a legitimate bodyguard figure in the eyes of his new best friend by beating the shit out of somebody vulnerable. He picked the wrong man. They'd read Reuben all wrong. When the sergeant began pounding on Jez Gavan, Hollow saw only another bully. The DS ended up in hospital and Hollow requested a new cell alongside Gavan. He saw himself as Gavan's protector. The whole damn operation was wrecked before it began. Then his lawyer began raising hell. A judicial review found that Hollow had been imprisoned on the back of potentially falsified evidence. Cotteril took enough pills to kill an elephant and left a suicide note on his home computer, admitting he had told nothing but lies and that the truth was all going to come out. Hollow was freed. Came home and the next moment he's on *Look North* like some bloody pop star.'

McAvoy presses his lips together into a tight, bloodless line and thanks his lucky stars that he will never be a detective superintendent.

'Aberlour was incandescent,' says Pharaoh, licking her teeth. 'He had to salvage something. Decided his best card was me. Hollow had warmed to me, according to Aberlour. For all that Aberlour's a prick, he has good contacts. He knew that Hollow had been sending me these little carvings . . .'

McAvoy turns away before she can see his displeasure. She notices anyway.

'I don't know what was in his mind,' she says. 'We talked a lot and I was civil with him but I don't know when he started thinking he could read my soul. Either way, he saw something in me and Aberlour wanted me to exploit that. That's why they let my name be put through the wringer. That's why it looks to all and sundry as if I'm done for. They thought he would swoop in. If all had gone right I was going to tell him about some fellow officer who was making my life a misery. That would be one of Aberlour's team. When he went for them they could make an arrest. Get him to confess to all of it. But none of it's gone to plan. I still don't even know what I believe he's guilty of. All I know is that somebody has taken him and I've got another body to deal with. And I have a horrible feeling Aberlour's going to wash his hands of the whole damn affair.'

She breathes out, slowly, as though telling the story has exhausted her. She looks for a moment as though she is going to put her hand on McAvoy's arm and squeeze it, both to give and receive reassurance. She holds herself in check. Unbidden, McAvoy gives her a clumsy pat on the shoulder. He looks at her in a way nobody else does.

'How did they meet?' he asks, half to himself and half to her. 'He corrupted her.'

'Ava?'

'Hannah. He offered her a chance at revenge. Made her sell her soul.'

'We don't know what happened yet.'

'Yes we fucking do,' says McAvoy, and he is breathing hard. There is a light in his glare that could be flame. Pharaoh holds his gaze for a full ten seconds, then breathes out.

'Do you want to go and piss off a much more senior officer?' she asks, turning away and heading back towards the crime scene. 'Keep that look on your face. Keep that fire stoked.'

'Ma'am?'

'Come in the van,' she says. 'Best behaviour. Fuck this up and you are so bloody dead.'

Pharaoh flashes a smile at the young officer who is leaning out of the back doors of the shiny white technical support van parked just inside the police cordon. She has a little more swagger in her hips and he is only too happy to confirm that yes, the secure line is set up. She's required to brief the man who has been fucking her life up for the best part of a year.

She allows the constable to help her into the van. Hears the thud as McAvoy bangs his head, followed by the sharp intake of breath as he absorbs the scene. It's a computer geek's paradise. Circuit boards blink and twinkle around a bank of computer monitors. Behind a sliding glass screen door, a small laboratory gleams with pristine whiteness. And then there's *him*. The oily prick who slithered into her life and told her that she was duty bound to let him fuck her over.

His name is Detective Chief Superintendent Aberlour. Iain, to his friends. He's perhaps fifty, with a lugubrious, sallow face, a mouth like a child's drawing of a clown and hair brushed forward in a Mod cut. He has dark, attractive eyes, and though his belly is never in shot, Pharaoh fancies that he has a loose gut, sticking out from a pencil-thin body like a petulant lower lip. She knows little about him, but rumour has it that in his youth, he was a member of the Young Conservatives and is a regular dinner party guest at the private quarters of the Home Secretary.

'Trish,' he says, as if they are old friends. 'A treat to see you, even considering the circumstances. You look tired. Pull up a chair. Any sign of Dawn yet? She said she was en route, but it's a hell of a drive. And I see you've brought a giant. I trust there are operational reasons? You remember the part about "absolutely nobody", yes?'

Pharaoh plasters on a smile. Pulls up a swivel chair and sits in front of the computer monitor. Wonders if it would be a sacking offence to light a cigarette.

'Sir,' she says, in the non-committal voice of somebody who has been dealing with superior wankers for twenty-five years. 'No sign of Dawn, no. I've sent a patrol car to guide her in from the bridge. The fog is getting thicker. She may struggle. This is my sergeant. He is here because he has my absolute confidence and respect and because he is dangerously close to working this all out for himself.'

Detective Chief Superintendent Aberlour sucks in his cheeks. Then he gives an appreciative nod.

'Keep trying Dawn, yes?'

'Yes, sir.'

Neither officer admits it, but they would not trust DCI Dawn Leather to find her way in from the city limits if it was broad daylight and she was following a marching band. She is good at one thing only, and that is agreeing with Aberlour. It is a skill that has seen her rise high.

'We're alone, yes?' asks Aberlour, giving a theatrical peer down the lens. 'And Sergeant, may I impress upon you the absolute secrecy of what you are about to hear?'

Pharaoh turns and rolls her eyes. She's about to give the universal sign for "wanker" and try to make McAvoy laugh, but she sees he is earnestly staring at the computer screen and nodding his assent. She feels like sighing. Instead she gives the van another once-over. The young science officer has closed the door behind him. There is nobody to interrupt them. Nobody to back her up, come to that.

'We're alone, sir.'

Aberlour gives a long sigh. 'Bad business,' he says, shaking his head. 'You remember the word we used a lot when this began? "Containment"?'

Pharaoh allows her temper to become a quick, angry smile. 'I do, sir. And I remember saying how hard it was going to be.'

Aberlour sits forward. Shows his distaste at her answer. 'Nevertheless,' he says, in clipped tones, 'we didn't expect this.'

'No?' asks Pharaoh, feigning innocence. 'Extraordinary.'

They stare at one another through the computer screen. Pharaoh met him once, as a younger man, but recalls little of consequence. Has vague memories of oily hair and manicured nails. Remembers the way he spoke to her, as if constantly on the verge of saying his goodbyes. Here was a man whose time was precious, and who only employed good manners when he needed to.

Despite his surname, he has no Scottish accent. If he is Scottish, he has rubbed the brogue off his shoe.

'We're certain, yes? No room for doubt?'

Pharaoh shakes her head. 'A single gunshot was reported at just after four p.m. Patrol car despatched immediately and the Armed Response Unit was immediately notified. They found the victim. Found Hollow's car.'

Aberlour digests this. 'Any of his blood?'

'Your people are working on it, sir. They're faster than ours but it still takes time.'

'And the victim?'

'Hot off the press, sir. Dorian Foley. Twenty-four. Released last year from Belmarsh. Thought to have a couple of hits to his name and we know for a fact he's dabbled in dealing and armed robbery. May have come to the attention of some serious players recently. Talent-spotted, you might say.'

Aberlour nods. Sucks his teeth. 'Usual MO?'

'Irritant in the eyes and back of the head caved in? Yes, sir. Looks like Hollow went down fighting.'

Pharaoh tries to remain impassive as she speaks, but something inside her creaks a little. The dam she has built around her imagination begins to give. For a second she imagines Hollow, bound and vulnerable, having his beautiful face turned into a mosaic by men he would never have encountered had she said 'no' all those months ago. Guilt dances in her eyes. She has to fight not to let it control her. Thoughts flash like tongues of fire in the back of her mind. She remembers Roisin's garbled message. Thinks fast. Talks fast.

'Foley's associates?' asks Aberlour.

Pharaoh breathes out slowly. 'I'm sure you know them better than I do, sir.'

Aberlour considers this for a moment. In the cool of the van, Pharaoh watches LEDs flicker. Watches tiny test tubes shake and spin beyond the glass door; DNA evidence being fast-tracked by the kind of mobile support vehicle her team could never afford.

'Teddy Tracy,' says Aberlour. 'Forty-eight years old. He's spent twelve years of his adult life in prison for various spells. Last known to be working for Dieter Helfrich. East European. Rumoured to have recently gone into business with some old friends of yours.'

Pharaoh makes a fist beneath the level of the camera. Digs her nails into her knees and ladders her tights.

'They're no friends of mine. The Headhunters abandoned Hull when Piers Fordham died. We know that. If they've moved on then Humberside Police can offer nothing but expertise. Drugs and protection are back in the hands of morons in this area, sir.'

Aberlour allows himself a smile. Nods in appreciation.

'We won't be getting Hollow back,' he says cautiously. 'He's dead already, we can say that with certainty. From here on in, this is a damage limitation exercise.'

Pharaoh pulls a face, unable to hide the strength of her disagreement 'We don't know that at all. What about the damage to Hollow?'

'He's a killer,' says Aberlour, with a warning note creeping into his voice. 'He got longer to play than he expected.'

Pharaoh's thoughts speed up. She had expected this. Knew, when she got the call and an urgent request to head to South Dalton, that a covert operation was about to become an exercise in media spin.

'We don't do that, sir,' she says, tight-lipped. 'We don't leave people to their fates. I don't, anyway. I joined the police to stop bad people doing bad things.'

'Then you can sleep easy, Detective Superintendent. Come tomorrow, Hollow will be doing no more bad things to anybody.'

Beside her, she can feel McAvoy's presence. She wants to reach out and squeeze his hand. Resists.

Pharaoh cannot help but remember her first conversation with Aberlour. Cannot help but remember the way he sailed, elegantly, into her life, and told her that she had unwittingly got involved in a case she had no business investigating.

'You're going to lay this at my door,' says Pharaoh. 'I can see it in your eyes. This was your baby, sir. You were the one who was supposed to monitor his every movement when he got out.'

Aberlour looks as though he has just swallowed something a millennium or two past its sell-by date. 'We have a skeleton crew in the north,' he says, bristling. 'And in the fog, he was impossible to follow.'

Pharaoh can contain her temper no longer. She reaches into her handbag and pulls out a cigarette. Lights it and angrily inhales.

'Have you read the papers, sir? Do you realise what I've had to put up with for this? My name is synonymous with being shit. I'll take that, if it gets a bad man off the streets. I'll be the laughing stock. But since Hollow came out, we've found two bodies. Two innocent girls with links to him.'

'I'm well aware of the cases you're referring to,' Aberlour retorts. 'What's your point?'

'My point, you ineffable dickhead, is that we allowed this to happen. These girls are dead because we were worrying about how this would all play out politically rather than locking up a man we knew to be a killer. And I swear to God, if you hang Hollow out to dry, I'll tell anybody who will listen that you were the one who made the decisions that left bodies all over the fucking county.'

There is silence in the van. Aberlour seems to be working out the different permeations of his next words. After a spell, he gives a half-smile.

'We still have a trace in his phone,' he says. 'If Hollow's alive, it would not be hard to find him.'

Pharaoh gives the tiniest of nods. Smokes her cigarette down to the filter. Licks her palm and stubs it out.

'It would be better if he didn't come back,' continues Aberlour. 'Despite our best efforts, this hasn't worked out as we had hoped. I realise it has been especially difficult on you, given the very public nature of your humiliation over this case. Despite that, I am aware that you feel some degree of responsibility for his wellbeing.'

Pharaoh says nothing. Wonders who was listening as she tried to get Hollow to trust her. Wonders who was laughing and elbowing their mates as she tried to kiss her prime suspect, and was knocked back.

266

'He doesn't deserve to die,' says Pharaoh eventually. 'We can't do that. We don't do that. He has a daughter . . .'

Aberlour gives the tiniest of shrugs. 'This game is built on favours, Trish. Favours and reputations. I can help you. I can help you in your ambitions. I can help those close to you.'

'Don't start that shit,' says Pharaoh, waving a hand. 'My team are all good officers.'

Aberlour stares back at her, sucking on his lower lip.

'I can't be a party to Hollow's death,' says Pharaoh, and it takes an effort for the words to come out strong. Her affection for him has been genuine. Her desire authentic. But she would never have allowed anything romantic to happen. She only gives a damn about one man: a man she is about to send into a hell she only wishes she could accompany him through.

'You said you could find him,' says Pharaoh. 'You want me onside, you let me try and save him.'

'Hollow?' asks Aberlour, incredulous. 'He's already in the ground. You know that.'

Pharaoh shakes her head. 'You clean up this shit the way you see fit. But we're as guilty as Hollow over this whole mess and I won't sit idly by while somebody kills him. His daughter deserves the chance to understand him properly. So do I. I need a grid reference, that's all. Then I'll say what you fucking want.'

Aberlour remains silent for a long time. Clicks his tongue against the roof of his mouth. Plays with the name badge on his black suit.

'Kid gloves, Patricia,' he says at last. 'Just you and your giant, here. Don't make waves. Your only brief is to find him. We can tell you where his phone is, if not necessarily him. But you need to limit your resources. You need to leave the media to us. You do what you must. If you somehow get him out alive, he's going to prison for whatever the hell we can get him on. He can't be on the streets to tell this story.'

Pharaoh isn't paying attention. She's pushing McAvoy out of the van; all but slapping his back in her haste to get back in the fresh air. She slams the door shut behind herself. Turns to McAvoy and gives him her most penetrating glare.

267

'Somebody has to be with his daughter,' she says, chewing her lip. 'Somebody she knows. She'll be scared. She'll need to talk.'

McAvoy considers her. Feels shabby even as he asks the question. 'You think she knows what he's been doing? That she'll give a statement?'

Pharaoh looks away. 'She's a good girl. She's already been through hell. And she's all alone in that place.' She looks up at McAvoy, her eyes intense and ferocious. 'You don't have to do any of this. You don't have any sins to atone for. But if you save him, you'll help me atone for mine.'

McAvoy stays silent for a minute, then, 'I'll find him,' he says. 'We can atone together.'

Watching him run to his car, Pharaoh realises she has never had a better offer.

PART FOUR

28

Teddy pulls the paper towels away from his temple and looks at the ugly blot of blood. It resembles Australia. There's a patch of skin somewhere near Brisbane.

He scowls. Spits. There is a jagged white line of pain down his vision, as though the scene before him is a photograph, ripped in two and then placed back together. He feels as though there is a creature inside his skull, kicking at the bone as if it were a stubborn door. He tries to ignore it. Teddy has always been known as a hard case. He can take this. Can do what must be done, even with a suspected skull fracture and an overwhelming urge to lie down and fall asleep for a very long time.

He screws up his eyes. Focuses on the man who lies on the cold floor of the big empty barn, which is patterned with straw and dried shit, like an uncooked joint marinated in too many herbs. His wrists and ankles are bound behind him with tie-wraps. He's lying half on his side, staring up with blue eyes that put Teddy in mind of a Siberian husky. Despite the blood crusted in his hairline, he is smiling a little, staring up at Teddy as if this is all part of the plan.

'Comfy, you fuck?' Teddy kicks him in the ribs. 'Don't you dare smile at me.'

Hollow grunts with the impact. Presses his lips together and folds the smile into a tight, thin line.

It doesn't smell as bad in the barn as Teddy had anticipated. He doesn't know how regularly it is used but the cow shit has long since dried and the overwhelming aroma is of damp straw. Occasionally, the stench of the nearby pig farm assails Teddy's nostrils but he is too far gone on adrenaline and temper to pay it much attention. He doubts they will be interrupted. The building lies down a pitted track, half a mile to the rear of Humberside Airport. The planes have all been grounded due to the fog, which has rolled across the Humber and into this patch of Northern Lincolnshire. Teddy struggled to find the turn-off from the country road. Had to double-back and risk collision with an oncoming 4x4 before he swung the car onto the narrow track and began jolting, painfully, towards the building that Foley had identified soon after their arrival in the area. They had planned to teach Trish Pharaoh about respect within its confines. Had planned to have themselves quite the time. Instead, he needs to get his hands dirty with the stranger who made him and his partner look like fools, and who left Foley dying on the ground.

As he stands above Reuben Hollow, Teddy feels sadness bloom inside his chest. He had cared for Foley. Cared for him more than he allowed himself to acknowledge. Teddy has several children by different women but has never been a part of their lives. He realises, too late, that he had come to think of Foley as a son. Enjoyed his company. Liked the way he talked. Sure, he'd fucked the young lad more times than he could count while they were cellmates, but that had been more about comfort than control. It was different on the outside. They were more than friends. They shared something. Trusted one another. And Teddy had been forced to watch him die.

He boots Hollow in the ribs again. Enjoys his grimace.

He walks back to the car. The doors are open and the headlights are on, throwing a sodium glow into the mist and darkness. Shadows play upon the rear wall of the barn. Each time Hollow moves his bound legs, his knees cast the silhouette of a mountain range onto the corrugated iron and brick of the curving roof.

Teddy reaches inside the car. Pulls out the nailgun and blowtorch. The two items had cost him more than £300. He'd made a mental note at the time to add the expense to his tab for the job. Wonders, for a second, how much more he is now going to make given that he won't need to pay Foley.

'You ready for this?' asks Teddy. As he walks into the patch of light cast by the headlamps, he feels as though he is walking onto a stage. Feels as though black velvet curtains are parting for him. He's tempted to take a bow.

Hollow isn't gagged. Teddy wants to hear him scream. He'll only shove the paper towels down his throat if the noise makes his headache any worse.

'We doing a spot of DIY?' asks Hollow, from the floor. 'It's not really my speciality. Can't even change a bulb, though I could sculpt you a beautiful replica.'

Teddy gives a slight shake of his head. He has stood over plenty of hardened criminals who have tried bravado in the face of pain. Their eyes always give them away. By the end, they are invariably snivelling and begging for mercy in a pool of their own piss. He sees none of that in Hollow's face. Sees absolutely nothing in those cold, blue eyes.

'I've never tried this before,' says Teddy, giving the nailgun a theatrical flourish. 'I've kicked people's kneecaps off before. Once had a job where I had to break an amateur boxer's hands and unhinge his jaw. That was a bit unpleasant. I think he'd won a fight he wasn't meant to. Can't really remember. They all blend in and you shouldn't really ask too many questions. This nailgun stuff turns my stomach, if I'm honest. Can't think of it without wincing. But these are changing times and old buggers like me have to evolve. Adapt or perish, that's what they say, isn't it? So I've just got to go through with it.'

'You don't,' says Hollow, raising his head. 'You could leave well alone. You could get yourself back down south and disappear for a while. I promise you, this isn't going to end well for you. You don't seem a terrible person. Your partner, he struck me as a bully. You just seem like a pragmatist. And the pragmatic thing to do is get in your car and drive away.'

Teddy chews his lip. Realises he's doing it. Stops and shakes his head.

'You've got balls, mate. You do intrigue me. I've done my reading up on you and there's no doubt you're an interesting man. I don't blame you for smashing the shit out of those lads who messed with your daughter. I don't know how any of that could be considered a crime. But you got in the way. Foley and me were only here to do a job. That copper. Her husband owed a lot of money to a very important man. We were here to get it back. I'm told that you're quite the rich man, so you've got a golden opportunity here. You can save her life by giving me your account details, or telling me where it's stashed. That was all we wanted. But right now, I think I want to hurt you more than I want to rob you. So I'm going to do some horrible shit to you and any time you feel like telling me where you keep your money, we'll have a little break, yeah? And if you're telling the truth, I'll stop hurting you. I'll still kill you, but the pain will be over.'

Hollow keeps his eyes on Teddy's. From the floor, he gives a little nod, as if they have reached an understanding.

Teddy moves forward. Reaches down to grab Hollow's shirt and drag him into a seating position. Gets a smell of him. Sawdust and soil. Varnish and metal. Takes his switchblade from the pocket of his trousers and cuts the tie-wraps that hold Hollow's wrists behind his back. Places the blade to his neck and speaks, slowly and deliberately.

'Put your hands on your knees. Palms down. You move, I'm going to open your throat and deal with the consequences later.'

Hollow licks his lips. The blade is already pricking at his skin.

'You're going to kill me anyway,' he says. 'Why put myself through it?'

Teddy digs the knife in. The tip slides a few millimetres into his throat. Warm blood runs down his neck and over Teddy's hand.

'Where there's life, there's hope. You've got a daughter. Your only job is to stay alive as long as you can. And to do that, you've got to put up with what's about to happen.'

Slowly, Hollow brings his hands forward. Places his palms over his kneecaps. Teddy readjusts his position. Keeps the blade against Hollow's throat and flicks the safety on the nailgun. Brings it around and places the point on the back of Hollow's hand. Winces as he pulls the trigger.

Nothing happens. Teddy tries again. Curses as he raises the

weapon to his face. Blows on the muzzle, as if trying to dislodge fluff. Looks at the safety catch and realises it's stuck between two settings. Pushes it all the way across. Looks down the barrel again and sees the nail, long and deadly, waiting to be fired through skin and bone.

Realises, despite his headache and his churning guts, that he's rather looking forward to this.

29

McAvoy holds the mobile phone in his left hand and swings the Volvo through the gap in the hedge with his right. He shouldn't be driving. The world is dirty glass and cobwebs. He can barely see more than a car length in front of him and he keeps losing the signal from his sat-nav.

The front tyre hits a pothole and he lurches to his left. Drops the phone in the footwell and swears. He feels sick. Adrenaline is making his hands shake. He's making fists with his toes inside his boots. Sweat is running into his eyes and making his shirt stick to his skin. He knows these feelings too well. Has been here, in this world of fear and duty, too many damn times.

From the footwell comes the beep of a new message. Probably Pharaoh again. Another plea to be careful. Another demand for an update. He takes a moment's glee in making her wait and knowing she's worrying about him, then feels wretched for the cruel impulse. He has every right to feel less than generous towards Pharaoh. She has played on his emotions. Played on what she knows about him. Played on his feelings for her and the fact that if he ignored her plea for help, he would never sleep well again.

He tells himself to relax. Hollow's phone is somewhere up ahead. Whether it is still on Hollow's person is anybody's guess. If the men who have him are true professionals they will have dumped his phone the second they took him. But as far as McAvoy knows, this track is not a through-road. He can see no good reason why Hollow's captors would drive down this muddy strip at the back of Humberside Airport just to dispose of his phone.

Through the fog, he sees the shape of a large, abandoned farm building emerge from the mist like an iceberg. He slows down.

Drifts forward and sees a patch of light and a nondescript vehicle with its doors open.

McAvoy stops the car. He wishes he had a plan. He has read every guideline and textbook on the importance of waiting for backup. He doesn't even know how many people he is facing, or whether they are armed. A gun was found at the scene of Hollow's abduction. A whole armed response unit should have been mobilised. But Aberlour is trying to limit the damage and refusing to make a move until he has worked out every possible angle. Hollow could be dead before then. Could be dead already. He doesn't know how he feels about that. If Hollow killed Hannah and Ava on top of all the men he is suspected of bludgeoning to death, McAvoy needs to see him in the witness box, being sent down for life in front of the families of his victims. He cannot bring himself to wish death upon him.

He forces himself to move. To do what he must.

Instinctively, McAvoy flicks the headlights of the car to full beam as he opens the door. Steps onto a patch of uneven ground and stumbles a little. Looks up just as a nine-inch nail whistles past his ear and smashes the glass in the door.

He throws himself to the ground. Looks at the scene illuminated by both sets of headlights.

A figure, crouching behind another. He has a blade in one hand and a large, fat-barrelled nailgun in the other. Dangerous, but not necessarily deadly.

He ducks back behind the car door. Wonders what the hell to do. Thinks about reaching down for a stone and throwing it at the gunman and finds himself laughing at his own hopelessness.

From the barn, there is a sudden, angry shout. McAvoy ducks his head out from behind the car.

Hollow has smashed his head back into the jaw of the man behind him. The blade has gone skittering away into the dark.

McAvoy runs through the blinding light and launches himself at the two men scuffling on the floor.

The trio go down in a tangle of limbs. McAvoy feels his head bang against a kneecap. Feels damp clothes and cold skin.

Scrabbles to his feet just as Reuben Hollow grabs the nailgun and swivels away.

Teddy's scream is a raw, animal thing that rips through the fog and the darkness and causes the pigs in the neighbouring field to screech in accompaniment. He looks down. Blood is already seeping through his shoes to puddle on the dirty floor. It comes as a relief when Hollow hits him in the face and unconsciousness takes him. He collapses to the ground, nailed to the floor.

Hollow turns to McAvoy. Smiles, as if they are standing at a bar.

'You're that copper. Her friend.'

McAvoy feels as though he is going to collapse. There's warm blood on his face where his wound has reopened.

'Give me the gun,' says McAvoy, and there is no disguising the tremble in his voice.

Hollow looks at the weapon as if seeing it for the first time. Then he hands it over, obediently.

McAvoy wonders what to say next. Wonders if he should arrest him or tell him that it's all okay and he's going to be safe.

Hollow makes his mind up for him. Drops his head and his shoulders begin to heave. His legs give out and he falls to the ground.

'Thank you,' he says, snuffling into his hand. 'I thought I was going to die.'

McAvoy stands still for a moment. Then he surreptitiously finds the knife with his boot and stands upon it. He crouches down and pockets the blade.

He feels the adrenaline begin to leave his system. Feels the familiar sickness and weakness. Feels the same damn need to fall on his belly and let Roisin stroke his hair.

He moves forward and puts an arm around Hollow's shoulders.

Doesn't notice the lack of tears as the smaller man weeps against his chest.

30

9.06 p.m.

A strip of road with no real name, somewhere grim off the A18.

An abandoned outbuilding between an old dairy farm and Humberside Airport, its metal roof rising above the trees like a bald scalp.

Three men, in a dying circle of light. Two lean against the bonnet of a sensible family car, staring at one another like chess masters. The third is a little way behind them, in the open doorway of the barn. He's sitting up, clutching at his foot, threatening bloody murder and shielding his eyes from the glare of the headlamps.

Helen Tremberg climbs out of her Citroën. Takes in the scene before her and decides she will leave the most intense of her questions until later. Penelope is with Helen's dad, who was good enough not to sigh when Helen called him and told him she needed another favour.

'Sarge,' says Helen, raising her torch and flicking it on to illuminate the broad back of her superior officer. She flicks the light upwards. Takes in the familiar face of a bleeding man. 'Mr Hollow.'

Helen turns towards the dark opening of the barn.

'He won't give us his name,' says McAvoy, gesturing at the man, who is baring his teeth like a cornered fox. 'His wallet belongs to an Edward Tracy. South London. He's not poor. Belongs to a couple of private members' clubs with names that rang a bell. I thought you might like to make the arrest.'

Helen holds her sergeant's gaze. He's fuzzy and indistinct in the fog. There's blood on his eyebrow. Blood on the neck of the man to his left.

Another scar, she thinks. *Another bleeding medal.*

'This is the gentleman who abducted you?' asks Helen, looking at Hollow. He's good-looking, up close. Dazzling eyes. But she'd expected more swagger. More style. He looks humbled and broken. His eyes are red-seamed and his lower lip seems to tremble as he nods.

'And he isn't running away because . . . ?'

McAvoy looks momentarily awkward. 'He's nailed to the floor.'

Helen sucks her teeth. Looks impressed. 'DIY can be fraught with danger – my dad told me that. He's a clever guy. He's the one who told me never to cut the grass in flip-flops.'

McAvoy pushes himself off the car bonnet. He looks tired, dirty and sad.

'The boss?' asks Tremberg.

'Following a lead,' says McAvoy, looking away. 'Going to tell Mr Hollow's daughter that he's quite well.'

'Going to be fun for the press,' says Helen, looking around. 'I'm picturing a zeppelin full of shit and a desk fan the size of Scunthorpe.'

'It doesn't need to be,' says Hollow quietly. He's taken his box of tobacco from his back pocket and is trying to roll a cigarette with shaking fingers. 'There are ways to play this right. I need to speak to Delphine. There are things that need to be sorted out . . .'

McAvoy turns fierce eyes on Hollow. Shakes his head. 'You received help because that's the way things have to be. But don't go thinking you're the victim here. You have a lot of questions to answer.'

Hollow looks puzzled. He hasn't spoken much, just sat and stared. A little while ago he remembered his mobile phone was still in his pocket. Took it out and looked at a smashed, dead screen.

'Questions?'

'Hannah Kelly,' says McAvoy. 'Ava Delaney. So many more.'

Helen steps closer. Tries her luck. 'Bruce Corden. Dennis Ball. A dozen damsels in distress. There are jigsaw pieces slamming together like tectonic fucking plates in my head, matey.'

Hollow lights his cigarette. Takes a drag that seems to calm him.

'I'll talk to DSU Pharaoh,' he says. 'I need to talk to somebody who understands.'

'You can talk to me,' says McAvoy, changing tone and suddenly addressing him the way he would talk to a nervous animal. 'A lot of people find me a good listener. And you can get it off your chest without there being any tape recorders. I don't know how this is all going to play out. You're a killer. I don't know how many bodies you're responsible for or how you turned Hannah's head but I know for a fact you've got blood on your hands.'

Hollow looks at Helen. Gives her the briefest once-over. Cocks his head and talks only to her.

'How's the baby?' he asks.

Helen looks surprised. Wonders whether McAvoy told him that the colleague he called in to help him clean this up was going to be a while because she has a new kid.

'She's well, thank you,' says Helen warily.

'A girl, then.'

'Yes.'

McAvoy catches her eye. Shakes his head. He hasn't told him.

'You smell of formula,' says Hollow gently, by way of explanation. 'And baby wipes. Can't be easy, looking after a child of that age and being a cop. You have my respect.'

Helen stares into the man's blue eyes. She's been charmed by slick bastards like him before. Won't be charmed again.

'This bollocks usually work, does it?' says Helen, looking hard at Hollow. 'Works on impressionable, frightened women, right? Do I look fucking impressionable, matey? Do I look frightened? Tell us the truth.'

Hollow seems taken aback. Drops his head a little. Looks up at her with his head on one side again, like a puppy begging forgiveness. McAvoy wants to hit him in the face.

'I've spoken to David Hogg,' says McAvoy, staring at the side of Hollow's head. 'He told me everything.'

Hollow wipes his face. 'Who's David Hogg?'

'He drove his car into a horse and rider out towards Great

Givendale. Somebody took revenge on him. Smashed him in the face with a horse-shoe in a sock.'

'Sounds like he deserved it. But why are you telling me?'

'The horse used to belong to Hannah Kelly.'

Hollow looks blank.

'She went missing several months ago. Her body was found yesterday, lying on a bed of flowers outside my front door.'

Hollow grimaces. 'That's horrible,' he says. 'This Hogg character. Did he do it?'

McAvoy catches the aroma of pigs as the breeze picks up. Feels it upon his face. Hopes, for a moment, that the wind will blow away the grey clouds that tangle around him in tattered folds and make him feel as though he is wearing a monk's sodden habit.

'You knew Hannah Kelly,' says McAvoy. 'I'm sure you did.'

Hollow looks from one officer to the other. Turns his head to where his former captor sits, still clutching his foot, upon the barn floor.

'Why do you think that?' he asks, pinching out his roll-up between finger and thumb and putting the stub in his pocket. 'I've been in jail for months.'

He seems cross, just for an instant.

'This is a set-up, isn't it? You're recording me. Does this prick work for you lot? I've made you look silly and you want me back inside. Christ, I'd have thought better of Trish. I thought we were getting somewhere.'

McAvoy stands up. Begins to pace. Stalks towards the barn and slaps some tie-wrap cuffs on Teddy's wrists. Teddy accepts it, offering his hands without complaint. McAvoy gives him a companionable squeeze on the shoulder. Makes sure Hollow can see.

'It's Detective Superintendent Pharaoh,' he says, turning a hard stare on Hollow. 'It's not "Trish". She's not your friend. She was the senior officer who charged you with murder. I was away at the time. I didn't get to know you properly. But I'm starting to. And I think in your own mind you're some sort of hero. You kill bullies. Nasty people. You do it for pretty, vulnerable women, and you bask in the glory of knowing that you're some modern-day Sir

Lancelot. I think that if Helen here told you about some scumbag in her life, before long, that scumbag would end up dead. I think that somehow you met Hannah Kelly and she told you about how David Hogg had got away with killing her old horse. You battered David Hogg half to death. Made a video of it on Hogg's phone and sent it to Hannah. But she asked you not to kill him. Rang you straight back and said that he had suffered enough. And because in your world you're some sort of knight errant, you did her bidding. You let him live. She fell for you. Persuaded herself you were her knight in shining armour. And she became a nuisance. So you arranged to meet her, and you killed her. Kept her body God knows where, then decided to start playing games as soon as you got out. You left her for me to find.'

Hollow is rolling another cigarette. His face is impassive but his eyes are hard.

'You did the same with Ava Delaney,' says McAvoy, talking faster than he can think. 'Killed her ex-boyfriend because he was battering her. And I think she wanted money to keep the secret. So as soon as you got out of prison you drugged her and killed her. You've tricked us with the dates, somehow. You must have done. We've got your DNA on a handkerchief we found at her home.'

Hollow holds up a hand. Lights his cigarette. Takes a drag and pushes out a lungful of grey.

'You're wrong,' he says. 'DNA? I've told Trish, I met Ava at the hospital. I dried her eyes.'

'That was almost a year ago.'

'No . . .' he stops himself. 'I wiped her eyes with my handkerchief. Like people do. I must have not got it back from her. That doesn't mean anything. It's horrible that she's been hurt. I felt like crying when I heard.'

Hollow puts the hand holding the cigarette to his forehead. Looks, briefly, like a pilot fish.

'You've been doing this a long time,' says Helen, thinking of how the pieces slot together. He fits the description. Would have been able to read Yvonne Turpin's soul in her teary eyes. 'I don't think you've killed anybody that the world would mourn. I think you've probably done a lot of people a lot of good turns. But those girls . . .'

Hollow stands. Winces, as his bruised ribs sing with pain. Takes a hard drag on his cigarette.

'I need to talk to Trish,' he says, looking agitated. 'She understands. She understands me . . .'

'Detective Superintendent Pharaoh is with your daughter,' says McAvoy. 'She's going to tell her that Daddy was hurt by some nasty men but he's okay now. A bit shaken up, but okay.'

Hollow sneers. Grinds his teeth. 'That's not what happened.'

'She hero-worships you, that girl,' says McAvoy. 'She'll be pleased to know you're safe. Pleased you didn't get hurt.'

Hollow is shaking his head. 'You're setting me up. This wasn't me.'

'You've killed a man already today,' says McAvoy, pulling out his phone. 'Dorian Foley. Bad lad, but it's still murder. Manslaughter, at the very least. I doubt a jury will buy another case of self-defence. I mean, lightning does strike twice sometimes, but it's hard to accept. The top brass would love to show they were right about prosecuting you. You're just too dangerous to be allowed out on the streets.'

Hollow's stance changes. He looks as though he is preparing to lash out or run. Subtly, Tremberg reaches into the pocket of her raincoat. Closes her fingers around the extendable baton and wonders, for a moment, how badly she is going to get hurt.

The three stand in silence for a moment, considering one another. In the darkness of the barn, Teddy bleeds onto the floor. In a dark corner of the building, his phone is silently ringing; a demand for an update from his employer, amid worrying whispers that one of his boys has got himself killed in the back of beyond.

'Let me see my daughter,' says Hollow, and his shoulders seem to sag. 'I can explain. I just need to see her. And Trish, too. Sorry, Detective Superintendent Pharaoh. I can't have them thinking I'm some sort of thug. It's not like that. You don't understand.'

McAvoy turns to Tremberg. Wishes, as he does so, that Pharaoh were standing next to him, telling him what to do. He imagines, for a moment, how it would feel to walk into the custody suite at Priory Road with Reuben Hollow in handcuffs and a case for serial murder already made against him. Wonders if it would be enough to wipe away the last smudges of stain upon his name. Whether Pharaoh would thank him or curse him. He closes his eyes. Knows how it would play out; how the brass would respond. Knows that before dawn, Hollow would be out, talking to the press about the rogue elements within Humberside Police who continue their vendetta against him. McAvoy is confident they have enough evidence to charge him but he knows himself to be hopeless at all the politics that come with a high-profile case. Pharaoh is his guide in all things hierarchical and until he takes her advice, he isn't sure what to do next. He needs to see her before he acts.

'We need to get medical help for this bloke,' says Helen, nodding towards Teddy. 'He's bleeding. We're shooting holes in our own prosecution if we don't start doing some of this properly. Sarge, right now Hollow is a victim. He's been abducted and hurt. You haven't read him his rights and you've questioned him on a double murder. This isn't how you do things. He needs to be checked over. Needs to give a statement. Leave me with this guy. Get Hollow to hospital. Get him in the system.' She stops herself. Looks hard at Hollow. 'Raymond O'Neill. He one of yours?'

Hollow holds her gaze, the faintest of smiles at the corners of his mouth.

'Is there anybody you think I didn't kill?'

'I don't know,' says Helen, looking at his hands as if expecting to see them bathed in blood. 'Sarge?'

McAvoy looks at her as if seeing her properly for the first time. Sees the young, ambitious detective constable who has suffered time and again through her willingness to do his bidding. She's right. She's here, now, standing in the dark and willing to do whatever he says, when she should be at home with her baby, or at the very least, safe behind a desk. And then he winces at his own thoughts. Realises how easily he could convince himself to think like Hollow, that he could too easily see the women in his life as frail and vulnerable flowers who need the protection of a big, strong man, and hates himself for his instincts. He remembers the stories his dad used to tell him, all about knights and noble warriors. Remembers the zeal in his father's eyes as he recounted yarns about Rob Roy MacGregor, Wallace and De Moray. He wonders if he became a policeman for any other reason than a need to see the gratitude of damsels in distress. McAvoy met his wife by saving her. There's something more than admiration in the eyes of Helen Tremberg because he has saved her, too. He wonders, here and now, whether he would kill for Pharaoh, but he knows the answer in his bones.

'I need to see Delphine,' says Hollow again. 'Please.'

McAvoy gives the slightest of nods and turns to Helen.

'Babysit him,' he says, nodding at Teddy. 'Make the arrest yourself, so whoever gets to run with this has no choice but to involve you. Do things properly. I'll try and do the same.'

Helen wishes he would look at her properly, but he seems too lost in his own thoughts. She wishes he would shake her hand or slap her on the back. Forces herself to think professionally. She has an opportunity here, the chance to put herself back on the frontline. She has no doubt that the man on the floor of the barn is linked to organised crime. She knows little of the incident at South Dalton but it has the feeling of a gangland piece of work. And the presence of the nailgun is significant. The weapon was the favoured tool of the gang that she and Colin Ray helped bring down. She has seen it used on the outfit's enemies and competitors. If this man has some link to the Headhunters, she wants to question him. Wants to ask him about Colin Ray. She realises just how hard she has worked to avoid thinking about her former boss. She does not believe Shaz Archer. Does not believe that Ray is sunning himself somewhere with another future ex-wife. She last saw him on his way to tell Archer that they knew who was behind the organisation. That same night, the suspect was beaten to death and Colin Ray disappeared. Half a picture forms in her mind. It disappears, snatched away like a flame on the breeze, but she keeps pushing. Keeps trying to make connections. Barely registers McAvoy's hand on her shoulder or his words of thanks as he leads Hollow to his car.

Helen walks to the barn. Flashes her torch in the face of Edward Tracy.

'Headhunters,' says Helen, as she hears McAvoy's car pull away. 'You heard of them?'

Teddy looks at her quizzically. Registers something in her gaze and gives a sigh. 'Is it always like this, up here?' he asks, through the pain. 'North, I mean. It's fucking mental, love.'

Helen finds the enthusiasm to smile. She squats down in front of the bleeding man and stares into a face that looks deathly pale. There are bags under his eyes and blood on his face.

'Your friend didn't make it,' she says, not unkindly. 'I'm sure you already knew that. But if you thought he might have pulled through, you were wrong. Why did you want Hollow?'

Teddy rolls his eyes. 'Like I'm going to tell you. I'm not speaking again until my lawyer's next to me, and even then, I'll only say what he tells me to.'

Helen nods. She stands up, and her knees crack as she does so. She thinks about how to proceed. Has the first spark of an idea.

Out of the corner of her eye, she sees a spot of blue light, flickering in the darkness. She crosses to the rear of the barn and finds Teddy's phone amid a mess of straw and dirt. There have been several missed calls. Half a dozen texts, each containing nothing more than a question mark. A picture message, showing the front of a run-down, three-storey house, all loose gutters and dirty curtains. She crosses back to Teddy. Shows him the picture.

'What does this mean?'

He manages a laugh. 'Lawyer.'

Helen wonders if she should lean on the nail that is still pinning him to the ground. Wonders if she should set about him with a blowtorch.

'I'm about to call in the troops. This place is about to get very busy with blue lights and uniforms. And you're going to get to

287

meet a real piece of work. She's my boss, kind of. Really snotty bitch. But she's very thorough. She'll do whatever it takes. And she won't unpin you from the floor until you start giving us something useful.'

Teddy shakes his head, though his strength seems to be weakening. Eventually, he shrugs his shoulders. Looks down at the mess of his foot.

'I can help you,' says Helen. 'I can make a lot of this shit go away. We sign you up as an informant. We can pay you. I know you know who I mean when I say the Headhunters. Not everybody calls them that – that's just the police name. But they're lethal. They steamroll through existing outfits and cream off the ambitious and the hungry. Those who don't bow their head end up nailgunned and blowtorched and very, very dead. They started up here but they've gone quiet on us. I reckon they've moved on to pastures new. You know things. You can help yourself.'

Teddy's head slumps forward. He gives it a shake, as though trying to stay awake. Helen knows she needs to make a decision. Needs to call a superior officer and get this man some help. Takes off her coat and presses it to the sodden laces of Teddy's boots. Winces as he gasps in pain.

'I'm no grass,' he says hoarsely. 'This outfit you're talking about, I'm not saying I know them. But you have to adapt or fucking perish. I'm adapting, love. You think I like all the theatrics with the DIY tools? You think I could see the point in making an example out of Hollow? We don't need that. It's cost my mate his life. The boss is making bad calls because he's scared to death. You think you can keep me safe? You think they wouldn't know I was informing? Christ, I'm a dead man whatever happens. They don't mess about. That house in the picture? Me and Foley were due there when this was all done. Babysitting job. They've been moving him from house to house, shot full of every drug you can name. Foley and me were due to take over; show the new firm what we can do. Make him forget. That's what the boss said. Make him forget who he fucking is. Foley had plans for that. He'd been reading up about memory on the internet, reckoned if he put a screwdriver in the right part of the skull he could make him forget just about anything. Poor bastard. Why don't they just kill him, eh? You think I want that for me? I upset these bastards and the next thing I'm hanging in a cellar next to some ratty copper who these Russian fuckers simply cannot break . . .'

Helen feels a chill across her shoulders. Can smell the blood and the pigs and hears thunder in her ears.

Later, she will wonder if this was when everything changed. If it would not have been better if she had simply misheard, or misunderstood.

But she is too busy hauling the nail through tissue, blood, bone and brick, listening to Teddy's hiss of pain as she frees him.

She needs him to trust her.

Needs him to spill his guts.

And then she needs him to show her where to find Colin Ray.

31

10.16 p.m.

Trish Pharaoh and Delphine Hollow are sitting in high, hard-backed chairs, watching the glowing coals in the fireplace.

The only other light in this square, sturdy room comes from the fat church candles at the centre of the long table. Shadows dance upon a ceiling the colour of home-made butter. The room smells of bread and fresh flowers, of Pharaoh's cigarettes and the perfume she has sprayed in her hair. Smells of a teenage girl who spends her days outside and didn't shower this morning. Smells of dried grass, burning on hot stone.

It's a hot, dark and comfortable space, and makes Pharaoh imagine horse brasses and cider. She feels somehow transplanted, as though she has been shoved, bodily, into another time, where women darn socks by the fire and the men swig ale from pewter tankards.

Both she and Delphine are drinking pear brandy. Pharaoh is holding her customary black cigarette in her right hand and her mobile phone in her left. Occasionally, she reaches up to push her hair back from her face, or to bat at the moth which keeps fluttering against her cheek.

'He's coming,' says Pharaoh again, looking at her phone. 'The fog's not getting any better. They're taking their time.'

Delphine nods. Her cheeks look red and sore. She has cried a lot this evening. First, when Pharaoh broke the news that her father had been taken. And then, an hour ago, when Pharoah's radio crackled and the news came through that he was safe. They had a man in custody, and McAvoy was bringing her father home.

They are waiting for the menfolk like fishermen's wives. They take it in turn to stand and cross to the window, to stare through the trees and the gravestones at the dirty track, hoping for the gleam of headlights.

'I can make you something to eat,' says Pharaoh, looking over her shoulder at the complicated, old-fashioned stove. 'I'm not quite sure I could work that thing but I don't think I could mess up a sandwich.'

'Dad can make something when he gets back,' says Delphine. 'Thanks, though. Thanks for being here with me.'

Pharaoh shrugs. 'Couldn't leave you with a stranger. And I need to talk to your dad when he gets back.'

'He won't be in more trouble, will he? I mean, he's only just got out.'

Pharaoh considers the girl, with her unkempt hair and freckles. She's wearing jodhpurs and a man's lumberjack shirt. Her socks don't match. There is hay in her hair. Although they share no blood, she has her stepfather's mannerisms. She looks at Pharaoh with the same intensity. Holds herself with the same stillness.

'We don't know what happened yet,' says Pharaoh tactfully. 'The man who was killed seems to have been trying to abduct your father, so it could be that the prosecutors will have no interest in making a case – especially given his current profile.'

'You said that last time,' says Delphine, turning away from her to stare into the fire. 'You said it would be okay and he went to prison.'

'Sometimes things don't work out the way people expect. That's life. And he's out now.'

'He's only been out a few days and already people are trying to hurt him,' says Delphine, swilling the brandy in her glass. 'What had he done? Who were they?'

Pharaoh joins her in staring at the fire. Watches the moth flutter upwards towards the scarlet and gold of the low flame. Wonders, for a flickering instant, what will happen to Delphine if Aberlour manages to prosecute Hollow as a serial killer.

'We don't know that either,' says Pharaoh, leaning forward to toss her cigarette into the fire. 'There are questions to answer.'

'And he's not hurt?'

'He's had a few knocks but he doesn't want to go to hospital. Wants to come and see you.'

Delphine smiles, suddenly shy. Hides the flush of pleasure.

'You're close,' says Pharaoh, making conversation. 'It's lovely to see. I sometimes get that from my girls. Other times they look at me like I'm a demon. Sometimes, I get both on the same day.'

'What did you say your eldest was called a moment ago? "Sophia" was it? You looked sad when you said it. Is she okay?'

Pharaoh shrugs. Pulls a face.

'It's not easy, being a parent to a teen with her own mind. I gave her a kiss on the head when I got in last night and she pretended to be asleep. Same again when I left in the small hours this morning. I hope it will pass. She's my oldest, y'know? My mate. She's got good reason to be cross with me but I never said I was perfect. I do my best.'

Delphine nods. 'She'll be fine, I'm sure. Dad and me don't argue very much. When I do get told off it's usually because I deserve it and he feels awful afterwards.'

'You're a good team. Still, you must miss your mum.'

Delphine pulls a face. 'She wasn't always easy to live with. She liked to drink. Liked it too much, if you know what I mean.'

Pharaoh indicates her glass. 'We all have our vices. I knock back too much of this stuff, I know I do. I don't make excuses, though. I know it's becoming a problem. I just look at my life and imagine it without the wine and the vodka and I wonder if I'm brave enough to try.'

'Mum wasn't brave enough,' says Delphine, with a note of bitterness. 'The doctors told her to stop but she wouldn't. She got nasty, towards the end. She was so horrible to Dad, after all he'd done for us. I really thought he might leave.'

'That must have been hard for you,' says Pharaoh, nodding. 'We can all be horrible buggers, sometimes. I bet she felt awful for the times she let you down.'

'So what? She still did it. Still pushed and pushed at him. The things she said to him. Things like him not being our real dad. She'd sneer in his face. Hit him, even. Say things to Aramis and me about him being all talk. That we didn't know what he was really like.'

'What do you mean?' asks Pharaoh, sitting forward, as subtly as she can.

'She said they might as well have separate beds, if you get what I mean. Said that he wasn't interested in that stuff. I don't like to remember the other things but it was very personal. Stuff about what he did like to do.'

Pharaoh watches the light dance on Delphine's irises. Watches her pupils dilate. There is a sheen to her skin; a lustre. Perhaps a shortness of breath as she speaks.

'I didn't like to hear it,' says Delphine. 'We were just kids. She spent her last days in a hospice and wouldn't even let him visit. Said all this stuff to Aramis about promising we would go and live with her sister. We didn't understand it. We didn't want that. We loved Reuben.'

'Your brother felt the same?'

'Totally! I mean, he could be a bit of a baby about some things and he fell out with Reuben more than me but he still knew that he was a good person and a good dad.'

Pharaoh looks into her glass. Looks at the sediment and the smear of liquid. Here, in this light, it is dirt and blood.

'It's awful what he did,' says Pharaoh drowsily. 'It must have been terrible for you. Had there been no signs? I mean, did you have no clue he was so unhappy?'

Delphine considers her for a long moment. Cracks her shoulders as she yawns languidly, like a cat awakening from a nap.

'He was a black cloud for weeks before it happened. Made it quite unpleasant to live here, really. Reuben and me were trying so hard. It could have been lovely. We started spending more and more time in the gypsy wagon and gave Aramis the run of the house. We still had horses then, you see, and me and Reuben spent most of our lives outdoors. It was nice. Homely, just the two of us. Aramis was spoiling it.'

Pharaoh yawns, then apologises. Her limbs feel warm. There is a strange light-headedness stealing into her consciousness. 'Teenagers can be like that,' she says, and yawns again.

'Most suicides take pills or hang themselves,' says Delphine, matter-of-factly. 'He drank hoof-shine. Just gulped it down.'

'You saw it?' asks Pharaoh. Her face feels numb. She can't feel her hands. Hears her phone clatter onto the stone floor.

'Of course I saw it,' says Delphine, standing up. 'I was sitting on his chest and holding his mouth open, you silly bitch.'

Pharaoh feels herself slithering onto the floor. Feels a sudden cramp in her guts, as though she has been punched in the belly. A sudden stab of nausea, as though dirty fingers are stroking the inside of her throat.

'He was spoiling it,' says Delphine, rubbing her nose. She squats down. Picks up Pharaoh's phone. Starts scrolling through the recent messages. 'Boring, boring, boring. Let's have a look at what you've been sending, eh? What you've been saying to Dad. You're disgusting, you know that? You should be ashamed.'

Pharaoh rests her face on the warm stone. She can feel the grooves. The inscriptions. Lies on a carpet of tombstones as a murderer stands above her and the light from the fire turns her eyes to points of flame.

'They never realised,' says Delphine, shaking her head. 'None of them. All the people he helped. They never accepted it for what it was. They all needed more.'

Pharaoh tries to speak. Manages to slur a name.

'Hannah? Yeah, she was like a groupie. Innocent little thing; all big eyes and posters of kittens. She kept texting him. Kept saying she would do anything to say thank you. Would do whatever he wanted. Sent him pictures of herself. He must have told her what he was into. Said he liked smells and hair and sweat. She played up to it. Sent him all these pictures of herself looking like a cave-woman. She didn't get it. She was making his life miserable but because she was this pretty little thing he couldn't just tell her straight. He had to keep stringing her along. He would never have done what he needed to.'

Pharaoh feels another thump of pain in her stomach. Feels moisture fill her mouth and a sudden rush of acid and bile. Retches and heaves onto the floor.

'You killed her,' says Pharaoh, between desperate gulps of breath. 'Set her up . . .'

'It's you I should thank,' says Delphine, smiling. 'You had Dad in for questioning. I had his phone. I got to play with precious little Hannah's heartstrings for a couple of days. She believed it all, that he would run away with her. Believed he would be her knight in shining armour for the rest of her life. You should have seen her face when I got there. It was like somebody had squeezed a sponge, the way the colour ran out of her face. She didn't even try and fight. Just ran the second she saw the knife. Silly cow tripped in the big shoes I'd told her to wear. She was dressed exactly the way he likes. I've seen his internet history too, you see. I know what he's into. I hadn't planned on taking the souvenir but it just seemed right. She was on her back, you see, and her arms were up, and it was just like a slap in the face, the way she had tried to manipulate him. So I sliced her. Took her hair and her scent and put them in my pocket. Took a while to get the fat bitch back to the car but it's a quiet spot there and I'd parked in among the high corn.'

Pharaoh lies on the floor, gasping for breath. Delphine had been only sixteen at the time of Hannah's abduction. She had no licence. But she lived in the countryside. Had probably been taking joy-rides in Reuben's Jeep since she was a child.

'I was in two minds about whether to tell him,' says Delphine, squatting down to poke the fire. 'He had so much on his mind with you and your bloody investigation. You do know he didn't mean to kill that man, don't you? I mean, talk about irony. He really did fall and hit his head. But we haven't lost a brain surgeon, have we? I mean, he was shit. His family was shit. Those lads made life unbearable for Aramis and me. I know that Reuben would have done something about them if I'd told him, but then I wouldn't have got to see it, would I? He'd have sneaked out in the night or done something on one of his trips away. This way I got to see him hurt them, and it was all for me.'

Pharaoh rises to her knees, fighting the pain in her stomach. 'Ava,' she spits, and bile runs down her top.

'Dirty bitch,' says Delphine, and an expression of pure hatred fills her features. 'Tried to blackmail him even while he was in prison. Wrote to him with all these veiled threats about telling people what he had done for her. I mean, he got rid of the bloke who was beating the shit out of her. Bumped him off, no questions asked. Beat his head in with a rock and dumped him in the river. Did it brilliantly, don't you think? All your experts and nobody thought it was anything but a hit-and-run. She needed money, or so she said. And she thought she could manipulate him just like Hannah did. Dad was never going to do what was necessary. We were working on an appeal and she was going to fuck it all up. We paid her what we could but we're not rich people. And she was going to keep coming back for more. She even had the rock that Dad had used to smash the bloke's brains in. He'd given her it as a token. Wanted to show her he trusted her, but it was a daft thing to do. Silly sod, needing to show off. And then we got the news that Dad was almost certainly getting out and it seemed like the only thing getting in the way of life being brilliant was that bitch. She'd written to him, telling him all these dirty things. How she stunk. Would be waiting for him, ready to press his face into her hair and let him get himself off . . .'

Pharaoh retches again. Tries to pull herself up and takes a short, deft kick to the ribs for her troubles.

'How did she know,' gasps Pharaoh, 'that he killed for her?'

'Ego,' says Delphine brightly. 'We've all got our faults. Dad needs the odd moment of adoration. I found the message he sent her. Didn't even delete it from his email account. Asked her if life was better now that some knight in shining armour had stepped in and ended her suffering and killed her bully. He all but confessed. She must have recognised the way he phrased it or something because she asked him for a number she could call him on. Soft sod went weak at the knees. She sent him pictures. Got his motor running. It was when he went inside that she started using it to her advantage, the grasping cunt.'

'How?' splutters Pharaoh. 'How did you kill her?'

Delphine gives a childish grin at the memory, as if recalling a great day at the beach.

'She recognised me when she opened the door, but I can do sweet so well. Dad had shown her my picture. She let me in. We shared a drink. She began to feel unwell and I put her out of her misery. Took another little trophy. To be honest, it had been so long since Hannah I was grateful for the chance to do it again. Dad would have liked the smell, that's for sure. She pissed herself as she choked on her own puke. I heard her windpipe crack as I pushed the toilet seat against the back of her neck. It sounded like chopping wood.'

'How . . . ?' splutters Pharaoh. 'How did you find out about Reuben helping these people?'

Delphine smiles. She spits into the fire and watches the saliva sizzle on the hot stones.

'He needed a special somebody,' she says proudly. 'I was just a little girl when he came into our lives but I knew from the first day that he was mine and nobody else's. We saw something in each other. I wasn't an easy child, I know that. I was into things that nobody else was into. I remember the slapping my mam gave me when she found me digging up the graves in the garden. I'd found finger bones, you see. I was playing with them, in the dirt, happy as you like. Dad never told me off for things like that. When I got sent to bed he'd come up and tell me stories. They would be about good people and bad people and white knights and black knights. It would always be damsels in distress and good, pure-hearted warriors saving them. As I got older the stories changed. They weren't men on horseback. They were here and now. And by the time I was a teenager we both knew what he was telling me. We both knew what he did when he had to. Mum was so jealous. It got so that me and Dad were together all the time. She drank and drank and turned on him so horribly. I just kept topping up her glass. Hiding her pills. I even started putting extra salt on her food when I read that it could speed up the effects of cirrhosis. She was in the way. She was forcing him away from us.'

'Cotteril,' says Pharaoh, and her vision blurs, mixing with the pictures in her mind. She sees the dead copper, typing his suicide note on his home computer and downing his whisky laced with enough painkillers to murder three men.

'Lying bastard!' whispers Delphine, her face turning ugly. 'Dad never confessed – he had nothing to confess to! Everybody knew about Cotteril being Mathers' relation. We kept waiting for you lot to find out. You never did. I had to phone the papers and tip them off but it took an age before they ran with it. Waiting for a slow news day, Dad said. It should have been enough to get Dad released but nothing changed. It made me angry. We still had a lot of Mum's old pills left. It wasn't difficult persuading the dirty bastard to let me in his house. Told me it was a bit naughty of me to be there in my short skirt and holding a bottle of Scotch. But I said I wanted him to know there were no hard feelings. So we drank. He fell asleep soon after. Never woke up again.'

Pharaoh feels her throat begin to close up. Feels a tremor in her chest. 'Hannah,' she says weakly. 'Her body . . .'

Delphine is still scrolling through Pharaoh's phone. She's pulling a face at whatever she is reading.

'Why do you never put a kiss on the end of your texts to Hector? You do to everybody else. You're dead mean to him in some of these messages. Then you're all apologetic the next moment. This is the one who's bringing Dad back, yeah? He's going to be in for a treat. I hope he's grateful for all Dad and me did to bring him a little peace. It broke Dad's heart hearing you talk about how much Hannah's disappearance had affected Hector. He kept going on about it after you left. Dad had always known what I'd done, of course. He'd never said as much, but he knew about her and about Ava. He mentioned it for the first time last night. Said that it would be nice if her family at least had a body. If your Hector got to sleep a little easier. Only took a couple of Facebook searches to find him. When I saw the flowers it just seemed perfect. I was happy enough leaving her where she was, in the pile of horse shit in the bottom field where she'd been lying since I killed the dirty cunt, but Dad likes things to be artistic and sweet. I dug her up. Laid her

298

out like a princess. Dad was pleased. Said there was no need to talk about it again. I don't know who these people are who took him, but they're going to be sorry. He's the good man in all this.'

Pharaoh drops her head back to the floor. Feels as though she is burning up. She tries to wipe sweat from her face but struggles to move her arms.

'You think I didn't see what you were trying to do?' asks Delphine, glaring. 'Flirting with him in those interviews. Smelling like a whore for him. Showing him your hair. I tried, you know. Tried to be what he likes. Let him see me time and again – dropping my towel, positioning the mirrors. It didn't work. Too much like a little girl. Couldn't grow hair for him, not properly. Look at me now, though. You think he'll like it?'

Delphine raises her arms above her head. Pushes her clothes back to show the mangled, matted strip of hair and skin she has cut from the body of a dead girl and glued to her own naked flesh.

Pharaoh grimaces as pain racks her. Manages to find some anger. 'You're insane.'

'You got under his skin. Messed up his head. Took him away from me. And whenever I saw him in prison you were all he would talk about. He was carving you. He didn't know whether you were a victim or a target. Didn't know how he felt about you. Still doesn't. But I know he only needs one person in his heart and that person is me. I know he wants me. He's always wanted me. But he resists. I've done all the things I know he likes. Worn the clothes; the boots and little dresses. I've tried so many times to get him to look at me the way I want him to but he's too good a man for that. But I'm a woman now. He won't have to fight it forever. Won't have to keep himself busy with slags like you. He'll have me, and I'll be all he'll fucking need.'

Delphine reaches up to the mantelpiece and pulls down a small, wicked-bladed knife with a wooden handle and a missing tip.

'He gave me this when I was eleven,' says Delphine. 'Showed me how to carve. I've made some beautiful things. You should go and see the little patch of woodland where Dad and me used to go to get some time together. It's beautiful. Peaceful. He'll probably tell me to stick your body there, but I don't think I can do that. I'll find you somewhere more suitable. Somewhere cold and dark. I'll plant you. Use you to fertilise the flowers.'

Delphine bends down. Squats over Pharaoh and pulls her arms above her head.

Grins in the firelight as she brings the blade down. Places the steel against the flesh of Pharaoh's armpit and begins to carve.

32

'You're bleeding.'

'It'll stop.'

'I can drive, if you want. I know this road . . .'

'Mr Hollow, I would advise you not to distract me. Or speak at all, really. I'm doing this because I believe you're going to be sent to prison for a very long time. I'm doing it because this is DSU Pharaoh's case. Be quiet, please, sir.'

'I haven't done anything wrong, I've told you. Trish will understand.'

'Please . . .'

'The surname Pharaoh. She's never told me. Unusual, isn't it? And her husband has a different name.'

'Mr Hollow . . .'

'I googled her when I was in prison. Impressive career. She's an impressive person. You're a good friend to her. Loyal. I'll make sure there's no trouble for you over all of this.'

'Trouble?'

'When the press run with it.'

'You may well be under arrest by then.'

'We'll see. There is so much I want to tell you, but you're holding back. Why are you a policeman?'

'To help people.'

'Seriously? You can't just leave it at that. Are you a copper's son, or anything?'

'My dad has a croft. He's a caretaker. Electrician. Sells old rolls of carpet. He's many things, but never a cop.'

'Nobody else? No hero?'

'My dad.'

'No, I mean somebody to emulate. Granddad?'

'My great uncle was a constable in Glasgow for a couple of years. Came down from the Highlands with dozens of others to help get the gangs to let go of their hold. Ultimate hard-line, zero-tolerance policing. He came back more worldly-wise and cynical. He told me some stories when I was a kid. Stories about locking up villains. Maybe it started there.'

'Thank you. That's interesting. And Pharaoh's name?'

'Not a chance.'

'We're nearly there. There's a right turn coming up just ahead.'

McAvoy turns the car into the pocket of darkness. Feels a change in the texture of the night air as the vehicle bumps over potholes and fallen branches and enters the woods. Turns the headlights to full for a brief moment so he can take a mental snapshot of the obstacles ahead. Sees the outline of Pharaoh's car. The curved bow-top of the wagon. The rotten teeth of titled headstones.

He pulls to a halt. Turns to Hollow and glowers. 'You'll do what you're told,' says McAvoy, 'or you'll be in cuffs until backup arrives.'

He climbs from the car. Feels the fog reach into his throat and nostrils, and the pain in his shoulders rise to his temples. Moves his head slowly, left and right, wincing. He feels somehow hungover. There's a dull throb at his jawbone and behind his eyes.

'There's a light on,' says Hollow, climbing out of the car and gesturing towards the cottage. 'Delphine will have a fire on. We'd probably read to each other tonight.'

McAvoy starts to picture the scene. Blinks down hard on it and kills it before it can fully form. He doesn't want to imagine it. Doesn't want to think that the girl inside the perfect little cottage is about to have her life shredded and crumpled like damp paper.

Hollow goes first, shouting his daughter's name. He reaches the door three steps ahead of McAvoy. Turns the handle and enters the kitchen.

Sees.

Delphine Hollow, her knee beneath Trish Pharaoh's throat. The blade he gave her, pushed into the skin of Pharaoh's armpit, lost in a pocket of blood, skin and hair.

Hollow turns, raises his boot and kicks the door shut. Hears the thud as the ancient wood slams against McAvoy's shoulder. Slams home the bolt and spins back to look at his stepdaughter as she goes about her work.

Delphine looks back over her shoulder. She locks eyes with her stepfather. She grins girlishly, guiltily, as if she has been caught stealing biscuits.

Wordlessly, she offers the knife.

'This wasn't what we agreed,' says Hollow gently as he walks forward, eyes on the red-soaked blade. 'This wasn't supposed to happen again.'

'She's been lying from the start,' says Delphine, applying more pressure to Pharaoh's throat. 'The messages are all in her phone. She's been running an operation to catch you for all the bad men.'

Hollow considers Pharaoh. Her eyelids are fluttering and there is red at the corner of her mouth. She's still squirming beneath Delphine, seems to be struggling to control her limbs.

'Things aren't always what they seem,' says Hollow. 'You've been wrong before. You were wrong about Hannah. She would never have told anybody.'

'You're too trusting,' says Delphine, looking back down at Pharaoh. She changes her grip on the knife. 'You think people are like you. They're not. That's why you're special.'

Hollow stands above his stepdaughter. Her pale skin is flushed and that stale, sour smell of sweat and turned earth is rising from her bare flesh. He reaches forward and strokes her hair. Takes a handful of it. Looks down at Trish Pharaoh and sees revulsion in her eyes.

'She'd have understood,' says Hollow, and when he gently pushes Delphine's head against his hip, he sees goosepimples rise on her skin. 'She still could. We have to think. To talk . . .'

McAvoy comes through the window as if launched by a catapult. He slams into the table in a storm of flying glass, crashing down onto the tombstones with a thud that smashes his teeth together and sends pain coursing into every part of his body.

On the floor, Trish Pharaoh manages to get a hand free and hits Delphine at the hinge of her jaw. She pushes the heel of her hand against the teenager's nose, forcing her backwards, registering the sound of the knife clattering onto the floor.

Hollow watches as Pharaoh pulls herself upright, blood and dirt and vomit streaking her hair and skin; pure, ferocious anger in her blue eyes. Sees her grab Delphine by her gorgeous, unruly hair and slam her head into the edge of the table.

Hollow turns. Jumps past McAvoy's outstretched hand. Crunches on broken glass and hauls open the door, disappearing into a swirl of black and grey as if tumbling into a tomb.

'Get after him!' screams Pharaoh. 'I'm okay. I've got her. Get the bastard right fucking now.'

McAvoy puts his hand down on broken glass. Feels pain and wetness and doesn't give a damn. He pulls himself up and splutters forward, tripping on the stones as he stumbles back outside.

Shivers with pain and cold as the mist closes around him. Hears a low, rustling whistle as the breeze moves the trees and leaves fall like dead skin.

McAvoy pushes forward, hands out in front, running blindly, ducking branches and skipping over tree roots; the whistle of the wind inaudible over his own breathing and the rushing of his blood.

For a second he fancies he can see the outline of a figure. Hears a branch break. Cloth tearing, as a shirt catches on rough wood and splits to the seam.

McAvoy wonders if he should yell. Wonders if he should lie and tell Hollow that if he does not stop, the officers behind him in their night-vision goggles will bring him down like a stag.

There is a movement to his left and McAvoy turns, just as Hollow smashes him across both knees with a branch as thick as an arm. He hears the snap of wood before the pain hits him and by then he is on the ground, slithering about in leaves and dirt. When the pain comes, it is an explosion. It feels as though the top of his head will blow off to allow the high-pressure steam of agony to escape.

'Tell me what to do next,' says Hollow flatly. 'Go on. Tell me what a good man does now.'

McAvoy's words are a hiss. He pulls his legs up to his belly. Holds his knees like a baby.

'She didn't want to do any of this,' says Hollow, hefting the remainder of his club. 'I did wrong. I could see what Delphine was from the beginning. I thought that if I told her my stories she might see that it doesn't have to be good people that she hurts. But it didn't matter to her in the end. It wasn't about anything but killing. I could see it in her eyes. I should have stopped her then. But I love her, you see. Not in the way she wants me to, but I love her. I'm not like other people, Hector. I can't care the way other people do. I do try. I did my best to be the right person for my family. Tried so hard. But it wasn't what I lived for. I lived for that moment when a pretty girl told me they had a problem. I killed my first one when I was still a boy. Did you know that? When I got out of prison I knew I'd do it again. I just had to wait. It's amazing how strangers will share things. They would tell me their worries. They'd see me in a bar or on a train and they'd start chit-chatting about the men who were making them miserable. And then we'd go our separate ways. And I'd log it in the back of my head. And then I'd go back and fucking kill them.'

McAvoy tries to put his feet down and feels a white-hot strip of pain run up his legs.

'I should never have done it so close to home,' says Hollow.

He seems angry at himself. Lets his feelings out by bringing the club down across McAvoy's shoulder and ribs. It feels like being hammered flat.

'Hannah. Ava. I met Hannah out at the church at Great Givendale. Lovely, lovely person. A really pure soul. She had tears in her eyes. Had been laying a wreath for her pony. I was working on some new carvings for the church. We sat out on the grass and shared stories. I did what I knew she wanted. I should have put Hogg in the ground, but there was something about

Hannah that made me think twice. She would carry the guilt of his death. She had to choose. She chose to let him live. And then she wouldn't leave me alone. It wasn't fair on Delphine. I tried to hide it from her but she kept reading my messages. Perhaps I knew what she would do. But when I got arrested there was no restraining hand. She killed her. Buried her. What could I do? Turn her in? She's the love of my life. I made mistakes. Ava – I was showing off. I should never have helped her. She wasn't even a good person. That was desire, plain and simple. I wanted her. She was in hospital when we met, battered and bruised and still the sexiest thing I'd seen in years. I was kind to her. I dried her eyes and wiped the dried blood off her face and she looked at me like I was special. I wanted to help her. She deserved to be helped. But with her, it was more than the fact that she was fragile or pretty or vulnerable. She was sexy as hell, Hector. I made a mistake by claiming the credit for her ex's death. I should never have contacted her again. But I did. I made a mistake and hinted it was all down to me and the next thing we were chatting and I told her what I was into and from there she knew how to play with me. I don't have sex like other people. I like smells; I like hair. I don't know why. I should never have shared that confidence with anybody. But I told Ava and I told Hannah and they used it to try and own a piece of me. Delphine didn't like that. And now they're dead, and I've got nowhere to go. I don't know if I want to kill you or not. You seem like a good person. I feel like there's something between us. I see the same thing in Trish's eyes that I see in Delphine's. I see it in your wife, too. She's killed, hasn't she? Tell me. She would. She'd spill her guts and look at me with those beautiful eyes and I'd do things that nobody else would . . .'

McAvoy's fury comes from a place within him he does not acknowledge. His shout is an untamed animal roar of pure and absolute rage. He lunges at Hollow just as he's preparing to bring the club down again. Grabs it in his great, bear-like hands, and thrusts it backwards into Hollow's face. Hears cartilage crunch against wood.

McAvoy grabs Hollow around the knees and smashes him to the ground with an impact that drives the air from both men's lungs. Hollow recovers first. Punches McAvoy in the top of the head: hard, ferocious right hooks that make McAvoy's head ring. McAvoy reaches up and tries to grab Hollow's wrists but Hollow squirms beneath him and manages to boot him in his damaged knee. McAvoy rolls away, reeling, bloodied, groggy.

Hollow is on top of him, raining down blow after blow. There is blood pouring down his face and into his mouth but his expression remains neutral. His eyes barely flicker as he grabs a fistful of McAvoy's hair and starts to beat the back of his head against the hard, compacted mud of the forest floor.

McAvoy hears his skull smack against the ground. He can barely see. Does not know up from down. Feels suddenly cold and weak. Feels wetness on the back of his neck. Feels his life pooling behind him into the dirt and shit where Hannah Kelly lay buried for those endless months of misery.

McAvoy throws his hand forward. Finds something soft. Pushes with his thumb and feels something give beneath his nail.

Hears Hollow scream.

McAvoy punches upwards. Lashes out, blind and desperate. Connects. Punches out, harder now, the weight on his chest diminishing.

And now he is on his knees, grabbing a handful of Hollow's shirt and pulling him close enough to hit. The other man has his hand pressed to his left eye, his face contorted in agony. McAvoy pulls him close. Puts his weight into the punches that he slams into the side of Hollow's head. One. Two. Three . . .

He collapses forward onto the unconscious, bloodied mess beneath him. Listens to his own heartbeat and waits for the pain to come back.

His world spins. Black and grey strobe in his vision. He can hear somebody shouting his name. Struggling to pronounce it.

'Hector!'

He lies on the forest floor and stares up into the fog. As if seeing shapes form in cloud, the swirl of mist becomes animal. He sees a wolf, turning its head, opening its mouth and swallowing the full moon.

And then he sees nothing but Trish Pharaoh, leaning over him and pressing her warm hand to the wound at the back of his head, screaming for an ambulance and telling him to hold on, to stay with her, to never leave . . .

33

'Any poison in this one?' asks Pharaoh as she twists open a bottle of elderflower gin and takes a sniff. 'Ah, fuck it,' she says, and takes a gulp.

Her gait is a little lopsided. She's holding a pressure pad under her armpit and looks as though she is wearing an invisible sling. She hasn't changed her clothes. She's still all mud and blood and puke.

Reuben Hollow sits at the table. His hands are cuffed behind him. His face is swelling, obscenely.

'You knew what she was up to, then,' she says, sitting down at the table beside him. There is a piece of broken glass on the wooden surface in front of her. It's shaped like a tooth.

Hollow raises his head. One of his teeth has come out at the back and his jawbone looks like a chicken leg. He looks broken. His voice contains the whine of a tired child.

'I never wanted this,' he says. 'I just tried to help people.'

Pharaoh takes another swig. There is a uniformed copper on the outside of the door. The grounds are swarming with Aberlour's team. But Pharaoh insisted she have this time, alone, with the prisoner. Nobody had questioned her. Nobody would dare.

'She didn't,' says Pharaoh, picking up the piece of glass and massaging it between her fingers. 'She killed people because she was obsessed with you.'

'That's not true. Not really.'

'How long ago did you realise?'

'Realise who she was? I don't know.'

'She killed her brother. Poisoned him.'

'We don't know that for sure. Teenagers imagine things.'

'She helped her mum on her way.'

'Like I said . . .'

'She killed Hannah Kelly for you.'

'Don't say that.'

Pharaoh tries to hold in her temper.

'It happens. Kids fall in love with older men. Long-lost siblings start sexual relationships. There's a precedent for every sick thing you can think of. She fell in love with her stepdad. And her stepdad showed her that it's okay to kill people as long as you believe you're doing right.'

Hollow drops his head to the table. Grinds his forehead against a tiny speck of glass.

'Hannah would never have told.'

'You sent her a video on David Hogg's mobile. He was begging for his life. She allowed him to live. Bet you weren't expecting that.'

Hollow manages the tiniest of smiles. 'I thought she'd want him dead. I had to honour her wishes.'

'You never involved any of your other damsels in distress the way you involved Hannah. Why not?'

Hollow looks around him. His hair flutters in the breeze from the smashed window. He looks at the mingled blood on the stone floor. His shoulders slump.

'With the others, I liked that they knew, but didn't know. They met a man, told him their problems, and those problems went away. Hannah saw the world differently. She wanted to believe in gallantry. Chivalry. The old ways. I wanted her to know that David Hogg was suffering for no other reason than because she ordered it. I wanted her to know I was hers.'

'You wanted to fuck her, Reuben.'

'No.'

'You might not want to admit it, but you wanted to fuck all of them.'

'I didn't. Not like you think.'

Pharaoh considers him, sucking on her cheek. 'Your internet history should make for interesting reading. Delphine says you're into all sorts of dark stuff. Smells. Hair. Hannah knew all that. She read up on how to become the perfect woman for you.'

'She was a good person. She was beautiful. But I wouldn't have ever let anything physical happen.'

'I don't think you physically could anyway, Reuben. I think you're impotent and you get your kicks seeing yourself as a hero. I don't think the woman you physically want actually exists.'

'I wanted you.'

'No you didn't. You wanted me to look at you with adoration and admiration in my eyes. You wanted me to know you were somebody spectacular.'

'You lied to me,' says Hollow, looking at her for a moment before turning away. 'You were trying to catch me. What did you really think of me? Underneath all the lies and pretending? Do you think I was doing anything bad?'

Pharaoh takes another swig of elderflower gin. 'You're going to go to prison for murder,' she says flatly. 'Lots of murders. So is Delphine.'

'She's not a murderer,' says Hollow. 'She made mistakes.'

'She killed Hannah because she knew Hannah better than you ever did. She knew she was a good person who couldn't live with knowing what she knew about you. Eventually, Hannah would have told somebody. Delphine stopped that. She pretended to be you. Set Hannah up and killed her. Brought her home and dumped her body under a pile of manure. When did she tell you about it? Were you supposed to be pleased? Did it make you twitch?'

'Don't say these things, Trish. Please.'

Pharaoh shakes her head. 'Ava Delaney,' she says, accentuating each syllable. 'She wasn't such a good girl, was she? She was much more honest about what she wanted. She wanted money to keep your secret.'

'She was confused. Life's difficult. She would never have gone through with her threats.'

'Delphine thought she would. She was so convinced that Ava would tell your secrets, she went to her home, poisoned her and killed her.'

Hollow looks down at the floor. Pharaoh would love to know what he is seeing behind his closed eyelids.

'I told Ava personal things,' he mumbles. 'When Delphine saw the pictures she sent me, it upset her. It upset her a lot.'

'She sent you pictures of herself looking vulnerable and helpless and with a full bush of armpit hair,' spits Pharaoh. 'She tried to win your heart, or at the very least, interest your dick.'

'You're spoiling it,' says Hollow. 'You're dirtying it.'

'It was fucking dirty, you silly bastard,' hisses Pharaoh. 'You weren't Sir Fucking Galahad. You were a creepy bloke in the pub who killed people to impress women. And when you impressed the wrong ones and they fell for you, your stepdaughter killed them.'

'I would have talked her down,' says Hollow, desperately. 'I'd never have let her kill you.'

'I saw it in your eyes, Reuben. You wanted to watch. You wanted to see her carve me up. I think you probably always wanted to fuck Delphine but it didn't fit with your idea of helping these poor desperate princesses. I bet when she told you how she felt about you, it half killed you not to let her have what she wanted.'

'No.'

'You did this to her. You tried to impress a young girl and you liked it when she fell in love with you. You helped her dump Hannah's body at Hector's bloody house!'

'She deserved to be laid somewhere pretty. Delphine was sorry for what she'd done. I was cross with her for leaving her body under the manure pile for so long. She deserved to be treated better. When you told me how much she meant to McAvoy it made sense to leave her for him. He would take care of her.'

'You half broke his soul, you sick bastard. I bet you stroked your stepdaughter's hair the whole drive there and back. I can see it. I know what you are.'

Hollow sneers at her, momentarily recognisable as the man who turned her world upside down.

'You wanted me,' he says defiantly. 'You know you did.'

Pharaoh considers this. Gives him a smile. 'Maybe. But when

we had our moment, I saw nothing but fear in your eyes. Fear that I would find out your secret. Fear that I'd realise you can only get hard for pictures on the internet and the look of adoration in women's eyes. That's why you rejected me. You were scared of me.'

'Don't say that . . .'

'A man called Aberlour is going to come and talk to you soon,' says Pharaoh, screwing the cap back on the gin bottle. 'I don't know what he'll want you to say. But I think that if you want people to view you the way you view yourself, you'll confess to all of your crimes. And if you want Delphine to spend her life getting help rather than counting off the days of a life sentence, you'll persuade her to do the same. I know that what matters most to you is the way women view you. You can be a good man in their eyes, or you can be a sick fuck. The choice is yours.'

Hollow cannot hold her gaze. He looks away but finds nothing to sustain him, so he looks down at the floor.

'It's not easy,' he says, almost to himself. 'Being good. Being the right kind of man.'

Pharaoh pushes herself back from the table. Looks at him with nothing but contempt.

'I know what a good man looks like.'

Hollow watches her turn her back and enjoys the shape of her. He catches her scent and savours it.

'You liked my sculptures of you,' he says, to her back.

Pharaoh stops. She turns. Sees nothing but a shrivelled, half-formed thing.

'They weren't sculptures of me,' she says, as she walks up the steps to the door. 'They were sculptures of a person only you could see.'

'You're beautiful, Trish.'

'Fuck off, Reuben.'

34

Wednesday morning, 9.04 a.m.

A private room at Hull Royal Infirmary. The smell of wet wool and dried blood. The trace of lipstick and machine coffee. Two types of perfume and cigarettes.

McAvoy's decision to wake up is an act of mercy for himself. He simply can't listen to any more.

He makes a show of opening his eyes. Feigns grogginess for a while. Allows the yellow light and the white walls to swim into focus. Stares up into the faces of two women who could be mother and daughter, but who would kill him for ever saying so aloud.

'You're back,' says Pharaoh, trying not to smile. 'Christ, you snore like a hippo.'

'Jesus but you scared me,' says Roisin. 'The coffee from that machine tastes like it's been stewed in a fecking sock.'

McAvoy screws up his eyes. Gives a groan as he takes stock.

'Broken ribs . . .'

'Broken hand . . .'

'Hairline crack to your shinbone . . .'

'Sixteen stitches in the back of your head . . .'

'They had to shave your hair . . .'

'You look great.'

McAvoy closes one eye. Wonders if he was better off pretending to be asleep. Then he remembers the agony of listening to his wife and boss make small-talk. Remembers their polite conversation; the sheer, desperate need to be civil. Decides he's marginally better off conscious, but that if it comes to it, he's not above passing out.

'Hollow,' says McAvoy. He swallows, painfully. 'Did I cuff him? Before I passed out?'

Pharaoh gives a grin. 'Broken jaw. Broken nose. Concussion. You beat the shit out of a serial killer, Hector. Even the people who hate you are drinking in your honour.'

'His daughter . . . How did we not know? Did Aberlour . . . ?'

Pharaoh looks away. 'She'll live. Don't know whether she wants to.'

Roisin considers him with soft eyes. She looks tired but has still found time to do her make-up. Examines him through long lashes and sparkly eyeshadow and grins at him with a mouth painted the shade of crimson that he likes.

'The kids are downstairs with your dad,' says Roisin. 'He was grumbling about having to come all the way back down here. I told him you were fine but he's not having it.'

McAvoy wonders how to feel about that and decides he has earned the right to have no opinion at all. Shifts his weight and gets a whiff of Issey Miyake and pungent Turkish cigarettes. He studies Pharaoh properly. She looks pale, but better than she has for a while. She's washed her hair and put on some blusher. Changed her earrings and undone a button on her white blouse.

'She killed the girls, Aector,' says Pharaoh quietly.

'Roisin?' asks McAvoy, confused.

Both women laugh. He feels a warm hand stroking his bicep, but couldn't say which of the women in his life is responsible for the act of affection.

'Delphine. She killed Hannah. Ava, too. She had an obsession with her dad. Couldn't stand anybody else having a hold on him.'

McAvoy lets Pharaoh's face swim into focus again. 'You always knew Hollow was a killer?'

She nods, holding his gaze. 'Him, yes. Her, no. Nobody knew that. Just him, and he indulged her. They'd probably have made a good couple if they weren't father and daughter. Or insane.'

McAvoy swallows again. Feels a sharp pain in his hand and raises it to see three fingers taped together.

'I thought you were going soft on me,' he says to Pharaoh, and

315

holds her stare for a moment longer than he knows Roisin would like. 'Thought he'd worked his way into your affections.'

'He was a charmer,' says Pharaoh. 'He killed bad people. I liked him a lot. But we can't live like that. We can't just do what we think is best.'

'Will he make a confession?'

'I think so. For her, he will. She was wearing Ava Delaney's armpit hair when she tried to kill me. That's not a massively normal thing to do. She might spend her days in a psychiatric hospital. She's been in the system before – she was reported as a minor. She dug up a school friend's kitten when they were seven and was found playing with the skeleton. Her mum did her best with her but she was always a good long bus journey away from being mentally stable.'

McAvoy lifts his head. Looks at the flowers at the foot of the bed. Heather and gerberas, gypsophila and irises.

'Helen,' says Roisin, by way of explanation. 'There are some chocolate strawberries from Sophia. Your mammy sent gift vouchers . . .'

Pharaoh looks at Roisin quizzically. Mouths, 'Mammy?'.

'She's always a bit lost when it comes to Aector,' says Roisin. 'They're not mad close. But I phoned her. You have to, don't you?'

McAvoy lies in the bed and listens to them talk. He tells himself that they like each other, deep down. Comforts himself with the knowledge that they are making an effort to get along for nobody else's sake than his.

'There's a card from Hannah's family,' says Pharaoh suddenly. 'It's simple but heartfelt. Just a thank you.'

McAvoy closes his eyes again. Swallows, and feels himself filling with a familiar emotion.

'Where was she?' he asks. 'Hannah. All those months . . .'

'Don't think about it now, Hector. She was dead before you even took a call about her. And we've got who did it. That's all we can do. We're police, not fucking saints.'

McAvoy lies still. Enjoys the attention and wonders who stripped him and put him in his pyjamas.

He looks at Pharaoh as she smiles, then winks. It's the closest she can get to saying she doesn't really know what the hell has happened these past few days. Doesn't know what to make of the world right now. He watches as she fights with her emotions. When she met Reuben Hollow he was just meant to be a new target. Somehow, he made her give a damn. Somehow, he made her want him. But whether she tried to kiss him to gain his trust, or because of something else, she will never truly know.

'I've got some fancy stitches in my armpit,' she says brightly. 'Going to be a challenge for my roll-on. I don't know what she'd have done with it. Sold it, maybe. Leo Sayer might be looking for a hair transplant . . .'

Roisin doesn't have much else to tell her husband. Feels a little left out. Sucks her lip and then feigns a sudden surge of excitement. She leans forward and kisses her husband, hard and hungry, on the mouth. Before McAvoy closes his eyes, he sees Pharaoh close hers.

'I'd best leave you to it,' says Pharaoh. 'Media are circulating. We don't know what road to take on Hollow. A former inmate has told the press that Hollow spent all his days sculpting miniatures of me, so that's going to require a carefully worded statement. Helen keeps trying to get hold of me, and I've got Shaz Archer bitching about being sidelined. I've got a million voicemails to ignore. The guy who took Hollow is only talking to Helen, but I've got a few questions for him myself, like what the fuck he was doing at my house. Shaz is doing her nut, which pleases me immensely. There's never a dull moment. Seriously, Hector – stay a sergeant. It's so much bloody easier.'

Pharaoh stands. Looks at Roisin for a moment too long. 'I'll sort it all,' she says, and her words are aimed at Roisin.

Roisin nods, managing a smile. Then she turns her attention back to her husband and Pharaoh heads for the door.

McAvoy says nothing. Drinks in his wife's perfume as she presses her face to his and inhales him. Listens for the door to close before he turns his head to Roisin and replies to her kiss.

'He wasn't a hero,' she says, into his ear. 'Not really. He found

317

an excuse to do what he wanted. You don't do that. You don't want to do this. You just have to.'

McAvoy pulls his other arm out from under the blankets. Holds her to him. Kisses her cheek and uses his bandaged hand to stroke her hair. Sees himself, laid out in his hospital bed, imprinted on her beautiful, searching eyes.

'I nearly lost myself,' he says. 'I nearly became something I always feared was in me. I could be him, Roisin. I could be him.'

Roisin smiles. She strokes his nose against hers, kisses him again and savours the feeling.

'Yes,' she says. 'But he could never be you.'

EPILOGUE

He'd half hoped for daylight, had allowed himself to imagine a brief splash of sunlight on his cheeks. But it's dark. Cold. He only has a moment between the back door and the car but it's long enough for him to get a sense of where he's been these past months.

He's surprised that the building is so palatial. He had expected a rubbish-strewn garden, rotten timbers and flaking paintwork. He figured, from the pervasive smells of ethnic food and the sound of video-games from the room above, that he was in a more broken-down neighbourhood than this.

Instead, he glimpses wrought-iron railings and sand-blasted brick. Snatches a look at a six-storey apartment building with a curved façade and neat balconies. He gets a glimpse of wealth and status.

'In. *Ublyudok!* Get fucking in.'

He obeys the well-muscled European. He's too weak to do anything else. His body doesn't feel like his own. It hasn't for a long time. His mind feels only loosely tethered to his own control; a kite, pulling and weaving on a frayed piece of string. He only half remembers himself. Recollections bubble up unbidden, gently breaking the surface of his consciousness like goldfish rising to feed. He has a memory of his second wife. She was Thai. They buried her in a bamboo casket and when the light shone on her coffin during the funeral, he could see the outline of her corpse. He half remembers a son. A lad who called him 'Dad' for a while and who asked if he would stay in touch if he and his mam ever split up. He doesn't know whether he honoured his promise.

He slithers onto luxurious leather. Presses his face against cream calfskin. Recoils, wincing, in anticipation of pain, as he realises that the mucus and blood from his nose might mark the sumptuous interior of the vehicle.

A part of him tells him to do it again. A part of him tells him to take a shit, right here.

The engine turns over with a soft, expensive-sounding purr. He feels the vehicle move away. Catches sight of himself in the blacked-out windows.

There's not much left of him, physically. He has a sensation that he has degenerated into something made of half-devoured food. His face is little more than a skull, covered with a meat that puts him in mind of gone-off ham. His remaining teeth protrude from gums of soft, over-ripe fruit. His eyes are olive stones, pushed into chunks of brie.

Through his own face, he sees the city beyond. Sees the wealth, the pleasure-craft that bob in the harbour and the Audis and Bentleys that sniff one another's bumpers at the kerbside.

'Head down.'

He obeys the accented voice. He can tell something is wrong. There is anger and fear in the voices of the two men in the front of the car. They have moved him before, but never so quickly. Never so openly. Never with such panic in their eyes.

He stares at his shoes. The leather is torn and blood has soaked into the uppers. His grey trousers are the colour of wine on stone.

A memory rises. A bearded man, wordy and arrogant, bleeding out in his arms . . .

Her. The blonde. His friend. Lying. Betraying him. Doing this . . .

The memory falters and fades. He doesn't know if he wants to bring it back.

He listens to the muffled voices coming from the front of the car. Hears the two men. He recognises one of them and thinks he can pick up an accent.

'Time for your medicine.'

He's been craving it. He fought it for the first months. Clawed and spat and lashed out whenever they approached him with the needle. Now he needs it. Needs the ferocious numbness that courses through him when the needle sinks into his half-collapsed veins.

He feels the sting as the hypodermic enters his neck. Feels a rush of nausea and exhilaration that propels him upwards. Then he seems to strike a flat surface and feels himself spread out and puddle against something unyielding. And he is falling. Sinking into himself and insensibility.

The chemical that pulses through his body is called Krokodil: so named because of the effect it has upon the skin. Use leads to discolouration and then breakdown of the flesh, leaving the skin looking like a crocodile's. It is an injectable drug, cooked up from codeine-based medication, iodine, paint thinner, lighter fuel and red phosphorus scraped from the strike pads on matchboxes. The result mimics the effect of heroin at a fraction of the cost. Wherever a user injects the drug, blood vessels burst and surrounding tissue dies, sometimes falling off the bone in chunks. The average life expectancy of a user is two to three years. His captors have been injecting Colin Ray for the last six months.

Colin Ray doesn't notice when the van ploughs into the side of the expensive 4x4 in which he is being transported. He feels nothing as it flips onto its side and bounces, again and again, down the opulent street in south London where it had been idling at the lights.

He isn't aware of being pulled from the wreckage or of the fingers pressed to his neck, searching for his faint pulse.

He won't wake up until he is miles from here, stripped and washed and resting in clean sheets.

Nor will he recognise the amber eyes of the old, half-crippled man.

Here, now, he is too far within himself to know what happens next. Perhaps later, he will have flickers of memory; snatches of swirling picture and sound. But he will never truly remember.

Such oblivion is a mercy. He would not want to see. Would not want to watch the old man drag the three Headhunters from the vehicle and begin his work on the sparkling, glass-jewelled tarmac of this graveyard-quiet street.

The man's weapon of choice is a cleaver; a rectangle of gleaming silver that reflects the cobwebbed beam of light that glares from the smashed headlamp.

Only one of the men has enough strength to put up much resistance, but he is quickly silenced. The handle of the cleaver thuds into his temple and his eyes roll back.

It takes the old man under a minute to complete his task. He has done this before.

A length of rubber tubing around the neck holds the blood in the bodies while he severs their throats and vertebrae. There is little mess until he releases the knots. Then the blood floods out, rushing onto the road to mingle with the black rainbow of petrol that sloshes from the crumpled vehicle.

He picks up the heads without ceremony. Two have hair, and he is able to hold them by their tresses in one hand. He has difficulty with the other; has to hold it like a bowling ball, with his fingers stuffed in nostrils and mouth.

He deposits his prizes in the boot of a nondescript car, parked just out of reach of the CCTV camera that monitors the road. Returns for Colin Ray and carries him like a bride. Places him in the back seat and climbs behind the steering wheel.

The man in the passenger seat does not need to ask if things went according to plan. He does not need to. The smudges of blood upon the older man's hands are proof enough.

The vehicle pulls away from the kerb just as the first police patrol car arrives. Of its two occupants, both will require counselling after tonight and one will never return to policing.

Both will be forever known by their colleagues as the poor bastards who found *them*.

The trio of decapitated Headhunters.

ACKNOWLEDGEMENTS

I have lots of people to thank for helping this novel become, well, a novel. Prior to their intervention, it was just an idea, and ideas are vague, nebulous things that tend to float away.

So . . . Ruth. Thank you. Truly. You're a joy to work with, a proper friend and you're taking my brain places I always hoped it would go. Thanks for putting up with me.

Oli. As ever. Agent, friend and fearless devourer of banoffee pie.

Val. Peter J and Peter M. Stav. Steve. Mari. Anya. Danielle. Mark B. You're inspirations, friends and dangerously attractive individuals.

On the research front, thanks to the people I can't name. Thanks to the serving prisoners and the internet performers who were kind enough to share their experiences. Thanks to the gangsters who told me how best to make somebody talk. Your secrets are safe with me until the point that somebody does what you suggested . . .

Jessica G. Babs. Gemma, you fox. Rob, of course. I'm not an easy friend so thanks for sticking around. Danielle and the girls. You're brilliant, and I say that as somebody who thinks most things are a bit shit.

Mam. Dad. Nana Milly. Nana Phyllis. This is all getting a bit like an Oscar speech but thanks for being largely useful and entirely weird.

Finally, Nikki. You're the gnomon on my sundial, and I'm not going to tell you what that means. George, you're my superstar. Elora, you're the best thing I've ever created.

Apologies to anybody I've omitted. If it's any consolation, you'll note that I didn't thank myself once, and I actually wrote the damn thing . . .

DARK WINTER

DS MCAVOY: BOOK 1

David Mark

Hull, northern England. Two weeks before Christmas. Three bodies in the morgue.

The victims – each a sole survivor of a past tragedy – killed in the manner they once cheated death.

Somebody is playing God. And it falls to DS Aector McAvoy to stop their deadly game.

AVAILABLE IN PAPERBACK AND EBOOK

Quercus

ORIGINAL SKIN

DS MCAVOY: BOOK 2

David Mark

Simon and Suzie are two pleasure seekers
defined by their flamboyant tattoos.

Peter Tressider is a plain-speaking
politician on the fast track to the top.

DS Aector McAvoy is a policeman with
scars to his body and career.

Each is marked in their own way.
And soon each will be branded
by the same sinister foe.

SORROW BOUND

DS MCAVOY: BOOK 3

David Mark

Philippa Longman will do anything for her family.

Roisin McAvoy will do anything for her friends.

DS Aector McAvoy will do anything for his wife.

Yet each has an unknown enemy – one that
will do anything to destroy them.

Sorrow Bound is a powerful thriller about how those
with the biggest hearts make the easiest targets; and
how the corrosive venom of evil can dissolve the bonds
between good people, until all they are bound by is grief.

ALSO AVAILABLE

TAKING PITY

DS MCAVOY: BOOK 4

David Mark

They have taken DS Aector McAvoy's family.

They have taken DCI Colin Ray's foundation.

They have taken DS Trish Pharaoh's fight.

Now the ruthless criminal network that has tightened
its stranglehold on Hull intends to take everything
that remains from those who dare to stand in its way.

AVAILABLE IN PAPERBACK AND EBOOK

Quercus